Songs of Bliss

Clive Gilson

For my darling wife, Karen, with us in spirit and without whom...

VAGABOND SHOES

"THESE DAYS YOU HAVE to stay in shape. My mother-in-law started walking five miles a day when she was sixty. She's ninety-seven now and I have no idea where she is…"

Polite but restrained laughter.

The comic sweats under the spotlights, his shiny grey suit starting to show signs of dampness around the armpits. He mops his brow with a handkerchief. One liners are his stock in trade, mostly borrowed from other, preferably dead, comedians.

Four seconds. Silence.

Ted Line, resident compere at Snuggle's Cabaret Bar, ploughs on.

"I remember the first time I had sex... I kept the receipt".

Deadpan.

Ted can't remember the last time he had sex. He's in free fall without a parachute, exposed and wounded, but Ted is a trouper and sticks to his script. Forged in the furnace of light entertainment, blending a vaguely remembered youthful enthusiasm and a brief middle-aged flirtation with the bright lights of television, Ted is like Excalibur; wet and drowning.

In a former life he was the straight half of Bread and Line, a comedy duo in the mould of Morecambe and Wise or the Smothers Brothers, whose main claim to fame was that their combined earning power was reflected directly in their amusing stage sobriquet. The duo were asked to do a pilot for the BBC in the seventies but they were not asked back to do a series. Lenny Bread gave his last performance seven years ago, falling off a stage in Lowestoft mid-way through a blonde joke. It was the funniest thing he'd ever done.

Lenny left Ted without an act. Prior to turning up on the doorstep at Snuggle's Cabaret Bar, Ted's solo career had peaked with a brief round of sombre interviews and one slot on a Channel 4 list program. Lenny, the funny man, lives on ambrosia with the great mother-in-law in the sky, while the straight man lives in a bed-sit in Barnstaple, on the North Devon coast, and keeps the punters from killing themselves in between acts of incredible bravado or, as is often more likely, awesome stupidity. Snuggle's Cabaret Bar is a tiny universe full of starstruck kids and failed contenders.

Ted readjusts. The great British public's appetite for sexual innuendo and smut is being irrevocably embarrassed into a state of silent nausea. There's something about a sixty-year-old, down at heel chain smoker that kills the comic effect. Ted decides that it's time for something more highbrow.

"What if there were no hypothetical questions?"

From the wings, hissed, "What if there were no shit comics?"

Ted's left hand is behind his back, casually formal in a minor royal sort of way. He mops his brow with a bright red handkerchief and as he does so his free hand, the one behind his back, twists and he raises his index finger towards the shadows stage right.

Billy Whitlow, known to his devoted audience as Billy Nero, the 'Don of Doo Wap', sniggers as he prepares to wow the girls with his star spangled, Bennettesque delivery of classic era crooning. Like Ted, he is a regular at Snuggle's.

The wings are cramped and hot, although wings as a term is ambitious, there being only the one. The acts have to squeeze past each other during changeovers. Props, instruments and the assorted paraphernalia of the lounge-bar spectacular come on and off stage the same way. Standing next to Billy is the lovely Leona, seventeen, and in her second year of theatre studies at North Devon College. Leona is the stage manager, which means she spends most of her evenings hissing into an old, ice-cream cone microphone, desperately trying to get the acts cued up for their moment of glory. The vibrating membrane in the speaker in the communal dressing room at the back of the club is badly frayed and the acts rarely understand a word Leona says. The running order, on the odd occasions that it gets typed up, rarely runs with anything approaching method or organisation.

Leona prods Billy with her pencil, giving him one of her well-practiced 'God' looks. Billy puts a finger up to his lips and nods.

The stage is set simply, Snuggle's having no pretensions towards the theatrical. The stage has no proscenium arch nor does it boast complicated rigging, fancy lighting systems or tabs. The stage is open and semi-circular, running along the back wall of the cabaret room. The backdrop consists of four ancient and torn blacklegs held together with gaffer tape, over which hang an indeterminate number of metallic silver drapes. The silver fabric is split, like a fly curtain, and now hangs twisted and bent after years of shimmering behind acts of appalling mediocrity, reflecting the worn-out spotlights in a thousand different directions.

Ted coughs in between jokes, partly because of his eighty a day habit, but mostly to fill the gaps where the laughter should be.

"Ever wonder about those people who spend two pounds on those little bottles of Evian water? Try spelling Evian backward."

This one gets a few tired chuckles.

At the far end of the room, sitting on a stool by the bar, Maggie Heard, the eponymous Snuggle, switches on a red shaded table lamp and drags a manicured, dusty pink fingernail across her throat. Ted knows the sign. Time's up.

"Well, ladies and gentlemen, it's time to serve the main course. You've been lovely, you really have, and I'll see you all at the end of the show."

There's a groan from the bar.

"One last little observation before I go. Have you ever noticed the one nice thing about egotists is they don't talk about other people?"

A group of ladies of a certain age and outlook edge their chairs a little nearer to the stage. Ted instinctively takes a step back, turns towards the wings and raises his handkerchief hand in welcome.

"Put your hands together for your favourite egotist and mine, Billy Nero!"

Billy enters stage left, waving to his audience. Ted starts to walk in front of him, a deliberate foul, but checks himself at the last moment and slides around behind Billy and off stage.

Mild applause.

Cigarettes blossom in the gloom.

Young girls in black skirts and white blouses deliver over-blown shorts and sickly cocktails to tables. Billy takes a bow and plants himself firmly centre stage.

"Ted Line, ladies and gentlemen, one of the golden oldies, talking of which, Maestro..."

Billy points at a three-piece band seated on the main floor by the far end of the stage. "*Spanish Eyes*".

Accompanied by the Snuggle's Show Band on Hammond organ, drums and lukewarm jazz guitar, Billy opens his set.

Billy segues straight out of *Spanish Eyes* into a medley of Nat King Cole standards, keeping the mood soft and his girls in direct eye contact. Girls. He likes to think of them in soft pink hues, although he knows the first blush of youth has faded from their cheeks. He has no illusions about his sex appeal. Way back in the late seventies, when The Don had his one and only minor hit with a saccharine version of *Let It Be Me*, he played games with mothers and daughters. The mothers are, for the most part, dead or institutionalised. A few of the daughters, matrons themselves now, keep the flames alive, and although they don't burn quite so brightly these days, Billy can still sometimes coax those old flames into a simulacrum of life so that they flicker gently on the dark waters of the Torridge Estuary.

Unlike Ted, Billy gets a good, solid, middle-aged round of applause. It helps to have the girls in the audience. Their enthusiasm and affection lifts the spirit of the rest of the punters, allowing him a certain degree of latitude when it comes to hitting the higher notes. Billy has a good head of hair, still looks fairly trim for someone in his mid-fifties, so long as he buys his suits from the more expensive end of the peg, and he doesn't sweat too much under the lights.

"Thank you, very much. The real King there. As ever it's a privilege to be back at Snuggle's, and I hope you're enjoying the show. I'm going to take you on a trip down memory lane on a journey to the stars." Billy winces inside slightly as he mixes his metaphors. "We'll be meeting up with Frank and Tony, Tom Jones, Vic, Matt Munro, Andy Williams and, of course, my own little offering to the wonderful world of song."

Billy smiles for Colgate and walks over to the band. The sound of the hurdy-gurdies cueing themselves in can just be heard over the clatter of pudding bowls and cheese plates being cleared from tables. Coffee cups and dessert plates full of house branded bitter-mints take their place. The drummer starts to slide his brushes over taut skin. A false start. Heads turn. The band paddle frantically towards the melody pursued by Billy's shark infested smile. The opening bars of *From Russia with Love* emerge from the chaos and Billy Whitlow dives back under the thickly silted, melodic waters that keep The Don of Doo Wap afloat.

As he sings, running on autopilot, his body and larynx accustomed to the task after thirty years, Billy watches the room, trying to gauge the mood. He also watches the bar at the back of the hall. The foreground offers its usual mixed bag of bodies and clothes, displaying every type of posh frock, from the truly elegant to the mutton. People sip coffee, some adding to the alcohol already in their blood streams with large cognacs, scotches or Cointreau on the rocks. Feet tap and the girls, who know the set like the back of their hands, mouth the words.

Although he appears to have eyes just for the front row, Billy's attention is firmly fixed on his employer. She sits, as she always does, on a stool at the bar where she can watch the room. The red table lamp that she uses to chivvy the acts along when she feels the pace slacken is off now. Maggie is in a half-life light, broken occasionally by the irregular crystal flash from her glass of apple juice. Maggie doesn't usually drink when she's working. She says it's hard enough running the place without adding maudlin hangovers to the mix. Her companion at the bar drinks enough for the two of them anyway.

The apple of Maggie Heard's eye is one Jock Cascarino, once a little fish in a big Glaswegian pool of criminality, now the fattest catfish lurking at the bottom of Barnstaple's muddy puddle. Jock makes up for the initial disappointment of his rotund body and his square, thick head through the sheer force of his personality, a force measured in irregular bouts of violence served cold by his two faithful employees, the smugly efficient Brothers Grim. Billy hates Jock Cascarino viscerally. He is, though, fully aware that Jock is the alpha male in the immediate locale and that he, the Don, has to pay his dues, picking at scraps once the carcass of life has been dragged through North Devon's thick red dust. The groans from the bar that pierce Ted Line's heart come from Jock Cascarino.

Billy's set drifts through the Vegas heartland, sometimes languorous, occasionally animated, and always accompanied by the mediocrity of the Three Musketeers in the corner. Their motto, thinks Billy, should be 'All for one, but never quite at the same time'. The only constant is Billy's smile. He wraps up the set with a full-blooded version of *My Way* and the band, who have meandered their way through classic arrangements like slugs in a beer mug, suddenly remember how to play. The audience cheers and Billy waves and bows, adrenalin pumping. He skips off, blowing kisses to his girls, and waits in the wings with Leona for his encore.

Some of the audience assume that it's time for dancing, time for the bar, and the applause dies off far too quickly for Billy's liking. Trust the girls, he thinks, and, true to form, as the volume of general applause fades he can hear their voices calling out his name.

"Bill-ee, Bill-ee, Bill-ee".

One of the girls waves her lighter in the air.

The band knows the score. *Let It Be Me* begins. Half of the errant punters return dutifully to their seats. The remainder, the socially dysfunctional in glad rags now finally released from the unfamiliar etiquette of public dining, are too concerned with their urgent need to visit the lavatory or to attract the attention of the two young men tending the bar. It doesn't seem to matter that the tables have waitress service. These paying guests need to work off the soporific effects of the limited repertoire that comes steaming out of Snuggle's kitchen. They want to put a little distance between themselves and the stage. Billy has to compete with the general hum of conversation coming from the back of the room, but slowly, as the song unlocks the heavy cell doors that incarcerate old memories, he wins back their attention.

Ted Line rolls on as soon as the last bar of the last song has been absorbed by the walls. He smells of cheap blended whisky. Ted thanks Billy, makes one last attempt to be funny and admits defeat, introducing the house band and inviting everyone to enjoy the facilities and the dance floor. The spots fade down to their dull gels and the cabaret is over.

Billy says thanks to Leona when she tells him how well it went and strides down the back hall to the communal dressing room. He changes his shirt, sprays on a little deodorant and checks his hair. In the old days, when he was a shooting star, he had the luxury of time and space. Now, desperate to avoid the ancient comic and his bad tempered, alcoholic ramblings, Billy makes a perfunctory visit to the world of personal hygiene, straightening his cuffs just as the old man wanders into the room.

"Nice one, Ted. Got to dash".

"Bastard", Ted mumbles to no one in particular as he walks over to a rickety refectory table and fills a plastic beaker with liquid rust. "Got to play the big-I-am with his fucking fan club. Has he seen the forearms on those women?"

Leona, who has followed Ted into the dressing room, grimaces as she switches off the tannoy speaker. Like Billy, she'll carry out her final duties of the evening with the minimum of effort and then head for the bar, although unlike Billy, who has no particular place to go, Leona has a crush on one of the boys serving drinks. She gives the back room a fleeting check over, fixes a straying strand of hair in the liver spotted mirror propped up at one end of the refectory table and makes her own exit, leaving Ted to his own declining devices.

The only way to get to the bar from the dressing room is across the stage. After the show and with the lights set for dancing the stage takes on a derelict ambience. Billy gets a slightly hollow feeling in his legs, as if he is about to leave fairyland and enter the land of mortals for the first time. Billy feels as though he is stardust caught in a decaying gravitational field. Billy lives in Bideford, just a few miles down the coast, so he is used to that peculiar West Country feeling of the down at heel, but he always feels discomfited when he leaves Billy Nero's comfort zone. He is fully aware that this part of the world has a special affection for the slightly weird, for the wanderers of the twenty-first century, and while he knows that his happy face will see him through the next hour, he has to admit to a slight sense of fear. There is a screw loose out there. The world smells of wet rot.

A quick check of shirt collar and trouser hang and over the top he goes, moving across the abandoned theatre of dreams with his smile intact and already reaching for his pen. There are five of his girls waiting for him, table menus in hand, each one of whom he knows by name. He signs his stage name, pecks them on the cheek and invites them to join him at the bar. Wedding rings. A quick glass of something bubbly and a story or two. It's the game that pays his wages. It's been a long time since he felt true desire. Billy has little need for groupies, not now, not like he did when he was younger. Just occasionally, when the fire is in danger of dying down to the last embers, but not tonight.

Surrounded by other men's wives Billy berths himself on a stool, and orders a bottle of Cava and six glasses. The drinks are on the house. Sat in her corner station like an empress presiding over the games, Maggie nods and smiles. Publicity. Word of mouth. Every little bit helps and they won't be on the good stuff.

Billy glad hands, tells stories, cabaret tales and outrageous slanders, and takes the time to look like he is listening intently when appropriate. There are a few more autographs to sign, one of which, he is delighted and touched to find, is on the cover of his long-playing record. A thirty-three and a third. Remaindered. A modern antique.

Speaking fluently while drinking little, he fulfils dreams, making a few low local horizons glow just that little bit brighter, thinking all the while of Bex, his daughter. Billy has to drive to Oxford in the morning to pick her up for a two-week holiday with him in rainy Bideford. Tonight helps to pay the maintenance. She wants to be a vet, which means another five years of talking to her mother. Billy feels smugly warm inside when he thinks about Bex, his one lasting success, his sole real achievement in life, his sole number one.

One of the girls is about to leave and he gives her a little hug, a squeeze that she returns, and only then does he realise that she thinks the hug is really for her. He smiles back as she swoons and then totters homeward through the thinning crowd at the bar. Another Saturday night done and dusted. Tomorrow is Billy's day, the day when he sees Bex for the first time since Christmas.

The loose screw is Jock Cascarino.

At one-thirty the lights go up, encouraging the punters to collect their coats and head for home. By two o'clock, the club's licensed hour of closing on a Saturday night, the place is clear of people but littered with crumpled cigarette packets, discarded napkins and half full glasses. The low light, dreamlike ambience has been replaced by full strip light nakedness and the room smells of stale smoke. The doors are locked. Ted Line is asleep on the sofa in the dressing room, where he'll be left, as usual, to sleep through Saturday night and well into Sunday morning. The boys from the bar are stacking glasses, brushing a thousand cigarette tabs into buckets and, whenever the door is opened, disappearing in a cloud of steam that billows out from the wheezing cavern of an old, industrial dishwasher.

By the doors there are two frowning Colossi in black polo shirts and leather jackets, their arms folded across their chests. The brothers McCoist, Ken and Davie, are standing guard. They are a cliché, a lethally hackneyed idea.

Maggie is checking through the till rolls and sorting floats. Billy, Leona and Jock sit at the bar nursing drinks, that lock-in privilege of the inner circle. Leona, sitting to the right of the group, pays no attention to the two older men. She takes regular swigs from a bottle of some impossibly blue vodka kick and makes eyes at the lucky lad behind the bar who will drive her home when the glasses and ashtrays are gleaming.

"Not bad tonight", says Jock after a long silence. "Heard it all before, of course, but not bad. Could do with a bit of sprucing up, though, something new".

Billy can put up with Jock if Maggie is in the room. Nearly. The bait has been offered and although Billy sees it for what it is he can't resist taking a bite. "You'd know all about that, wouldn't you?" he says.

Delighting in Billy's obvious irritation Jock carries on in his flat Glaswegian demi-brogue, "I would, yeah. Something new, something a bit more up to date. Mind, I suppose when you're trading on the past like all those dead guys you talk about up there, it must be difficult to keep up with the times. That's the difference between you and me."

Billy groans. "Oh God, not the self-made man speech."

"Why not? It's important. Take Maggie, for example. She's got something concrete here, literally, if you follow". Jock chuckles, warming to his task. Snuggle's is housed in what was once a mid-sixties estate pub, the perfect place to wind down a life as a nearly man. Suburban mediocrity writ large. "Some things stay the same, but she's always trying new stuff too, new menus, new acts, battle of the bands in a month or so. You should come along, by the way. Might be some new material you could borrow".

Billy shifts in his seat, staring straight ahead at the optics.

"I mean, I can see how tradition and style and that keeps you locked down, Billy, I really can, but you've got to have a plan for the future. Have you got a plan, Billy?"

"What?"

"Have you got a plan for the future Billy, something up your sleeve?"

Billy wishes he had an ice-pick up his sleeve and tries to savour the gore of a familiar image, of cold steel buried in Jock's forehead. He turns to look at Jock, picking his spot and catches sight of the McCoist brothers over by the door. He sighs, disappointed. The Glaswegian takes it to be a sign of defeat, but Billy smiles, drifting for a moment in the snapshot of Jock Cascarino lying prostrate in a pool of blood before he answers.

"Well, yes, I do have a plan. Not the sort that needs gorillas or steel toe caps, just a simple little plan. I want to earn enough to pay my way and see Bex through college".

"Noble", says Jock as he casts a well-practiced eye over Maggie's comfortably proportioned body as she moves behind the bar, checking the optics, "but predictable. I mean, that family stuff is all very nice, but isn't it just another way of saying you're giving up, that you're handing on the baton to another generation and waiting to die?"

"I think you're confusing me with Ted", says Billy draining the last of his scotch. He puts the glass down on the bar and pours another slug from the bottle that he and Jock are sharing.

"Aye, maybe, but you are living in the past. For Christ's sake, look at the birds hanging on your every octave. Not one of them under fifty. They're dinosaurs, man".

Billy feels compelled to come their defence. "They're lovely. They're not eighteen-year-old nymphos, but what would I do with one of those? I've got nothing to say to kids. You can't be a teenager forever, well, most of us can't." He looks straight at Jock. "I like a woman to look like a woman, not a stick insect. Anyway, you're with Maggie and she's hardly a spring…"

Jock wags a finger under Billy's nose. "Off limits."

Billy looks away. He always does when Jock slides the hook deeper into his flesh.

Silence.

At times like this, with Jock's blunt needle wedged firmly under his fingernails, Billy hates himself. He'd swap any one of his girls for a night with Maggie. Billy and Jock trade blows with each other for this one simple reason. Jock is with Maggie. Billy has wanted her ever since he turned up for his first gig. He can see the moment clearly. He can still see her smile as she bought him a drink after that first show. That's the only real reason why he turns up once a month and sings in this God forsaken hole.

In spite of the Glaswegian gangster's goading, Billy feels as though he's doing all right, that he's getting through the swansong days of his life with a degree of dignity. He has a few regular spots in clubs around the Southwest, and he makes a nice living out of some of the region's more pretentious weddings. He gets invites to guest in Bristol, occasionally even London. The Palladium might as well be on the moon, but for a jobbing crooner he gets by. More importantly, he contributes to his daughter's well-being and education.

The boys have finished clearing the bar. Ted and the cabaret room will be left for the morning cleaner. Leona and the boys say goodnight and are let out into the early morning darkness by the brothers McCoist. Jock deigns to offer a patriarchal wave to Leona as the door shuts and then turns back to the business in hand, back to Billy Whitlow.

"No, you should try harder, Billy. I'll admit my early days down here were a bit awkward. Drugs, girls, a little bit of this and that, but I changed. That's the point I'm making. I changed, Billy, got into property, bought up failing farms and converted them into holiday lets, second homes, you know the score. Wait for the daft old cowshed buggers to get in debt or for their bloody sheep to get sick with some fucking disease or other, move in, tidy up and pick the pockets of the stupid bastards pouring out of the Home Counties."

Billy has a question. He's asked it more than once, because he knows it's a way of returning Jock's fire, and that makes a little bit of a difference. It makes Billy feel as though he is fighting at the same weight. Jock is a self-satisfied thug, who delights in winning, but the question keeps Billy in the game for a while. Billy knows that it's all smoke and mirrors, but he can't stop himself from playing the game. Ultimately, he loses because Jock goes home to Maggie, but for a few moments he gets to watch the man squirm.

"Why did you really come down here?" Billy asks.

Jock sits, silent for a moment, a moment that Billy seizes.

"You've always said you were a player up there, so why come all this way to sleepy little Tarkaville? Something happen? Bit of bother with the polis?" That last word is emphasised in a cod

Scots accent.

Eye contact. Flat and glassy. But then Jock smiles and says, "You need to get out more, pal", and with that he downs his drink, rises from his stool and wolf whistles at Maggie as she puts the last of the till rolls into her briefcase. The tills are cleared and the takings are in the safe, although with Jock Cascarino as her boyfriend, there is little likelihood of robbery. Even the local kids know not to mess with the club. It helps that the brothers McCoist live in the flat above the shop.

Jock blows Maggie a final kiss and says, "See you later babe, bit of business to do."

He and Maggie have obviously already discussed the matter. Maggie puts the briefcase on the bar and sighs. "Yeah, have a ball. Don't wake me when you get in."

She walks round to the front of the bar as Jock and his goons unlock the doors and leave. She locks up again and, as Jock's Lexus pulls out of the car park, she pours herself and Billy one for the road.

Billy is the first to speak. "I just don't get it. What do you see in Kray Minor?"

Maggie sits on Jock's still warm bar stool and leans against Billy's shoulder. "Security. And he wouldn't hurt me, Billy, not in a thousand years. He'll hurt anyone else who gets in his way, but he'll never lay a finger on me, which is more than I can say for some. He's not so different from you, you know."

Billy is appalled that Maggie should think of him in the same light as Jock, but he doesn't let it show. The conversation drifts and ebbs away, spiralling down through Billy's plans for Bex and the state of his love life. Maggie knocks back the dregs of her first and last drink of the evening, a little luxury at the end of another long week. Her bobbed, dyed blonde hair falls away from her head, revealing the soft skin of her earlobes. Billy wants to kiss her, imagines himself doing it and blanches.

Maggie straightens up, stands and says, "Come on, you old groaner, time to hit the road".

Maggie and Billy kill the lights and walk out of the club. Maggie sets the alarm and puts the keys into her briefcase. Once outside Billy offers Maggie his arm, which she takes, and they walk across the car park to her car, a bright blue Mini convertible.

"You're a good man, Billy Whitlow", she says as he turns to leave. "Don't let Jock get to you. In his own way, he's a good man too. See you soon."

This is the moment, the minute when he breaks the spell. Alone in a car park under sodium orange lights, with the world tucked up and Jock out of sight, Billy can feel Maggie in his arms, can see her brief but ultimately useless protest fade away as she realises that Billy is her man. He hesitates, checks his step and wills Maggie to say something, anything that might call him back to her side. All that he hears is the beep of central locking and a car door opening. His foot falls back to earth with a dew damp, tarmacadam slap. He coughs and heads away from the woman of his dreams, whispering a gentle adieu.

"Take care, Maggie".

It's three o'clock on Sunday morning.

Billy has a choice of route home. He could take the coast road that runs through Fremington's quiet little world of bungalow boredom, but he prefers to see the lights of Bideford scatter along the Torridge Estuary as he breasts the last hill on the main trunk.

The Little White Town has tucked itself up for the night and the roads are clear. Billy's Vauxhall is the only car on the new bridge, a perfect time for suicide. The Samaritans sign is positioned at the apex, the reading of which offers a last moment of redemption to the jumper. Jumping is not uncommon.

The tide is in and the streetlights along the quay are reflected on gentle ripples. Rope lights are strung in the rigging of the Kathleen and May, the country's last operating merchant schooner, and they're switched on at night now to advertise the boat as a tourist attraction for Easter.

At the roundabout, just after the bridge, Billy turns left into the town centre, slows as he passes a speed camera and at the next junction, where a second-hand car dealer spends his days polishing tired paintwork, Billy swings right and up the hill. The headlight beams from his car narrow and concentrate on to a green painted garage door and Billy pulls up on the drive-in front of a compact, thirties, bay window semi-detached house. All of the neighbours' lights are out bar one house a few doors down. Saturday, sex, late night flicks, who knows. Billy yawns as he puts the key in the lock. The house is dark and quiet. Billy drops his keys on a glass topped telephone table, hangs his jacket on the banister and visibly sags as he walks into the sitting room.

Instead of Jock Cascarino's preferred tipple, a reasonable blend but a blend nonetheless, Billy pours himself a stiff single malt, picks a well-thumbed copy of his favourite record from a shelf and slides the black vinyl from its cover. It's an act of love. Careful not to touch the record's grooves he places it on a Linn Sondek turntable, one of the few indulgences in an otherwise spare and simple interior. He sets the sound system so that his final memories of another long Saturday night will be soft and mellow. Billy lets Vic Damone sing him lullabies.

The record is his favourite, the one he always plays to himself after a show. *Linger Awhile with Vic Damone*. It's one of his hero's better recordings for Capitol from nineteen sixty-two, the stuff of dreams. Damone was signed by Capitol in sixty-one when they lost Sinatra to Reprise. Not bad for a boy who had to drop out of school and take a job as an usher and elevator operator in a movie theatre, the Paramount, in Manhattan.

Billy thinks about Bex, about the Gingerbread House, a term he uses to describe the place where his ex-wife spins her sugared web, and about the good old days. Like Vic, Billy bummed around in dead end jobs, singing in pubs for a few beers and little bit of cash on a Friday night, but unlike his hero Billy never did bump into Perry Como. He took the traditional route; working men's clubs, hard grind and a little luck.

He was spotted in summer season in Eastbourne by a producer looking for the new Tony Orlando. The build-up was fun, but the choice of songs was poor and the timing sucked. They broke him with *Let It Be Me* the same week that the Sex Pistols split up in America.

The carousel starts to spin. Vic Damone, born Vito Rocco Farinola in nineteen twenty-eight, reaches track five, *Stella by Starlight*, and Billy reaches a state of grace. His soul reels in the thread by which Billy has dragged it around since waking, settles on his shoulder and together they fall asleep in the armchair as Vic croons softly into their cotton wool ears.

THE NIGHT HAS A THOUSAND EYES

A STEEL GREY MERCEDES taxi swings round and leaves a solitary male figure standing at the kerb of the Avinguda de la Mar. It's early April, three o'clock in the morning, and the temperature is even and comfortable. Lights flicker in dilapidated shop windows. The threat of garish neon that fills most of the visible street front signage hangs cool and dull. The late traveller picks up a single sports holdall and starts to trudge down the Carrer de L'Inginyer Serrano Lloberes, towards the harsh brilliance of the lonely, night-owl bars that stay open into the small hours for insomniac sailors working the aggregate freighters along the Mediterranean coast and beyond. This is the Paseo de Bonavista and the Factoria Rio Tinto, Castellon de la Plana, Spain.

Apartment lights sneak out through shutters closed to the night above the shop facades, and in one of them a crooner sings gently through a tinny transistor radio speaker. American schmaltz. A fifties throwback. Alex Berisa stops at the traffic island at the end of the Serrano Lloberes and watches a lone scooter whine along the Paseo. The sound of drilled out baffles echoes off the stripped back and bare sides of the empty street. A fine layer of dust from the Factoria's processing and shipping of aggregates mutes the surfaces of the street furniture. Shop windows show streaks and diffused shades of colour under the streetlights. Everything that Alex looks at or touches is coated in a whimsy of pulverised stone dust and he wonders what the place is like in high summer when the heat stifles and the breezes off the sea carry thick, choking clouds of powder into the lungs of the local inhabitants. The low level industrial rawness of the port area does not seem so very different from home.

Home is where the heart is, except that Alex's heart is broken. It is not the breaking of bonds with a lover, nor is it the failure of family blood that erodes care and tenderness with the dull edged disappointment that hollows out the soul slowly over the years. Alex is tired. The family, the blood and the honour, the unswerving loyalty are all that he has to sustain him. The empty streets down which he walks at the dead hour of the night are a fitting place for the terminally ill, and he feels as though he has a cancer in his bones, a tumour of hate and revenge placed there by Arbnor Jasari. A doctor. The family doctor. The magician. The chemist. Betrayal lies at the heart of it all, betrayal and a sister who is condemned to spend what remains of her life living like a vegetable. Betrayal and shame. Alex is the Capo Bastone, the trusted captain, the man in day-to-day charge of affairs, managing the family's business interests in the coastal Adriatic clubs and bars that sit within his family's sphere of influence.

The port area around the Factoria is brutally familiar, just like

Durres, a place that Alex has already visited and left behind in his search. Arbnor Jasari is on the run, on the high seas with a satchel full of the family's dollars and little regard for the damage that he has done, for the destruction, for the living death that he has inflicted. Alex nearly chokes on the pain of it all as he heads along the Paseo. A bright red and yellow sign draws him down the street. At arm's length, in places where people make their choices and live with the consequences, Alex has never before given a second thought to what he does. He cannot afford the luxury of sentiment. It is business, a chance to put the record straight, to make good the loss of honour, to avenge.

The ritual of death, the killing of a couple of family soldiers, is something to be expected. These things happen from time to time in the Berisa family business. For Alex, the betrayal is in the doctor's running, is in his failure to face up to his responsibilities. It is why Alex is here now, at this late hour, in an industrial dust bowl in a foreign country. He is facing his own responsibilities, and in the facing of them, although he might not mend his heart, he will take a grim satisfaction in doing the right thing. It will sustain him through the hard months and years to come, through the inevitable moments when he has to look at his sister. Rezarta. Beautiful, vacant Rezarta.

As he walks away from the Factoria towards the late-night bars frequented by a polyglot sea of sailors and the hardier members of the local community, he turns to look at the lights on the cargo ships that lie at anchor, loading and unloading, ploughing their way through blue Mediterranean waters. Jasari made his way from Vlore to Durres and hooked up with one of the freight lines, Med-Seva, Russian owned and Maltese registered, spending dollars on a private passage out of Albania. Alex has called in favours to get this far and now he too must spend dollars. The doctor can run, but he can never hide from the Berisa family. Not now. Alex tells himself this again and again as he steps in and out of shadows, but in truth Alex feels the trail already wearing thin. The doctor has a head start of almost a week and Alex is certain that his quarry is already running again.

Low lights and hunched shoulders. Some of the conversation in the bar stops as Alex enters. He is out of place, a tourist, a lamb for the slaughter. He is sporting a day's stubble and he knows that he looks like a fool with a wallet full of hard currency. Alex surveys the room, looking for the tell-tale signs of fellow travellers, ideally someone from his own place and people, but the pale base skin of a Russian will do. In the deep gloom of the bar everyone looks weather beaten, but Alex has a keen eye and a sensitive ear. Slavic undertones. Mannerisms out of place. Alex is also aware of the atmosphere, of the calculations being made about him. He walks up to the bar and orders a beer in faltering Spanish. A table to his right, towards the back of the bar, has a half-finished bottle of vodka on it. Two men sit at the table in quiet conversation. Polo shirts and jeans. Jackets on the backs of their chairs. Western styles. Unmistakable.

Bottle in one hand, bag in the other, Alex walks to the table at the back of the bar and speaks Russian clearly and concisely, "Are you Russian? May I join you for a moment?"

The two men turn silently to look at Alex. They remain seated and soundless for moments that seem to thicken around Alex. The man furthest from him is the first to break eye contact, turning back to his drink, which he downs in one. The second man replies in a thickly accented English accent, "Who wants to know?"

Alex maintains eye contact with the second man as he walks around the table and takes a chair from another empty booth. He sits, putting his bag down between his feet and his beer on the table next to the bottle of vodka. His Russian is accented but technically almost flawless, an essential skill in his line of family business. "No one in particular". He reaches into his inside jacket pocket and pulls out a rough Polaroid picture and a crisp hundred-dollar bill. "No one at all".

Away from the table the conversation levels rise again. It is nothing new, just Russians playing their games in the dark. The locals steer clear. A couple of anonymous merchant marine boys pay for a bottle cheap Spanish brandy and leave the bar. Alex passes the picture to the two sailors at his table and they both stare at the face in the picture for a few seconds. The man in the picture is Doctor Jasari. He looks almost emaciated, but has bright eyes. He has a receding hairline, but the hair is still long, like a prematurely ageing teenage rocker. Dark skin. A smile on thin lips. They both make the same monosyllabic reply to Alex's unasked question; "No".

Alex stands and reaches forward to pick up the picture, but before he can the second of the two Russian sailors slams his hand down on the hundred-dollar bill. Alex smiles and nods. The man's hand closes over the foreign currency, leaving the picture for Alex to pick up. The first sailor looks up at Alex briefly and makes a movement with his eyes towards another group of three men sitting next to the bar's window. "Albanian fucks, like you".

Alex continues to smile at the two Russians. He can feel eyes on his back. A television set on a wall mounted bracket behind the bar is playing satellite Eurosport. A Spanish commentator is going into overdrive about a sweating pack of cyclists. Alex picks up his drink and his bag, steps away from the table slowly and walks towards the front of the bar. The owner of the place is starting to get the fidgets. People asking questions at three-thirty in the morning freak him out. Alex puts his bottle of beer on a free table, walks over to the bar, asks for a bottle of brandy, pays with another hundred-dollar bill and tells the bar owner to keep the change. Greenbacks always take the sting out of the situation. Nearly always. Alex takes a second to lock down the faces and shapes of a couple of guys falling prey to money-lust over in the far corner. For their sakes, he hopes that they don't think him easy to shake down.

The group by the window respond to a familiar accent. One of them is even acquainted with the family name, which helps to lubricate those parts of the conversation that the brandy and three further folded bills cannot reach. The picture is passed round the group, but none of them have anything positive to say. Alex is already scanning the bar for other likely sources of information as the men take a second large shot from the bottle of brandy. The conversation drifts to stories of home, Tirana, Vlore, dreams of fishing boats and fat, fecund wives. The travelling world is full of stories of home, stories of darling little girls ripped from the bosom of beauty. Alex bids them have a good night and, spotting no more likely targets, picks up his bag and heads for the door.

He is followed. Alex knows that he is being followed. The tail is good but not good enough. In fact, thinks Alex, oddly not good enough, as though his shadower is trying too hard not to be spotted. Alex has flown to Spain and he is relatively unarmed, carrying only a knife borrowed from one of the airport canteens, which makes it a difficult but not an impossible situation. He heads for the Factoria. There are no cars on the road, no mopeds, nothing but the lights along the Paseo. Alex is in no mood to play games. He is tired and frustrated. He turns to face the following footsteps. It takes Alex a second to recognise the face of the second Russian. He was expecting one of the green-eyed boys from the table in the far corner of the bar. The Russian sailor beckons Alex into a doorway beyond the dim street lighting.

"You have more money?"

Alex nods slowly but he doesn't reach for his jacket pocket. "Depends on what you've got to say".

The Russian considers this for a moment and then shrugs his shoulders. He whispers in good English, "This face, I saw it. We are held up here by another ship. Kozlov line. Some problem with engine. This face, he was on board. Paid big dollars to one of her officers, a stupid Ukrainian boy who fancied himself and had a big mouth. The man in the picture sailed on that boat. He left some days ago, maybe two weeks, for England."

Alex can feel his heart rate quickening. The man has yet to give him any detail that can be corroborated, but the smell of Jasari is suddenly in the air, in his nostrils. Alex needs facts.

"Yes, that's good, but how, where did you see him, what was the ship's name, where was it heading?"

The Russian looks at Alex and then at his jacket pocket. "I give you information. You want more you pay".

Cold, hard cash. It is what it all boils down to every single time. Alex feeds the man one more bill and holds another four in his hand. "So?"

"I say, Kozlov line. Valentin. I know this man is on board. I saw him one night in ship's mess. We played cards, to take this Ukrainian boy's money. Your man was sitting quietly in a corner reading a book. I'm sure it was him. The Valentin goes to Bideford, Devon and then on to Lovissa, Finland"

A grand. Ten big ones. The world turns on every black and white, Bogart cliché and every one of those old, worn out phrases is worth the breath and billfold. Alex has a destination, somewhere to aim for, a target upon which he can train his sights. He is on his way, walking the empty streets of Castellon de la Plana with a spring in his step. A taxi. A train. A flight to Paris and the Eurostar. How long, he wonders, does it take to sail from Castellon to England? He forgot to ask.

Alex makes a call on his mobile, long distance, roaming the night's dusty airwaves for the comfort delivered by a familiar voice. The receiving phone rings ten or eleven times before someone picks up and a woolly voice answers.

Alex gets down to the gist of it without delay. "Xhev, it's London. Meet me as soon as you can. I'm going to be travelling for a couple of days so call me with the details. Oh, I'll need a hire car and the proper equipment. Make the arrangements, Okay?"

WHY WAS I BORN?

THREE MEN SIT IN silence. No conversation. The Lexus hums quietly. The only other audible sound is the rumble of rubber on tarmac. Ken McCoist, driving, manoeuvres the car to avoid potholes and sunken drain covers. White lining. Jock Cascarino sits in the back.

They pass a mock Gothic bus stop at Fairy Cross, heading out towards Hartland peninsula. Jock stares straight ahead, letting the soft digital glow from the dashboard wash through his thoughts. There's nothing worth looking at through the side windows. The North Devon Expressway is, for the most part, unlit. Trees line the road. The ghostly shapes of cream rendered houses flash by. Devon is a rural county, spread wide and thin. Jock hates the great outdoors.

The car speeds along the winding road, dipping down into a hard right at The Hoops Inn and on through Bucks Cross, ignoring the speed limit, lurching slightly on a tight left-hand bend. On the right, lit up and festooned in banners, Bideford Bay Holiday Park announces yet another sale of chalets and static caravans. Jock's meditation is broken.

"Have you phoned ahead?" he asks.

"Aye, he's ready", replies Davie from the front passenger seat.

"Good. Did you make the deliveries like he asked?"

"Oh, aye, picked up three on Friday night. They should be tucked up safely by now".

Jock moves to the centre of the rear bench seat, sitting forward so that he can look through the windscreen. The car takes a series of sharp curves. Ahead the lights of Clovelly Cross stand out in the darkness. A couple of miles to go.

"The good doctor seems to be settling in," he says, and chuckles. The brothers McCoist chuckle too.

Jock considers the workings of providence and finds that all is well with the world. The good Lord is in his heaven and the good doctor is on the farm. A perfect combination. Jock runs through the story again, scarcely able to believe his luck.

The good doctor is a refugee, but not of the political kind. True, thinks Jock, he'd qualify. There's every likelihood he'd be tortured and killed by his own government, but then again, he's as likely to be tortured and killed by his old friends. And now he's mine, and, for the moment, I choose life.

Arbnor Jasari is on the run. Arbnor Jasari is valuable. Arbnor Jasari is known locally as the good Doctor Albania.

Ken McCoist sends the Lexus barrelling down a narrow lane, spraying loose chippings into the hedgerows. This spindle thin thoroughfare is the main route into the ancient market town of Hartland, now nothing more than a large village. Lundy can usually be seen from this road during the day if the mists and the rain keep away, but it's pitch black now.

Full beam on the headlights announces their arrival even though there's still half a mile to go. The farm sits on a gentle down slope that has been scoured by Atlantic squalls for centuries. The trees are twisted, pushing their branches out towards the south-west in the direction of the prevailing wind. The rain when it falls, which it does more often than not, is almost horizontal.

The farm. The old Sillick place. Built in the late nineteenth century by a fanatical gentleman farmer as a model of classical Victorian modernity, adorned with brick arches and eagle topped buttresses, the farm is a wreck. Jock bought the place six years ago, one of his first ventures in the property market, but the sheer cost and scale of the renovation work means it will stay derelict. It keeps the tourists away. Jock has other plans for the place now, anyway.

The site consists of a large, seven bed farmhouse, part of which has been made habitable again, and a range of huge, stone built barns, each one of which has walls three feet thick. The Sillicks raised pigs and the remains of sties decay in the winter gales. Abandoned machinery, seized solid with rust, litters the courtyard around which the barns are arranged. The house is in darkness. Doctor Jasari prefers to sleep where he works.

"I hate this place", says Jock as the car bumps down an unmade track, passes the old farmhouse and pulls into the courtyard. "Fucking albatross. A licence to burn money. Did I tell you about the Sillicks. Mad as hatters. The old man lost an arm in a combine. Could still knock seven shades of shit out of his boys and the wife, though. She, so they say, ran off with another woman. Can't say I blame her. When the old man died the brothers took to drink. I bought the place for a hundred and forty grand, lock stock and barrel. Reminds me of Glasgow after the ships went to Korea. Fucked."

The walls, which should be rendered, show salt leached brickwork in huge, naked patches. Window frames rot. Doors hang loose. To the left of the car is the old dairy, a two-storey stone megalith just like the barns. At first glance, it too looks like a shell, like a skeletal memory, but the car headlights reveal solid metal doors and steel shutters on the windows. From the upper floor a thin sliver of electric light can be seen where one of the shutters has warped slightly. Doctor Albania is at home.

Ken McCoist gets out of the car and opens the rear door for his employer. Davie stays put like he always does, on duty, watching. Simple Davie. All grunt and gristle.

Doors slam. Footsteps echo off barn walls. To reach the upper level of the dairy Jock and Ken go down a narrow passage at one end of the building. As they enter the passageway a motion sensor triggers a mesh encased light. The passageway leads to a staircase. Ken takes point, climbing two steps at a time and knocks on the door at the top, while Jock waits at the foot of the stairwell.

There is a closed-circuit television camera mounted on the wall above the door. A few seconds pass. The door is unlocked from within and bright fluorescent light floods the staircase. As Jock follows Ken up the stairs he hears a low groan emanating from the lower level of the building, once the Victorian milking parlour. To the right at the foot of the stairs a wooden stable door is padlocked. Jock raises an eyebrow, pauses for a couple of seconds on the stairs and then hurries on up towards the light. He enters a room that, apart from a small kitchenette and bathroom at the far end, the fruits of an early attempt at holiday conversion, runs the full length of the upper storey. He lets out a surprised whistle.

"You've made yourself at home, then", he says walking up to a thin, dark skinned man with long but receding hair. He extends his hand. The thin man looks at it for a second, shrugs and turns away.

"Yes. It's okay."

Doctor Jasari retreats to the back of the room and sits at a desk. A computer screen is on. Jock has no idea what the graphs and the figures mean, only vaguely recognising the shape and structure of Microsoft Excel from Maggie's domestic accounting. Next to the keyboard and mouse is an empty glass tumbler.

Jock walks around the room, which has tables arranged around the outside walls, with two more set end to end in the centre. Laid out on the tables are a range of scientific devices, glass jars, tubes, a centrifuge, a hundred and one pieces of equipment, none of which Jock understands. He has no need to. The whole thing is accounted for as capital expenditure in books that are wrapped up as tight as a drum, expenditure written off against tax bills, an investment, research and development, a pension scheme top up. On the tables in the centre of the room are sachets of the only thing that Jock has any real interest in.

"Is this it?" he asks, staring at the sachets. Jock feels like a kid in a sweetshop, a deadly serious confectionery emporium designed for one purpose; child catching. His eyes narrow. He calculates.

"Yes, it's ready. Sorry it's taken a bit longer than I said, but, you know, I only have the basics here. Takes time to get it right. A few mistakes, but we're ready now".

The doctor waves a hand towards the far wall, against which there are two metal cages, built from floor to ceiling like old fashioned Deadwood gaols. These chic additions to the accommodation have served Jock well in the past. He likes to know that he can put people on ice if he has to. Each cell contains a camp bed. One of the cell doors is open and the bed unmade. This is where the doctor sleeps. The second cell is occupied by a young girl. She lays on her back, one arm crooked behind her head, oblivious to their presence.

"Twenty-four hours, no side effects, just endless bliss", says the doctor, admiring his handiwork.

Ken McCoist wanders over and rests his forearms on the cell bars. He looks at the girl. Seventeen, maybe older, puncture marks on her arms, unkempt, dirty clothes, an MP3 player hooked up, smiling, gone.

"Pretty", he whispers, and wonders just how blissful she really is.

The milking parlour. The naming of it fills Jock's head with images of rosy cheeked girls resting their heads against warm cow hide, but the bucolic charm of the image is warped by the groan that he heard when he started to climb the stairs to the laboratory. Jock knows not to ask. Business is business. You can't give people steak to eat on a Saturday night without fattening the steers.

As Jock, the doctor and Ken McCoist discuss business on the upper floor, creatures shift in the darkness beneath the makeshift laboratory. The building's upper floor has been made habitable, but by no means luxurious. Decades of dust are being sieved gently through the floorboards as Jock and the boys move around upstairs. The sound of boot heels on timber echoes through the lower level, dragging the livestock from sleep, or whatever approximation of it they might have found. Without light, locked away, immune to the seasonal shades of day and night, these creatures lose track of themselves, reverting to a simple, feral consciousness.

One of them struggles forward on hands and knees, an arm outstretched, warding off cobwebs, using a thin sliver of light from the padlocked stable door as a guide. The sudden appearance of light fires neurones, causing primeval instincts to urge the creature on. As though emerging from evolutionary autism, the creature recognises a subtle shift in the nature of the world and tries to respond. It has no words. It groans again, crawling on its belly now, its head on the floor, pressing its cheek into the dirt. Through the gap under the stable door it sees a concrete floor and the bottom layer of a bare brick wall. The creature coughs, spits and tries to make shapes out of random thoughts.

Movement. Voices in the heavens. A second creature stirs, waking, scanning the world, unseeing, apparently looking straight ahead but really trying to view the room from the corner of its eye. It too sees light by the door. Orientation. It sees a break in the light, torso shaped. Dust falls. It moves, unwrapping itself, uncurling, stretching. Unlike the first of its kind, evolution has taken a step forward. The creature stands and limps towards the door, slowly, carefully, crouching.

A foot drags. A stone turns. The creature by the door spins round, arms up and covering its head, knees drawn in, foetal. It cries. Tears run like flash flood streams through the dirt on its cheeks.

The walking creature reaches the door, feels in the dark for the source of the mewling, finds a head and cradles it. Slender fingers become tangled in matted hair. Stroking. They are both crying. Evolution takes another step forward.

"What the fuck have they done to you?" says the second creature. Light and soft. Female.

She is the last of the tribe, the last of the three souls delivered on Friday night, two females and a male. One lies in bliss in the room above the milking parlour. The male lies in the dirt in the middle of some demented local death and she, the last innocent on earth, the boy's comforter, has no idea what's happened to him, except that he was the first to walk up the stairs. When he was brought back he was as high as a kite. Since coming down he's been insensible, a mute child.

The girl upstairs is a junkie. It only took a couple of hours for her to start crawling up the walls. She'd probably been looking for a hit for a while. When the thin man with the strange accent told her she'd get a fix if she went upstairs, the girl didn't hesitate, but then they all have some things in common, she guesses; homeless, hopeless, dossing, drunk, high and stupid.

The boy convulses, coughing again, a deep, rasping belly bark. The girl feels something warm on her arm, and assumes it's spittle. She rubs her hand over the sputum and raises it to her nostrils. She's sober now. Stone cold sober and, like all livestock, petrified by the smell of fresh blood.

"Oh, my God, oh my God", she sobs, chilling, feeling her skin turn to goose bumps. The volume rises as her heart rate leaps. A step change. Exponential. She's screaming at the top of her voice.

She doesn't hear the sound of heavy footsteps. Her world is one of riot and panic, of the vast sound in her head. Outside in the passageway Ken and Davie McCoist arrive by the door at the same time. Davie hits a light switch on the wall. Inside the room two builder's floodlights, fixed to the joists, glow and then burst above the girl's head. She is blinded, her eyes scorched, full of needles. She buries her head in the boy's neck. Behind her, the padlock is ripped from the lock and the door flies open.

She is vaguely aware of hands dragging her up, holding her under the armpits. As she rises she feels the boy's head roll down her stomach and onto her thighs. There is a dull thud. Ken McCoist hauls her out of the room. Her feet scrabble in the dirt. Hard, cold images of solidity crash through her tears, images in strobe light; the doorway, stairs, denim, brickwork. She chokes. The air has left her lungs. She deflates. Her left knee cracks against concrete. Unseen by either the girl or Ken, Davie is nearly retching as he kills the lights and locks the door. She and the vomiting man share a physical connection. Their eyes are full of water, full of tears.

As she is dragged up the stairs and across the makeshift laboratory she gets a vague impression of something fantastic, a Frankenstein world, half remembered from childhood. She sees the outline of two men walking towards her, one short and thickset, the other tall and thin. She wants to scream, but the muscles in her throat have constricted around her vocal chords. She hears muffled words. She feels the pin prick of a needle.

Now she wants to laugh. The room fades out of her conscious thoughts and she is lowered onto the spare camp bed. The last thing she thinks is that it's snowing blue-black raven feathers.

Davie stands watch in the courtyard. He is tired. It's late. Not cold enough for breath to steam, but there is a chill in his bones. He can't be sure whether it's the hour or the slaughterhouse air. Time and place. The wrong time and place. He wants to stand in the light, in the passageway, but it's too close to the stable door. Don't ask questions. Do your job and don't ask questions, he thinks, trying to blank out the image in his head of the girl's terrified face.

Upstairs three men stand by a camp bed, breathing rapidly. Jock Cascarino's forehead glistens with a thin coating of sweat. He is agitated.

"For Christ's sake. Do they always scream like that?" he hisses, staring at the doctor. The doctor shrugs. Jock continues, using the sound of his own voice to reassure himself that he is in control. "No way, no way am I risking all this so some fucked up bitch can ruin it all. And how come you don't seem to give a toss?"

"No one hears. It's too late, the walls are very thick, and no, they don't usually scream. Usually they're just happy zapped". The doctor points at his temple and makes a circular motion.

"What did you give her?"

"Just a little sedative, for emergencies. Very effective. Short lived. She'll come around in ten minutes. Ketamine and Midazolam. Don't worry if she sees pink elephants when she wakes up. A side effect, back to normal quickly." Doctor Jasari leaves Jock and Ken standing beside the bed and goes back to his desk.

Jock turns and follows the doctor. Ken takes up his usual pose, arms folded, standing by the door to the stairs. Jock picks up one of the sachets. "So, tell me about the mistakes. What, exactly, are we dealing with here?" he asks.

The doctor sighs, pushes his chair away from the desk and stretches out his legs. "Okay", he says, waving his left arm in the general direction of the tables. "You give me basic stuff, yes? I asked for more, but I understand this is quiet place, this is difficult. I make do. I ask for people, pigs, I think?"

"Aye, guinea pigs".

"These things, yes, and your men bring me so far nine. So, I have equipment, I have medicine and vet drugs, basic chemicals and I mix. I make potions like at home. But it's difficult, getting the right balance, you know? Too much and the kids overdose. Too little and they get a bad headache and demand their money back. It has to be right. So far, you've got six bodies out back, one zombie downstairs and one good girl over there. We'll try the new one on same mix. If it works we're ready to go."

Jock watches the doctor carefully. He tries not to show any emotion at the mention of dead bodies. Collateral damage is to be expected, but he needs to balance the books. "Ready? We'll get to that in a moment. First, Doctor, some details. About these bodies out the back?"

"Yes. Okay. In the pit, you know, when you bought this place and dug a big hole in the yard for the toilet shit. They're in there, with plenty of quick lime, soaking away." The doctor puts his hands together in front of his nose as if praying. He glances up at Jock to watch the man's reaction. This is a stepping stone, a way to make some money so he can disappear. The deal is simple. Jock gets his own local source of superheated Ecstasy, they all put some cash in their pockets and once the lab is established, the good doctor heads into the sunset.

Except the sachets contain a powdered form of something called Kitty Flip, Ketamine and MDMA mixed with a little additive of the good doctor's own making. He's done it before. He has a reputation. He likes his work. So much so that he spent a brief spell in prison number Three Hundred and Two in Tirana, from where he was bought for his expertise by a local hood. Shortly after that clubs and raves the length of the Adriatic rocked the dawn away, fuelled by Doctor Jasari's euphoric cure-all. The problem here is that he's having to guess. The Ketamine is good and his own additions are fairly straightforward, but the quality of locally supplied E is patchy. Get it right and the kids fly. Get it wrong and they fry.

"Why? I need to know why I'm dealing with the bones out back", demands Jock.

"Are you a chemist?" It's rhetorical. Doctor Jasari sighs and continues. He feels like a primary school teacher. "No. Look, at home I had a proper lab, proper equipment, made good pills.

Here it's not so good. I understand. But this stuff is difficult. I know the rough ingredients and quantities, but the stuff messes with the head. Serotonin and Dopamine. You've heard stories of kids getting bad reactions. It's the same thing. Unfortunate but necessary. I've had to experiment and there have been a few accidents, a few reactions, hyperpyrexia, in bad cases hyponatremia, retention of water, brain swellings."

Blank looks. Poker-faced. The deck is stacked in the house's favour and the doctor wins. A straight flush.

"But now I have the right mix. I make notes on the computer." The doctor glances at Ken. "Once we get the right feedback from the clubs, we can make enough, and I can train your boys. A monkey can do it. I'm sorry, but shit happens. It's a small price. No one loves these kids, anyway. They die happy this way".

Ken grimaces. He understands the reference. He thinks about the gonzo boy downstairs and marks it down for future pay back. Jock swallows his pride. He can't argue. The whole thing has been done on a wing and a prayer. One last fling. One more deal. He needs reassurance. Kids, drugs and death. Shit happens, but this is getting too close to home. He turns to Ken. "You're sure these kids won't be missed?"

Ken unfolds his arms and takes a step forward. He feels awkward. Thrusting his fists into his trouser pockets, he says, "As I can be. We followed instructions. Shop doorways, that sort of thing, made sure they were all junkies or winos. And they came along without too much persuasion. The van works a treat."

The van is a Ford Transit crew bus painted up in the multicoloured rag of Jehovah's Brigade, an evangelical missionary group working the Southwest, saving the fallen. Jock has even made sure the registration number is the same as the one on the real van used by the local branch. The kids board the happy-clappy bus to be taken for a meal, a drink and free methadone. Ken McCoist takes them for the ride of their lives.

Jock turns back to the doctor. "And you, you're happy with the results?"

Doctor Jasari sinks down into his chair, letting his head fall back, closing his eyes. "Now, yes. The equipment is good enough, we have good base drugs, so we have no problem. All we need now is professional distribution."

The Doctor raises an eyebrow as he finishes his last comment. Mocking. It's enough. Jock hates being made to look a fool. He moves with surprising speed and lashes out, kicking the seat of the chair. The doctor jerks forward, eyes open, glaring.

"And I don't like fucking foreigners, pal", Jock roars, "but we can't always have what we want. Cut the whinging. Are we ready?"

Doctor Jasari holds Jock's dog eye for a couple of seconds. He looks down. Now is not the time to upset his host. There will be plenty of time for that later. He stands, picks up one of the sachets from the table next to the desk and walks over to the cells. Jock follows. Ken walks over, curious. Body language. The doctor checks the new girl, sees that she's beginning to stir and licks his index finger. He puts it into the sachet, picks up a small amount of the yellow powder on his fingertip and dabs it on the girl's tongue.

"This will make her very happy", he says, "easier to deal with."

He turns to Jock and smiles. "I'll explain." Pointing to the blissed-out girl in the other cell, he continues, "She is deep, won't come out of the hole for a long time. I've kept her blissed all day, all night, to see how she reacts. She's fine. I'll let her have a few more hours, then give her some red powder. Like the boy downstairs. They'll go down the rabbit hole to join their friends." He shrugs.

"Now the new girl is waking up, I'll show you how it works. It's good stuff. If the kids take it in the clubs like the girl did just now, or perhaps a little more, the effect lasts maybe two hours, and the come down is gentle, no hangover, no depression. Very nice stuff. One sachet, five good hits, maybe more, you get a whole night. Like E, they should drink only water, but not too much. Very important."

They're back on track. Jock asks the next obvious question. "What does it do?"

"Like I say, same as E, you know, euphoria, energy, big senses, plus a little bit extra. Pretty pictures in your head. Music, even sex, this stuff makes it so much better."

The new girl tries to sit up. Her mouth is dry. She feels as though she is wrapped in cotton wool. The doctor squeezes past Jock and Ken so that he can sit on the camp bed next to her. He whispers something. She shakes her head. He whispers to her again. She looks haunted. Her eyes are still glassy, but Ken fancies he can see someone very small and very frightened looking out at him, which is just the way he likes to deal with the big wide world. The doctor places her hand in his own, extends her index finger and raises it to his lips. He licks her finger, dabs it into the sachet and raises it to her mouth. She has no power to resist. The doctor repeats the action a second time and then, as the first rush starts to hit home, lets her make herself comfortable. The full effects take hold quickly.

From beneath the camp bed the doctor fetches a Sony Walkman, hits the play button and hands it to the girl. She looks at him through dreamy, floating eyes. He gestures to her to put the earphones in her ears. The metallic hiss and thump of a trance bass line fades. Her foot starts to move in time to the phantom hook. She closes her eyes. Doctor Jasari stands and ushers his partners out of the cell.

"Here there's not too much stimulation so she's relaxed, happy. In a club, lights and sounds, people, so much input, she'll be in heaven." He looks back at her over his shoulder. She is attractive in a basic, unscrubbed way. "Shame. No more clubs for her".

The rest of the conversation is brief and to the point. Jock wants one hundred sachets. If all goes well, they will run a little marketing campaign over the following weekend. It's Easter. The summer season builds up from here. All those kids, all that seaside rock, all those ten pound notes.

Jock and Ken pocket a few of the sachets and leave, shutting the door to the laboratory behind them. As they pass the padlocked stable door neither one of them will look at it. Davie has the car doors open for them as they leave the building. Car doors slam, marking their exit just as they announced their arrival.

Upstairs Doctor Jasari looks at his lab rats. He makes a choice. The new girl. He goes over to her cell, sits on the bed and gently, very gently, starts to stroke her thigh.

Jock and the brothers McCoist retrace their outward journey. As ever, the homeward trip seems to take less time. Jock sits forward on the rear bench, his arms running along the backs of the two front seats. He is strung out. As the digital clock on the dashboard counts down toward five o'clock in the morning the sky begins to lighten. They are all fighting to stay awake.

The coming of daylight, which Jock thinks should refresh them, seems to weigh them down. He won't let his boys see how frayed he is. One last move. He's planned for this. He has three farm complexes under renovation and a number of other properties coming up for sale. It's the right time of year. Finish the work and sell. By Autumn he wants shot of the lot, shot of the cash flow problems, shot of the whole bloody place. He's under pressure. He feels his age. One more deal and he can quit. Cash in the bank and Spanish horizons every morning. Things to tie up. Loose ends. The toss of a coin.

"Davie, I want you out at the farm first thing Monday morning. Check the grounds, make sure our mutual friend hasn't left any shit lying around. Make sure the bodies are disposed of properly. I don't want fucking rats dragging fingers off into some gobshite farmer's barn."

"Aye, boss". Davie yawns. He's only just getting the feeling back in his toes. The car's heater makes him feel heavy, as if he's sinking. He's ready to submerge. Drowning holds no fear, especially now that he has realised what the Boss wants him to do. He shudders at the thought of visiting the farm again.

Jock turns towards Ken, who seems less inclined to throw the car around now. "Ken, we need to call Shaun in next week,

Wednesday probably. We'll need to give him a taster, work out where to shift the gear, how best to run our wee test. Tell him I'll see him at the club, early doors. Price it down to start with, same as a couple of E's, ramp it up later when it gets a bit of a reputation."

Ken nods, concentrating on the road. They're hitting the main trunk road now on the outskirts of Bideford. He and Davie will drop Jock off at the house in Westleigh before heading back to Snuggle's and the flat above the club that they share. Added protection.

"All we need now is a name", Jock continues, "something to create brand loyalty, if you get my drift."

Davie has dipped beneath the plane of creative thought. Twilight. Ken spots his younger brother drifting away and shakes his head. The boy has no stamina, but there's nothing new in that. He makes a left, heading down towards Instow. "Won't the stuff do that?" he asks.

"No idea. Never thought to ask. Good point, though. But we still need a name, something for the kids. What did the doc say? Kitty Litter?"

Ken smiles, checking the rear view, full of his employer's ugly mug. "I think he called it Kitty Flip. But it's not. Similar, but better. No, what about what he said, about the girl, you know, blissful?"

"Fuck off. That's the seven dwarves. Sneezy, Snorty, Dopey." Jock is silent for a moment, thinking, cogs whirring. "Mind, it's not that bad an idea. What about Bliss? Am I right or am I fucking right? Bliss. That's it."

"Aye", in stereo.

The car slows as it enters the narrow village lanes of Westleigh, passing the Exeter Arms and on, up the hill to Jock and Maggie's house. Sitting behind the wheel, Ken feels crowded in by the jumble of painted terraced cottages. He finds the chocolate box congestion of renovated Devon villages claustrophobic.

Once they are through the village, Jock makes Ken stop at the kerbside so that he can walk up the drive and not wake Maggie. He knows she'll be asleep. Nothing disturbs her once she's off. He believes sincerely, though, that small kindnesses like this are what make the difference. He'll sleep on the sofa just to make sure that nothing disturbs her sleep. Business is one thing, but you don't have to live like that all of the time.

SOMETHING'S COMING

LILLE IS NOTHING MORE than a vague memory of sidings and dirty buildings running along the edge of a railway track. The Pas de Calais is being rolled up by the minute as Alex Berisa yawns and reaches out for a cup of coffee. He is being lulled into a sleepy haze of half remembered truths and personal, unreliable interpretations. The Eurostar seats are large and comfortable. The gentle hum and click of high speed rail travel seems incongruous. He drains the last of a double shot Americano, shuddering slightly as the bitter grounds in the bottom of the cup strain onto his tongue. He needs to sleep, if only for an hour or two.

Alex closes his eyes and tries to let the lullaby smother him. Just as the orange glow beyond his closed eyelids starts to fade to black he hears a familiar ring tone. He fumbles in his jacket pocket and pulls the phone out, back to front, and struggles to find the green connect button. Contact. Caller identification. Xhev. Alex clears his throat before speaking softly.

"Xhev, how are you? Where are you?"

The voice in Alex's ear is thin and digital but unmistakably that of his brother.

"I'm good, Alex, good. In London, staying with Pjeter. Got in late last night."

"That's good. How is the old man?" Alex can feel the warmth of his brother's grin across the digital divide.

"Never changes. He's still a randy old goat, but always a gentleman. He's been very helpful so far."

"Okay, what have you got for me?"

"Pretty much as we agreed. There'll be a driver waiting for you at St. Pancras. He'll bring you down to Pjeter's place. I've got a car ready and some equipment. Glocks, silencers, the works, just as you ordered. And I've got some information."

The doctor. Pray to God, Alex thinks, pray to God that Xhev has found him.

"Go on".

Xhev hesitates, reading hastily scrawled notes from Bideford's shipping information website. "Val...Valentin docked nine days ago. She's moved on to Finland, now, but our guess is that our man put ashore. Can't see much scope for him way up there in Finland. It's nice and quiet down there in Devon, just the place to lay low for a while. Pjeter has put the word out here in London, but there's nothing to report up here. My guess is he's still down there. He's got no papers, so he'll struggle to turn the dollars he stole from us into sterling, at least legitimately, so I don't know. He can't have gone too far yet."

"He won't. He knows we're following. He knows he has to lie low. He'll probably try to do a little dealing, something to earn enough local cash so that he can survive. He'll watch and wait, try to let the trail go cold."

A long inward breath. Xhev sighs. "It won't go cold, will it? You won't let the bastard go, will you Alex?"

Alex is feeding on scraps. There is no certainty in the chase. All that he has is his family name and the spur of revenge and hot blood in his veins, blood shared with his beautiful little sister, Rezarta, who is destined to spend whatever life she has left being spoon fed and dribbling onto her blouse. Alex is the eldest, is the captain.

"We'll find him, brother, to the ends of the earth if we have to. This story has one ending. You know it. Keep the faith."

Xhev's voice is quieter, less certain than before, the bravado of the moment and the mission shattered. "I know it, Alex."

Alex has to put steel into his voice. Like his brother, he too feels the despair that comes from looking into his sister's black and vacant eyes. It is a mill stone, a yoke.

"Xhev, concentrate. Remember, I need you in London. Double check everything. Get me maps and directions, as much as you can find. Check the pieces, whatever you can do. I'll be with you and Pjeter for Quofte and Raki tonight."

A pause. Xhev's voice comes back stronger. "Yeah. God speed. See you tonight, brother."

"Tonight".

Alex waits for the line to drop and shuts his eyes, but the smell of the doctor is with him again. The miles are closing down and there will be no sleep now. He puts his mobile phone back into his jacket pocket and rises from his seat. He needs another hit of that good old, caffeinated wire in his blood.

YOU'RE BREAKING MY HEART

THE MOTORWAY STREAMS BY. The Archers are in full rural swing, the omnibus edition rambling through the private tensions of country life. Wind noise. Billy indicates and overtakes. He glares at the driver of a Korean economy hatchback, who is steadfast in his blinkered, sixty-five miles per hour, middle lane certainty. As soon as Billy is clear of the hatchback he indicates again and swings right across all three lanes, making his point. In his rear view mirror he sees the man, the object of his immediate, irrational road rage, turn to his wife and mutter something about impatient road hogs. Billy is tempted to slam on the brakes and beat the dim-witted moron to a pulp. He vents, letting out a stream of oaths and curses, and, feeling slightly ashamed, reminds himself to breathe deeply, to relax.

He catches half a sentence of dialogue on the radio, something about cell counts in Ruth and David Archer's herd, and the rage is forgotten. Billy drifts back to his original train of thought. The radio, the wind noise and the thump of tyres on white lines are nothing more than background static. Billy is running old movies in his head. Home movies. Slices of history in which he is the centre of the universe. He cringes, visibly flinching as he opens the can marked 'Happy Families' and loads the eight-millimetre spool onto the projector in his head.

Billy had woken up just after eight, still sitting in his front room armchair. His neck was stiff. His clothes looked like they had been lived in for a week and his mouth was full of cat litter. He sat in the half-life of waking, trying to remember who and where he was. Everything around him, his possessions, his natural environment, seemed out of kilter with the world, as if spinning at a slower rate around the sun than the rest of the planets.

As the reflux memories of his waking spill into his gullet, Billy coughs. The smell of stale scotch on his breath nearly makes him retch.

The record player has an auto return mechanism, so Vic Damone's long player had finished side one and clicked its robotic way to silence without mishap, but when Billy had first stirred the low-density hum from the speakers beat against his head like an incoming tide on a breakwater. Too much to drink. Always too much to drink.

Back in the here and now Billy tells himself that he ought to cut out the late nights, maybe buy some cocoa. This morning he feels as though he has abused every single day of his fifty odd years on the planet. This is the cardiac nightmare. He holds his breath, counting the pulse at his temple as it becomes more frantic. He exhales heavily. Still alive.

He had showered, dosed himself up on caffeine and stopped at Taunton services for a full helping of cholesterol. Now that he has passed Bristol, he feels marginally better than he did. He will probably do without alcohol today. Probably.

The images in his head flicker back and forth. He imagines conversations the way they should have happened. There is a dull ache in his vital organs, which lowers his defences against these viral memories. Every sign on the motorway proves that he is drawing closer to his destination, and with that closing out of options the memories become stronger. It is inevitable. Familiar. Unnerving.

Billy is torn.

He speaks with Bex every weekend on the phone. He understands that she is in her final year of A Levels and needs to study, but they have not seen each other since Christmas and he desperately wants this time with her. Knowing that he is loved, knowing that he can make a difference to her life is one of the keys to his survival. As a lone male in his mid-fifties he is high on the list of those lonely souls who die too early, but Bex helps to keep him well. She gives him purpose. She stops him from turning the car around, from disappearing down the rabbit hole.

Equal and opposite force. Every time that Billy speaks with Bex he invariably has to speak with her mother, Carol, his first and only wife. She is the opposite, the converse, the flip-side. Bex pulls him towards Oxford with unstoppable force. Carol blocks the road, the immovable object. Bex always proves the stronger. Billy wants to be with her. He thought about trying for custody when she was small, but so did Carol. She made it plain, given their shared experience, that she would cut him out of their daughter's life completely if he ever tried to do that to her. Billy tells himself that the compromise they reached all those years ago was in everyone's best interest, and it probably was, but he still thinks of himself as a coward.

This is what unnerves Billy. This is the story in his head:

He met Carol after a show in eighty-five. Let It Be Me had already become a nostalgic pub quiz question. Billy Nero was back in summer season, hitting the high notes at the end of the pier, warming up for the headline comics. He sang the standards at holiday parks. He worked the clubs. Billy Nero was right back where he started. The bright lights of stardom were dimming under the clouds of Billy's personal history, although you could just make out the fading tail of his comet if you knew which part of the darkling sky to stare at through a telescope. Faded he might be, but his one-time chart entrance helped his billings, helped to keep his head above water, and paid for cocaine.

The club where he and Carol met was in the Lake District, Billy being the main attraction at a caravan park where they held a regular Saturday evening cabaret. Billy Nero headlined.

Carol was a groupie, in that off-hand way that some people have. She had never seen Billy perform before, and as far as either of them were concerned at the time, she would never do so again. She wanted a little bit of glamour. Billy wanted a shag. Simple. Except that the simple things in Billy's life have a habit of going pear-shaped.

It was the mid-eighties. Everyone had a habit. Billy had two; cocaine and women. The drink would come later. Billy was in that downward spiral loved by the red tops and show business gossips. It was a strange and unexpected whim of his muse that Carol should save him. She was trim and petite, fashionable in leggings and bangles, and good, easy company. The sex was great, and Carol worked hard to ensure that Billy had someone to share his hopes, dreams and drugs with. She got a sniff of the good life and followed the scent like a Bisto kid.

For a while Billy was grateful. Carol soothed him, and although money still ran through his fingers like water, she did, for a time, manage the chaos. By eighty-seven they were married and, in a rare period of calm during which they were both bewitched by the prospects of simple domestic pleasure, they bought a house in Oxford, settled down and produced a daughter, Rebecca. Nineteen-ninety. Billy came to terms with the shift in his career. He was content to abandon the stars, settling for a low atmosphere flight plan, and it was a comfortable place to be.

For a while.

Billy feels cramped and compromised. The story, as he tells it, unravels at this point. There is no going back. Geographically, too, he has just hit the point of no return. He is on the A34, thirty minutes away from Summertown. Whichever way he looks at things, the truth turns his stomach. Maggie's comment from the early hours of this morning bites down hard.

A year after Bex came along, Billy pressed self-destruct. He tried everything he could to rekindle the flames of his career. He changed agent. He pestered television production companies. He was convinced that if Lenny Bennett could make it on to Celebrity Squares and Blankety Blank then so could he. Nothing happened. Nothing constructive. Pushed back by the indifference of his peers, Billy's bad habits kicked back in. His period of remission was over. He continued singing, started drinking, hit the coke with a vengeance and ended his marriage with a string of abrupt and soulless affairs.

Carol put up with it for six months. For a while it helped that she could turn a blind eye to Billy's self-destructive ways, wrapped up as she was with a new baby. She stopped touring with him, battened down the hatches, and lashed the cargo of their lives to the deck of their wallowing coaster, but the storms still came and blew everything away. They ran aground. Billy came home in the small hours after a gig on the twenty-third of October, nineteen ninety-two and topped himself up with a cocktail of vodka and barbiturates. Bex slept in her room. Carol told him to leave. Billy broke her nose with his fist.

Billy has tears in his eyes. He lives on his own and has done ever since he saw Carol's blood on his hands. Billy Nero has girls. Billy Whitlow watches from a safe distance. Not once with any of his occasional girls has he dared to touch a button nose. Carol fell in love with Billy Nero rather than Billy Whitlow, and they probably would have drifted apart under the weight of that disappointment, but the man behind the mask is the one who smashed his fist into her face.

It is a matter of trust. When Billy looks in the mirror he sees a man without conviction. Without Bex, without her simple, uncomplicated love, he is nothing.

Billy takes the exit at Peartree, swings the Vauxhall down to the Wolvercote roundabout and follows the northern ring road until he gets to the Kidlington turn off. Instead of heading out of town he takes a right down the Banbury road and just before the shops, opposite the BBC radio studios, he turns left into Lonsdale Road. As he turns he sees the road sign opposite. South Parade. He laughs. It always amuses him. South Parade runs to the north of North Parade between the Banbury and Woodstock roads. Bex explained it during her last visit to Devon. During the Civil War, when Charles I was besieged by Oliver Cromwell at Oxford, South Parade was the Roundhead southern front, while North Parade was the location of the Royalist's northern lines.

Carol and Bex live towards the bottom of Lonsdale Road, with oblique views from bedroom windows over the river Cherwell to Old Marston. Billy drives past suburban gardens and the artful gothic density of Saint Michael's church. The house is of a type typical in North Oxford; semi-detached, three bedrooms and quietly solid. Billy knows from looking in estate agency windows that the place is probably worth half a million. Carol kept the house as part of her second divorce settlement. Billy is thankful for that, and for the fact that Bex has always managed to distinguish between Billy and a small number of surrogates.

Billy always feels as though he is walking on eggshells when he heads for the front door. The time is arranged and Carol will be waiting, watchful and primed. After the initial anger, after the worst stages of antagonism, the worst excesses of separation and grief, Billy cut the drugs and the hedonism. He tried to make peace, but he failed to bridge the chasm within his own head. His stumbling, confused apologies came too late, and he has never been able to lay the ghost. He knows that as soon as he sees Carol he will see her ruptured and bloody face. It's obvious to Billy that she too sees what he sees. The only way they deal with it now is to draw a line under it, to talk as if their shared time leading up to the assault simply doesn't exist. Billy attempts to make restitution by paying the maintenance on time.

Carol opens the door. There is no visible sign of injury. Billy smiles and the dance begins.

"You look rough", she says by way of greeting.

"Late night, you know, the clubs and all that". He sounds as if he is apologising for his life. It has become a habit when talking to Carol. He avoids confrontation, telling himself that things are better for Bex this way. Another proof of his cowardice.

Carol steps back into the hall. "Still haven't got a proper job then? Well, you'd better come in. Teenage girls. Never ready on time. Cup of tea?"

She pads down the hall to the kitchen. Carol never did wear shoes or slippers in the house. Billy watches her. She has that effortless grace of divorced women who are comfortable in their own skins. Carol has no need of a man. She knows how to plumb in the dishwasher. She chooses the company of men because she has the strength to say no, to be alone. Carol is confident in her years, a confidence born out of the combined experience of two marriages and two divorces. Carol is six years Billy's junior, turning fifty in the summer, and she has lost none of her innate appeal. Her hair is highlighted blonde, shoulder length, showing faint hints of grey. She has barely put on any weight.

Billy enters the house, not sure whether to wait by the stairs for Bex or follow Carol directly into the kitchen. He loiters. Disembodied, muffled by open wardrobe doors, a voice calls out from upstairs, "Hi, Dad, be down in a sec, Go and talk to Mum".

The house is full of clutter. Pine. Two tone walls and dado rails, but never untidy. Carol collects things, tastefully abandoning hand carved boxes and odd candlesticks on every available surface. Books line one of the sitting room walls. By the stairs there is an art nouveau stand for shoes and coats. Billy goes to hang his jacket on one of the pegs and notices a pair of boots. Male. There is a Barbour, far too big for either Bex or her mother, evidence of male occupation. This unsettles Billy. He hangs his jacket over his arm and heads straight for the kitchen.

As Billy enters the kitchen Carol is pouring hot water into a mug. A single mug. "Don't make one just for me", Billy says, trying just that little bit too hard to be polite. He is gasping. Dehydrated. Carol looks at him as if he is mad. She mashes the tea bag, spoons it out of the mug and drops it into the sink. A dash of milk. She always remembers.

Handing it to Billy she begins the inane pleasantries that mark out conversation between people who have known each other intimately but whose lives no longer touch. But for Bex there would be no contact. "So how are things in the wild west?" she asks.

"Same as usual, really", Billy replies, "got a few weddings booked up, private parties, Lord Lieutenant's charity bash. Monthly slot in Barnstaple, so not too bad. Hardly the big time, but mustn't grumble. And you?"

"Good".

Silence.

Discomfort.

Billy spots what he thinks is a new toaster on one of the kitchen work surfaces. "New?" he asks pointing at it.

Carol laughs. Typical man. The toaster isn't new. "You'll never change, will you! Never were very domestic. No, Billy, it's the same old toaster. The kitchen..." she says sweeping her arm through an arc. It sinks in. Painted. The toaster looks new because the work surface has changed. The cupboard doors are different. Subtle. Clean.

"Sorry". Billy smiles again. That apologetic voice.

They have found the essential point of entry. Carol continues, "Dave, he's a friend, sells kitchens, bathrooms, that sort of stuff. Hand built. He had some stuff left over when a client changed their mind and bailed out. He thought of us. Very kind".

Billy looks more closely. Solid wood doors. Granite surfaces. Properly finished, no half measures, no filled angles. The boots in the hall are the type used by workmen. Riggers. Dave. Just a friend or is he in residence?

Although he knows that it's irrational, that there's no possible point to it, Billy feels jealous. Despite the evidence and the logic, he still feels as though he has unfinished business here. The heat of the tea in his hand, in his gullet, makes him sweat. "This is stupid", he tells himself.

"Good job", he says, running his hand over one of the work surfaces. The tile grout is white and uniform. The silicone sealant around the sink is perfect. "Very good job".

Billy struggles to think of something else to say, something complementary, and is saved by the bell. Feet clatter down the stairs. Elephant feet. Something scrapes along the banister. There's a dull thud on the hallway floor, and skipping, freewheeling, Bex hits like a goose winter.

"Dad!"

Arms around his neck. Seventeen. Alive. Bright and fresh. Billy's heart skips a beat. Suddenly, and despite the aching weariness that he has been feeling all morning while driving up to Oxford, he feels that every single second of his life has been worth the struggle. He wants to pick her up in his arms just like he used to do when she was five years old. Bex. His darling, his princess, his blessing.

They kiss. Bex babbles on about bags full of books, about school, about Mandy Hollins, about a party the previous Saturday, about anything and everything, jumping to and fro between subjects like a firecracker. The discomfort evaporates. Carol relaxes. The conversation and the smiles between the three of them are, for a few simple moments, genuine.

As he puts her bags into the boot of his car and waves to his former wife, Billy thanks God for the love of a daughter like Bex. She is a single child, mature beyond her years, who holds the green line between adults who have forgotten what the war is about. What would he do without her? All thoughts of Dave and his boots are vanquished. Billy settles down in the driver's seat and kills the car radio. Depending on the traffic, on the caravan hell that holidays bring to the Southwest, they have three, maybe four hours on the road.

Bex fills the airwaves. By the time they get to the motorway, Billy knows more than he could ever wish to know about Mandy Hollins, her boyfriend, Rashid, and their doomed love affair, consummated, as far as he can tell, all too frequently behind the college bike sheds.

Billy and Bex are cruising across North Devon, curving across the edge of Exmoor, lights on, wipers clearing rain from the windscreen. They are at the end of a pulse of traffic. Taillights snake red as the road bends, dips and rises. The light is failing, the world is turning and colours are assuming that natural state of daily decay, grey-black, under rolling banks of cloud. The wind whips in, buffeting the car, pushing it towards the centre line. It's Sunday evening and homeward bound weekenders flood out of the county, heading for civilisation. Grockels. Love them or hate them, Billy's livelihood depends on them.

As far as Billy and Bex are concerned the only weather relevant to their existence is inside the car. They are bathed in sunshine, soaking up ultra-violet, warm and safe. The rhythm of the wipers mimics the gentle rush and draw of soft waves on a perfectly white sandy beach. Blue skies. Bex has introduced Billy to her friends, to her teachers and to a world of gravel voiced young men and their crying guitars.

They stopped for coffee and petrol at one of the motorway services and she spotted a radio adaptor for her iPod on special offer.

"Please? Pretty please!"

How could Billy resist? In between stories she selects tracks by bands and artists from another universe. They laugh. Billy points out where these youngsters are going wrong, where their craftsmanship is lacking. Bex calls him a Muppet, a dinosaur, and as she does so she holds his hand tightly.

Ordinarily Billy would be watching the streams of oncoming traffic, dodging in and out, overtaking slower moving vehicles, but tonight he is in no hurry. He wants this time, wants to enjoy Bex without interruption, but it's a wonderfully lost cause. Bex bubbles along beautifully beside him, fielding a seemingly incessant stream of teenage exuberance on her mobile. Texts, messages and calls fly through the rain-heavy air, bouncing off cells and masts. Holding a conversation with her is like trying to herd bees, and Billy is in seventh heaven, even when the conversation gets round to her mother.

"You should try a bit harder, Dad, she's not a monster", Bex says quietly as they reach South Molton.

Billy acknowledges this simple, obvious fact with a monosyllabic grunt, concentrating on the looming chaos of the next roundabout. He has never spoken to Bex about the fury. She knows about the basics of it all, but she was eighteen months old when he left and she holds no direct memories of his wayward existence. Bex has heard at second hand most of the published stories. Billy is grateful for that, at least.

He has no reason to lie, although both he and Carol are complicit in the conspiracy of omission. By the time Bex was old enough to understand both he and Carol realised what their anger might do to her. Best interests. Bex knows just enough about the affairs, knows about the drugs and the personal battles, but not about the fury. Billy often wonders about it. When should he tell her the full story? He needs to.

"It's not always as easy as that", he replies eventually. "At your age things are black and white. When you get to my age history tends to obscure things. You get lost in the past".

"Grey areas?" Bex is teasing him.

"Something like that. Short term memory loss. You forget why you're thinking about something. Memory plays tricks. It wasn't…easy back then."

"It never is, Dad. If things were easy everyone would be happy all the time. All I'm saying is you've punished yourself enough. Why do you think I'm so hyper when you pick me up. Someone's got to lighten you two up. It stands out a mile"

Billy is touched. How can someone so young be so bloody sensible? The milkman's daughter? A changeling? Who cares.

"If you say so. It's just…there was stuff going on back then. We were in a bad place. I lost control and I'm never quite sure whether I've got it back."

"It doesn't matter. That's what I'm saying, Dad, it doesn't matter anymore. Mum is fine. She's over it. Dave is good for her. Be pleased for her and let it go."

Bob the builder, thinks Billy. Can he fix it? Yes he can. He holds the thought, trying to get back on track. Bex is right. Let it go. But no matter how hard he tries to bury the past it won't stay six feet under. The freshly levelled soil starts to boil and broken bones jerk through. Boots. Kitchen work surfaces. Dave is all the things he could never be, will never be.

Bex holds the moment too. She turns to face him. He looks at her out of the corner of his eye. He sees a soft, pale, youthful face full of hope. He smiles.

"The way I see it we have a very short time on this earth. We have to enjoy it. We owe it to ourselves. And I've decided. For the next two weeks I'm going to make sure you enjoy yourself", she says.

"After your revision", Billy counters.

"Don't!" Bex grins.

Billy's hand is resting on the gear lever. She takes hold of it again. "I love you, Dad".

Bex disarms him totally. The car slides through the rain. "And I love you. You're right, Princess, but I still blame myself. Your Mum...well, she's done pretty well. Let's leave it at that. I'll try, for you, but I can't promise".

The conversation drifts a little. Billy is tired. That last haul up to Barnstaple always drags. He needs a drink. A proper drink.

Mornings, especially Monday mornings, are not one of Billy's strong points. By the very nature of his profession he is a night animal, having spent thirty years living and working after dusk. He wakes to the sound of the toilet flushing, which, while not totally outside his experience, is unexpected this morning. As far as he knows he is the only person in the house. He rolls over in his bed, dragging the duvet up and over his shoulders. Wiping crusts of sleep from his eyes he tries to focus on the alarm clock. Digital figures swim. He screws up his eyes, yawns, and as his sense of time and place returns he remembers.

He and Bex stopped off at Mister Hu's on the quay. It is one of her favourite treats. As far as Billy is concerned Mister Hu cooks the best Chinese takeaway this side of Peking, and he should know. One of the perks of living the light entertainment cavalcade is that you get to travel and you get to eat food out of cartons. Billy has a mental map of a thousand disposable towns which uses clubs, pubs and restaurants as points of reference. He has eaten Chinese meals the length and breadth of the country. The one safe place in a sea of grease and boiling chip fat is a Cantonese harbour. Mister Hu is, without doubt, the best Chinese chef in the world. Billy could eat his Hong Kong style sweet and sour chicken until he bursts. Bex too.

His head feels remarkably clear. A set meal for two. Drinking tea. Choosing tea.

Billy wanted a drink, a real drink, something that burns, but he chose tea. Instead of sitting on his own on a Sunday night playing records or grazing satellite channels, he enjoyed the simple delight of his daughter's company. They ate. They talked. They both went to bed before eleven. Billy feels self-contented and happy. He rolls onto his back and stares at the ceiling rose. He can just make out the plaster pattern in the shadow world of early waking. He stretches, wiggles his toes underneath the duvet and breaks wind. Simple things.

Footsteps. The third step on the stairs creaks. Billy hears the kitchen door open, hears cartons being shovelled into a bin liner and he waits, luxuriating in the stuffy warmth of his bed. Cups. Water. The sound of a filter coffee machine brewing up. Eight o'clock. By ten past the smell of fresh coffee gropes its way under his bedroom door. Humming, Billy flings back the duvet, puts on last night's boxer shorts and grabs his dressing gown from the back of the door. He nips in to the en suite, plays tag with a stray hair in the toilet bowl and, doing a dreadful impression of Paul Robeson, starts to sing; "Oh, what a beautiful morning, oh, what a beautiful day..."

The kitchen is a classic example of minimalist, bachelor life. Billy is halfway through Delia Smith's *Learn To Cook* video course, but has yet to invest in all that cooking paraphernalia. The work surfaces are largely bare. He has a kettle, a toaster and a white china pot inscribed in blue with the word 'Tea'. He has been stuck halfway through the course for two years. His requirements in the culinary department are largely catered for by the places he works in. Part of the deal is a free meal. Billy is king of the sliced ham and ketchup sandwich.

Bex is struggling. She opens a cupboard and finds assorted, mismatched pieces of crockery. In the next cupboard there is a jar of marmalade and a jar of strawberry jam. The marmalade will have to do because the jam is two years out of date. Bread. Billy has forgotten to buy fresh bread. She finds a pack of crumpets in the bread bin. The coffee flask sits steaming on its hot plate. Billy walks in.

"Morning, love".

"Hi, Dad, bit early for you, isn't it? Where are the knives?"

Billy thinks. Where are the knives? It takes a second or two. It jars him slightly that his daughter doesn't automatically know where he keeps his cutlery, but he has to let it pass. He isn't entirely sure where the cutlery lives either.

The morning is too bright, too glorious, to waste. "Second drawer along, by the sink". He sits at a small pine table, rubbing his knuckles through his hair. "Sleep all right?"

"Like a log. This place is a disgrace. As soon as you've showered we're going shopping. If I'm stopping here for two weeks I'll need some decent food. You can't revise on an empty stomach". Bex fills two mugs of coffee, puts them on the table and starts searching the cupboards for sugar. Neither of them take milk. "Sugar?"

"Oh, probably not. Stopped taking it." Billy pats his stomach, holding it in as much as he can. She takes a sip of coffee and makes a sour face, as if she has swallowed diesel. They laugh. She drinks it anyway.

Bex stuffs four crumpets into the toaster and gets a tub of margarine out of the fridge, which is, save for a small lump of Cheddar with a hard rind, and a couple of half cut lemons, almost empty. When she peels the lid off the margarine tub she discovers mixed-in toast scrapings.

"Dad!"

Billy looks sheepish. The toaster pops. Bex puts two crumpets each onto side plates and dumps them on the table. "Hail fellow, well met", she says, levering off the lid of the marmalade jar. Breakfast is a brief affair. Father and daughter bicker amiably about the state of Billy's culinary supplies and of his being a total boy. At his age he should know better.

With the second, slightly stewed cup of coffee Billy asks, "So, what's the plan? How much work have you got to do?"

"Quite a lot, really. Chemistry, physics and biology. It's not like English. I wish. I actually have to know this stuff. I reckon I ought to work most of this week. Boring." Bex makes big brown cow eyes at him. "What about you?"

"Easter holidays. The clubs are ramping up. I've got gigs in Taunton, Paignton and Bristol, Thursday, Friday, Saturday. Nothing else till then. I've kept next week free apart from the Saturday, though. Figured we could do something." Billy sips at his coffee, which is just turning bitter.

"Like what?", Bex asks.

"I thought Padstow, Rick Stein's, the bistro. Or we could head into Exeter for a bit of shopping, whatever you want to do. It's your break. We can sit on the beach at Instow for a week if you want. I'm your slave, within reason." He grins. Billy has been many things but never anyone's slave. "Is there anything you want to do?"

Bex considers her options. Better come clean. She has already made plans. "Well, apart from work, I'd like a quiet week. Could we stay in, watch a bit of telly, play a few records. You could teach me stuff. It's really cool having a Dad who's a singer, even if your stuff came out of the ark. I thought we could we go and see Maggie at the club on Wednesday. When you're away I'll do my revision and playhouse."

Everything comes out in one long stream. Bex pauses, takes a breath and before her father can interrupt she lays out her plans for the following week.

"Next week, I'd love to do Padstow, Tintagel, maybe the Eden Project. Definitely the Eden Project. And Newquay zoo. Vet stuff." Billy looks impressed. Organised. He has yet to visit Cornwall's indoor jungle.

Now for the big one. "And then I've invited a couple of mates down for the last weekend. I want to go surfing. Tod's wicked. And Lizzy, you know Lizzy, they're both from school. Westward Ho or Baggy point. Bigbury, yes Bigbury. A night out on the town. That club in Bideford. And the pub with all the moon boots. Lobster Jack's. Tod and Lizzy need some relaxation as well. You don't mind, do you? Say you don't?"

"Tod?", Billy gasps, quite out of breath with the sheer rapidity of his daughter's suggestions and orders.

"It's cool. He's just a mate, nothing heavy, none of that deflowering stuff. You'll like him. He plays guitar and the piano. Please?"

Billy makes the usual parental sounds. He asks a few questions, knowing that the answers are irrelevant. He listens to his voice as if it is coming from another room. It is a tone of voice, an act that all parents learn to some degree. How can he refuse?

"Yeah, yeah, Bex, all right". The sound of her voice in his kitchen is better than Vic Damone's lullabies, is better than ambrosia. "Actually, it'll be good to have some people in the house. I'd like that."

Bex stands up, skips around the table and plants a huge kiss on his forehead. "Brilliant. I'll call them, let them know we'll meet them at Tiverton. Thanks." She trails one hand across Billy's shoulder and makes a pumping fist movement with the other, the one that Billy cannot see. "After you've showered", she says, "you can take me shopping."

As Bex takes the stairs two at a time Billy smiles. Little girls. All grown up and hell in the bathroom.

IT'S MAGIC

THE FIRST MIGRANT HOUSE martins are skimming the rooftops, fattening themselves up before finishing their journeys to summer homes, to familiar eaves and overhangs. With the steel shutters permanently closed, Arbnor Jasari works by electric light. He has no interest in the beauty of the morning. He takes a brief walk around the courtyard when he wakes to clear his head and then tries to settle into his routine. This morning he is distracted.

The cells opposite his desk are open. The one formerly occupied by the blissed-out girl is now empty. The camp bed has been made and, apart from some scuff marks on the wooden floorboards, there is no sign that the cell has recently been occupied. The second cell, the one which the doctor normally sleeps in, is occupied by the last of the lab rats. She is awake and curled up under a threadbare blanket on the camp bed. There are two MP3 players on a wooden chair next to the bed together with the spent casings of two tea lights. On the floor lie two empty bottles of cheap, screw top red wine. Beside them there is a crumpled plastic sachet. The girl's naked shoulder is covered in bruises. Her knee aches. The doctor talks to her while he works.

"No repeats, please, it's no use", he says, counting out empty sachets and putting them in lines of ten on an old, painted wooden tray. The painted outlines of fat, red hens on the tray are flaking with age.

"Enough yesterday. I told you, the other girl has gone home. If you scream, I'll have to hurt you, but if you're a good girl, I'll make more powder for you. You do want to be happy, yes?"

Silence.

"I think so. You're very young, very pretty. You don't want me to make you unhappy. I think it's really very simple."

The doctor finishes with the sachets and takes the tray over to one of the tables in the middle of the room. He picks up a set of kitchen measures and selects the one marked up as tablespoon sized. He scoops up a full measure of yellow powder from a stainless steel bowl and carefully fills the first sachet. Then he runs his finger along the grooved seal at the top and places it in a plastic Tupperware box next to the tray. There are two Tupperware boxes.

The girl stares straight ahead and says nothing. Her hair, which is shoulder length and mousy brown, is matted and dishevelled. She is too thin to be healthy, a sign of the times, of squats, drugs and the occasional meal.

"Not so loud today? Good. Face the facts. You live a shit life, yes? Sleeping in doorways, begging, thieving, getting bad stuff. This is a chance to clean yourself up. You're dirty, your hair is a mess. After a shower I'm sure you'll look much prettier. So, we'll make a deal. You won't scream or try to run away. I'll feed you, and I'll provide drink and free happiness. You help me, I help you. It's lonely here sometimes."

Arbnor Jasari looks up from his work and grins. He is not seeking permission. This is a one sided deal. The house wins again.

"If you make me mad it will be very bad for you. I'm sorry I hurt you last night, but it was necessary. It's like training a dog, you have to learn the rules. A dog is only as good as its trainer, and I'm a good trainer. You understand? You help me, I help you. We make money, we go away, far away, no more shit."

The girl rolls onto her back and pulls the blanket up under her chin. She is slowly getting to grips with the slight modulations and vowel deflections in the man's voice. In another place, at another sunset time, with sangria and the sound of waves breaking on clean white sand, she might even find it attractive. Holding the blanket in place she raises herself up into a sitting position, adjusting the pillow so that her back is protected from the cold stone wall. She watches the doctor as he continues to fill sachets with yellow powder. There are needle scars along her right forearm. Waking is agony. She needs a fix and there is something gnawing away at the back of her mind; this man, a strange taste in her mouth, lights, sounds and the smell of unwashed bodies.

The doctor carries on chatting, making small talk. "In my country I also had a very bad time. I was a bright student, expected to do well, but for me it was drink. Then drugs. I was a doctor in a small town, Gjirokastër, built by farmers. It's an old Ottoman town and I hate it. Very boring. So I drank and made good drugs. Then I had bad day. I was performing a minor operation, a wart on a woman's neck, and I had a muscle spasm." He mimics his right hand locking and makes a slashing movement. "Big mistake. They arrested me, locked me away in prison Three Hundred Two, Tirana."

He has the girl's attention. In spite of an urge to bury her head deep under the covers, to run and run and run, the girl is fascinated and she finds herself listening to his story. Self-preservation. So long as he talks, so long as he works, she can keep him at a distance. She tried screaming for help last night. She tried to fight him, tried to make a run for it, but the door was locked. He looks like an eight stone weakling, tall and weedy, but he is strong and sinewy, like a cat. He plays with you. His eyes are cold and calculating. Sudden movements, she has learned, make him extend his claws.

"But prison wasn't so bad. I have skills and I sold them, making simple drugs for the other prisoners." The doctor stands up and looks at the girl. He has a faraway look in his eyes. He is homesick. Nostalgic. Then his face darkens. "This makes news, underground news. One of the local bosses bought me and took me away to Vlore on the Adriatic. They gave me a proper lab, good ingredients, and told me to make fine drugs for the tourists in Croatia, Italy, you know. You'd think I should be happy, no? Well, I wasn't. Things were still very bad for me. I had no freedom. I had to make drugs or I die, but one day I chose another way. Now I can't go back. You can't go back when you've killed members of the family, when you steal a load of dollars and run away. Omerta, as the Sicilians say. So, here I am. Homeless, like you."

The girl speaks softly. "My name is Helen".

Arbnor Jasari looks at her, making an assessment, regarding her as once he might have watched a patient, reading between the lines of described symptoms, looking for a signature.

"Good. Helen. A nice name. I am Arbnor. Arbnor Jasari. Doctor Arbnor Jasari." He walks around the table and enters the cell. He sits on the edge of the camp bed, takes the girl's left hand in his and raises it to his lips. "Pleased to meet you, Helen".

She looks down at the blanket, down at where it rests between her thighs. Now that the fog is lifting she remembers him there. She looks up and forces a smile. Selling herself to live, to get a fix is something she has done before. This time, she thinks, the stakes are higher.

"I'm sorry. I was scared yesterday. Confused. Maybe we've both been fucked by life".

"By life…yes, but things change. You help me, I help you." He gestures back towards the tables full of basic brewing equipment. "All this stuff makes good money, and our colleagues are not so bright. Mostly they're full of shit. Big muscles and little brains. They think they own me, like before in Albania, but maybe it is not quite so cut and dried. If you'll work with me, here, now, then when I decide to go I could take you with me. We could both be free. That's a real deal. What do you think?"

Helen doesn't move. She makes no sound. She stares into Arbnor Jasari's eyes. He stares back. Somewhere in the back of her head, remembered from a time long ago and a place far away, she hears the opening bars of The Good, The Bad and The Ugly. It seems appropriate. "Can I have a shower?" she asks, "and my clothes?"

The doctor holds her hand tightly for a few seconds more then lets it fall back into her lap. They appear to have an understanding. They're both in a place of need. He doesn't trust her, and he knows that she doesn't trust him, but so what? The world is far from perfect.

"Yes, yes, of course. There are some clean towels in the little cupboard by shower. Your clothes, too. Dirty, I'm afraid, but I'll ask the stupid Scotch men for new clothes. They'll bring them soon."

Inwardly he chastises himself for burning the other girl's clothes. Then, with a moment of reflection, he decides that new clothes will be much better, much safer.

"Shampoo, soap, it's all in there. Please..." He stands and helps the girl up from the bed. She wraps the blanket around her body, but not before the doctor sees a flash of perfect white buttock and the naked snake of a young woman's soft-skinned back. He steps back to allow her free passage out of the cell. A gentlemanly gesture. She manages to smile weakly at him and trots down to the far end of the room where the shower, toilet and kitchen are located. As she passes the open kitchen door she makes a mental note. Cutlery.

The doctor returns to his work. As he fills the remaining sachets he talks loudly so that she can hear over the sound of the boiler as it wheezes into life, telling her how he bought a ride on a smuggler's boat to Italy and how he worked his passage on various ships, until, after some weeks at sea, he made landfall in the little white town of Bideford. He had been expecting Bristol or Southampton.

"So, when they come back, you say nothing, yes?"

The taps are on. There is a toothbrush in a chipped mug on a ledge above the sink. She shudders, thinking about where the toothbrush has been, but her need to clean herself, to descale her mouth is greater than her distaste for the strange, thin man in the laboratory. She can just hear what he is saying. Her mouth is full of toothpaste. It feels wonderfully sharp and hot on her breath. She makes a noise in the affirmative.

"And no more funny business!"

The doctor hears the shower gurgle and kick in. Pipes rattle. The wall mounted boiler in the kitchen rattles and groans as it heats the water. It is one of the two concessions that Jock has made towards home comfort for his pet scientist. The other concession is two gas heaters, both of which are on permanently. The sachets are ready. One hundred perfect packets of extreme pleasure in a plastic food box. Next to them is the second box. It contains fourteen sachets. They look identical to the others but they are not the same.

These sachets were made up early on the Sunday morning, straight after the good doctor and his spaced out good time girl had played their little game of fair damsel and evil ogre. He was high on adrenaline after her screaming fit. He was bruised. She was confused and battered. He had no choice but to force feed her yellow powder and lock her away. He has the scratch marks on his upper arms and chest to prove how strong and forceful she had been. To calm down he mixed up a little potion and drank red wine.

In the excited aftermath he misread his own notes and spiced up Jock Cascarino's mixture just a little too much. He was going to throw the batch away, but, on mature reflection, he decided that having a little stock of something criminally mind-bending might prove useful. If the girl tries to cross him again she will regret it. When the time comes to deal with Jock Cascarino and his hired thugs, what better way could there be than to make them crash and burn with their very own rocket fuel.

He leaves the two plastic boxes at the front edge of the table and walks to the far end of the room. The shower door is closed. He leans against the wall, shuts his eyes, and draws mental pictures of his good time girl washing herself down in the shower.

The girl stands under the hot stream of water for twenty minutes. She washes her hair three times before attacking the bar of soap. She wants to be clean. She wants to wipe away every last trace of that thin bastard. She wants to cry but knows that she cannot allow herself the luxury of emotion. She scrubs herself raw and then lets the water flow over her body for another ten minutes. She counts the bruises on her arms, legs and abdomen.

First thing of a Monday morning means different things to different people. Davie McCoist is scrubbed, dressed and on the road by twelve noon. The sun is shining. Early April. The Easter weekend approaches. Billy Whitlow and his daughter are in the kitchen unpacking the shopping. Davie is just setting out on his principal errand of the day and there are days when he hates his job.

The journey out to the farm takes longer during the day,

especially in the school holidays. Cars, laden with bags, kids and panting dogs clog the roads. Motorhomes squeeze down narrow lanes. Caravans snake their way up hills and inclines, slowing as supermarket rigs coming from the opposite direction scrape along the hedgerows, devouring tarmac between their trailer wheels. Davie has no desire to rush anywhere this afternoon. Doctor Albania gives him the creeps. He tries to think of other things, of trips out with his mother on sunny days in East Kilbride when he was seven or eight, of sunlight on leaves through a bus window. The trouble with these long distant memories of innocence is that they inevitably involve Ken, big brother Kenny, Chinese burns and rabbit punches, making him do the dirty work, nicking chocolate bars and making smaller kids cry.

The North Devon roads close in on Davie's thoughts, the high banked hedgerows limiting his vision. Green rolling fields extend all the way to the cliffs that run round Hartland Point, but all that Davie can see are tailgates, stands of daffodils and plastic bags snagged in hawthorn branches. Opposite ends of the country. Same old shit.

Brake lights. The tail of traffic comes to an abrupt halt. Ahead of him, obscured by a bend in the road, he hears the hiss of air brakes. They wait for a few seconds. The cars in front of him pull away again slowly. As Davie rounds the bend he sees fresh roadkill. The remains of a cock pheasant glisten in the sun. Feathers blow on the slipstream from the accelerating cars. It reminds Davie of the purpose of his visit. Dead bodies. He opens the driver's side window to let some fresh air into the car.

Ten minutes later Davie pulls into the farm courtyard and parks next to a piece of old farm machinery. There are hundreds of metal tines on a large, circular wheel, and the entire contraption is pitted and brown with rust. He has no idea what it was used for. To Davie the thing looks like an instrument of torture or the skeleton of a defeated alien invader. He gets out of the car, careful not to snag his jacket on the beast's ragged teeth. Everything seems idyllically peaceful underneath the dilapidation of decaying human ingenuity. He glances up at the top floor windows of the dairy but makes no sign of recognition. He is sure that they have heard him pull up. Instead, he walks round to the back of the car, opens the boot, takes off his shoes and puts on a pair of Wellington boots. Then he walks round to the back of the barns and the milking parlour, treading carefully through pools of semi-liquid mud and loose gravel. The place is a mess, covered in abandoned building material and rapidly shooting clumps of dock and nettle, which are spreading across the broken and barren ground.

Rotting timbers lay scattered across the old pig rearing area. Concrete breeze blocks are covered in lichens. Lengths of scaffolding stick up at odd angles from water filled trenches. Orange safety netting hangs from a metal spike at the edge of a half dug pit. In the middle of the yard, surrounded by uneven piles of earth and the fresh green heads of pernicious weeds, there is a black plastic manhole that shows signs of recent, repeated use. Next to the manhole is a crowbar. Davie wedges the crowbar into a slot in the manhole cover and levers it up and off the septic tank.

Davie begins to heave as soon as the lid moves away from the tank. The stink of stale air and decomposing green matter mixes with rat piss and the decay of human flesh. Davie is engulfed in an invisible cloud, the unsubtle aroma of rotting meat. He has no need for a torch. The chamber of the glass reinforced plastic tank is full of naked skin. Scratched and broken. Sucked dry of colour. Marbled with mortification. Arms, legs, a bloated stomach, he can see them tangled together a couple of feet below the manhole pipe. There is no room at the inn. The eyes of one of the homeless kids are open and they stare up into the bright spring sky beyond Davie's shoulder. He vomits, adding his own foul odour to the already putrid air.

"Fuck", is all that he says, repeating the word again and again, whispering it so as not to disturb the boys and girls beneath his feet. He feels faint. He has seen bodies before, but nothing like this. Davie has ended lives on Glasgow's heavy, swollen streets, but he has never observed death as part of an industrial process. It has always been personal, a thing done between individuals, usually on behalf of someone else, and always in the company of Ken. Davie has always known the names of the people he has killed. What he sees now perverts his sense of honour, twisted though it is. It's like being in a classroom at school where someone is repeatedly scraping a fingernail down a blackboard. He wants to end this now. Davie steps back, wiping saliva from his chin with the back of his hand. He breathes deeply, swears quietly once more, and promises himself that he will never work for foreign bloody bastards again. They are animals.

There are traces of quicklime on the bleached arms of the fermenting corpses. Outside, on the ground and on the manhole cover, the rains have washed away any residue. Davie slams the manhole cover back into place and stamps it down to keep the dead from rising. He checks the surrounding area for scraps of torn clothing, for personal items, but finds nothing other than puddled boot prints and the tracks of a wheelbarrow tyre. Police forensics might find enough to hang a man, but to a casual observer there appears to be nothing amiss. It's a derelict building site, nothing more, nothing less.

Roof slates lay smashed beneath the overhang of the main barn roof, and on the opposite side of the yard are the rib thin remains of pig units. The old boiler room still contains a series of unconnected pipes that radiate out from the centre of the back wall like the arteries and veins from a transplanted heart. Davie guesses the boiler was sold for scrap. Sheep bleat in the distance, beyond Davie's line of sight. A seagull wheels away to the west, and disappears beyond the roofline of the old milking parlour, while crows mob a buzzard above the tree line that runs the length of the field below the farmhouse. Davie hears the buzzard's high pitched squeal of annoyance and imagines the bodies in the pit, in their death throes, pleading for light. The crows caw incessantly. Life is like that. He wonders if the kids were dead before they were dumped in their plastic grave. He hopes they were.

Davie makes his way back to the car. Just below his knees, where his trousers have brushed the sides of his Wellington boots, there are damp, muddy stains. He changes his footwear and puts the boots into a plastic carrier bag, which he drops into the rear passenger footwell. Spotting the mud on his Chinos, Davie raises his eyes to the heavens and swears. He is not happy.

He crosses the courtyard, walks down the passageway by the

old milking parlour and sees Saturday night's padlocked stable door flung wide open. He pokes his head inside the makeshift prison, where faint slivers of light shine weakly from the edges of the steel shuttered windows. The room has been swept. Doctor Albania has been busy. Davie trots up the stairs, knocks and waits for the good doctor to unlock the door to his temporary laboratory.

The good doctor's little reverie by the bathroom door is broken by the rap of knuckles on wood. He checks the closed circuit television monitor on his desk and sees one of Jock's goons standing at the head of the stairs. He sighs. All work and no play makes Arbnor Jasari a very tetchy boy.

The door is unlocked and Davie enters the lab, still brooding over the novel use that the waste disposal system is being put to. The doctor moves to the centre of the room and stands by the two tables.

"You here for the samples?" he asks, abrupt and sharp.

"Aye, and for a look round. Jock wants some reassurance. Any more bodies for the morgue?" Davie can hear the shower running. Doctor Jasari is fully clothed. He looks like he needs a good scrub, but Davie doesn't think the doctor is preparing for his ablutions.

The doctor cuts in immediately. "Morgue?" As he says it he remembers. An American word. Mortuary. "Oh, yes, I understand. No more bodies. They've all gone home. Very cosy." The sound of the shower cuts out.

"So I saw" says Davie with marked ill humour. He checks out

the room, approaching the tables in the centre of the room on which the sachets are being stored, all the while watching the far end of the laboratory and the bathroom door. "These the ones?" he asks pointing to the Tupperware boxes on the table.

The doctor moves away from the table, carefully keeping sufficient space between himself and the hired muscle. He stands beyond the table, between Davie McCoist and the door to the bathroom. "Yes. You want to try some?" He laughs. "Good stuff. It'll give you big balls."

Davie nods, picks up one of the sachets from the box containing the bad mix and turns it over in his hands. Rough hands. Heavy and powerful. "That good, huh?"

Nerves betray Doctor Jasari. He starts to move forward. It is an overreaction and he is telegraphing anxiety, thinking too quickly to be certain of his next step. Betrayal. "No, no, not that one. The other box, please! This is for later."

Davie looks at him quizzically. "Later? What do you mean?"

Arbnor Jasari tells himself to breathe, to slow down. The doctor tries to smile, buying time. "What I mean is this is for the next batch, for next week. The full box is for you. One hundred sachets, just like Jock asked." He makes a movement with his head indicating the closed bathroom door. "The girl from room downstairs, like the ones you've seen this morning. She's the last one. I'm going to keep her for a while, like a pet. I get lonely out here on my own all day."

"Big balls, eh?" Davie sneers. "You dirty little shit."

A pause.

Davie checks his natural sense of disgust and tries to focus on the job at hand. Be professional, he tells himself, rise above it. "It takes all sorts. You don't mind if I hang around, check her out. Can't be too careful, can we."

Sweat breaks out at the doctor's temples. He can feel a trickle of perspiration running down his side, making the material of his shirt cling to his damp skin. He feels hot and uncomfortable. He runs a hand through his hair. Lank. Greasy. The bathroom door opens. The girl appears wrapped in a bath towel with her hair piled up in a hand towel. She is playing the game, but the rules have changed. She sees Davie and stops dead in her tracks.

Davie recognises her; the girl from Saturday night, the screamer. He remembers holding her. She felt so fragile and small. Now she is awake and stone cold sober, briefly free of any substance. Davie sees the bruises on her arms and shoulders. He knows that he probably caused some of them when he dragged her up the stairs, but cannot believe that he caused them all. Too many of them are vivid purple and fresh.

The girl recognises Davie, too. He is the son of a bitch who tricked her into the van. He had a friend. They drove them all out here and now the rest of the poor lambs are gone. She remembers the boy coughing up blood in the room downstairs, remembers how heavy he felt in her lap.

"What the fuck is he doing here?" she hisses. She looks at the doctor. Davie stands quite still. The doctor is trapped between them, playing piggy in the middle.

Davie bats the ball back into the doctor's hands. "Your new best friend? Not sure Jock will be too happy. Does she know what's going on?"

"She's seen all this", replies Arbnor Jasari, "but it's no problem. She understands. Her friends have gone home and she's going to stay for a while, keep me company. As I said, it's not a problem."

Stalemate. No one moves.

"Gone home?" Davie feels like a second rate cop in a sick situation comedy. His world is full of questions, but very few answers. "Does she know where home is? Does she know that mum, dad and the rest of the fucked-up Brady Bunch are waiting for her with open arms? Shame about the digs. Does she know that, doctor?"

"Know what?" Helen asks. There is something she is missing, something important. All this talk of home makes her uncomfortable. She left home two years ago and she has absolutely no desire to see the place again, especially not her stepfather and his wandering hands. Sweet talk when the lights were out.

The doctor ushers her towards the cell, keeping between her and Davie, the interrogator. "I've told her what she needs to know. And she will help me. I have keys and I have drugs. She knows what will happen if she upsets things."

Helen walks slowly, warily back towards her cell, treading with bare feet on the rough wooden floorboards. She edges past the table and makes a dart for the cell door. The doctor follows her and closes the cell door behind her.

The matter of fact tone in the doctor's voice makes Davie's blood run cold. He struggles to keep a lid on his anger, hissing at the man through clenched teeth. "I can see that. Nice set of bruises, miss."

Safe behind bars Helen turns and spits at Davie. "You should fucking know", she yells. "Kidnapping. That's what this is. That's what you are. Bastard."

It's water off a duck's back. Davie has heard it all before. He ignores her. It's Jock's call, not his, and if she wants to play with the Devil, then that's up to her.

The doctor stands with his back to the cell door, hands in pockets and shrugs. "So what? If Jock wants the drugs, he'll give me the girl. No girl, no more work. You got that?"

Davie can take any amount of shit from working girls, pissed-up lads on the lash and fellow travellers on the dark side, but he doesn't like taking Class A crap from the third world. He goes quiet. His voice drops, low and monotone. "Yeah, I got that. You'd better hope Jock is in a good mood when I tell him."

A fake American accent. "Whatever".

The doctor watches Davie as the blood rises, colouring the goon's cheeks and forehead. He, the doctor, blessed with natural gifts that spin beyond the other man's low orbit, is back in control. He likes the feeling and lets it show. The doctor likes to rile people.

"Unlike you, Davie, I can count to more than ten. I have a brain. It doesn't matter if Jock is unhappy. I'm the one making drugs for him. One day, maybe, when this is simple enough for a monkey to do, he'll give you the job." The doctor points at the first plastic tub full of sachets of yellow powder. "Until then you fetch and carry and right now I want you to carry those to your boss. You can fetch her some new clothes as well. Understand?"

Davie has had enough. The bodies outside, the stink of vomit on his breath, the girl's bruises, it all wells up. He takes a step towards the doctor, who shrinks back against the cage but doesn't take his eyes off Davie. The doctor grins. It's a come on. Davie's thigh catches the corner of the table and the whole thing lurches with the impact. Dull pain. Another bruise. Davie's leg burns. He stares at the doctor with pure, unadulterated malevolence. The pain in his leg digs down to the bone.

The girl in the cell watches the two men intently, not at all sure what is going to happen next. Will they stand their ground, will the doctor win through sheer bloody-minded goading, or will he be nursing a flat nose and broken ribs? What about her own immediate future? Shit.

Doctor Jasari stares at the plastic boxes on the table. The impact of Davie's leg carries sufficient force to make the boxes slide forward with enough lateral thrust to tip them over the edge of the table and onto the floor. The carefully segregated sachets, the good and the bad mixtures, scatter across the floorboards. The Doctor lets out a howl of anger and pounces on the debris, desperately trying to identify the different batches of powder.

"Fucking ape!" he hisses.

Davie's momentum carries him around the table and he grabs the doctor's collar, yanking the man's head back. "Serves you right, prick. Shut up and put the shit back in the box. Fuck you!"

"Leave him alone" Helen screams from the cell. "He spent all morning on those". She chooses her team. The weird man.

Looking after number one. There is no future with thugs, but there might be a way out of this mess with the drug maker.

Davie slams a flat hand against the cell bars to make the girl shut up and it works. She steps back in fright. "Why are you so friggin' worried, pal? What's the story?"

The doctor has to think quickly as he wriggles out of Davie's grasp. Kneeling, he looks up at his assailant and smiles thinly. He holds his hands up, making the universal sign of obeisance. "Different batches. Quality control. We have to see if batch one is good. Then we can use batch two as the control when we get into full production. If it's all okay, we're on the road, but now I don't know which ones are which."

He scrabbles through the sachets, but there is no way to tell them apart. Fortunately the second box, the one containing the brain-fry mixture, hit the floor and tipped to the left and the doctor thinks that most of the bad sachets have fallen to the left of the skewed table leg. He scoops them up and counts them back into the box. There are only eleven sachets. He has no choice. He has to guess.

"Just sort it." Davie moves back to the far side of the table. He has shown the gook. No one calls him an ape and gets away with it.

The doctor fills the first box, counting out one hundred sachets, and puts the remaining three with the others from the second box. There's probably a killer or two in the batch that Davie will take with him, but there's nothing the doctor can do about that. They will just have to live with the bloody mess. What does it matter, he thinks. Some poor kid has a bad trip. Shit happens.

He hands the box to Davie, who looks at the doctor and then at the girl. "You'd better be careful", Davie says and turns to leave. As he reaches the door he adds, "I'll be telling Jock about this".

The door closes. Doctor Jasari goes over and locks it, returning the key to his jeans pocket. The girl sits on the camp bed and he goes over and sits next to her. His heart is racing. He touches Helen's arm and feels little tremors running through her bones. Goosebumps.

"You see what I have to deal with. It's always the same, but this time I'll take enough money, take enough of everything."

He rests his head in his hands. He is shaking. Now that the muscle-man has left the building, now that the threat is gone, he is in a state of shock. Adrenalin pumps through his system. The girl puts her right hand on his shoulder. He shivers.

"I am tired of being alone", he whispers.

She stands, pulling the hand towel from her damp hair and shaking it loose. She lets the bath towel drop. "You don't have to do it on your own. I'm here now."

He looks up and lets out a long, slow breath. "I must take a shower. For you."

Helen takes his left hand in hers and pulls him up from the bed. She leads him out of the cell and towards the bathroom.

"I'll scrub your back", she whispers.

MUSIC BY THE ANGELS

MONDAY ROLLS INTO DARKNESS and Tuesday dawns. Billy and Bex enjoy the smallness of domesticity, breaking the back of a confusing, sometimes threatening world by carving life up into manageable chunks. The bonds between them have remained strong in spite of Billy's frequent and sometimes prolonged absences. Their separation is legal. It is understood.

Between household chores, unpacking the shopping, brewing tea and the constant cycle of preparing food and stacking the dishwasher, they discuss the future. For Billy these are poignant moments. He is on the downward slope, aware that his time is growing short. He has no desire to do great things and the lure of bright lights is less compelling than once it was, although he cannot imagine life without a faint echo of music and sing-along girls. Fatherhood and divorce changed him. He grew up. He had to. He indulges his passions lightly now rather than burning himself at the stake, making a living doing something he loves. Billy has learned to be grateful.

Billy finds it strange that Bex is the one who, despite her common sense and grounding, seems, on occasion to be fearful. Sometimes he feels as though he ought to become maudlin, regretting the passing of time and the rising call of the pine box, but he has no fear of death. He has done things, many of them the wrong things, but he sees little point in regret. Bex, on the other hand, carries hope and fear in her hands, balancing them constantly. She has so much to do and she is in such a hurry.

They discuss school and university. Bex describes how her teachers fall into one of two categories; the ones who have come to resemble their books, hidebound, stiff of spine and congenitally dusty; and those who's pages get dog eared and torn as they try to remain part of the ever-changing youth culture that surrounds them. Most of the boys at her school are laughable, full of seventeen-year-old menace and spots, with legs and arms that they have not quite grown into. One or two are the real deal, though, and Billy will meet Tod in a few days.

Bex is not ready for the sex thing. She is quite matter of fact about the whole issue. She reels off reasons as if she is reading a list of faculties in a university prospectus; qualifications, boys rather than men, too young to really know her own mind, being frightened of the responsibility. It is Billy who is uncomfortable. He has a history, a list, a little black book chock-full of names from his illustrious past, but like his own parents, as he grows older he finds the subject increasingly difficult to talk about to people younger than himself, especially those he loves. He feels inadequate. He should be able to pass on the benefit of his experience, but it seems so sordid. The thought of Bex in the arms of some heathen called Tod begins to form in his head and he changes the subject.

Results. Bex wants to take a year out if she gets good grades, a year doing something somewhere. She has yet to make up her mind. A year on the tiles before taking up the books again. She wants to be a vet. Billy revels in her optimism, in the sheer range and exuberance of her take on possibilities. The world beckons and she is ready to follow. Billy tries to explain how careful she must be and how she must try to understand the questions before assuming that she has any answers. He still has nightmares about his little girl being led away by a Pied Piper.

How do you live with love, he wonders?

Bex wants to know about his past. Billy plays a game with her, one they have enjoyed for some years now. He selects records from his collection, talks her through the stories and the lives, and pins the melody to his own life. Bex has an aural map of her father's history.

They always end up with Vic. As the last bars of *On the Street Where You Live* fall away, Bex asks, "Can we go out tomorrow night? I want to see where you work".

Billy protests. "I wouldn't call Snuggle's the place where I work".

Bex insists and Billy bows to her youthful enthusiasm. "Okay, okay. Tomorrow night. Actually, it's not a bad idea. Open mic night. You'll see how terrible most people are, and just how talented your old man is."

"Modesty", says Bex, smiling up at her father. She is sitting on the floor, resting her head on his knee as he selects records and tracks, and cues them up on the turntable. "And it'll be nice to catch up with Maggie. Haven't seen her since last summer. How is she?"

Billy puts a hand on his daughter's head and strokes her hair gently. "Same old Maggie…"

The old Sillick place continues to rot. Each season brings with it clifftop weather. It almost never snows and frosts are rare, but it rains hard and often. When the wind blows the rain billows across the fields in great sweeping clouds. It seeps into the fabric of anything man made, finding the smallest cracks and gaps. For Doctor Jasari and his good-time girl the early part of the week passes without weather. They have an accommodation to make.

They also have drugs to make and the equipment in the lab is makeshift and basic. Although the process of making Bliss is fairly straightforward, being a blend of already formulated substances, to produce it in any quantity is labour intensive. Doctor Jasari is, in his watchful way, grateful for Helen's company. He has shown the girl how to grind tabs of MDMA. He mixes and measures. She spoons the stuff into sachets. Together they finish the second batch and are well on the way to building up stock levels for the summer season.

The door keys remain firmly in the doctor's pocket. When he wants to sleep he locks the girl in one cell and he beds down in the other cell. When he wants company he asks and she gives. There is a freezer in the old farmhouse and a proper, full size bed. They have discussed their options. When they need to fill the fridge in the lab kitchen the doctor accompanies the girl to the farmhouse. He is usually friendly, but then he can afford that little luxury. He has a small Beretta tucked into the waistband of his jeans.

The girl has suggested they sleep together in the farmhouse. It would be more comfortable and they could spread out. The lab is depressing, but Doctor Jasari has yet to make a comment. He says, "We'll see". He is uneasy in the open air. Windows without shutters disturb his peace of mind. The girl finds it amusing and gruesome. He makes no bones about his contempt for Jock Cascarino and his boys. They are a means to an end.

Life is about choices, choices and consequences. Compared to the street she is relatively safe here so long as she plays the deadly game, so she concentrates. She does the work as directed. She pleases and teases. She makes drugs, makes basic meals, makes the doctor smile, and when the moment softens she makes him sweat. When she gets scratchy, when the itch is in her bones, he makes one of his potions and she feels alright. As a special treat, when the day and the man are done and the cell door is locked, he gives her good, clean smack. She spends the small wee hours over the hills and far away.

It helps to take her mind off things. She can deal with the situation most of the time. Freaky it may be, but she is in control. She is a woman and, fragile as she may seem, she has power over men, and she believes she can make that count. This man, her new lover and benefactor, is distinctly odd, too familiar with death, impassive in the presence of abuse, but he is still a man. What concerns her are the small things. In the farmhouse there is a room, a bedroom, bare and unfurnished. In the middle of the floor she has seen a pile of personal effects; a wallet, cheap beach jewellery, a hair scrunchie, a pair of red trainers and a small pink teddy bear with a heart shaped patch of red silk sewn on its chest. For the time being, she has decided, these are questions for another day.

The doctor sleeps soundly. He finishes each day in the arms of his good-time girl. He drinks red wine, the bottles coming from a diminishing store under the stairs in the farmhouse. He drinks just enough and then he tucks her up for the night and finishes the last bottle in his own cell. They drift through chemically enhanced conversations until their drug of choice carries them away.

Jock and the boys keep busy with the humdrum routines enjoyed by local businessmen everywhere. Property requires management. Contractors need chivvying along. Bills need paying. The sane world revolves around the treadmill of death and taxes. If you don't keep on top of the buggers they will rip you off and Jock keeps on top of them all. If a difficult situation arises he has the brothers McCoist sit on people. A technical term. The application of pressure works wonders during awkward negotiations.

Of the three farms under renovation, two are nearing completion, being on second fix, bathrooms and kitchens. The third will be ready by the autumn. Jock makes his legitimate money by buying up failing farms, selling off the land and converting house and barns into holiday homes. He only buys when there is potential to create seven or eight homes on a site.

His first successful development turned a clear million in profit, thanks to a gambling debt and the brothers McCoist, and the deal allowed Jock to buy two more farms. That was six years ago. There is enough cash in the bank to retire, but Jock has ambition. He also has a history. Like Billy's it is one of missed opportunities and cold shoulders. He should have been big in his hometown. Instead he ran south with his tail between his legs. He wants to make one more killing before he starts taking golf lessons in the sun.

Doctor Albania is a sign, a mark of providential favour. He turned up in a pub, trying to buy whiskey with dollars. The British are sceptical about funny money. Euros are the devil's own currency. The good doctor clearly had an eye for the using type, however, picking Shaun Lloyd out of the crowd and trying to sell him a hundred Ecstasy tablets for twenty quid. Shaun pocketed the tabs, shared a drink with the man from out of town and phoned Ken McCoist.

It was meant to be a shakedown. Jock's boys control the distribution of certain substances in the North Devon Triangle; Barnstaple, Bideford and Torrington. Thankfully for Jock, Ken was on form that night and rather than deposit the foreign gentleman behind the recycling bins at Morrison's he took him to see his boss. Doctor Albania was christened. The albatross, Sillick Farm, suddenly had a purpose.

On a day-to-day basis the brothers McCoist run errands, supply wholesale drugs, ensure that local coppers turn a blind eye and deal with any unexpected situations. In their spare time they go to the gym and try to impress young women in that depressing way that forty-year-old alpha males have. They love the holiday season as it provides them with a chance to wear singlets and impress dumb blondes. They have no particular hobbies and Jock keeps them busy. As for ambitions, Ken wants to buy a pub on foreign soil when his boss retires, while Davie dreams of being able to return to his beloved Ibrox in a British Racing Green Jaguar XJ6. For all of his summer singlet bicep flexing, Davie's dreams are heavily populated with sheepskin coats and pints of Heavy.

Jock is out of the brothers' hair today, visiting Brownsham Top, one of his investments. He needs to explain something to the happy-go-lucky crew of local builders doing the renovation. The terms 'presently' and 'directly' commonly used by the usually invisible human beings that Jock calls the 'turnip-heads', terms that mean sometime in the next three weeks, do not feature in Jock's dictionary. He wants the kitchen tiling finished and the final units fitted. He is releasing the details to the estate agents on Wednesday, just in time to catch the Easter parade of eager house hunters. Welcome to the glossy Good Life.

Jock's absence leaves the world of Snuggle's Cabaret Bar in a comfortable state of flux. Maggie Heard loves Snuggle's best on a Monday and Tuesday. The club is shut. The lights are out. She can sit in the office and book acts. She can plan menus. She has time to chase up corporate reservations. When the sun shines and dust motes spiral, when the smell of stale smoke mellows and becomes almost pleasant, that is when Maggie loves the place the most.

On Tuesday afternoons Maggie gets her hair done and spends an hour or two at a local beauty salon. Nails. A facial. A fake tan. It's all show business. She insists on looking her best. The first full flush of youth may have passed, but she works hard to keep herself in trim. She is high maintenance and loves looking good. The bob cut has served her well, but her stylist is working on her layers. She'll wear her hair at shoulder length by the Spanish autumn.

It is tradition at the club that Wednesday night, the first show night of the week, is dedicated to local talent. Open mic is held every two weeks. On alternate Wednesdays Maggie tries to support local amateur dramatic and operatic societies by inviting them to sing songs from the shows. She also scours the local papers to see if there are any visiting celebrities, but they rarely attend and almost never perform. She nearly tracked Judi Dench down once, but her telephone message was never returned. Maggie would love to ask Joss Ackland over. He lives locally. Somehow, though, she has never plucked up the courage. Does he hoof? Maggie doesn't know and thinks, on balance, that he is probably getting on a bit. In fact, she is not entirely sure that he is still in the land of the living.

She gets back to the club around four in the afternoon on a Tuesday and by rote she checks that the bar is stocked for the following day and gives the place the old once over, the finger on the bar test. Cleaners. The answer phone in the office is flashing. She checks the message.

"Hi, Maggie, it's Leona. Just thought I'd check you remember that I've got Saturday night off. My birthday. I'll see you Wednesday after college. Any problems give me a bell. Bye-eee."

Maggie has watched the budding romance between Leona and one of the regular boys behind the bar with a small degree of fascination. People watching is a hobby. It's a shame that the boy has to work on Saturday. She thinks about giving him the night off too, but she has no cover. Maggie prefers working with people she knows, which is probably why Billy has such a regular slot.

Ted Line is an altogether different indulgence. That is care in the community. If she let him go he would drink himself to death. He probably will anyway, but at least he gets four nights a week when he has to slow down.

Billy and Bex arrive at Snuggles just after eight. The tables are mostly empty and a few punters mill around the bar, most of whom have stars in their eyes. The show kicks off in half an hour and regular attendees know this period as The Mumble. Conversation is limited and nervous. Hopeful comics rehearse jokes, careful not to say anything above a whisper in case one of the enemy nicks a punchline. Bathroom singers run through lyrics. At the far end of the bar a boy of sixteen takes anxious swigs from a bottle of orange juice. He has a large cardboard box of props by his feet. The magician.

The audience is made up of two distinct types; tourists and locals. When Billy and Bex turn up the few poor souls in the bar are tourists. Grockels. The atmosphere is as thin as consommé. The locals drift in around the time the show gets underway, having experienced the build-up too many times to want to participate. They will be sampling the wares of the town's pubs, getting tanked, ready and primed for heckling. Maggie usually holds the first act until there are enough people in the place to make the heckling enjoyable. She sees no point in having an open mic night without audience abuse. The artistes have to learn the hard way.

Billy takes Bex to the end of the bar where Maggie usually sits by the red table lamp that she uses to remind Ted Line to hurry things along. Tonight the lamp will stay off. Performers get five minutes. If they go the distance they get a voucher for a free meal and drinks, and an encore later in the evening, but if the act bombs Ted Line rings a bell and they are hauled off stage with extreme prejudice. Billy moves one of the prototype comics along and he and Bex settle down on bar stools, ordering a couple of beers and a packet of smoky bacon for Bex.

The young lad behind the bar acknowledges Billy and takes an immediate interest in Bex. In between pouring pints and dealing with the steadily increasing trickle of voyeurs and masochists, he tries to get Bex into conversation. He has to tone his usual patter down a little, and his sincere belief that fathers should never accompany their teenage daughters in public is suitably reinforced. Bex thinks differently.

They get through two bottles in short order and Billy suggests that Bex has a Coke next. Strictly speaking she is underage. His suggestion carries the full weight of genuine parental concern, which hits Bex like a feather duster. Beers all round. The topic of conversation is marriage and Bex is explaining to her father why she will never accept that women need to do the meringue thing. Billy loves the primary colours that teenagers use when daubing the world with their opinions. He gives her current convictions a month at most.

The bar is filling. The atmosphere thickens. Just before half past the main door flies open and twenty young lads bowl into the room. The bartender looks totally dismayed, but Maggie appears in the nick of time to give him a hand. She makes a point of greeting a middle aged man in a blue fleece, shows him and the lads to a group of tables in front of the stage and suggests that they give her an order so that she can bring the drinks over. It is a pointless gesture. The lads are already crowding out the bar, yelling orders and intimidating some of the tourists. Maggie spots Billy and waves as she beats a hasty retreat and helps with the serving.

Shouted out from the crowd, "Four Buds, love!"

"Buds, right." Maggie picks the bottles out of the cooler cabinet, flips the tops on the bar's bottle opener and says, "Ten pounds, please". A note changes hands. "You going to give 'em hell tonight, lads?" she asks. The lads leave her in no doubt about their intentions. Maggie works her way down to Billy's end of the bar and serves one of the tourists. Service is gradually becoming less hectic, but she waits and watches, making sure the hired help can cope.

"It's like the bloody Coliseum". She has to shout at Billy and Bex. The noise level is rising by the second. Snatches of conversation and good humoured insults break through from all sides. Maggie fights to make herself heard. "Barnstaple Town. That bloke in the fleece is Terry, the manager. He wanted to get them out for the night. Bit of team bonding. Should improve the bar takings."

Another order comes across the bar. Maggie deals with it, telling Bex that she will be round for a proper chat in a second.

As Maggie walks round to the front of the bar, chatting with a couple of regulars on the way, Leona pokes her head out from the wings and points at her wrist, making the universal sign that says the evening is running late. Maggie doesn't see her but Billy does and he manages to catch Maggie's attention. She turns towards the stage and gives Leona the thumbs up.

Leona's head disappears for a few seconds. Ted Line is primed.

Then Leona skips down to the main floor and sits poised over the sliders of a small, portable mixing desk. The musical acts have to provide their own backing tracks, which she cues up for them on a compact disk player. She opens the main faders and Ted Line wanders out onto the stage to a cheer from the footballers, who are revelling in the opportunity this evening gives them to sit on the terraces and barrack. A *Chumbawamba* track booms out of the main stage speakers. "*I get knocked down, but I get back up again.*" The evening's signature tune. First up is a regular, a would-be new wave politico comic.

He is greeted by jeers and cat calls. Maggie makes her way over to Billy and Bex now that the punters are firmly focussed on the stage. She gives Bex a huge hug. "Lovely to see you, darling. You're looking so well. How's the old man treating you?" She winks at Billy.

Bex grins. "Same as usual. No food in the house. Embarrassing. Everything you could possibly want in a Dad."

Billy sits back and takes it on the chin. Maggie goes with the flow. "Typical man. You take your time and find a good one when you're ready. So, how's the studying. Billy tells me it's crunch time. Doesn't seem five minutes since you were all buck teeth and braces."

Maggie and Bex hit the catch up button. Billy tries to watch the act on stage, but keeps one ear tuned in to the conversation just in case they start ganging up on him again.

The act. "What's wrong with this country?

Barnstaple Town's centre forward. "You are!" Cheers, jeers and laughter.

The comic has enough chutzpah to ignore the almost constant stream of interruptions. "I'll tell you what's wrong. Gulf War. Iraq. What was all that about dossiers."

Boos from the audience. Old news.

"Weapons of mass destruction. Weapons of mass destruction! Said so in the dossier but they never found them, did they! So, how did they know old Saddam had them? Tried to make it all official, didn't they. Nicked a student thesis and put it in a posh report, when all they needed to do was look at the bloody receipts!"

The guy on stage has a monotone voice. The material almost works but he loses his audience through the diesel drone. He makes every topic sound so boring, which is of itself a talent, but not one appreciated by tonight's punters. The football boys are in full cry. Swept along on a tide of alcohol and the untethered horseplay of ridicule, the rest of the audience join in. Ted rings the bell and actually has to push the man away from the microphone. The crowd, responding to the emperor's question, jeer and give the comic the thumbs down. Leona fades the microphone out and plays in a recording of police sirens. The poor sod has never got beyond two minutes and he has been trying for a year.

Next up is a girl from the checkout aisles, a karaoke queen. Someone has told her she can sing but she warbles and Billy can't watch. He wishes he was deaf. She reaches for the high notes but they are kept in a box on top of the wardrobe and she has forgotten to bring her step ladder. The bell goes again and Leona hits the sound effects. There is general, raucous merriment in the audience. Faces screw up in pain. A steady stream of orders flow to and fro across the bar. Billy re-joins the conversation between his daughter and Maggie Heard.

"…yeah, Jock's fine love, like your Dad, set in his ways and a pain in the backside, but better the Devil you know."

Billy realises that he has not seen Jock since he arrived, which is most unusual. "Talking of little Devils, where is he tonight? It's not like him to miss a chance to have a go at the acts and Ted?"

Maggie suddenly looks hard and cold. "Round the back. Actually, I'm bloody furious with him. Swanned in here at seven o'clock, picked up a bottle of Grouse and said he had some business to do. Could he use the office? He's been in conference with the Brothers Grim ever since. And he's expecting a visitor. I wouldn't mind but he knows how busy we get when the Muppets are on the bill."

Billy prefers not to ask about the business and Maggie wouldn't say anything, anyway. Billy knows how much Maggie hates Jock using the club as his office. Sometimes he treats the place like a personal fiefdom. Jock would have made a fine Robber Baron. Maggie started the place with her husband, and while that relationship might not have been the best, Snuggle's is her baby, is the good thing that came out of all that hurt. She and Billy exchange a sharp glance. The subject is changed. Back to Bex.

"So, darling, do you take after your wonderfully talented father? Fancy a go?"

Bex pulls a face. "The singing vet? Not for me, Mags, never."

The sixteen-year-old boy is on stage. He sets up a camping

table and mumbles something about the Sands of the Nile. He takes a large transparent bowl out of his props box and puts it on the table. Then he pours out three small piles of differently coloured sand from plastic carrier bags. Finally he signals to Ted, who brings out a pitcher of water.

The boy begins by pouring water into the bowl and he has to stand slightly awkwardly to use the microphone while performing his trick at the camping table, but he soon starts to gain confidence. He tells a story about an ancient Egyptian ritual, and he stirs the water with his bare hand. The water turns black and opaque. As the story unfolds, the boy places a handful of each colour of sand into the bowl of dark water. Then he extracts them, one by one, dry and unmixed. To finish he stirs the water one last time, and it becomes completely clear.

A klaxon sounds. The audience, most of whom have been watching intently, quickly realise that the boy has done it. Five full minutes. There is something utterly compelling about this ingénue, something naïve and spellbinding in the way that he speaks and moves. Ted walks on and claps. Cheers all round. The boy blushes spectacularly and nearly runs off stage, only to be called back to clear away his props, and suddenly he loves it. Adrenalin. Applause. A star is born.

Blind hope fades. Gags go flat. Melodies are betrayed by shocking timing. The only success of the night so far is the teenage magician, and on stage now another stand-up is dying. His routine consists of rehashing skits from films and shows. Billy has found a new low. He has just endured the 'Dead Slug' sketch. Monty Python's legacy is safe.

The door to the main bar opens halfway through a dreadful parody of the Two Ronnies' Pispronunciation sketch and in walks a sallow-skinned young man. He is at least six foot four. His head is shaven, but shows a couple of days of growth. There is a bald patch at his right temple. The young man is thin and his clothes hang on his bones as he scowls at the crowded room, and as he walks past people he makes them feel dirty. If he has slept in the last week he shows no sign of it. The crowd at the bar parts as the youth's brooding smell drifts before him like a force field.

Rising up from behind a wall of sound, standing tall on ramparts of abuse, the comic spots the boy and goes for the obvious put downs. "Bloody hell, it's one of the walking dead. Oi, Lurch, over here, mate!" he yells, pointing at the youth. Heads swivel. Ted Line holds his bell hand still for a moment. A group of the footballers in the front row stand on their chairs and chant, "You're not welcome at the bar...you're not welcome at the bar!"

The young man ignores comments from punters and comic alike, leans on the bar, and orders a pint of snakebite.

Maggie, who has watched his progress in horror, gets up from her chair and signals to the barman that he shouldn't serve the boy. She walks over, watched by the crowd and the comic, who provides a running commentary. Maggie hesitates, steels herself and then reaches up to tap the young man on the shoulder. Billy's move to her side is instinctive. Bex feels her heart skip a beat.

"Sorry, love", says Maggie, trying to conceal the edge in her voice.

Where are the McCoists when you need them? Billy sets his feet wide. If it comes to push and shove he wants to be ready for it. His right fist is balled. The young man turns slowly. He is trying to effect narrow Clint Eastwood eyes.

"Sorry, love, but there's a dress code. I'm going to have to ask you to leave."

The young man stares at Maggie for a few seconds and then turns to look at Billy. "Here on business. Mister Cascarino wants to see me. Tell your poodle to back off, mate."

Maggie stands her ground, going toe to toe. She is fuming. Billy recognises the look in the young man's eyes. It is a look he has worn; despair in the soul. The kid is either high or just sufficiently drunk enough to take Maggie on. Beside him Maggie is caught in the spotlight and Billy decides that it would be better if he directs her fire away from the druggie. Better for everyone. Better for Billy. He asks a question, "Where's Jock?"

He lights the blue touch paper and steps away. Maggie stands stock still for a moment, then turns slowly away from the boy and, without saying another word, she walks parallel with the bar, heading towards the far end of the room. She walks at a measured pace, letting the rocket fuse reach its zenith. Her scream is internalised, is stored and primed for another target. She disappears into the corridor that connects the main function room to the kitchen and the office while the young man resumes his place at the bar and gets his pint. Billy retreats to his seat, smiles at Bex and says, "Who'd run a pub?"

The boys are in conference and the door to the office is shut.

Maggie explodes through it and the door slams into the whitewashed brick wall. Everyone in the room jumps. Maggie plants her hands on her desk, leans forward and measures her words. Venom. Dripping. "Who the fucking hell is that in my bar?"

Jock looks at her. He asks himself a question. It takes a moment for him to spot the answer burning in her eyes. He is genuinely dismayed. "Shit, babe, I'm sorry."

He rises from the chair and starts to move round to the front of the desk. As he does this he glances at Ken and motions to him to go and fetch the little toe rag. "I told him to use the back door, love, not the front."

Maggie stands up straight and spits out the words, "And I've told you never to use this place for that kind of stuff. I don't want it here, you understand. Not here. Why can't you meet him wherever it is that sort hang out. Under a stone. Anywhere. But not here!"

Jock holds out a hand. Placatory. "Babe, I'm really sorry. It's business. I needed somewhere private."

"Don't you bloody touch me. Private! Some fucked up druggie walks into my bar mid-show, and you call that private. Sort it, Jock, then get the hell out of my sight. I'll deal with you later."

Maggie turns to go and almost walks into the young man as he is being pushed into the room by Ken McCoist. Enough is enough. She takes one step forward and slaps the boy across the cheek. Snakebite slops out of his pint glass onto the carpet tiles.

"If you ever do that again I'll break both your legs", she says to the boy, her voice dripping with cold menace.

Ken steps back out into the corridor and watches Maggie stalk back to the bar. He licks his lips.

Out in the main auditorium a bell rings and Ted Line announces a twenty minute break. Punters and performers make for the bar. The interval scrum. Maggie flips up the countertop, hits the optic at the bottom of one of the bottles of Scotch three times and glares at a man who has the temerity to ask for three pints of bitter. She thinks about joining Billy and Bex, but decides that she needs a moment to herself. She crosses the room, steps up onto the stage and heads off towards the dressing room. Behind her the sound of normality, the sound of alcoholic conversation, continues as if nothing has happened to disturb the awful equilibrium of the evening.

Ted has a thirst on. He fancies a cold pint but doesn't want to wait for a suitable break in the crowd at the bar. Not a problem. He heads for the kitchen and breaks out a can of lager from one of the fridges. He pulls the ring slowly so as not to make a noise. The office next door used to be a dry store for the kitchen and although the conversion work was carried out some years ago, the old access hatch between the two rooms still exists. It keeps prying eyes at bay, but not prying ears.

Ted leans his elbows on the stainless steel work surface underneath the hatch and takes a gulp from the can. The sound of his own swallow is unnerving. He thinks about lighting up a cigarette, but decides not to. The smoke would drift into the room next door. He settles for a little snooping. Working the clubs and drinking in Barnstaple's many pubs gives a man a chance to see and hear a great many wonderful things, and Ted has seen the young man before. He knows the game, and a little juice on Jock might help to keep the wolf from the door.

Jock is back behind the desk. Shaun Lloyd is sitting in Ken's chair, next to Davie. Ken is leaning against the door to prevent any more disturbances. Shaun is halfway down his pint and the bottle of Grouse has sustained substantial damage. Jock has laid out a small number of plastic sachets on the veneered chipboard top of the desk.

"Nice. That red mark on your cheek suits you. Makes you look strangely healthy." Jock raises an eyebrow.

Shaun Lloyd always looks like a cadaver. He is one of the middlemen. Jock never deals directly with the low-life scum who inhabit pub toilets and waste ground. Dealing for pennies is a mug's game. Shaun is one of a select few to whom Jock supplies in bulk. What they do after that is up to them, as long as Jock and the boys are left well alone by all concerned.

Shaun touches his cheek. He can still feel the sharp, smarting pain of Maggie's slap. He says nothing. Shaun lives a twilight life, moving through the rock pools and shallows of the Atlantic coastline, selling directly sometimes, but usually preferring to move the merchandise on quietly through his own network of club and playground contacts. Shaun is learning the trade, marking time while he builds a future, well aware of the rumours that Jock is getting ready to sell up. Shaun has plans.

Shaun is probably cool under pressure, Jock thinks, because he smokes weed like it is going out of fashion. Shaun never touches anything else. Never has. Pills and potions are for the boys and girls in the happy zone. Jock hates the possibility that there might be a connection between his own early life and that of the boy dealer, but nevertheless he has to admit to a sneaking regard for the sallow skin sitting in the chair opposite Maggie's desk. Shaun is a bright lad. Jock gets down to the brass tacks.

"It's simple. This stuff on the desk is called Bliss. We have an arrangement with a certain gentleman, a mutual acquaintance if I remember correctly, who will supply us with as much of this shit as we can shift. Clubs, raves, wherever there's a market for E, there's a market for Bliss. Our good doctor is a little odd, but he's tucked up and we'll sort him out later, won't we Davie?"

"Aye, boss, with pleasure." Davie puts real feeling into that last word.

Shaun leans forward and picks up one of the sachets, turning it over in his hands, watching the yellow powder spill back and forth within. "So?" he mumbles.

"You're to try it out this weekend. This is the first batch we've received and we want to do a little market research. If it's really any good, if you do this for us, we'll give you an exclusive on distribution in and around Barnstaple." Jock leans back in his chair and stretches out his legs. He rests a tumbler of Scotch on his belly.

Shaun considers the offer. "Need to know some stuff. How it works, how much to charge, percentages."

The McCoists wait quietly. There is a background hum from the bar. The football lads are getting boisterous, chatting up girls. One or two have given Bex the eye, but she has, so far, ignored the come-ons. Leona is showing the left back how a sound desk works. Ted Line takes another swig of lager and leans a little closer to the plywood door of the serving hatch.

Jock does a smugly competent impersonation of a city slicker. "Our investment. We give you one hundred of those sachets for free. Gratis. You flog them on for a tenner a go. There's enough in each one of those sachets to blow their tiny little minds all night long. Simple as well. They just lick their fingers, take a sherbet dab and off they go to la-la land. The stuff is ninety percent MDMA with a few additions. A wee dram of Ketamine for the bells and whistles and some stuff the doctor does. All we want is everyone having a good weekend and coming back for more. You get a freebie, we create a buzz and then we ramp up. What do you think?"

Hard currency. Jock has never given Shaun anything for free. He looks for the catch, looks for the hook and line, but apart from the obvious shit associated with dealing in this sordid little world, Shaun can think of no good reason to refuse. "You're saying I get to make a grand this weekend just from this stuff and all I have to do is tell you all's well with the world?"

Jock reaches down by his chair and picks up a plastic food container full of sachets of bright yellow powder, which he puts on the desk in front of Shaun. "That's exactly what I'm saying. Give the good children of this parish a weekend to remember if they can. Probably best to hit a couple of clubs, Friday, Saturday. Caligula's Friday. The Basement Saturday. One thing, though. The doc says to avoid booze. Give the kids the word. Water, not booze."

"That's cool". Shaun runs his fingers along the tops of the sachets. A grand in his hand. "They're used to it. Will your boys be around?"

Jock looks at each of his minders in turn. "No. On call, though. Any shit you give them a bell."

Ted's hearing is not what it was and he missed the names of the clubs. He leans still closer to the wall. He is so wrapped-up in the gathering of secrets that he doesn't notice a tub of ladles and slatted spoons standing directly to the left hand side of the hatch. He catches the tub with his upper arm, feels the pressure of contact and withdraws, moving his right arm across his twisting body to steady the thing before it makes any noise, but he is too slow. The tub has tilted too far. Disaster moves in painfully slow motion. The sound of metal rings out on hard, cold floor tiles.

Ted stoops to pick the spoons and ladles up, to hide the evidence, but he is far too old and far too clumsy. He tries to straighten himself up so that he can move away from the hatch but the door to the office is already open. Ken is in the kitchen before Ted can think. The old man's arm is twisted up behind his back and he is manhandled into the office.

Shaun slips out and this time he does take the rear exit. Tucked under his jacket he has a plastic box full of rocket flavoured sherbet. He can think of a couple of mates who will try it out for him. Always best to do a little research.

Ted is pinned down in one of the chairs with Jock snarling in his face. "Been having a good earwig, have we, Ted? Having a good fucking time? Maggie was right. Private my fucking arse. What did you hear, Ted, what did you hear?"

Ted feels Ken's full weight on his shoulders. He cannot breathe and his heart is racing. He needs a cigarette, he needs nicotine now. "Don't know what you're on about. Wanted a cold drink, that's all. Just wanted…"

"Check it out". Snarls Jock, and Davie leaves the room and goes into the kitchen. "There's a whole fucking bar out there. You know, the place you'd never leave if you could exercise what's left of your free bloody will. What were you doing in the kitchen?"

"Drink, Jock, a drink. It's heaving out there. Got a can out the fridge, turned round to leave and bumped the stupid fucking spoons." Ken digs his fingers into Ted's bony shoulders. Even though he is wearing a sports jacket, Ted can feel Ken's nails as they plough the material into his skin.

Davie returns with an open can of lager. Jock looks at the can, feels its weight and nods to Ken, who, although he does not let go of Ted, relaxes his grip.

Maggie is back in the main bar with Billy and Bex. She apologises for the disturbance and orders another large scotch. She is breaking her personal rule. She doesn't want apple juice right now. She checks her watch and looks round for Ted Line. Time to get the show back on the road. The audience is getting restless and with most of Barnstaple Town's first team squad in attendance she doesn't want any more trouble. Billy tells her to sit tight and goes over and interrupts Leona and her newly discovered football beau. She tells him that Ted went for a drink, that he's probably down in the kitchen having a fag.

Billy checks the bar again and then heads down to the kitchen, but he finds nothing there except a load of cutlery on the floor. He hears voices in the next room. Billy knocks on the office door and enters, finding Ted surrounded by the local hoods. Jock is speaking.

"If you weren't so bloody lame and decrepit I'd have the boys take you for a ride. You're a fucking liability…" Billy is in the room now and Jock's train of thought is broken. "What the fuck do you want?"

Billy sees the look of desperation in Ted's eyes. "Him", he says, gesturing to Ken McCoist so that he will move away from the terrified funny man. Jock nods when Ken looks at him for instructions. "Maggie's already spitting bricks, Jock, you don't want to upset her anymore. Come on Ted, time to introduce the next star."

The shakedown of a defenceless old man serves only to confirm Billy's already well developed sense of prejudice. Jock Cascarino is a bully and Billy is secretly glad that the skin-headed youth has slipped a sliver of ice into the bosom of Jock's relationship with Maggie. It serves the bastard right, and if it all goes pear-shaped, Billy will be there to pick up the pieces, just like he is doing now. He has no particular liking for Ted Line, but even Billy Whitlow can feel sorry for an underdog.

Jock sits on the desk, arms folded across his chest, and smiles. "Just making sure the old duffer wasn't going to do himself any harm". He shakes his head. "Piss off Ted, go and give them what they want."

Billy opens the door for Ted. Just as he is about to walk out into the corridor Jock says, "You're going to be okay? You're not going to have any more accidents, are you?"

Ted understands the difference between a consideration and a question delivered with menaces. He smiles weakly at Billy and together they hurry down the corridor and into the main bar. Billy asks him what the hell is going on, but Ted shrugs and makes his way to the stage.

Leona says farewell to her new admirer and resumes her position at the sound desk. *Chumbawamba* blares out of the PA one more time as Ted checks his list and calls up the next act. A young girl in tight jeans and a tassel fringed jacket climbs onto the stage. The music stops.

Ted steps up to the microphone with the girl in tow. "Tell us your name love and what you're going to do."

"My name is Tania Watson and tonight I'm going to be Shania Twain".

Groans from the audience. Ted winces. Leona cues up the backing track. Tania starts to wiggle her ample hips.

The show is over and the sound of cat calls and claxons are a memory. The football boys have gone home with team bonds much as they ever were, but Leona's new sound engineering protégé has a beer mat with a phone number tucked into his trouser pocket. Bonding of a different kind.

The young magician gave a creditable encore, performing most of Fearson's Hook-up without mishap, although he did miss his mouth with the cigarette at the end. He finished with a series of Productions and Vanishes amongst the audience, the old coin behind the ear stuff, and then, like Cinderella, he left with his meal and beer voucher before last orders when his Dad turned up to give him a lift home.

Jock has left the building too. Once the business with Shaun was concluded and Ted Line's cards were marked, he slipped out the back door, choosing discretion rather than confrontation. Like the boy magician, Jock is tucked up at home with a hot drink. He will wait for Maggie, and has already practised his apology. It will never, ever happen again. Right now he means it.

Ken has been given the job of keeping an eye on Ted. Jock has no doubt the old comic overheard some of the conversation with Shaun and he also has no doubt that the bugger will try to use the information, although he has no immediate fears regarding sirens and tyres crunching on gravel. Ted could be tricky once in a while, but most of the time he was predictably manageable.

Punters drift away until only the hard-core remain and the last hour of the evening unwinds. Leona packs away the sound desk, running cables back up to the wings of the stage, while Ted broods quietly at the far end of the bar. From where Billy is sitting at the other end of the bar he cannot help but catch Ted's eye. He finds himself drifting in and out of the conversation. Bex is being introduced to Leona by Maggie.

Comparisons. Two seventeen year old girls with lists. School and College. Boys. Music. Hunks. Clothes. Leona and Bex flare, covering the ground like a bushfire. Words come out in staccato bursts, punctuated by laughter and the favourite contemporary phrases of the day; "Oh my God... Wicked...Cool". Billy lets the sound waves crash over his head, thoroughly enjoying every moment of the drowning, until his eyes drift back to shore and Ted Line.

Ted has finally caught Billy's attention and he beckons Billy over, mouthing something that Billy cannot understand. Ted is wreathed in cigarette smoke. Billy smiles at Bex and the ladies, and excuses himself, picks up his beer and walks over to where Ted is sitting. Ted offers Billy a vacant bar stool, but Billy prefers to stand, leaning on the bar. He has to bend forward to hear Ted, who speaks in whispers. Furtive. Nervous.

"Can I get you a drink?"

Billy looks at his bottle of beer, which is nearly empty. "Yeah, okay. You alright?"

Ted nods, raises his hand for the barman and puts Billy's beer on his tab. He stubs out the last knockings of a cigarette, reaches for the pack and stops. Ted fidgets on his stool, looking down all the while at the polished wood of the bar. He coughs. "I know we're not exactly the best of...well, you know. But I need some advice. Artiste to artiste, like."

Billy has watched Ted on stage since the incident in the office. The man might not be funny, but he is a professional, time served, and he has stumbled over lines and introductions all the way through the second half of the show. Something is on his mind. Billy assumes it's the muscle.

"No problem, Ted. I know what you mean. I don't think either one of us is a fan of the Wiegie Weirdo." Ironic smiles all round. "Personally I'd ignore the bastard. Just throwing his weight around. You know how he likes to be the Big-I-Am."

Ted can still feel the squeeze in his shoulders. Should he tell Billy or should he cut and run? "Any other time and I'd do just that. I'm not scared of him, you know. The world is full of scum like him. Always got something to prove. I'm just sick and tired of this shit, and the point is, Billy, the point is I'm not sure what to do next."

Billy is starting to feel a little confused. What is Ted driving at? "Do next? Nothing, I suppose. Put it down to experience." He drags a vacant bar stool over and sits down. This is going to take longer than he thought.

"No can do, mate. I know a secret. A big fat secret. Question is, how much is it worth?"

So, thinks Billy, the old bastard wasn't as innocent as he made out. "I can't help you. I don't know what you're talking about. You'll have to explain."

Ted considers this. No names, no pack drill. He doesn't want to dilute the potential proceeds, but he needs a point of view. "I didn't mean to do it, but we all saw that kid in the bar. Then he gets escorted down to the office by one of Jock's gorillas. Come the interval I came over for a drink but the bar was a mess, so, I popped down to the kitchen and grabbed a can. Overheard voices. Next thing I know I've got my ear against the wall."

"Yeah, and your arse in a vice". Billy sees an opportunity, a chance to open up a route to Maggie. Just maybe there's something in this.

"Yeah, that as well. Anyway, turns out the boy is a dealer. Jock is setting something up this weekend, something to do with nightclubs." Ted is not being entirely frank, particularly as he already knew who Shaun was. "As I say, the question is, what is that sort of information worth?"

Billy sees another opportunity. Broken kneecaps. "Count me out, Ted. I don't want anything to do with it. We all know Jock's money is dirty, so what's the point. The Old Bill know. Shit, some of them are probably on the payroll. I think the question should be, who are you going to tell. Might as well be Ghostbusters for all the good it'll do."

Ted is like a gambler. He's lost his shirt but he's convinced his trousers are lucky. "Jock doesn't know that. I could make a few bob, afford a nicer flat maybe."

"Piss it away, more like."

Ted looks sour. "Whatever. Anyway, who said anything about the Old Bill? There's other firms."

Billy takes a swig of beer and shakes his head. He suddenly feels tired. The old comic is one punch line short of a joke. "Come on, Ted, get real. So what if Jock is dealing. Everyone knows. You're talking about blackmail. That's a one way ticket. You know it."

Ted sighs, reaches for his cigarettes, flips the top of the box, takes one out and taps it on the bar so that it slides vertically through his nicotine-yellow fingers. "That's the problem. But he wouldn't expect it coming from someone like you. Not if you threatened to tell Maggie. She'd believe you. She's Jock's Achilles." Ted smiles. Stained teeth. The viper in the nest.

Billy stands. He leans forward and whispers in Ted's ear. "Fuck off, you old git. Do your own dirty work."

As he walks back to the girls, signalling to the barman to top up their drinks, he wonders whether Ted really has the balls. Useful, though. Information is power. A bit of gossip to store away for a rainy day. He re-joins the girls' conversation and it's like he has never been away.

Leona breaks the flow. "Thanks for the drink, Billy".

"Yeah, thanks Dad. We're just comparing notes. Can't wait to get the summer over. Exams and then travel. Leona wants to go to Africa."

Billy looks surprised. "Africa? I thought you were set on London. Get your qualifications and hit Shaftesbury Avenue."

Leona looks at him, head tilted slightly sideways. "Yeah, I did, sort of, but Bex has been telling me about her gap year. Sri Lanka to work with turtles and elephants. Sounds a bit Discworld, but brilliant too. It would do me good to see a bit of the world and there's so much I could help with. You know, voluntary stuff, well-drilling or something. It would be so cool."

Full steam ahead. The girls head off in a thousand different directions, leaving Billy's middle aged paunch trailing in their wake. He feels like a baiter being dragged along behind a yacht, swamped by the swell of their surging chatter. Brilliant. He loves the sheer audacity of youth.

They head off on a new tangent. "Oh God, yeah, home is where the heart is, but you've got to get some distance. Don't get me wrong, I love it down here, especially in the summer, but it's so parochial. Half the kids at college have no idea. They're going to live and die within sight of their parents. And don't get me going on the Cornish. Jesus." Leona laughs out loud. A local flavour. Prejudice of a kind.

Bex agrees. "I know. It's just the same in Oxford. Dreaming spires and all that, but you do get to hate the students. All that town and gown nonsense. And they despise those good old Bucks boys. Local rivalry is great. When Wycombe and Oxford meet at football there's always trouble. No way am I going to study at home. Mum wants me to 'cos of the loans, but

I fancy Edinburgh or Belfast."

Billy has never quite been able to shake off the provincial history of the six counties. Despite the peace process his first thoughts are always of paramilitary graffiti, marching bands and shots to the back of the head. He sort of knows this is one of those generational divides, but the basic prejudice lingers. "Not Belfast. Anywhere but Belfast!"

Bex winks at Leona. Conspiracy. "Anywhere? Okay, Baghdad University. Student exchange."

A pincer movement. "Or what about Tehran, or Sarajevo, no, I've got it… Mogadishu!"

Billy rolls his eyes and gives in. He settles for a full tactical withdrawal and goes back to thoughts of Maggie and Jock. The girls laugh raucously. Not a bad night, thinks Billy, when all is said and done. A few points scored. He can't see Maggie anywhere and it occurs to him that things might have gone too far. Should he be worried?

Leona is getting serious. "I mean, college is great, I'm doing something I love, but it's only this place that keeps me sane. Snuggle's makes my world go round. How sad is that? Your Dad's not bad, well, pretty bloody amazing actually, but it's hardly the bright lights, is it. Africa and then London. That's the plan. For the moment this will do. It really helps with my studies and it pays for some fun."

Bex is pleased with the compliment about her Dad. It makes her feel warm and close to him, and appreciative of Leona. "That's the only problem with my stuff. You can't really get proper experience when you're still at school. The nearest I get to fixing-up animals is the Saturday job at the stables. Mostly mucking out. But I love it. It's great when we do the schooling for kids. All those little faces perched on great big ponies, and they learn so fast at that age."

The girls are finishing their drinks. Both are on vodka kicks. It's almost time to hit the road.

"Hey, what are you doing on Saturday?" Leona is asking the question. "Only Maggie gave me the night off for my birthday. Trouble with this job is you work most weekends and I've sort of lost touch with some of my friends. Even the boys are working."

Bex pricks up her ears. "Boys?"

"Yeah, I'm sort of seeing one of the boys who works here. But they're working. Dave and Rob. But the guy from the football might be there and he might bring a friend or two. We're planning on meeting up at The Basement. Fancy it?"

Bex is shocked. Leona seems so straight. "But if you're seeing, Dave…you naughty girl!"

Leona grins. Wicked and warm. "I'm far too young for all that serious stuff. Anyway, I don't sleep with them, well, not with most of them. This girl just wants to have fun and when you're a poor student it helps if the boys have a few quid in their pocket. Say you'll come, please."

Billy pretends to be equally shocked, but can't keep it up for long. He will be in Bristol and he has no right to insist that his seventeen year old princess sit at home all alone while he is out and about. Of course she can go. He will give her enough cash for a cab if she needs it, although The Basement, pulsing as it does at the heart of Bideford town centre, is on home territory for Bex.

Bex tugs her Dad's arm as she replies. "On one condition. You come over in the afternoon and we get all girly. Hair, makeup, all that. Then you can show me Bideford in all its glory." She checks with her Dad. "That's okay, isn't it, Dad?"

It is a deal. Lobster Jack's followed by The Basement. Billy will be home by three. The clubs go on until at least then so he should be back in time to make sure his darling girl and her new best friend are safely tucked up for the night in the land of innocent dreams. Billy is a father, and although every woman that he has got drunk with, slept with and fought with is another man's daughter, he still believes in miracles. The immaculate Bex, and, by association, the sweet but slightly flawed Leona.

As they get up to leave Billy looks for Maggie but he still can't see her. He quickly checks the corridor and sees a thin slice of light shining out from under the office door. She doesn't need to hang a do not disturb sign on the door handle. Maggie wants to be alone. Billy sighs and then holds the main door open and the girls walk out into the night. Billy and Bex are giving Leona a lift home. Walking across the car park Billy hears one word echoing off the inside of his skull.

"Shit!"

MY TRULY, TRULY FAIR

DOWN ON THE FARM life is lived by routine, by cycles of growth and decay. Helen works hard. She learns how to be useful with a pestle and mortar. She learns about measurements and combinations. Helen works hard at the business of living and through hard work she thrives. She blossoms. It helps that the reward for her hard work can slide into her veins and take away the drudgery of this modern farming life. The good doctor makes the world go round and for Helen, anyone is a friend if they supply free gear.

She finds herself coming to terms with the strange, thin man in the other cell. Most of the time she can make herself believe that they have something in common, that they are both prisoners, that he is not so bad. When he is in a good mood she likes his company. He is educated. Arbnor Jasari can be cultured. His conversation has range and depth, although the world that he inhabits has been warped out of shape, but such weird meanderings are nothing new to Helen. Most of her life has been spent fitting herself into oddly shaped spaces and her new friend has a certain naïve, if deadly, charm. She is by degrees excited and terrified.

"Helen. No, not like that."

The doctor reaches round from behind her and shows her how to tilt the bowl that she is holding so that the mixture is easier to work. She remembers images from a television childhood. Rosy cheeked kids and grandmothers making cakes. She feels the warmth of his skin. His forearm. Breath on her neck. He watches her as she tries to do as he has shown her. It is good. His lips brush her neck. She shivers.

"Very good. I'll make a real chemist out of you. You see how well we work together."

Helen concentrates on the mixing. It's like grinding flour and she is the mill wheel turning at the constant urging of the flowing water course that provides life. In the derelict surroundings of Sillick Farm she thinks it appropriate that the work is being done by hand. It's organic, a labour of love. She works on one of the tables set against the wall at the opposite end of the barn to the small kitchen and bathroom. On the tables set in the middle of the room there are four plastic food tubs, each one containing one hundred sachets of Bliss. She and the Doctor have been busy.

To make the time pass more productively the doctor allows her to take an occasional sample from his supply of MDMA. It takes the edge off. She feels a sense of wellbeing out of all proportion to her surroundings and circumstance.

This morning, Saturday, she thinks, they took a walk around the courtyard. Exercise hour. Clockwise. She thinks she has been here for a week, but her appreciation of time down here on the farm is a little out of joint. She thinks about running away every time he lets her out of the workhouse, but it's a fleeting consideration. She has felt the hard steel of the Beretta tucked into the back of his jeans. She has felt the caress of the needle. She makes a choice every morning.

"Okay, that's enough. Take it over to the other table and we'll take a break."

Helen carefully wipes the serving spoon that she has been using to blend the various ingredients of the good doctor's happy cake mix on a sheet of kitchen roll. She carries the bowl to the table and then joins the doctor in the kitchen. He spoons instant coffee into two chipped brown mugs and waits for the kettle to boil.

"Please, sit down."

"It's okay, Arbnor, I'll stand. You've had me sitting at the workbench all morning. I need to stretch my legs."

"Whatever".

The automatic switch on the kettle flicks off and water bubbles out of the spout. He always overfills. He lets the water settle down and then pours. Two spoons of sugar. "I've been thinking. You work very well. I'm happy you're here, so long as you remain a good girl. I'm going to make you an offer."

When the doctor is in a good mood he makes offers. Helen thinks that he is sincere when he says he needs a friend. She is coming round to the idea.

"I can get you off smack. If you really want to I can do this. Not now, though. We have to stay calm. There's too much work to do."

Getting off smack is the last thing Helen wants to thinks about right now. That is something you have be committed about.

Jesus. That is something really scary. Humour him. Say the things he wants to hear.

"I don't know. I mean, yes, but the come down is shit. Sort of freaks me, you know."

The coffee burns the inside of her mouth.

He smiles. It's a start. "Let's go outside. It's a nice day and I want to breathe fresh air."

Taking their coffee with them Arbnor Jasari and Helen, his Girl Friday, unlock the doors and venture out into the bright sunshine of a clear Spring day. There is a low wall at one end of the courtyard where they can sit. They squint up at the sky. The house martins have been joined in flight by swallows. The eaves of the old barns are spattered with droplets of mud where the birds are building nests. New life.

The two of them bathe in the fresh warmth of the day. Eyelids close and burn orange. They can hear the sound of a tractor in the distance. Gulls surge up into the bright blue sky and drop down again to feed on the bugs and worms turned up by the plough. Through cracks in the concrete floor of the courtyard Campion has sprouted and is in early bloom. Cuckoo-flower. Helen soaks it all in. She will say anything so long as it guarantees her another moment like this.

The doctor watches her as she leans her head back and opens herself up to the sun. He too feels the warmth of a new growing season in his bones. He sighs and allows his otherwise taut and watchful soul to appreciate this simple moment of happiness. He is growing to like this girl. Affection. He thinks about basic lessons in physiognomy. Light penetrates the skull, triggering physical reactions. Mating instincts. For the first time since he spiked the coffee of his guards in Albania he feels as though he might be able to relax.

"I mean what I say. When all this is done I can help you. We're good together. Maybe we can be partners. I make good stuff, no? For you. All I ask is a little kindness in return. No more shit. I've had it with arses making money out of me."

The tone of his voice, the subtle foreignness of it fascinates Helen. She is growing to love his oddly cultured yet innocent use of the English language. She corrects his latest minor transgression. "Arseholes".

"Arseholes? That sounds much better." He laughs out loud. "Next time I see him I'll tell Jock he is an arsehole. When we have enough money."

Helen laughs too. They infect each other. Out here in the sunshine she feels alive. The bastards who brought her here will have to pay, on that she is settled, and the doctor seems like her best bet, at the moment. He has dealt with real mafia hoods already. Between the two of them they ought to be able to deal with the Three Stooges.

Dates and days merge in Helen's mind, but something about the way the sky twists above her makes her start to count. Clouds in high wispy layers. It must be eight, nine days since she accepted a ride in the Jesus bus. That definitely makes it Saturday morning. The seventh. Tomorrow is Easter Sunday. Chocolate. She feels a need, a craving.

"Arbnor, what sort of stuff have you got in the house? Food and stuff?"

"Hm?" He breaks away from thoughts about Jock's arsehole.

"Oh, you know tins, a few bits in the freezer, the usual stuff. Camping rations. Why?"

"Just a thought. Tomorrow. Easter Sunday. Chocolate."

"Easter? Ah, yes. I know about this. Back home my family is Muslim. Me, I gave that up. Too much trouble. The devout know too many truths. Easter. Chocolate. Yeah, I have chocolate. Do you want some now?"

Helen shakes her head. "Tomorrow. A treat. A day of rest and chocolate."

Arbnor Jasari moves a little closer to her and brushes a stray lock of hair from her eyes. "Okay. I tell you what. We'll bag up this afternoon, maybe have a drink and a smoke tonight. Tomorrow I'll bring chocolate and the television from the farmhouse. There's even a DVD player and I have a couple of films. Chocolate, television and films all day. Like big kids. A deal?"

Helen leans forward and kisses her doctor softly on the lips. Patient familiarity. Breaking the rules. "Doctor Jasari, it's a fucking deal."

The brothers McCoist go their separate ways for a couple of days. Jock has Ken tour the property developments, giving him a chance to don a hard hat to go with his hard man image. Fluorescent yellow is not Ken's colour but he perseveres. The site foremen can run rings round him when it comes to projects and schedules but they choose not to. There is an implied threat, covert but ever present. Jock pays well and expects results. The converted farm buildings are starting to look really good.

As the work progresses, as tiles are grouted and kitchen units are fitted, Ken edges ever closer to his bar in Ibiza. He has been looking through travel brochures and has decided that the rave capital of Europe offers his best bet. He can always find work there if things are a little slow behind the taps. Pretty girls and spotty boys. Senoritas and long dark nights. Cold beer and tapas. He is going to call his bar The Straw Donkey, a paean to millions of package trips and the souvenirs that litter lofts throughout his homeland.

Ken's brother is less inclined to dream of foreign shores. The closing down of the Cascarino Empire means that an end is coming, but Davie has never been quite sure whether his glass is half full or half empty. Sometimes, when he listens to Ken when they're alone in the flat above Snuggle's, he thinks that maybe he should broaden his horizons, but he knows in his heart that his crock of gold lies at the end of the lane, not at the end of the rainbow. With his pay-off from Jock he is going home. He has a couple of debts to pay, a couple of issues to resolve from the old days, but once everything is sorted he wants nothing more than a season ticket to Ibrox, and, anyway, things have a habit of turning down at the corners when Ken gets involved.

For Davie the round of check-ups at bars and the odd meeting with Jock's business contacts moves him that little bit closer to the streets of Glasgow. As much as he will miss his brother, he is convinced that East Kilbride will cure the darkness that he feels in his soul.

He collects a little cash here and there. He delivers a little weed and a few pills. The firm supplies cocaine but has for a fee relinquished its monopoly on heroin. Part of Jock's handover. Saturday morning keeps the wheels greased. MacDonald's at Roundswell and envelopes for a couple of boys who wear blue on duty. A fair exchange. Everything stays sweet.

Saturday afternoon finds Maggie at the club. She inspects the bar, checks table layouts and reservations, and spends an hour with chef. There is a problem with the salmon starter for tonight's dinner. There's not enough to go round, an order from the supplier fouled up, so they decide to offer a choice. Pâté or salmon mousse. Maggie wants everything in its place before the start of the evening. With Leona off, Maggie will have to manage the backstage area. Keeping costs down. This season is all about maximising revenue and profit.

Just after three the phone rings and Maggie takes it in the bar. It's Billy. She transfers the call to her office. She can hear the rumble of tyres on tarmac and wind funnelling around glass. She sits at her desk.

"Hi, Billy, that's better. Won't be disturbed in here. Are you in the car, love? What can I do for you?"

"Yeah, running some errands, but it's okay, I'm on hands free. Just thought I'd say hello. Make sure everything's okay after Wednesday."

Maggie holds the phone under her chin and starts to make a daisy chain out of paper clips. "Wednesday? Oh, yes, everything's fine."

"Good. Only I was worried, you know, about that kid. What

you said. Slapping his face and that."

Eight clips in the chain. "There's no need, love. Jock has sorted it."

"And Jock?"

Maggie laughs. "No need to worry about that either. Hard Paddington stares. Cold silences. Poor lamb has had the works. He hasn't been out for two days. The brothers Grim are holding the fort. Do you know, he even made me lunch yesterday. Proper lunch. Puttanesca. Spaghetti with olives and capers."

Billy hits the breaks and swears. The hands free set in his car means Maggie gets full blast. "Sorry, Mags, sorry. I'm not swearing at your lunch. Bloody lorry pulled out. Yeah, sounds great. Haven't had tart's spaghetti for ages. I didn't mean to cause you and Jock any trouble, you know."

"What? Nothing to do with you. I've told him a thousand times. Not in the club. He's only got himself to blame. Anyway, it's all done and dusted. By the time we wake up tomorrow I'll have forgiven him. Have already, actually, but I sort of forgot to tell him, if you know what I mean. It's not often I get the chance to be Lady Muck."

She gives up on the daisy chain at twenty paper clips. Displacement activity. Maggie picks up a ball point pen and starts to doodle three dimensional boxes on a scratch pad. Billy is glad that Maggie can't see the colour of his cheeks.

"Yeah. Know what you mean."

There is a pause. Billy still has not worked out how to broach the subject of Ted Line.

"You still there love?"

"Sorry Mags, bit of traffic. There's one other thing."

"Go on".

"Ted. Got a bit confused on Wednesday. Jock had to have a word. Has he mentioned it?"

Jock has not mentioned it and now it's Maggie's turn to stop and think. Is Ted becoming a liability? "How do you mean?"

Billy clears his throat. "Seemed to think Jock was doing a bit of the old business. I told him to forget it, but I don't think Ted likes Jock very much at the moment. Just wanted to warn you in case he says something out of line."

Ted will have to go. Maggie's charity doesn't extend to those suffering alcoholic dementia. "Darling, Ted is always saying things that are out of line. I'll bear it in mind."

Another pause.

"Billy. About the kid on Wednesday. I know you worry about it and I'm grateful, I really am, but can you leave it alone. Jock is sorting it out."

The sound in her head, the sound of her own voice, is wrong. Maggie hates telling Billy to shut his eyes to the obvious. She likes him. He has been a friend for some years now. She makes a choice. "Look, can I trust you?"

Billy sounds slightly aggrieved. "Of course, Mags, you know you can".

"Okay. You and I both know Jock used to be into some heavy shit. But he's stopped most of that. Yeah, there's still some stuff hanging around. Dope. A few girls. But all that's changing. By the end of the summer it'll all be closed down. Everything. The farms will be sold and the money will be in the bank." Maggie takes a deep breath. "Even Snuggle's, Billy. I'm packing the club in as well. Jock and me, well, we're heading off to sunnier climes. One more season here for both of us, cash in our chips and Mercia here we come. That's why the kid was here. Closure, Billy. It had to be done. Jock has explained it all to me. I hated the kid being here, but needs must."

Silence. Billy doesn't know what to say. Maggie has dropped a bomb shell. He sees brake lights in front of him but the colour red does not compute. He has to slam on his own brakes at the last minute. Cones. Speed restrictions. Cameras. "Fuck!"

"Jesus, Billy, are you alright?"

A moment. Deathly. Images flash up in Maggie's head, images of burning fuel and twisted metal. But there is no sound of squealing tyres, no rending of metal.

"Mags, sorry. That's all I seem to be saying this afternoon. Lost it there for a moment."

"It's me who's sorry, love. I wanted to tell you to your face. You do know you'll always be welcome for a holiday, don't you?"

Billy looks for a way out of the conversation. He feels as though a part of him is dying. Shrivelling up. He could cut the phone and blame it on a loss of signal, but he doesn't. Billy tries to stay calm, straining the boundaries of his own voice now. Take it like a man.

"Sure. Sure. Look, Mags, can we talk about this another time. Road works. Cop car up ahead. I hope everything works out. We'll talk next time I'm in the club, okay. Got to go. See you soon."

Maggie starts to reply but the line drops. "See you…"

The ballpoint pen nib rips through two layers of paper.

Sat at home in the conservatory Jock watches the horse racing with the sound turned off. He is on his mobile and Davie confirms that Shaun has had a good night at Caligula's. Five hundred in his pocket. Fifty sachets palmed. Word getting round. It all sounds highly promising. Jock checks his watch. Four o'clock. The flowers should have arrived.

"Davie, got to go, pal. Expecting another call." He hits the red button.

The last two days have been hell on earth. He's cooked for the woman, for Christ's sake, pleading guilty, under house arrest, but he loves her and he wants to make amends. He told her that he was sorting out some trouble, the old business, kids trying to muscle in. Shaun keeps watch. Jock thinks that Maggie bought it.

One more summer. Six months. Sell everything. The units, the house, the club, the drugs. Take the money and run. On the wicker coffee table in front of the television is a brochure from a Spanish property development company, which is open at a page showing glossy pictures of a villa with a pool. On their last trip over he and Maggie bought one just like it off plan. It should have been ready in May, but now the Spanish developers are saying August. Jock reckons that by the time they have cleared the decks, maybe in October, it should be complete. Even if it's not, they will have enough money to move out there, rent somewhere and give the bloody builders hell.

Thinking about a new life helps to relieve the tension. He wants to put everything cold and miserable behind him. Building sites. Johns. Junkies. He wants to wake up with Maggie where the sun shines every day. He wants to make love to her by the pool on balmy summer nights. One more hit. One more deal is all it will take. The combined rewards from all of their hard work will let them live like kings and queens.

He turns the sound up and watches the four-twenty from Haydock. He has forty on the nose. Red Rose Amigo to win. The house phone rings. Jock is up and out of his chair like greased lightning.

"Hello?"

Maggie's voice is soft and gentle, and Jock knows that the worst is over. "Hello, darling. They're beautiful. Thank you."

The release of tension in his shoulders is patently visible. "I'm really sorry, pet".

"I know. And I do know you're working for our future, love. Thank you. What a lucky girl I am."

"No, Mags. I'm the lucky one. Shall I come in tonight?"

"Yeah. Forgive and forget. See you later, love. Thanks again. Bye."

"Bye".

Jock gets back into the conservatory just in time to see Red Rose Amigo win by a short head at three to one. That makes twenty one red roses in all.

The reality that underpinned her tutor's words hits home for Leona when she wakes up on Saturday morning and looks in the mirror. She has dark rings under her eyes from too many late nights under bright lights. She got home at three in the morning after finishing the show at Snuggle's, wrapping everything up and spending a gorgeous hour with her pet bartender in the front seat of his Fiesta.

Her parents slept peacefully through Leona's long goodbye on the doorstep. They sleep through everything including, as far as Leona can tell, their waking hours, as though they are both simply waiting out the days until they die. They appear to have settled for their lot and put their hopes and ambitions in a shoebox under the bed. It's all a waste of time. There is no point in saving for a rainy day in Devon unless you're planning to enter into bankruptcy.

So far this week Leona has hit the sack after two o'clock in the morning three times already. She has exams in six weeks and London depends on her grades. She starts to feel uneasy. Her body is still growing and maturing and she drinks too often. She smokes as well, although at present this is under control. Two or three a day. The face in the mirror is telling her to get a grip. Her tutor was right. She looks for smoker's pucker wrinkles.

She was called into her tutor's office on Friday afternoon after her last lecture. She is supposed to use free time like this for library study, but on a Fridays she usually goes home and tries to grab an hour or two in bed before the night shift begins. Yesterday she spent an hour being told in no uncertain terms that unless she reined-in her extra-curricular activities she would fail.

The possibility of failure is not one that Leona wishes to contemplate, bringing with it the prospect of a dizzying career at window two of the drive-thru obesity factory; that or Snuggle's *ad infinitum*. Resolve. She tells herself to try harder, tells herself that this is real life in a world full of opportunities. Falling at the first hurdle is not an option. The face in the mirror brightens. Leona has an innate ability to find the brightness even when the sun is obscured by clouds. When she is pissed-off her face darkens like a wet Wednesday but when she smiles she can light up a room.

First things first. She needs a cup of tea and some chocolate biscuits for breakfast. The television in the living room is tuned to Sky Sports. Breaking football news. Her father is living the dream. His Saturday afternoon exercise regime is kettle, fridge, armchair. Circuit training for the morbidly comatose. Leona tells him to sod-off when he calls out and asks her to make him a bacon sandwich.

Back in her room she gets an overnight bag down from the top of her wardrobe and selects a range of tops, skirts, dresses, undies and shoes. Makeup goes in next. She applies the minimum amount of slap to get her through to the afternoon and remembers, having finished the last of the biscuits, to brush her teeth. The toothbrush goes in as well.

Cash. Maggie gave her a birthday bonus as she was leaving the club on Friday night and Leona has a hundred in her purse. She puts forty away in her dressing table drawer, a little something to add to her savings for her new life in London, and leaves the rest in her purse for the coming celebration. If she plays her cards right, if both she and Bex pout and pirouette, most of it will still be there in the morning.

She has reached a compromise. She will try harder, but not until Monday. This is the weekend and it's always better to make resolutions on a Monday. Leona calls her boyfriend on her mobile and he promises to come round and give her a lift. He will be there in half an hour. She takes her bag downstairs and dumps it in the hallway before joining her father in the living room. One of the curtains is drawn to keep the brightness of the late morning sun off the television screen. A recently retired footballer is telling her Dad that Manchester United must push up and pressurise their opponents today if they are going to keep their title ambitions on track. Manchester United, it would appear, must try harder too.

"Anything I can get you before I go?" she asks.

Her father is silent. Concentrating. It takes real effort to summon up the answer. "Cup of tea would be nice".

As Leona walks across the twenty-year-old paisley patterned carpet to the kitchen she says, "I'm leaving home today. Joining the circus. I've always wanted to work with lions."

There is just the faintest flicker of a smile on her father's face. It is a reaction. She wants more but she has concluded that the muscles in her father's face have wasted away. She sometimes daydreams that he has a disease that is gradually destroying his motor neurone system. The happiness of the dream is fleeting. She is coming to terms with the fact that he is just a grumpy old sod.

From the kitchen. "I won't be back tonight, remember. Staying with a friend. Bex. From the club. Try and remember to tell Mum when she gets back from work."

Silence. She makes tea in the cup and drops the teaspoon in the already crowded sink. The linoleum floor covering is rolling back from the kitchen cupboards. On the wall opposite the door, surrounded by cracked beige tiles, an old Rayburn back-burner is choked with winter ash. Her Father will be in a foul mood when her Mum gets home. The last of the milk has been poured into his tea.

"Thanks". Mumbled. The pundits have moved on to Aston Villa's chances against Liverpool, which are poor, it would seem. Leona files her nails, filling time with the sound of voices in stereo on the flat panel LCD television and the rasp of glass paper on her cuticles. Everything else is falling apart, everything else needs a handier man than her father, but the television is state of the art and digital. It's all a question of priorities.

A knock at the door.

"I'm off. See you in the morning, Dad."

She leaves him with his thirty-two inch view of the world, picks up her bag and heads out into the bright blue sun-stream of possibilities. As she opens the door she thinks she hears him speak.

"Take care. Have a nice time, love".

The door slams halfway through the longest sentence that he has uttered in the last hour.

At the regular morning briefing Sergeant Miller runs through the usual range of operations for the oncoming day shift. Barnstaple Town are playing at home against Frome, a top of the table clash in the Western League Premier Division. To describe the matter in hand as crowd control would, in Liverpool or London, be worth a laugh, but the boys in blue prefer this duty to patrolling the high street and shopping precincts in the town centre. There is far more trouble associated with retail therapy in North Devon's regional capital than there is with football. The combination of fat wage packets and all day drinking in town centre pubs makes Boutport Street particularly hairy as the day draws down.

He concludes with a notice about missing kids. "Details are on file and you should all study them before going out on patrol. In particular, one of the workers at Fourways drop-in centre has reported that a number of regulars, both male and female, haven't been seen for over a week. They've probably buggered-off somewhere more interesting, it being Easter weekend and all, but if you do come across them have a word. It's logged and you know the drill. That's it. Have a good one."

The officers file out of the room, chatting in groups and preparing for another day on the streets. On the way out the Sergeant collars a couple of bobbies rostered for one of the mobile patrols.

"A little job for you when you get chance. This bloke at the drop-in centre reckons that one of his customers has seen a painted van picking up kids late at night. Could be something and nothing, but he did give us a partial registration. The vehicle check shows the van as being registered to the Jehovah's Brigade. Some sort of Christian group. Preaching on the streets. You know the sort of thing. They've got a place out on Westacott Road, down near Tesco. Might be worth a nose."

Raised eyebrows. Saving the great unwashed. One of the constables makes a note of the road name. "How urgent?"

The Sergeant is already distracted. He is due in the control room this afternoon but thinks he can swing it to get to the match. "If you get chance. I don't suppose the God Squad are bumping-off sinners. See how it goes."

"Okay, Sarge. Will do."

A silver Ford Mondeo pulls into the deserted weekend car park of the Traveller's Inn at Roundswell services. The car has new plates, although it shows the typically mud-slung signs of a substantial journey. On the windscreen there is a branded tax disk holder. AirCars. On hire. A Mondeo in a cheap hotel's car park. A simple statement. A travelling man. The only odd thing about it is the day. Mondeo drivers tend to go home on a Friday night.

The driver of the car gets out, opens the rear passenger door and takes two sports bags from the back seat. He unhooks a suit jacket from the rear grab handle and slips it on. Picking up the bags, he walks into the reception area and finds it deserted, but there is the sound of a television playing in an office at the back of the reception area. A door with a mirror strip window slides back and a young woman walks to the front desk, smiling. Uniformed. Blue. Attractive in her pony-tailed neatness..

"Hello sir, can I help?"

Her smile is genuine. The man at the desk is tall and tanned, well dressed and well groomed. He has thick black hair that would be unkempt and full of waves were it not kept immaculately short. He is clean shaven and dark eyed. She likes what she sees. He looks fit and lean. Hard, mid-thirties, so unlike most of the salesmen and shop fitters who clamber out of their cars and vans reeking of cheap cologne or cigarette smoke.

He returns her smile. "Yes. I'd like to take a room. For ten days if that's possible."

Most people stay for a night. You get weekenders, the odd romance, even the occasional, furtive day booking, but rarely ten nights. It seems an odd number. "Oh, well, I'll have to check. We get pretty busy during the week. Smoking or non-smoking?"

"Non-smoking, please."

The receptionist sits at the desk and hits the spacebar on her computer. The screen saver disappears and she checks bookings. "You're in luck. Sort of. I can put you in a smoking room on the first floor."

He frowns for a moment. "I'd really appreciate a non-smoking room on the ground floor if at all possible. I can't stand the smell of other people's stale cigarette smoke and I'm not very good with heights. Even looking out of an upstairs window makes me feel a bit queasy. Couldn't you do something? The last place I tried was fully booked next week."

The smile returns. Eye contact. The receptionist can feel herself blushing. Strictly speaking it's against company policy, although these sort of requests come across the desk often enough. She hesitates, swimming in his unblinking gaze. A mouse click. Then another. Moving data. She looks up and says, "Seeing as it's such a long stay I'm sure I can work something out."

They both relax. In the centrally heated lobby she can feel herself starting to glow. Data re-organised. "There, all done. Room nine. At the end of the hall. Turn left through those double doors." Now to the business part of the transaction. "How will you be settling your bill?"

He reaches into his inside jacket pocket for his wallet. "Do you take Amex?"

"We do. I can take an imprint now and you can pay when you leave or, if you want, you can settle the bill up front. We do have broadband in the rooms but you pay for that using the phone and your credit card. You get the weekend discount rate for next weekend, but unfortunately you have to stay Friday night to qualify so it's the full rate for this weekend."

"Yeah, that's fine. I'll pay now. Saves any hassle later on."

He hands her his American Express card and she puts it into the card reader. First impressions. A gold card to go with his golden tan. Rafal Petrov. An expiry date two years hence. His name sounds foreign as she rolls it around her tongue, although he speaks without any accent. Metropolitan. He is certainly not a local man.

"If you could just enter your pin number, Mister Petrov".

He keys in the four digit code and presses the green button. The display on the reader confirms the transaction and a printer on a desk behind the receptionist churns out two copies of his invoice. The receptionist staples the charge card receipt to one copy and hands it to her guest.

"There you are, Sir".

"Thanks".

The moment of connection is ending but she wants it to carry on. She wants to know more about him. Stock question number one. "Are you here on holiday?"

He bends to pick up his bags and replies as he straightens. "Not really. I have some business to attend to in Bideford next week. But I do hope to see something of the countryside at the weekends. Through there and turn left?" he nods in the direction of the white swing doors to the right of the reception desk.

"Yes, last door on the left. Facing the car park. If you need tea or coffee, anything, just ask at reception. Enjoy your stay."

He leaves her with another broad smile. "I'm sure I will. Thank you."

Rafal Petrov, known to family and friends as Alex Berisa, locks the door after he has entered the room and hooks up the security chain. He rolls up a small piece of toilet paper and plugs the spyglass in the door. Then he checks the room. Standard fare. The bath is too small and shallow to lie out in. The window is double glazed and has security catches to prevent it opening more than six inches. He inspects the mechanism, but there is no obvious release. Cross head screws. He rummages in one of the sports bags and pulls out a small black case, which he opens. He takes out a screwdriver and makes sure that it fits the screw heads.

Satisfied that the room is safe and clean, he unpacks the other bag, putting jeans, underwear and tee-shirts in drawers. He unfolds five or six shirts and hangs them up with his suit in the wardrobe. The kettle sings and he makes himself a cup of black coffee. Stripping down to his boxer shorts, Alex takes the coffee into the bathroom and fires up the shower, testing the water until he can feel the heat stinging his skin. The bathroom fan kicks-in as the mirror steams up.

After ten minutes under the jet stream of the electric shower, Alex dries himself, wraps a towel around his waist and returns to the bedroom. The sports bag with the screwdriver case is on the bed. He empties it. Black combats. Black jumpers. Gloves. A Beanie. Black lace up boots. Alex takes a second black case, larger than the one containing the screwdrivers, out of the sports bag.

Alex puts this case on the bed and unzips it. The case is six inches deep and the bottom half is sculpted. It contains a handgun, a silencer, two clips, magazine loader, cleaning materials and a plastic file of synthetic oil. Tools of the trade. He strips the Glock nine millimetre double action semi-automatic handgun down in less than a minute, checking each component in turn and reassembles it. The barrel is modified, being half an inch longer than the factory supplied version and threaded. Alex screws the silencer onto this thread and sights, feeling the weight of the loaded pistol in his hand.

He unscrews the silencer and repacks and closes the case. He repacks his working clothes, putting the bag down on the floor. He returns to the bathroom, rinses out his coffee cup, and completes his grooming. He dresses in jeans, a casual shirt and his suit jacket. Time to find out about the local nightlife.

Alex presses a buzzer on the front reception desk and the young woman comes out to greet him, rather pleased to be of service. He looks even better than he did before. Refreshed. Rough and smooth. Sparkling.

"Hi, sorry to bother you, but I was wondering if there's a supermarket near here? If I'm going to be here for a week I can't keep badgering you for more coffee."

"Of course. Sainsbury's. Back out onto the roundabout and turn left, then right at the next roundabout. You can't miss it."

Her name badge has Julie written on it in black felt tip.

"Great. I was also wondering about nightlife and food. To be honest I don't fancy the Wimpy across the car park. Can you recommend anywhere, Julie?"

First name terms. Familiarity. Julie feels the heat rising again. "Depends what you like. There are some good places in town. The Old Bank's nice and there's a new Italian by the museum. There are some interesting places to eat at Instow. The Schooner at the far end of the promenade is supposed to be good. Anywhere really. There's loads of places for food and there's always the pubs. Millions of them. Take your pick, really."

Alex leans on the reception desk. Julie notices that he has one of his bags with him. Probably putting stuff back in the car. "I wouldn't leave anything in your car. Not around here, Mister Petrov."

"No, I won't. And please call me Rafal."

Anonymity. One of the rules of the game. Singularity. The

solitary world of the professional. It's a shame, Alex thinks, because there are so many pretty girls in the world. Maybe he could break that rule during his stay. He turns on the smile.

"I was thinking of something a bit livelier. Music. That sort of thing."

Sustained eye contact. "Erm, The Monkey. On the old quay, but it's not really your sort of place. Sticky carpets." She makes a face and Alex responds by smiling brightly again. Definitely not his sort of thing. "Or there's a couple of clubs. Caligula and the Red Zone. A lot of the pubs have live bands at the weekend. Oh and there's Snuggle's if you like your Dad's music."

He laughs. "What about Bideford. I've heard it's quaint. The Little White Town. Anything worth sampling there?"

"Actually, it's not bad. Lobster Jack's is busy in the summer. Lots of live sport on satellite, though. O'Hare's on the quay has live music. Irish, obviously and there's a nice club. The Basement. Small and cosy. Like anywhere round here really, loads of pubs."

The main door swings open and an older couple come into the reception area. Julie smiles at them and they nod to her, waiting their turn. Alex turns and acknowledges them too. "Sorry, just getting some directions." He turns back to Julie. "Thanks. You've been a great help. I'll catch you later, hopefully."

As he picks up his bag and heads out to his car, Julie finds herself hoping so too. She is in a great mood. The older couple are staying for a long weekend and have a complaint to make about their shower. Nothing is too much trouble for Julie today.

Alex hits the remote and unlocks the car, throwing the bag onto the front passenger seat. As soon as he is cocooned within metal he flicks open a large road atlas. He turns to the pages covering North Devon and scans the map, familiarising himself with place names and road numbers. As he makes a mental note of his immediate locale he whispers to himself, "Arbnor, my friend, where are you hiding?"

He shuts the map book, puts on his sunglasses and turns the ignition key. Sainsbury's. He has an errand to run. A jar of coffee, muesli bars and shampoo. The stuff of everyday lives.

Coffee and toast eaten late on a Saturday morning. Billy is back from a brief trip to the supermarket. Bright sunshine floods into the room. The kitchen door is open and Bex leans against the door frame watching sparrows darting in and out of the shadows. The garden is long and thin, hedged on both sides with an old, mossy path of paving slabs running down the middle from a small patio area by the house. The grass is already in need of a cut. Last year's failed attempts at container gardening still bear the skeletal proof that Billy does not possess green fingers.

Since the night out on Wednesday the two of them have passed like ships ploughing on through rolling fog banks. Bex has been rising early and putting the hours into her revision, while Billy has risen late and busied himself with songs and shirts. Bex drains her mug of coffee down to the bitters and turns to join her father at the breakfast table.

"I never realised how nocturnal you are. Has it always been like this? Even when you were with Mum?"

Billy yawns and nods. "Yep. She loved it at first. The late nights, bright lights, parties and stuff. Too much stuff. When you came along she changed. Got priorities. I'm not complaining, love. I'm glad she's like she is. You've turned out brilliantly and it's mostly down to your Mum, not me. I don't have many regrets, but I do think back and wonder what things might have been like if I'd seen the light."

Bex sits quietly for a moment. "No point, Dad. We're here now." She pauses. "For a long time I didn't understand. Too many Dads. The boyfriends were a bit of a mystery because Mum always kept them at arm's length until she was really sure. Didn't happen very often. Simon was okay, but I was seven by then. I knew enough, though. After they got divorced and I saw Mum in her full, 'bugger it' independence, the one thing that seemed constant were the holiday visits and your phone calls. I used to wait all weekend for the bloody ring. What matters is we're friends."

Hand in hand. Billy lets the moment of self-pity break over him. Bex is holding him. He feels free when she is with him. "How is your Mum? This Dave, is he okay?"

Bex looks serious. A frown. "Yeah, actually he is. I think they might be alright. Mum likes him. Says he makes her feel wanted. Just seems a bit...I don't know. Not that there's anything wrong with him, that's not what I mean. It's more like I'm going away for a year and then to Uni. They'll make the place their home. It's like I'll become a visitor. Strange, I suppose. Growing up. Leaving home is suddenly becoming real. Scary and thrilling all at the same time."

Bex smiles at Billy. "You'll like him. He's very laid back. I'm not sure how they got together, really. You know what Mum's like. Hustle, bustle and Puritan work ethic. God knows what she does to candidates when she's interviewing them. She says Oxford is a nightmare. Too many graduates trying to be managers and foreign language students desperate to get into the media."

"So, you going to tell me about your gigs?" she asks after a second or two of quiet contemplation. Bex rises and fetches the cafetiere from the kitchen work surface. She finishes the coffee, pouring herself and her father half a mug each of the bitter black liquid.

"Much the same as it always was". Billy winces slightly as the coffee curls around the back of his tongue. "Well, sort of. Taunton went well. I think I mentioned it was a fundraiser for a breast cancer charity. You know the score, half fee and a donation. The place was packed. Auction fever, chiffon and champers, but it was fun. Foot-tappingly good, actually, and I had a few dances, got a phone number."

Billy looks slightly ashamed of himself.

Bex grins. "Typical".

"Not so good last night. Easter bonnets and knobbly knees. Cabaret for the terminally caravanned. Not one of my favourite things, but you can't argue with people who want to give you money for being a superstar. Anyway, once I get on stage I get into a groove. The club looked quite pretty, in an obvious way. Ceiling star lights glowing to full effect. The usual standards. I finished with a medley from My Fair Lady. Always get the grannies in a sing-along. They've asked me back. Once a month throughout the summer."

Bex looks at him over the rim of her mug. "Going to do it?"

"Mmm. Two-fifty a night and near enough to get home."

"Is that good?

"Two-fifty? Average for that sort of place. They'll take a couple of thousand at the bar."

"Plus the odd starstruck groupie?"

"No". Billy looks appalled, but not because Bex thinks he is incorrigible. "Have you seen the clientele? Give me a charity ball any day!"

Billy changes the subject. "How's the revision going?"

"Pretty good. Chemistry is a grind but I think I've got the basics. Ditto Physics. Biology's a doddle. I love it. Makes it so much easier. And then there's English. After the other three it's a bit of a relief to get stuck into a bit of literary criticism. I know I should be nervous, but I'm feeling okay. I've got a chance."

Billy sits back and looks at his daughter. How did he and Carol make such a perfect little creature? An 'A' grade student. What amazes Billy is that she knows she is a star pupil but has never allowed herself to become pompous or overbearing. The girl has always wanted to delve about in the guts of things, especially living things. When she was thirteen she set herself a task and has pursued it doggedly ever since. Her pin-ups include an Austrian specialist in elephant pregnancy.

Billy thinks back to when he got home last night. The lights were out and when he looked in on Bex it was like she was eleven years old. She has a habit of lying on her back with her mouth open, and with her long, dark hair splayed across her pillow. Billy always checks her before he turns in. He is stunned by his good fortune, by his darling girl.

Bex clears away the breakfast dishes and then hits the living room, where she sprawls on the sofa and flicks through the Saturday morning delights on the television. She settles for an MTV channel and a magazine. Billy showers, shaves and dresses. Light casual. He has a suit and shirt in a carrier hanging from his bedroom door. At two he takes his leave, heading for Bristol and his particular brand of Saturday night fever. He is leaving early to hit Cribbs and IKEA. He needs some new shirts and another rack for his compact disks, a large number of which are piled on the floor next to the stereo.

CINCINNATI DANCING PIG

THE DOORBELL RINGS AND Bex skips down the stairs in her dressing gown, her hair wrapped in a towelling turban. The house is full of sound. *Material Girl.* Bex is playing one of her compact discs very loudly on Billy's stereo. Through the frosted glass in the front door she can see the outline of a female head. Leona.

Bex swings the door open and is greeted with a hug and a still cool bottle of Chilean white. Leona persuaded her lift to stop off at a supermarket on the way over. The trauma of Saturday afternoon queues at the ten items or less aisle means she is gasping for a cigarette. Bex shows her into the kitchen and unlocks the back door. Leona slices through the foil sheath covering the stopper with the tine of a fork and uncorks the bottle. The girls stand in the garden in bright, late afternoon sunlight, dragging on Silk Cuts. Sunlight sparkles on wine glasses. Condensation dribbles over their fingers.

"I don't usually smoke. Just at the weekends." Leona giggles like a naughty schoolgirl. They are both high on anticipation, too young to know the perennial disappointment of night clubs and loud music, that hollow feeling that comes with age and an inevitable desire to snuggle up at home with the television.

"I'm just the same. Sorry we've got to smoke out here but Dad would go mad. His voice and all that. And he thinks I'm too young."

"Yeah, that and the stress".

Bex is at a loss to understand what stresses Leona is under. They are both seventeen. "It can't be that bad".

"People don't understand. I mean, it's not as though I'm a binge drinker or anything, you know, out all night boozing. I work at the club because of my course. I thought it would help. But yesterday my tutor gave me shit about my work and always being tired. I mean, bummer or what?"

The perennial student problem. Work, play and study. It seems that Leona is burning too many candles at odd angles.

"Anyway, I don't want to talk about it. It's my day off and we're going to hit the town. We'll start with another glass of this, get some bass thumping out of that stereo and hit the bedroom."

They finish their cigarettes, stubbing them out in a glazed blue pot full of last year's dead bedding plants, and take their glasses, the bottle and Leona's overnight bag upstairs to the bedroom Bex is using during her stay in Bideford. Towels are dug out of the airing cupboard and the shower steams.

With the basics done, both girls spend the next hour studiously making themselves up to look like they don't care; hair professionally unkempt, foundation, a hint of lip gloss, a dash of sparkle, nails scrubbed, and in Leona's case painted purple. *Madonna* gives way to the infectious groove of the dance floor. *Basement Jaxx.*

Bex fetches a box of her Dad's wine from under the stairs when they empty the bottle. Rosé at room temperature but they don't care. The sound of girls in full fancy echoes around Billy's normally silent bachelor home.

Clothes. Experiments. Leona has brought three tops, a short skirt, jeans, leggings and assorted shoes. The girls are roughly the same size, Bex being a little taller and more firmly toned than Leona. Swaps and combinations. A halter neck little black number from the bottom of a suitcase. Agreement and giggles. It looks better on Leona, less clingy, but her selection of shoes are wrong.

Bex hits the surf section of her wardrobe; cargo pants, a long sleeve, two-tone pink top, and pink canvas pumps, but it's all together too casual. The Basement has no formal dress code, but the girls have standards. Choices are made. Wine is drunk. Another break for cigarettes and formerly definite decisions are overturned. Raucous laughter. Strained top notes. The girls sing along to one of Billy's compilation discs; *Cab Calloway, Minnie the Moocher.* Hi-De-Hi-De-Ho dance steps in the bedroom.

In the end Leona goes for the little black dress, the pink pumps and a set of chunky costume jewellery. Her hair is styled in a sort of punk haystack and her makeup is understated except for eyeliner, which is thick and black. Bex opts for a splashed blue strappy top with a low neckline, short black skirt, black tights and her Doc Martens.

Reflections in mirrors. High fives. One more glass of Rosé. Seven o'clock. The light is failing and the Easter holiday influx into Bideford's drinking dens is in full swing. The girls are on a high and expectant, facing the eager prospect of boys at Lobster Jack's. The girls throw jackets around their shoulders, check the impossibly condensed contents of their infinitesimally small handbags and get ready to face the music and dance.

Mobile, fags, lighter, money, emergency repair kit and condoms.

The phone rings. Bex thinks about leaving it but remembers that Billy said he would call. He is in Bristol, probably just about to go to work, poor love. Bex kills the driving bass line of some blurred-out trance track and picks up the phone. Leona gestures towards the back door and Bex nods. A last cigarette. Bex mouths the words, "Out in a mo".

"Hello, Dad?"

"Hi, love, how's things? Everything okay?"

"Yeah fine. Nice and quiet. We're just getting ready to go out. What about you?"

"Not too bad. Traffic was fine. Everyone piling down the other way. Big queues at the bridge, as usual. Just arrived at the club. Wags. Footballers wives."

"Nice! Watch yourself. What time do you kick off?"

Billy wonders. Is there a faint burr on her voice? Drinking? "Yeah, very funny. The club is called Wags. Nine. Split set. Should be through around half eleven. Quick drink and on the road. Back around half-two. You'll be back by then,

I expect."

"Probably." Bex pulls a face in the mirror above the telephone table. "I mean yes, Dad. We'll do our best. The clubs start chucking out between two and three, so we might be a bit later, but not much."

"Have you put the cab money somewhere safe?" Billy gave Bex two twenties before he left.

"In my purse. Don't worry. I'm a big girl. Anyway, Leona will make sure I'm okay. We'll look after each other."

"Yeah, yeah, I know. Just being a Father. How is she, by the way? Should have asked."

Bex loves him for it, loves him for the awkwardness that separates their respective generations, but he seems a little flat, a little down, monotone. "She's fine. All dressed up. Says hello. Sure you're okay, Dad?"

He ignores her last question. Now is not the time to discuss Maggie's plans to leave the country. Billy suddenly wants to end the conversation, but he is reluctant to let Bex flex her bright young wings. There is something about telephone conversations that makes him feel protective towards her. It is, he thinks, the voice, that disembodied feeling you get when you hear someone close to you but cannot see their face. It is something he has to live with. Most of his parenting has been broken by static. Letting go is hard to do, even though he knows his little girl is growing up fast.

"Bex, be careful. Take care of each other and don't do…"

Bex makes a joke of it, cutting through Billy's self-conscious fatherly discomfort. "From what you've told me that leaves a pretty wide field of play, Dad. Don't worry. We know more about these places than you do. It's different now, different sounds, different stuff. We'll both be careful, I promise."

Billy doubts that Bex knows more than he does. He has enough experience of personal misdirection and abuse to write a graphically illustrated encyclopaedia. He lets it go. Now is not the time. Bex has worked hard all week and he loves her.

"Sorry. You know how it is. Your Mum and all that. Have a great time, both of you. Say hi to Leona. Love you, Bex."

"Love you too. Give 'em hell tonight, Dad. Bye."

"Bye, love, bye".

The sound of a mobile disconnecting. Bex puts the house phone back on its cradle and nips out into the back garden. Leona has two unlit cigarettes in her hand. As soon as she sees Bex opening the back door she puts them both in her mouth and lights them, handing one to Bex.

"Ta. Dad says hello and have a great time."

"He's nice, your Dad. Must be lovely to have a famous father."

"Well, he's not that famous, not really. He's just Dad to me."

The girls finish their cigarettes and stub them out in the same neglected plant pot as before. Bex collects the butts and puts them in the wheelie bin. Before they leave the house Bex checks to make sure that she has the cab fare and her mobile.

The girls are walking into town. From Billy's house they go down to the Northam Road, past a second hand car dealer and along past Morrison's. Crossing at the lights, they cut through the back of Bideford's narrow, overhanging streets and hit the pedestrian shopping area. Two thirds of the way towards the High Street they hang a left onto Cooper Street and smile sweetly for the Saturday night bouncers on the door at Lobster Jack's.

Moon boots. The first thing Bex sees in Lobster Jack's is a girl wearing moon boots and a short, faux fur jacket. Hilarious. The jogging-bottom girls are done up to the nines. Every table is taken, the place being full of loud teenager girls and the emerging surliness of young men in their late teens and early twenties out on the prowl. Every available surface is stacked with bottles and pint glasses. Ashtrays overflow. Boys crowd the bar and the steps that divide the two split levels of the room.

The volume of a hundred conversations is matched by the commentary that fills the upper atmosphere, an atmosphere you can see despite the hum of industrial filters hanging from the ceiling. West Ham are belatedly fighting-off relegation from the Premiership. Eyes turn upwards. Four giant plasma screens are mounted on the walls; North, South, East and West.

The bar has been created out of the shell of an old and derelict warehouse. Pre-combustion engine fittings still hang on the walls. Rusted chains and pulleys. Above the television by the main entrance Bex can see the old wooden loading doors for what must have been an upper level. The place is open to the roof now and themed. Ernest Hemmingway. Pictures of the man are screwed to the walls. From the middle of the ceiling hangs a glass fibre Marlin. Fishing poses. Boats. Hemmingway in a bush hat. Nowhere is there any reference to Hemmingway the writer.

The girls fight their way to the bar, gathering glances and undress-me looks like rosebuds in May. Armfuls of lust. Winks and nods. Elbows. Cheeky chappies revving up and burning imported beer like gasoline. Leona has to shout to make herself heard. The barmaids wear skimpy black tops and short black skirts. The barmaids look frayed, smiling for the customers as an afterthought. Leona orders a couple of Buds and pays. A leering boy to her right lights up and breathes smoke into her face. Looking cool. She gives him the brush-off. They spot an opening by a pillar with a narrow shelf and a half full ashtray, and stake their claim, but there are no stools left so they stand. The pillar is set towards the back of the bar and gives them free rein to people watch.

Bex points at the Marlin. "Bit up market, isn't it? Hemmingway?"

Leona bends forward so that she can make headway against the background noise. "Most of them don't know. Probably think he used to fish out of Clovelly. That or Lobster Jack was a character in Jaws."

There is a roar from the boys in the bar. West Ham have just conceded another goal. The picture cuts to their manager who is swearing blue murder. Leona waits for the roar to subside. A glass smashes on the opposite side of the room. A cheer.

"Came here in the winter. Empty. Like a morgue. If you think this is bad, though, you should see it in July. School's Out. Bloody heaving. It's monster."

"I bet. Did you see the sharks?"

"The what?"

"Predators. Eyeing us up when we came in."

"How could you miss it. Should be a good night."

Laughter. Raised eyebrows. Big tugs on their beer. Leona opens her purse and gets a cigarette. Flame and smoke. "Seen anyone you fancy yet?"

Bex shakes her head. "Far too early". She points to her half empty bottle. "Need some more of these first. Dutch courage."

Leona remembers the smoking gun at the bar. "Did you see that tosser at the bar. Thought he was so cool. Why are boys so childish? Don't answer. I want to live in hope."

The conversation spins along with sarcastic comments and dry observation. The boys in the bar are uniformly laddish; shirts worn loose and jeans, trainers, grease and muscle, full of attitude and unearned notions of respect. The girls target individual specimens and rip the piss out of them. Occasionally eyes meet across a crowded room. Brief encounters with a blue tinged facsimile of steam engine smoke hanging in the air. Bex finds herself avoiding one corner of the room where a couple of lads, brothers by the look of them, keep staring at her. The come on. Thought transference.

Having spent the afternoon on the grape juice both girls try to take it easy on the beers. Teenage constitutions are remarkable things, but even in their relatively short social lives both of them have experienced the fatal charm inherent in mixing the sauce. The process of getting tanked is being demonstrated more than adequately by a mixed group a few paces away. There are two girls, not much older than Leona and Bex, who are having difficulty standing. It is just after nine.

Another foray through the jungle of wandering hands at the bar brings two more beers. Bex buys her round. She hands a cold filtered lager to Leona. "So what was all that shit about college?"

Leona grimaces. "Don't. Poxy tutor. I'm doing my best. It's not as though anyone at home gives a fuck. My Dad thinks reading is for posh tarts, unless it's the back page of the Sun. Without Maggie's wages I wouldn't be able to go to college. That's what they don't understand. And it's good experience. I bet most of the kids up in London haven't got a clue. Paid up members of the local am-dram club, probably. I've worked with pros. At least I'm doing a proper job. Wankers."

"Yeah. Makes me feel inadequate." Bex tries to empathise. "Mum won't let me get a part time job. Says I've got to concentrate on getting good grades. It's not fair when my mates are doing stuff and I still get pocket money." Bex is exaggerating.

Two views, two different worlds, but neither Bex nor Leona have any particular axes to grind. It's all shades of karma, the greys rather than the black and whites.

Leona gives Bex a slightly deeper insight into her family situation. "Everyone's got their own shit. Take my Mum. Works her arse off for a pittance. Gets paid less than the men at the pottery and has to work twice as hard. When I was thirteen I took one look at them sand decided to get out. I'm going to finish my course and I'm bloody well going to be a stage manager. We've both got the same shit. It's just different shit. If that makes any sense? Being a vet is something special. Your

Mum's right."

Bex is bumped by a rangy youth on his way back from the toilets. A muttered sound. No recognisable syllables. He bumbles away into the crowd.

"Not even an apology. Jesus." She marks his card and returns to the subject at hand. "I know. Dad's probably glad I didn't follow in his footsteps. What's that saying, 'Don't put your daughter on the stage Mister Whitlow'. He tries his best. The last couple of years have been pretty good. It's like we're best mates."

"That's great, Bex. Enjoy it." Leona looks at the floor for a moment. "Shit. Enough family talk, girl. Let's just agree that life is weird. My shout."

Leona heads back to the bar to keep the juices flowing and Bex is left alone in a crowd. She fidgets, fussing with the shoulder straps of her top. Suddenly she feels as though she has iron filings running through her veins and as if drawn by a magnet she can't help but look into the far forbidden corner of the room. The brothers are still there with their mates. One of them is getting the rise. Tousled hair. Hair gel sticking to a fat kid's podgy white fingers. Good looking boys. The other brother is facing directly towards Bex and he sees her looking. He grins as Bex looks away, pretending to examine a picture of Ernest Hemmingway on the back of a boat holding up what looks like a reef shark. Grainy. Black and white. Hooked.

Leona shoves a shot glass into Bex's hand. "Come on, get that one down your neck. We can get in half price if we're there before ten. Chance to pick a good ogling spot. There's an upstairs bar with a balcony where you can watch the boys strut their stuff."

Heads back and fire on the throat. The girls trip out of Lobster Jack's and feel the chill of a Spring evening on their bare skin. Arm in arm they walk a couple of hundred metres through the pedestrian area of Bideford's main shopping drag until, on the High Street, they join the early doors queue at The Basement.

As the girls hit the end of the short queue outside the nightclub, Billy hits a top note on stage at Wags. *Moon River*. Silky smooth. It is a good night and the club is flush with well-heeled punters. Suits. Billy is on a roll. His voice is like thick double cream. The wine glasses on the tables gleam in the hushed, appreciative light. The toilets are a work of art. You know by the order and cleanliness of the place that the kitchens are spotless, that the food is top notch.

Billy is in seventh heaven. The world around him is a perfect place. Harmony and melody. He is soaring above the strings. A real show band. The Sultans of Swing. Happiness is a great meal, a good cigar and a polished crooner belting out the old favourites.

Bouncers with attitude. Paired off and cocky. Black jackets, white shirts and steroid ripples. The Basement is located in what was once the little white town's local cinema. The multiplex has yet to arrive in North Devon, but the old Odeon's and ABC's have fallen prey to the vicissitudes of consumer choice all the same. Barnstaple has the only commercial picture house in the area. The club is industrial, modelled on old machinery; scaffolding, mocked-up turbine housings and a science fiction proliferation of metal walkways.

Downstairs there is basically one large room with a coat check in one corner and a bar running along one third of the longest wall. Neon lights and LED wall panels flash incessantly. The Basement should carry a health warning for epileptics. The dance floor is at the far end of the room. The carpet in the downstairs bar area is dark and pock marked with cigarette burns and as Bex and Leona walk through the club they find their shoes sticking to the carpet. The drinking areas downstairs are divided by metal grates and there is hardly any furniture. A few metal seats are fixed to the outer walls. Iron pillars support the upstairs mezzanine.

The place feels hollow at this time of night. Most of the regular clubbers hit the queues outside around eleven and the punters on the early shift are still thin on the ground and coalesce into random groups. Girls mostly. The volume is subdued. Bex and Leona can speak without having to shout. Music switches between commercial dance tracks and RnB. Mediocre. The club is just waking up and shaking off the lethargy of the sleeping day.

The girls take advantage of 'Happy Hour' and buy a couple of vodka kicks each. After eleven the prices double and you need a good supply of cash to make it through to closing time. They climb a metal staircase made of welded steel with checker plate treads. Upstairs there is a small bar area and a narrow balcony that runs around three sides of the building. Opposite the bar is a chill-out room full of soft seats and bean bags, with space enough for twenty people. The toilet doors next to the small bar are scuffed and dented. Heel marks.

Bex and Leona wander over to the balcony and look down on the deserted dance floor. *Chopperchunk* flares out of the speakers. The volume increases. Through the main doors downstairs the trickle of clubbers is growing and they spot a girl in a *Kill Bill* catsuit, yellow with black stripes. Hen night fancy dress clobber. The girl is lithe and fits the cat suit perfectly. Sort of cool, especially when Bex spots Moon Boots from Lobster Jack's. The Basement is being flooded by short skirts, bare flesh and mockney accents.

The first intrepid boy hunters hit the bar. Poles apart. After twenty years of evolution in club land white stilettos and plastic handbags may have given way to belly button piercings and porthole dresses, but the ritual stand-off between groups of rhythmic girls and leery boys is alive and well. The sound of conversation rises with the deepening boom of the PA. The caffeine and alcohol mix in the girl's drinks is kicking in.

Leona spots something. "Over there". She points to a group of girls standing at the edge of the dance floor. "Only problem here is the kids. Underage. Lippy. The management turns a blind eye. Some nights it's like a sixteen-year-old's birthday party in here."

Bex nods. Then she realises that strictly speaking they are underage themselves. Ironic. Leona is serious, though and adds, "Shouldn't be allowed".

The current track is a cut above the previous ones. The girls sway in time to the bass line. This time it is Bex who spots something. The youth from Snuggle's, the one who upset Maggie, is at the bar. She watches him lean over and speak to one of the barmen, who nods a couple of times and then disappears through a doorway at the back of the bar.

She nudges Leona. "Isn't that the bloke from the club? Wednesday night?"

Leona takes a couple of seconds to orientate herself. Tall and thin with a crew cut. Long overcoat. "Yeah. Wonder what he's doing here? Wouldn't have thought he'd be hanging round with the underage Neds on a Saturday night."

Shaun waits by the bar, a bottle of water in hand. He likes to get in early. The management prefer it that way too because they can tuck Shaun away in his little cubby-hole without too much fuss. Shaun tries not to look obvious as he checks-out the groups of boys and girls on the ground floor. Kids. If the plain clothes boys are looking for a bust they usually try to fit in when the crowds are at their thickest, but Shaun can spot them a mile off. They're always slightly too old, slightly over or under dressed. It's something about the effort they make to look right. Shaun uses the kids as cover and there's nothing to worry about so far.

A tap on his shoulder. The barman. "You can go through. The boss is up at the top bar."

Shaun skips up the metal staircase and checks out the two girls leaning over the balcony. They have their backs to him. He is not sure, but it seemed as though they were watching him when he was waiting for the nod downstairs. They look vaguely familiar, but Shaun can see that they are way too young for the drug squad. He keeps a weather eye on them as he slides across the room and leans on the bar.

One of the two men behind the bar says something to his partner, who heads off downstairs to collect another box of plastic glasses. Alone with Shaun the barman offers him a drink.

"No, ta. Got my water."

"As ever. Sober little fuck aren't you, Shaun. Got the entrance money?"

Shaun reaches into an inside pocket in his overcoat and pulls out a deck of cash. He slides five twenties off the top and passes them to the owner of The Basement. "All present and correct. Usual place?"

"Be my guest".

To the left of the bar, next to the toilets, there is an alcove in the rear wall through which the punters would access the fire escape door if there was an emergency. A large yellow and black sign says that the door is alarmed but Shaun knows this is not true. The alarm is always switched off when the club is open. There is a stool in the alcove from where Shaun can watch the night unfold without being deafened by the soundtrack of people screwing up their lives. This position has a number of advantages. He can see the staircase clearly from here through one of the metal grid walls, which gives him time. If there is a raid he can be through the fire escape door and up onto the roof in seconds. From there it is up to him.

He checks his pockets. The usual range; E, dope, uppers, downers and the new stuff. The money that he slipped to the owner of the club is an overhead. Cash on the nose. An out of pocket expense. Routine business. A ton for his pitch. Shaun likes to think of himself as a market trader. A good one. He sells quality gear at a reasonable price. The rent means that he gets an exclusive between the hours of ten and twelve, which is more than enough time. The boys on the door know most of the local faces and keep them out until then. They also know the cops. As far as the owner is concerned it is money for old rope. Everyone has to pay their rent, but only Shaun gets the early shift, which is when the kids are still flush.

Bex and Leona watch the place fill up. The open acreage of the dance floor is turning into a sea of limbs blowing like grass in the breeze of driving bass lines. The groups of boys and girls in the drinking areas are gradually getting squeezed into ever smaller spaces. Standing room only. The heat rises. Foreheads glisten. The bars are under siege. There is always a crush in the first hour after eleven as the exodus from the town pubs hits full swing and boys start giving girls the glad eye. Jealous partners check out the opposition. Everyone has to shout to be heard.

Bex and Leona leave two empty bottles on the floor where they have been standing and move along the balcony so that they can see the dance floor and the bar area downstairs more clearly. Cigarette butts litter the floor around their new vantage point and their drinks are warm but that is the price you pay. If you order a drink that needs a glass you get a plastic one. Order a bottle and you get glass. For your personal safety. The weapon of choice.

Bex has to cup her hand and speak directly into Leona's ear. "I love this bit. All these people. When I was little Mum and I used to make up stories about people in the park. You know.

She's really a witch. You can see her broomstick poking out of her shopping trolley."

Bex points to a tall, thin boy on the dance floor. "He's an internationally famous limbo dancer."

Leona laughs. "Yeah, and her, the one in the black t-dress with the skull, she's a ring wraith. Only comes out after dark. Searching for a hobbit to take home and have her wicked way with. Likes midget sex."

Bex swings round and looks at the specimens in the upstairs bar. Through the press of sweaty bodies she can see Shaun's head in the alcove. It disappears as two of the club's clientele squeeze past a knot of female drinkers and talk to him. Their backs are towards her but she keeps watching. After a minute they head back into the crowd. Bex is fascinated. The gaunt boy from Wednesday night seems to know a lot of people, but he only ever seems to have a brief chat with them. Then it dawns on her.

She prods Leona and points at the alcove. "Stranger than fiction. I think he really is an international drug dealer."

"What, the bloke from the club?" Leona watches too. There is a brief pause. The DJ has got his timing wrong. The sound of voices without the back beat is weird. Clubbers are momentarily confused. Synthetic star shine bursts from the PA and the grind resumes. Another buyer visits Shaun in his alcove.

"You're right. Do you think that's why he went to see Jock? Drugs?"

Bex is shocked. Jock? By inference that means Maggie. "No.

Can't be." She thinks around the question for a moment. "No. Maybe Jock was warning him off. Maybe there's been trouble at Snuggle's. Maggie was pretty pissed-off when she saw him. I don't believe it."

Their story telling is interrupted. Two boys emerge from the crowd and, grinning from ear to ear, they hold out two bottles of blue wonder. "Weren't you at Jack's?" one of them asks.

Bex and Leona hesitate. The better looking of the two stakes his claim for Bex. "In the corner under the telly. I kept looking at you. Remember? I'm Jim and this is Darren."

Leona looks at Bex. She has no recollection of seeing these two, but then it dawns on her that Bex might be a bit of a dark horse, too. She whispers into Bex's ear, "What do you think? Yours looks like a laugh. I think mine's a bit on the shy side, though."

The boys stand their ground, smiling and still holding out the bottles. Bex decides. "Why not. Let's have some fun."

The girls return the boys' smiles and accept the offered drinks. Late teens. Good looking in a Mancunian guitar band sort of way. Cocky but not threatening. A certain swagger about them. The bolder one of the two does most of the talking and they exchange a few jokes and comments about the punters, all of which helps the newly founded foursome to settle into something approaching a rhythm.

After a few minutes Jim leans forward and whispers to Bex. "Fancy something a little more exotic?"

Bex is on his wavelength. She has tried Ecstasy a couple of times and is up for it.

Leona's radar is also picking up incoming signals. "What did he say?"

"Wants to know if we want some E. Up for it?"

Leona is unsure. She has never tried anything harder than alcohol or cigarettes. "I'm not sure. I mean…" Her body language is becoming distinctly awkward, caught between the delicious impurity of the moment and an inherited, innate reluctance to put herself in danger.

Bex reassures her. "It's okay. I've tried it a couple of times. Makes you feel warm. Sort of right with the world. And it's brilliant on the dance floor. I promise you, it's alright."

Leona feels nervous. This is unfamiliar territory. "What if I don't like it? You know, Yvonne thingy, brain damage?"

Yvonne Miller. At the time the press was quick to report that Yvonne's death was an obvious example of the dangers of illegal drugs in general, and Ecstasy in particular.

Bex has an answer. "Wasn't the stuff. She died because she drank too much water. I checked it out before I tried it the first time. Weird, I know, but I'm into all that stuff. Chemistry and shit."

Bex nods to the boy. "Okay. We're in."

He taps his brother on his chest and Darren pulls a tenner out of his back pocket. Jim does the same and says, "Look, sorry about this, but we can't afford to buy drinks and drugs. If we all put a tenner into the kitty, I'll go and sort it. I'll leave Darren here as security."

Leona fidgets and stares down at the dance floor. Bex puts half of the cab fare that her Dad gave her into the boy's hand, enough for both of them. "No problem. I know where you're going. I can watch you all the way. If you do a runner with the cab fare I'll kneecap your brother."

"Please do, he needs waking up." Jim gives Bex a star spangled wink and then disappears into the crowd, working his way towards the alcove through shifting gaps in the contra-flows of moving bodies.

Darren decides to make his move. He and his brother have already divvied up the spoils and he has been allotted the girl with haystack hair. He steps forward awkwardly and shouts at Leona. "So, what do you do?"

Billy finishes the second half of his act with a pared down arrangement of *Georgia*. It is not his usual sort of song, but he likes to experiment and he is getting into Ray Charles at the moment. Just Billy and a piano, sweet and soft. He can still put feeling into a lyric and there is not a dry eye in the house. Thumbs up from the owner. For a brief moment Billy almost feels like he is back in the big time. Five hundred in his pocket for headlining and that welling-up in the soul. This is what he was born for. As the song dies, though, the acid tinge of bitterness bites back and he can't help but feel the shame and disappointment of all those chances that he missed. He screwed up the big-time.

Off stage he has a drink with the owner and a couple of the owner's friends and they shake on a return visit. Billy has a Coke. He has a long drive and wants to be back in time to tuck his daughter into bed. Pats on the back and the punters get to mingle for half an hour. The best of both worlds. The drive home will fly by. Billy is looking forward to dealing with teenage hangovers in the morning.

It's all about the ups and downs of show business. One minute you're on top of the world, the next you're feeling like the fat kid picked last for the football team. He ought to pay more attention to simple domestic pleasures because the one thing that brings him real satisfaction is being constant for Bex. The thought of her needing him in the morning brightens up his mood, and as he glad hands and sparkles once again he is suddenly having so much fun.

Brief encounters make up the bulk of Shaun's working life. Happy shoppers. Low voices and the rustle of bank notes. Online transactions are all very well for posh tarts in London's city wine bars, but Shaun has one simple rule. He has to be able to smell the value of your money on his fingers, and trade is good tonight. A number of Friday night's rave crew have followed the supply down to Bideford and they are putting the word out. Bliss is shaping up nicely. Bex watches her beau slip between two groups of drinkers and slide into the alcove.

Jim knows Shaun by sight. "Hiya, mate. How's tricks?"

Shaun rarely smiles. Everyone wants to know your name when your pockets are full of Kryptonite, but he sees too many faces to remember features. The boy looks vaguely familiar, but it could be the setting or the background music that induces the image. Shaun has heard that smells trigger memories. The odour of rank urinals drifts out of the male toilet.

"Yeah, middling. What do you want?"

Long conversations bore Shaun. He has two hours to shift his gear and be on the road. He has spent too many years on the dance floor. Looking through people and at the fatuous décor inside night clubs has become a tedious necessity.

The boy gets the picture. Cut the crap. "Had a whip. Forty notes. Doves?"

Shaun nods and pulls four small plastic wraps from his pocket. Each one contains two tabs. Just as he is about to exchange them for the cash he stops and smiles at the boy. "Hold on. Got something else. New shit. Called Bliss."

He puts two of the wraps back into his overcoat pocket and feels for the plastic sachets given to him by Jock on Wednesday night. He selects two sachets and hands them over with the two other wraps to the boy.

"Basically the same but got a bit of an edge. All you do is lick you finger, dip and suck. One of these is the same as a couple of E's, only you get more control."

The boy looks at the sachet of yellow powder. He has heard of the stuff coming in powdered form but never seen it. It looks like the stuff in one of the jars in his mother's spice rack. Shaun takes the money from the boy.

"Oh yeah, one more thing. No Sunday blues."

Jim palms the gear into his jeans pocket and thinks about saying thanks but Shaun has already blanked him. The deal is done and Jim is history. Bliss. Jim has never heard of it and if it turns out to be washing powder he will murder the guy. Possibly. Then again Jim reckons that Shaun knows his stuff. Shaun has been dealing for as long as Jim can remember and never yet been busted. He skims the edge of the crowd and slips into a gap at one end of the small upstairs bar. After a few minutes trying to get the attention of the staff he manages to pay for four more vodka kicks and holding two in each hand by the neck he trips the slow waltz back to his brother and the girls.

Between deals Shaun sees the boy leave the bar with bottles. What the fuck. Jock can go screw himself. They always drink and drop. It is not his problem. What do these people want from him? He is not a bloody babysitter.

Raised eyebrows. Leona is spooked by the powder. She has been trying to get in the mood but is struggling. She feels disjointed, alone in a world full of foreign bodies, and there is none more foreign than Darren, who has been working hard but making little headway. Bex is in that comfort zone induced by just enough alcohol. Her defences are down and she is feeling the beat drive through her bones.

Jim pops the two wraps and offers the girls one tab each. He doesn't want to spoil the mood. Pissing the haystack girl off will inevitably lead to the two of them making their exit stage left, which would put a real downer on the night.

"Look, it's okay. No one's going to force you. If you don't want to try anything that's fine. Take a tab and do what you want. If you're not happy about it that's cool."

He drops a tab and swills it down with bright blue vodka. Darren follows suit, as does Bex. Leona can feel the weight of the thing in her palm and she looks at Bex for reassurance.

"You're sure you've done it before?" she asks.

Bex is letting the groove lead her body. She brushes against Jim and it feels good. She nods and says, "Positive. You just get euphoric, sort of into everything. It's not like acid or anything. You don't see pink spiders crawling up the walls. You'll be fine, promise."

Darren chips in. "And the touchies. Sometimes. It's brilliant. Like you can feel everything in the universe, right down to the atoms."

Jim gives him a nudge. "Ignore the stupid little…" Now is not the time for the C-word. "He's trying to be nice. Come on, lets hit the dance floor."

The boys squeeze out from the balcony and make a gap in the crowded bar area for the girls to squeeze through. Leona grabs Bex by the arm and together they make their slow passage onto the staircase and down into the heat of the main room. The dance floor is jam packed with bodies. Trashy, liquid synth loops fill the air. The nasal melody is underpinned by diesel bass lines thumping out at one hundred and twenty beats per minute. The boys merge into the crowd, gripping their drinks tightly. Leona and Bex pick up the vibe and as they too fuse with the mass. Leona downs her tab and submits to the infection.

Shaun gets the nod from one of the guys behind the bar. Time is up. He slips off his stool and works his way through the crowds. He catches sight of the girls from the balcony on his way out. Recognition. Snuggle's. Not a problem. The one in the little black number could do him anytime. Out on the street he thrusts his hands into his coat pockets and walks down to the quayside cab rank. No sweat.

Lights. Drowning in sound. As the drugs kick in Leona and Bex find themselves at the heart of something intangible. They become one with the pulse, losing themselves between the cracks in the world's tectonic plates. Eyes wide open. Huge grins. The electron web burns brightly. Body heat. The grind and flip. Zooming and peaking. Tracks coalesce, becoming a closed circuit of rhythm.

It is too loud to speak, but Leona feels no need for words. Bex was right. She is open. She can empathise with the universe and the rush is amazing. This first time hit burns her soul with love. The fact that Darren is a bit of a goon simply doesn't matter. He is here and he is flying with her. She is glowing, mesmerised and loving every second of it. The look on her face is all that Bex needs to see to know that the Rubicon has been crossed. Leona is just like her; a fully paid-up member of the adult race.

The night seems endless. They take a short break while Jim hits the bar again, this time for bottles of water. The alcohol has done its job in freeing them from base inhibitions and high on exaggeration, sitting astride the four points of their personal twinkling star, they don't need any more of that old shit. Bex encourages Leona to keep drinking water, telling her that dehydration is the biggest risk, but Leona is full of energy and bursting to get back to the groove. She leaves her bottle by a chair fixed to one of the side walls and dives back into the heaving press of bodies.

Bex is losing track of time. All four of them are pushing the limits. Bex and the boys take another break around two but Leona stays on the dance floor, determined to mine the night for every ounce of gold locked away in its black-hearted mother lode. Laughter all round. Exhausted but ecstatic. The DJ is playing club classics now and the dance floor is a mass of happy campers, up to their hips in love honey. The atmosphere on the dance floor is electric.

Out of breath, Bex and the boys lean against one of the pillars supporting the mezzanine floor above the main room. Jim fishes one of the sachets out his pocket and hands it Bex.

"Your share. Going to give it a whirl?"

Bex takes the sachet and grins back at Jim. "Yeah". Her eyes are gleaming under the spotlights. Her face and skin glow with rude, loop-enhanced health. Jim opens the sachet and licks his index finger. He dabs at the powder and makes eyes at Bex as he slides his finger into his mouth. Provocative. Darren wishes Leona was with them so that he could copy his much cooler older brother. Unlike the tabs the rush from the powder hits within a minute. Bliss. Jim is swept up on the rolling surf of the trance mix currently playing. On the dance floor he becomes aware of lights and vague distortions in peoples' faces. He can feel the weight of his body but it seems to him as if he is floating just above the crowd.

Darren drags Bex back onto the dance floor and they work their way over to Jim and Leona. Bex is holding her sachet in her hand and as they melt into the white water of electronic motion all around them she takes her first hit of the new yellow powder. Like the boys she is in the twilight zone within a minute. The roof opens above her head to reveal pure white star shine. The initial buzz cascades through her body and she becomes one with the dream. She dabs her finger in the sachet again and offers it to Leona, who is so far gone on her own physical and emotional trip that she accepts it without question.

The nature of the hit is different. Vision blurs. Colours seep into the world from the edges, bleeding. The next twenty minutes burn like flares and then fade, becoming reflections like spots on eyelids after looking at the sun. Another burst. Wet fingers trigger explosions. Hitting the transmit button. Pictures and tones. Every subtle nuance of the spectrum, of the broadcast wavelength. The kids are soaring over the rooftops on wings of serotonin. Synapses flash. Blue lightning in the brain. The dopamine dance craze. Receptors firing. Acetylcholine. One hundred percent proof adrenaline.

And then the bass line revolution blurs and starts to slow, becoming one long, low growl in Leona's head. She feels as if she is speeding up, as if her reactions to and perceptions of the world are so fast that everything around her is happening in slow motion. Someone is pulling curtains across the moon. Shadow puppets are dancing in her mind's eye.

The crescendo. Bex has her arms raised above her head. She knows this track. *United Noize; Fetish*. The main loop repeats over and over again, hooking her into the mix. She shuts her eyes and feels the flow. Sublime. She wants to share the joy and turns to where she last saw Leona. She opens her eyes and takes a second or two to adjust the colours being registered in her head. Strobe lights. Diamond white. Ultraviolet. Black. Empty space.

Something primeval kicks in. At the base of her skull, down

where the reptilian DNA regulates the basic functions of life, a small voice is calling her name. The primitive region of existence. Fight or flight. Instincts for survival. Bex is standing in the middle of a heaving dance floor, high on booze and doped up on MDMA. She should be in love with the world, but she feels dreadfully alone. The back beat gyre of sound and movement, of colour and smell, gives way to a void. She looks down and sees Leona on her knees.

Leona is kneeling up and is impossibly, unnaturally still. Her arms hang down by her side and for a moment Bex thinks that her friend is going to start praying, but as she looks into the girl's eyes she realises that the light has gone out of them. Bex stands there, motionless herself now, and wonders where Leona has gone. She is reminded of a toy robot on Boxing Day. The batteries are dry and lifeless.

Bex grabs Jim's arm and drags him down with her as she squats in front of Leona. The other dancers back away a little but keep moving. Spotlights crash through their never ending cycle of colours on the small patch of clear wooden floor around the kneeling girl. Electronic music fizzes and sparks, but Bex is no longer able to hear it as a coherent progression. Everything is disjointed and dissociated.

Jim puts his hands on Leona's shoulders and shakes her roughly, trying to get a response, trying to jiggle the batteries and switch the current back on. Clubbers on the dance floor and in the bar area are staring, all of them making the same basic assumption; stupid, pissed up kids with one mother of a hangover on the cards. No one helps. They know what to expect. As Jim and Bex call out Leona's name she vomits and Jim's shirt and jeans are covered in projectile alcopop bile. The dancing mass parts like the Red Sea. Jim falls back and spins away from the girl. He is dragged back onto his feet by his brother, and as he lurches backwards he instinctively pushes the nearly empty sachet of yellow powder in his hand into his jeans pocket. Like the rest of club land, the boys are staring at Leona and Bex, putting together the essential facts; it's time to make themselves scarce.

Jim has taken the brunt of the disgorgement and Bex is oblivious to the state of her own clothes. The shock and surprise of the moment makes her sit back on the dance floor as Leona topples forward, face down, into the remains of her evening session. Bex can feel the music pumping away around her but she can't hear it. She looks up at where she thinks the boys are and sees two of the bouncers standing by the edge of the dance floor, ready to hump and dump another lashed teenage raver into Bideford's Saturday gutters.

Instead of manhandling them both out of the club the bouncers are rooted to the spot. The older one of the two of them has his right arm across the chest of his number two. He has seen this shit before. He turns towards the main bar and makes two distinct gestures. He runs his thumb across his throat and then makes the sign of the Devil and puts it up against the side of his face. Telephone. Triple nine.

The seconds that follow seem like hours. Bex is aware of legs and feet moving around her where she sits. She knows that she is wired, that she should be freaking out, but all she can do is sit and stare at Leona. There is no movement from the prostrate girl. Bex is still holding the small plastic sachet full of yellow powder in her left hand.

The club's main lights go up. The world is filled with blurred voices. Shouts and screams. Bex is vaguely aware of people being herded. The bouncers and the bar staff are shepherding the punters out onto the streets. The owner of the club is standing over the girls, screaming into a mobile phone. He kills the call and turns to the senior bouncer, the one who hit the panic button.

"Get them the fuck out of here. Now!"

He means the crowds. This is his worst nightmare. He wants the kids out on the streets. Everyone knows the score. Blue lights. Paramedics. The Old Bill. If he can get them out of the place before the serious shit hits the fan most of them will drift away and it will be impossible for anyone to be a reliable witness. Most of them are blitzed up anyway and they won't want to hang around. Cabs are filling up. The alleyways and lanes echo with hurrying footsteps. A knot of the more morbid residents of the little white town hang around the entrance.

The club owner grabs one of the bar staff and barks out another order. "Get round this place now. Make sure none of the little bastards has dropped anything. Squeaky clean. Understand?"

Bex is aware of the change in ambience. The place looks like a mortuary in full light. The music is still playing. It is all too fantastical and her head is spinning. She looks for help again, looks for the boys, but Jim and Darren have cut and run, making a snap decision that no bit of skirt is worth this much shit. Instinct. Survival. Bex crawls over to where Leona is laying and cradles her head. Leona's small bag is still draped around her neck. In the confusion that survivalist reptile brain stem ensures that Bex slips her sachet of powder into Leona's bag.

At the same time that Leona sinks to her knees a dark blue Vauxhall Astra pulls up on a drive. Door keys. The lights are out. Billy guesses that the girls are still out but he checks the room where Bex and Leona are sleeping all the same. It is a mess. Clothes and makeup. Empty wine glasses. Typical girls having fun. Billy goes back downstairs and puts on the outside light so that they will be safe when they get home. He remembers that Bex told him the clubs chuck out around three. Half an hour.

He settles down in the living room with a large Irish and puts on the television. He flicks through the channels and finally settles on another rerun of *The Outlaw Josey Wales*. Billy has had a great night. The set went down a storm and he loved playing with a proper show band. He has a new contact and a firm booking for May. He has earned a grand this week and the season has only just begun. He knows it will be a good year and he can't wait to tell Bex about the gig.

On screen the two bounty hunters have just left Josey Wales in the saloon in some one horse, no hope Texan town. Billy has seen the film so many times before that he knows the lines. One of the two bounty hunters comes back into the saloon to challenge the outlaw. He has no choice. As Clint Eastwood says the line Billy joins in, drawling in his best gunfighter voice. "Dying ain't much of a living, boy".

Washes of blue light drench the rendered stonework of the shops and banks on Bideford High Street. An ambulance is parked outside the club's main entrance with its rear doors open and a uniformed police officer stands guard while the paramedics deal with the incident. A collapsible stretcher has been wheeled into the club, along with basic resuscitation kit and oxygen. The police are there to keep the local population from looting the on-board drugs cabinet. People hang around, ignoring every suggestion that they go home. Some of them peer into the ambulance with bald, video trained curiosity, while others try to get a glimpse of the bodies. Ghoulish fascination.

There are two patrol cars in attendance. One officer is directing late night traffic and moving people on. The remaining two officers from the first patrol to arrive are in the club. Questions. Notebooks. Kids and booze and drugs. The owner swears blind that he follows the rules. The punters are told not to bring anything in with them, but how can he know. Do they want sniffer dogs on the front door? Bar staff and bouncers hang around waiting to give statements. None of them have seen anything.

There is a hive of activity around Leona. She has been moved into the recovery position and one of the paramedics has strapped an oxygen mask to her face. The other member of the ambulance crew is with Bex.

"It's alright, love. Come on. Talk to me. I need to know what's happened. Tell me what she's taken."

Bex is confused. She feels as though her body is separating into its constituent parts and dripping away. She is cold. The ambulance man has wrapped her in a blanket but she feels numb and slow. What is he asking? He turns to his colleague.

"She's strung out as well. Not getting much."

"Yeah, I can see. Try and get her to show you what she's been on."

"Do you hear that, love. Have you got anything on you? Anything you might have taken tonight?"

Bex shakes her head. An idea is dislodged from one of the tightly packed shelves at the back of her brain. She shows the man her bag. Cigarettes. Cash. Keys.

"That's better. Now, can you tell me what she's taken?"

Leona is unconscious. Without knowing what she has taken the crew are having difficulty assessing the criticality of the situation. The ABCD's. Bex shivers. Her voice is broken and soft.

"E's. A…couple."

"E, Jack." The man tries to keep Bex on track. "Look at me, love. Anything else? Have you been drinking? How much? When did you take the drugs?"

Too many questions. Bex is struggling to stay awake herself. She feels heavy and light at the same time. Her body is made of lead. Inside her head there is a blizzard blowing. White Out. She tries to answer. Which question?

"Bottles…just usual…stuff".

"Okay, stay with me. Put this on." He places an oxygen mask on her face, turns and looks for one of the police officers. "Hey, could you get on the blower. We'll need another unit. This one's looking pretty flaky too."

Jack has collapsed the stretcher and is ready to move Leona.

The two ambulance men transfer her from the dance floor to the stretcher slowly and with precision. She looks desperately fragile but she is a dead weight. Her face is streaked with saliva and drying vomit. The stuff is in her hair. The police officer reports that a second unit is on the way.

"ETA?" asks the first paramedic.

"Five", is the reply. The officer is anxious to speak with the girls but he can see that they are both in a bad way. Static. Requests for backup are logged. It is early on a Sunday morning in provincial England and mobile patrols are busy. The officers in attendance will have to do their best and wait for support. The owner of the club and his staff are next to useless, whiter than white. Backsides are being covered. He can smell it.

Jack checks Leona's pulse. Weak. "As soon as the other crew arrive we've got to get this one to Barnstaple. She's unconscious and hypothermic. Respiration is impaired as well. I don't want her going arrhythmic or into convulsion in the back of the bus."

"Yeah, understood. I'll try to keep the other one awake."

With Leona on the stretcher the first paramedic takes a plastic vial from his kit bag and takes a sample of her vomit for testing at the hospital. The second man returns to where Bex is sitting and checks that the oxygen mask is still secure. Bex is drifting away. Her eyelids are drooping. She is starting to slide.

"Come on, love. Stay with me. No going to sleep. Not yet. What's your name? Tell me your name?"

Bex can hear a voice asking her questions again. She wants to get up and walk towards the voice but it sounds so far away. She can't see her own footprints in the snow. She is freezing. Aged seven and out in a blizzard. All around her are the dark shadows of night-black trees. She makes one last effort. In her dream she is shouting but the man who called to her hears nothing but a faint whisper.

"Bex…Bex…my name is Bex".

The voice comes again. Fainter. Moving away from her. "How old are you, Bex?"

"Sevente…"

Black snow.

"Fuck, she's gone too!"

Background noise. The sound of a dual tone siren. The club owner is being told to calm down.

"Calm fucking down. There's two stupid bitches dying on my fucking dance floor and you want me to calm down."

Hands on hips. The police officer who radioed for the second ambulance is joined by his colleague.

"Yes, sir. Button it, unless you want to go for a ride."

Doors crash open as the second ambulance crew wheel their stretcher into the club and barge through the staff to get to Bex. They are followed in short order by two plain clothes detectives. The club owner runs his hands through his hair in an act of despair. It is going to be a long night.

"Oh great. The fucking cavalry." He can read the body language. He changes tack. "Look, I'm sorry. It's just, well, it gets to you after a while. We run a clean place here. You guys know that. The door security team has been vetted. We tell you when we spot stuff going on. I'm not going to lie to you, though. I get pissed off by it, just like you do."

The two detectives walk over to the ambulance crews and check the details and status of the two girls. Then they rejoin the uniforms.

The new ambulance crew get to grips with Bex and move her onto their stretcher, exchanging information with the first crew. Jack checks Leona's handbag. He finds a sachet half full of yellow powder.

"What the hell is this?"

They don't have the luxury of time. He puts the sachet with the vial in his kit bag. As Bex is being stabilised they wheel Leona out to their ambulance and slide the stretcher back onto its runners. One of the crew climbs in with her and slams the doors shut. The driver climbs into the cab and turns the ignition key. Strobes. The wail of a siren. Leona's blood glucose level is already being checked and she is hooked up to the on-board oxygen supply. Under fluorescent light reflected off the wipe clean interior of the saloon she looks deathly pale. According to the on-board monitors she is tachycardic. Her liver and kidneys are in freefall.

Bex goes through the same set of procedures. Radio messages are sent. Crash teams at the North Devon Hospital are alerted. Billy is on his second large Irish. It's fifteen minutes past three o'clock and he is bored. He wants his little girl to come home.

CAN ANYONE EXPLAIN?

TWIN SETS OF HEADLIGHTS break across the new Bideford bridge. At the Instow junction blue lights flash and sirens scream through forty miles per hour warnings. Homeward bound drivers hug the kerb as both ambulances hit seventy on the dual carriageway section of the North Devon Expressway, heading for Roundswell and the welcoming sodium warmth of Barnstaple's empty streets.

In each ambulance, under bright fluorescent lights, the paramedic member of each crew tries to ensure that airways are clear and functioning. Oxygen is administered and brows are wiped to clear sweat-covered strands of hair from closed eyes. In the second ambulance Bex has her right arm exposed so that it lies along her side with her palm facing upwards. Although she is unconscious her pulse is strong. The medic finds a vein and despite the distraction of rapid motion caused by hanging drip lines he is deft and assured as he inserts a catheter into her forearm, hooks up a bag of saline and begins to administer four hundred micrograms of naloxone through the intravenous connection that is keeping Bex in touch with the physical world around her. A monitor pings regularly.

In the first ambulance the paramedic is working as quickly as he can given the constant subtle shifts of weight and force induced by the vehicle's furious pace as it crosses the narrow stretch of land between the Taw and Torridge estuaries. He can't find a vein in Leona's arm and struggles to raise the usual lines on the back of her hand. The trace on the monitor is showing all of the tell-tale signs of ventricular tachycardia. Leona is burning up as her heart races up to and beyond one hundred and fifty beats per minute. She desperately needs lidocaine. Her left arm and hand are bruised and stained dull purple from the repeated attempts to cannulate. Eventually he tags a valve in one of the collapsed veins in her hand and administers adrenaline.

The ambulance swings out and around a sharply breaking red Transit. Excited, surprised faces peer out of the front cab as the ambulance hurtles away into the darkness. Lights and sirens scour the edges of the road and as the paramedic braces himself the monitor flat lines. On board telemetry feeds the emergency report and electrocardiograph results to the team waiting in Accident and Emergency.

The paramedic moves into another sequence of practised procedures. He makes sure that Leona isn't wearing any metal jewellery, removing her watch and a costume bracelet from her left wrist. Time is critical. He attaches self-adhesive electrodes to Leona's chest wall, one at the base and one at the apex of her heart, powers up the on board defibrillator and runs an analysis of her condition. Shock is required. He hits the manual override button and sets the initial shock to two hundred joules. As soon as he is sure that he is clear of Leona's body he presses the button. Seconds tick away. The machine recharges and analyses Leona's output once again. She is still flat.

Over the next five minutes he increases the level by steps to three hundred and sixty joules, repeating the procedure again and again. Sweat drips off his forehead onto Leona's exposed chest. His movements are measured and concise. His own heart is racing and the ambulance is in full flight along Barnstaple quayside, braking hard at the right hand bend by the council offices and the main police station before accelerating up to the twin roundabouts at the junction with the Ilfracombe road. Siren wail bounces off building fascias, startling late night pedestrians as they wind their drunken way home. The route is clear. Both vehicles push hard through the traffic lights and up the hill towards the hospital where they swing round and reverse into the emergency bays by the entrance to Accident and Emergency.

Onlookers stand and stare as the crash team help to manhandle Leona's stretcher out of the ambulance and into the crash room to the left of the main entrance. She is transferred to one of the beds and as she is hooked up to the equipment and monitors one of the nurses continues to carry out basic life support procedures to try and prevent her becoming asystolic. Voices are raised. A second bed is prepared and Bex is wheeled into the room a few minutes later.

Plastic aprons shine under the strip lights. The pulse of machinery underpins the determined efficiency of the crash team. As doors swing to and fro with the constant movement of nurses and support staff, interested bystanders try to catch a glimpse of the drama, eager to compare the reality of television medical scenes with the fiction all around them. They are comfortable with screen doctors, watching them from the safety of well-worn armchairs and familiar surroundings. Anything that breaks the harsh aroma of the institution, that softens the lines in this house of pain, is a welcome distraction to the morbidity of their own skin.

Despite every effort of the ambulance paramedic and the nursing team no one can find a vein. Leona's body is in a state of total collapse. A consultant anaesthetist intubates and the crash team are able deliver drugs through an endotracheal tube. Epinephrine. Two milligrams.

The crash team repeat the staged, Frankenstein dance of defibrillation on Leona's pale skin and her body goes into momentary spasm with each fresh jolt of electricity, but the line remains stubbornly horizontal. In between charges the nurses compress her chest, counting out the rhythm of life in beats delivered by the heels of their hands. When the ECG fails one of the nurses double checks by feeling for a carotid pulse. Leona's heart is not responding. One of the paramedics steps out into the main entrance hall and hands a vial of vomit and a sachet of yellow powder to the triage nurse. Uniformed police officers are drinking stale coffee from a vending machine as they too watch the latest episode of real life casualty unfold.

"Stand clear!"

The whine of a charged defibrillator. The thump of the shock and a body reacting to the elemental charge. The raised sides of the emergency bed rattle with each attempt to bring the girl back from the mortuary slab, but there is no joy in the air. Leona is rolled onto her side, more gel is applied and the defibrillator paddles are repositioned.

In the next bay the nurses and doctor attending Bex are

considering other options. Shouts echo around them. Orders. Basic life support. Bex has her airway, breathing and circulation checked again. Her head is tilted and her chin lifted to avoid the danger of asphyxiation. She is on oxygen but breathing under her own steam.

The doctor assessing Bex peers round the curtain screening his charge from the other girl and asks a question of the first ambulance crew paramedic. "Have we got any history, Jack?"

"Not much. Booze and Ecstasy. I found something in her bag. Yellow powder. It's on the way to the labs now."

"Right. And were they both unconscious when you got there?"

"No, yours was still conscious. Seems this one just collapsed, but yours went down slowly."

"Have we got a name?"

"Yeah. She said her name was Bex before she lost consciousness."

"Thanks." He turns back to Bex and talks slowly and clearly to his own team. "Okay, drug related, probably a mixture of alcohol and MDMA, possibly something else, which suggests hyponatremia and possibly cerebral oedema. Check eyes, posture and muscle tone. Right Bex, let's have a look at your responses."

Coma. Bex is unable to respond to pain in a conventional way with purposeful movement, reacting by involuntary extension of her limbs only. Bex shows no sign of response to verbal stimulation. Her eyes remain closed. The doctor orders a blood count, blood sugars, paracetamol and aspirin, and makes a call to arrange an immediate CT scan.

The nurses attending Bex prepare for her to be moved for her scan and then on to the intensive care unit, where she will be managed until her protective reflexes begin to recover. In drugs related cases, where depression of the central nervous system is caused by external factors, there will be a battery of tests to complete before she can be classified. As long as she continues to breath she will not be declared brain dead. She has a chance. Recovery from coma or a persistent vegetative state is always a possibility.

As Bex is wheeled away past the main treatment area towards the lifts the urgency and the work rate in the crash room subsides. The waiting relatives and friends of the lesser, more ordinary emergencies watch, and those conscious patients still able to concentrate on realities outside of their own sphere realise that they may not occupy the centre of the universe. Sweat and tears. Leona's fragile body is wrapped in a blue blanket. Hands are still and voices lowered. The official time and date of death is logged as three fifty-seven on the morning of Sunday, April the eighth.

Leona's final curtain, her final bow is taken at the end of the Procedure Show. Leona and Bex are the subject of two Incident Reports alleging illegal substance misuse and detailing the actions taken by the medical teams. In Leona's case the patient progress notes are brief. Her death is recorded and her body is moved to the hospital mortuary to await the Coroner and police action to inform her parents. The senior manager on duty in Accident and Emergency authorises a search of her belongings. They make a note of a number stored on her mobile under the name Home and inform the two police officers. A call is then made to the Community Drugs and Alcohol Team.

For Bex the basic procedure is the same, although her patient record is as yet incomplete. They find two numbers stored in her mobile; Mum and Dad. By half past four the two detectives from the club are in the waiting area and are reading through the report. Their first inclination is to contact the mother through the Thames Valley force, but so far they have not done so. The father's number is local. The sachet of powder has been retrieved from the lab and is now locked in the controlled substance cabinet.

The older of the two detectives is getting fidgety. "Come on, let's take a look at our corpse".

His younger partner winces slightly. He has just transferred from uniform to plain clothes and finds the hard edges of the job difficult to come to terms with. The corpse was a teenage girl just an hour ago. He is still struggling to find his equilibrium in the world of criminal investigations.

The two detectives walk along empty corridors where the floor is scuffed and marked with black rubber skids from trolleys and wheelchairs. Their footsteps echo off matt blue walls as they pass wards and treatment areas signed in white lettering on blue metal. The mortuary is manned by two technicians. Warrant cards are shown. They check the report that will be sent to the Coroner. The body has not yet been processed and is still on a trolley wrapped in a blue blanket.

Leona's bag is at the foot of the trolley with the relevant paperwork. Her body has started to lose its colour. The senior man checks Leona's arms for needle marks and finding none turns his attention to the contents of her bag, which include a mobile phone, a half-crushed packet of cigarettes, a cheap plastic lighter, a little money and a packet of unused condoms. The junior of the two detectives hangs back a little from the trolley.

"What a fucking awful place to die."

His sergeant is brief and to the point. "Doesn't matter where you die if you go like that. At least she had a chance here."

The younger man steps forward, puts a hand out and hesitates. His hand is shaking.

The sergeant looks at him and says, "You shouldn't do that. No point. Just makes you mad when you need to be level-headed."

The constable can't move his hand away from the girl's pale face.

"Go ahead, then. I was like that once, but after a while you learn that it's best not to. You can sleep that way."

"I don't want to forget. For Christ's sake she's died here. She deserves…"

"She deserved, past tense, son. She deserved a big world, a better chance, a warm bed and old age. Now she deserves a decent burial, that's all. It's late and I'm tired."

The younger man drops his hand into his jacket pocket and feels keys and loose change. She looks so young and so innocent.

"That could be your daughter".

The older man looks into his colleague's eyes and recognises in them a fire that he has long since extinguished. "You'll have to try harder than that, son. It's not my daughter and that's what counts, not yours either, just a young girl..." He moves round to the foot of the trolley and checks the name on the patient record chart. "Leona Jeffery. I'm sorry she's dead but I'm not going to lose any more sleep over lost causes."

"If you said it with a bit of feeling I might feel better about it."

"I'm sorry, son, but that's just the way it is."

The detective constable falls silent for a moment. He feels desperately tired. He has not felt this unwell since his wedding. Smiling for all those happy snappers and their badly framed photographs wore him out. That rictus grin. After the ceremony all he wanted to do was find a comfy chair and take a nap.

"She's...was so young. Seventeen. It wears me out."

"Sometimes we all get tired."

"Yeah, but you're..."

"Old. Thanks. But who gives a fuck. Forty, fifty, it doesn't matter, but seventeen and everyone cries. You won't be invited to my funeral."

"I didn't..."

"Nobody ever does. Don't worry about it. I've got a thick skin." A moment of unwanted intimacy. Leona's eyelids still look soft and fresh. She has long eyelashes and delicate hands. Her skin is beautiful. Cold and damp. Blood stagnates in her veins.

The younger man moves away from the trolley and heads for the main mortuary doors. "I wonder if she had time to be loved?"

"Probably. But there's no point worrying about it. The rest of the boys and girls have run off to play somewhere else. It's some kind of love, I suppose. Better call in before we get up to ICU. They're a bit funny about phones near their machines. Put a call into control. Trace the parents and get cars out to their addresses. The Thames valley boys can do the coma girl's mother."

The detective sergeant pauses and turns to look back at Leona's body. "You'll need to tell them we're referring this one to the Coroner so no release until the inquest. Parents can ID but that's all".

Car doors are closed quietly. The first flicker of dawn light breaks on the horizon. Sparrows call and sing, preparing for another day and the business of nesting. Barnstaple. Bideford. Oxford. Next of kin. Bleary eyed parents stumble downstairs, wrapped in dressing gowns, squinting under hall lights burning far too brightly for the time of day. Walls, dado rails, furniture; it all seems harsh and angular. Latches and dreadlocks tumble. It's still too early for central heating systems to have kicked into life and the air has a slight chill to it. Doors open. The early morning chorus triumphs but no one hears the melodies. Dumbfounded. Shapes. Peaked caps. Black uniforms. Quiet voices. Bewilderment.

The Jeffery's are the first to feel the skeletal breath of dawn in their living room. Leona's father sits in his chair and stares at the blank television screen. Her mother sobs quietly on the sofa, one hand over her mouth as her eyes spill tears across her cheeks. A female officer sits next to her with one hand on the woman's shoulder while her male colleague struggles to form words. In the end he elects to stick to the facts. He puts the father's dumb animalism down to shock.

Tea is made by the female officer and the mother pulls enough threads of her life together to drink half a mug of the hot, sweet liquid and then get dressed. She wears no make-up and has skimmed her hair with the brush. She throws on a tatty pair of jeans and an old shirt. She cries again as she tries to rouse her husband from his stupor. She can't see through her tears to slip her shoes on properly and has to be helped by the female officer.

She leaves the house with the police officers, looking back at her husband of twenty-two years, who has not said a word since the male officer told him that Leona had died. As the patrol car pulls away from the kerb outside their house he gets up and turns on the television. He doesn't care what is on. After a minute or two of staring at the box he picks up his mug of tea and hurls it at the wall.

Billy wakes in his armchair. His head is fuzzed and he can feel the brittleness of the veins in his temples. The curtains are still open, the table lamp is still on, and half a tumbler of Irish sits on the occasional table beside the chair. There is a late night phone in quiz show running on the television. The doorbell rings. The answer to the question being posed by an impossibly bright wannabe is; A, Sulako. Billy can't be sure whether the chimes are part of the soundscape of edutainment addiction or the girls at the front door.

He tries to focus on the clock above the mantelpiece. It must be Bex and Leona, probably too drunk to find the keys. He is furious. What time does she call this? He makes two attempts to stand and as he does the blood rushes into the void behind his eyes. Whiteout. He steadies himself with the arm of the chair and shakes his head a couple of times. He catches a glimpse of someone peering in through the bay window. An unfamiliar shape. Leona. A boy. Boys and girls taking the piss. Except that there is something worryingly familiar about the figure. It is not the shape, but the colour. Black.

As Billy walks into the hall and towards the front door he is determined to give Bex an earful. She is still a kid, no matter how old she thinks she might be. As for Tod and Lizzy and clubs, she can forget it. He starts to build himself up for the moment, huffing and puffing, ready to blow her house down, but something is gnawing away at the soft tissue of his waking mind. Billy left the outside light on for the girls and silhouetted perfectly against the frosted glass in the door he sees the full profile shadow of his worst nightmare. He slows as he approaches the door. He struggles to make his hand work on the latch. Close up he can see buttons and the outline of insignia. There is a cap. Billy opens the door and stands open mouthed as the first police officer speaks.

"Mister William Whitlow?"

Silence. Billy steps back on auto pilot. He tries to remember; speeding tickets, unpaid fines, tax fraud, anything that might shut out the possibility of a name other than his daughter's being mentioned.

"Mister Whitlow?"

Billy dredges up a word but he can't say it out loud. Making a sound will break the spell and let the outside world flood in and drown him. He nods.

"Can we come in, Mister Whitlow?"

Billy leaves the door open and walks back into the living room, where he sinks back into his armchair. He has the tumbler of Irish at his lips as the officers follow him in. They sit awkwardly, fidgeting with their caps. Billy looks at one, then at the other and back again. They don't look like the arresting type. Billy hits the off button on the television remote.

"Mister Whitlow", one of them begins but Billy cuts him off.

"Bex? Is she hurt? Is she alright?"

The words that fled from him as he stood by the door are now crowding into his skull, jostling for position, desperate to gain access to the thin atmosphere that Billy is breathing. He feels faint. The liquor burns but it doesn't warm.

"Rebecca Whitlow. She is your daughter?"

Billy waits for another word. Death. Dead. Fatal. And then the tense used by the police officer sinks home.

"She's not dead?"

It's framed as a question but Billy knows that Bex is alive. Hurt, in pain, in need, but alive.

"Please, what's happened?"

It's the turn of the messenger to struggle for the right words. His partner looks at the bottle of whiskey on the table with a mixture of longing and approbation. Billy is over the limit for driving.

"She's in hospital, Mister Whitlow. An overdose, but she's holding her own."

Billy sinks the whiskey and pours himself another stiff measure. As an afterthought he offers the bottle to the officers, who thank him but decline. Down in one. Then he is on his feet and asking questions; when, where, how, why? He is not listening to the answers. He grabs his jacket from the back of his chair and pulls car keys from the pocket.

The second officer speaks for the first time. "I don't think that's a good idea, sir. Why don't you put those back in your pocket and come with us."

Carol was snugly asleep in bed with Dave, her handyman boyfriend. The shock of receiving the police at five am on a Sunday morning brings back every one of the hurts and slights that she suffered at Billy's hands when they were married. Time heals external wounds but the scar tissue is still red and raw on the inside. Dave has the luxury of being an outsider. He deals with the police calmly, making a note of the hospital address and ward name. While Carol packs a bag for them both, ranting at her ex-husband all the while, he puts the postcode into a driving direction website and prints out instructions for the journey. As they pull out onto the Banbury Road in Dave's Range Rover, Carol is in full flight.

"That fucking waste of time. How can he do this? How can he let something like this happen?"

"I know, love."

"No you don't", she snaps. "No you don't. You weren't there

when he screwed up. Screwed us all up. For Christ's sake, it was bad enough then, but at least I knew what I was doing. But his own daughter. Jesus!"

Dave understands enough to know not to react. Carol is right. He has no real means or motive for joining in with her rage. He can only play a supporting role in the drama that seems to go on, act after act, in the lives of Carol and Billy. She has told him things about those days, but he doesn't really know anything. Bex is a great kid and he likes her. He likes them both. But he doesn't really know anything about those times.

Carol continues. "I mean, he always fucked things up. It just happened. I should have known he'd do something like this."

Dave considers this. For all of Billy's history he doubts that the man made his daughter do anything. "I don't suppose he thought this would happen."

"Stop at the services on Pear Tree. I need a cigarette."

"But you don't smoke."

"I need a cigarette. Just bloody stop there."

Carol glares at the glove box. A glass wall descends between them. Ice on the inside of the windscreen. She realises that she has overstepped the mark and, risking frostbite, she puts her hand on Dave's leg and turns towards him. "Sorry. Not your fault."

Dave concentrates on the road. He drops his left hand onto Carol's and squeezes. "I know. It's okay. Any particular brand?"

"Yes, Silk Cut. It's just that shit always happens when Billy's around. He never means it to but it just does. I should know.

He didn't give her the stuff, whatever it was; he didn't force it on her. I'm enough of a realist to know she decided to take it. But it had to be there, didn't it. He had to be involved."

Dave indicates left. They pull into the services and he buys a couple of packets of cigarettes and a packet of cigars for himself. He has never smoked but always wanted to. Now seems like as good a time as any to try it out. The emotional maelstrom that he is feeling is nothing to the devastation that his partner must be enduring. All that matters now is that he is there, in the storm with her, shielding her as best he can from the driving winds and rain of shocking fortune. Dave can't quite get a handle on where they are; is he simply shocked by the melodrama? Is it sympathy or empathy or just plain old fashioned recklessness in the face of mortality?

As soon as they hit the four-twenty down to Swindon, Carol lights up. The passenger window is open a couple of inches and the sound of the wind catching on slabs of metal and glass rushes into the car.

"What scares me most", she says, "is that Bex might turn out like her father. What if she's inherited the self-destruct gene? I couldn't bear it, not again."

The wards begin their day around six in the morning. By seven Bex has been wheeled back from her scan and is being introduced to intensive care. Billy sits in a waiting area in a corridor outside the main unit. He can feel stubble on his chin and neck and he is exhausted and grubby. His breath smells. He has watched nurses hurrying through doors for an hour, and he has asked and answered the same questions over and over again. Medical staff. Police. More police. How could he possibly know about Bex and her use of drugs? They have his contact details. They will be in touch.

Shifts are changing. Notes are checked and instructions given. A cleaner wheels a mobile cleaning trolley along the corridor towards Billy. His head is splitting. He is compensating for the silence in his heart by singing quietly to himself in a vain attempt at reassurance. *You're Breaking My Heart*. Vic Damone, naturally.

You're breaking my heart 'cause you're leaving (1)

You've fallen for somebody new

It isn't too easy believing

You'd leave after all we've been through

It's breaking my heart to remember...

Billy is helpless. This is a world that he knows nothing about, with its strange terminology, frightening machinery and hushed atmosphere. The nurses have been sweet and one of them made him a mug of coffee which is on a small table next to his chair. It's stone cold and untouched. Billy is waiting for the medical team to finish connecting Bex to their magic boxes. Maybe then someone will tell him what is going on.

No one has explained anything to him except that Bex is in a coma. Such a simple and short word. As he reaches the end of each line of the song Billy fights back tears, fights back images of artificial ventilation and a hand hovering over an electrical switch. Persistent Vegetative State. Out of hope. Kill the lights on your way out. Tests and potions. They might as well be putting leeches on her arm for all that Billy understands of the three ring circus going down all around him. When he asked one of the nurses what a coma actually is she told him that it's a state in which a patient is totally unaware of both themselves and their external surroundings, and they are unable to respond meaningfully to external stimuli. Billy feels as though he has a migraine coming on.

Time moves in sporadic jumps. The clock on the wall above the nurses station at the entrance to intensive care taunts him. Every time he looks at it the hands seem to stick. Slow motion. Every time that he watches the damned thing crawl through the seconds he gets that drowning feeling again. Then, when something happens, when some random action catches Billy's attention, the hands on the clock sneak forward in five minute increments. The secret of immortality is to be found while sitting on a plastic chair in a hospital corridor. The lyric repeats in Billy's head. He leans forward, resting his elbows on his knees with his chin in his cupped hands, and starts to count the scuff marks on the floor.

"Mister Whitlow".

Billy looks up from his counting game and sees one of the nurses who has been treating Bex standing beside his chair. Her hair is tied tightly back and she is wearing the standard light blue scrubs. For someone so used to dealing with the underbelly of the world Billy looks pathetic; unshaven, crumpled and hangdog. He stops singing and waits for the girl to speak. She smiles and sits down next to him.

"She's doing okay, Mister Whitlow, really."

She puts her hand on Billy's sleeve. Her fingers are slender and her skin is warm and healthy. Youthful. No rings. Nails clean and short.

"Your daughter is breathing on her own. That's good, Mister Whitlow. It means she probably hasn't suffered any brain stem injury. There are more tests to do but the consultant will explain. Right now she's in a very deep sleep."

The song is still playing in Billy's head but he manages to turn the volume down. "Can I see her? When can I see her?"

Billy feels the lightness of the girl's touch on his arm. An angel. A cliché but one that Billy grabs hold of. He tries to smile.

"Not long now. As I said, there's a few things to do but as soon as she's settled and stable I'm sure they'll let you sit with her. I know it's hard but keep singing that song. What is it by the way? I don't recognise it."

The smile comes. Faint but noticeable. "Just an old love song. Nothing much. Just words."

"You've got a good voice. I can tell. I love a bit of karaoke. Anyway, your wife is on her way. She called in a few minutes ago to see how your daughter's doing."

Billy is well aware that the good ship Carol is steaming across the Western approaches at full revolution. He is still smarting from the call. There was nothing he could say to her. Every word that she hurled at him hit home like a shell and exploded with the full force of the simple truth. The clock hands have stolen another five minutes out of their lives. With every beat of his heart Billy wishes that he could make them spin back through the night, all the way back through Saturday so that he could call the club in Bristol and cancel the gig.

"Ex-wife", he says to the nurse and looks away.

The nurse pays no attention to Billy's comment. She can't fix broken hearts. "Shall I get you a fresh coffee? That one's stone cold."

Billy nods. As she picks up his cup and heads off towards a small kitchen area behind the nursing station Billy leans back and stretches his legs out. He shuts his eyes and lets the melody swell and blacken like a bruise.

It is just after nine when the consultant emerges from the main care unit and wakes Billy. The second mug of coffee is cold and stagnant, just like the first. A different nurse stands next to the consultant; older and harder than Billy's angel. The man in front of Billy is tall and just starting to go bald. It won't be long before he has a pronounced widow's peak. Billy stands and apologises.

"Not at all, Mister Whitlow. Probably the best thing you could do."

Billy feels adrenaline pumping through his system. This is it, the moment when worlds collide.

"Can I see her? Can I see Bex?"

The consultant nods. "Yes, but first I want to run through a few things with you. Do you want to sit down?"

"No, no, I'd rather stand. You get a bit stiff on those chairs."

The art of polite conversation. Billy is procrastinating.

The consultant folds his arms across his chest. A distancing motion. Body language. Time to get serious. "Do you understand what coma is, Mister Whitlow?"

As best he can Billy repeats the explanation given to him earlier.

"Basically, yes. Your daughter has ingested a combination of drugs. Methylenedioxymethamphetamine, or Ecstasy in other words, and Ketamine together with some traces of amphetamine. Mixed with a not inconsiderable intake of alcohol. She is lucky to be alive. I'm afraid the same can't be said of her friend."

For the first time since he saw black shapes at his living room window Billy remembers that Bex went out with Leona. The significance of the doctor's words worm their way through Billy's selfish layers of self-preservation. Leona. Unlucky. The enormity of the concept looms over Billy like a super tanker shadow falling across a dinghy in mid-Atlantic. It is too much to handle. Billy filters it out, storing the words and the details for later assimilation into this new version of the world.

The consultant barely notices the flicker of horror in Billy's eyes. "We are still waiting for the full pathology report, toxicity etcetera, but early indications are that this combination has caused a degree of cerebral oedema..."

Billy gives the consultant a blank stare.

"I'm sorry. A degree of swelling in the brain. The CT scan isn't too bad and we hope, as long as we can keep her stable over the next couple of days, that the amount of damage done won't be significant. Right now both of her cerebral hemispheres are impaired. Her Glasgow Scale is down at four or five, which means that she is deeply unconscious, with no response to pain. It's what we call a Stage Four."

Coma. Damage. Simple words that describe someone who is not Bex. Billy asks the obvious question. "When you say damage you mean brain damage, don't you? She was going to be a vet. She was going to university. She will go, won't she?"

The consultant unfolds his arms and thrusts them into his lab coat pockets. He looks down at the floor for a couple of seconds before answering. "It's impossible to say, Mister Whitlow. We'll just have to keep her stable and make an assessment when she wakes up. As I said, the swelling could be a lot worse. There is every possibility she'll come out of this without too many complications."

Billy's head is spinning. The super tanker shadow cuts him off from the light. Leona died. Bex is going to be a vegetable. Darling Bex. Beautiful, sweet Bex. He can't think. Sirens wail and lights burn brightly in his head for a second or two before snapping to pitch black. Words and images hurtle along his neural pathways. He feels numb, barely hearing the final words of the man in the white coat.

"You can sit with her if you like. No need for aprons. Just make sure you wash your hands and use the gel."

The consultant pats Billy on the shoulder once and turns away. The nurse shows Billy to the gentleman's toilet where he washes. Then, once they have both applied gel to their hands and buzzed for access to the main intensive care unit, she shows him to a room full of screens and monitors. Every sound and every readout seems to scream one word at Billy; Bastard. And there in the middle of the room is Bex, cannulated, intubated and hooked up with wires and tubes.

Billy pulls a plastic chair up beside the bed and sits. He takes his daughter's hand in his and rests his forehead on her wrist. The lyric starts up again in Billy's head and as he gets to the line where Bex breaks his heart the tears begin.

"So you're here."

Visiting hours. Only two relatives are allowed at any one time in the intensive care unit. Billy has been sitting alone with Bex for an hour. Carol is the second visitor. Her mood is one of controlled anger. The journey has given her time to prepare herself for seeing Billy, but like her former husband she is petrified by what she sees happening to Bex. It's a scene from a film. Electro-mechanical life. Billy rises from the chair, lingers a moment holding his daughter's hand and then steps back.

Carol can feel revulsion rising in her throat and she wants to gag. She has to fight to keep the controls in place. Every ounce of her body, every muscle and sinew is straining to break free and launch itself at Billy, but she manages, through sheer iron will and from a deep sense of respect for the institution that they find themselves thrown together in, to keep things in check. Bex is part of the machine, the ghost in the machine, but she looks peaceful, as if she will wake any moment, smile and ask for a cup of tea in bed on a Sunday morning. Carol takes Billy's seat and strokes her daughter's hand.

"Bex, Bex, Bex, what have you done?"

Human silence. The sound of breathing. Billy leans back against a wall, head tilted upwards, staring at the ceiling. Electronic sound. A pulse. Monitors. Computer fans. Silicon control. A nurse appears in the doorway, says hello and checks charts and displays. Billy listens as Carol coos and clucks. He wants to hug Carol, desperately wants to bury himself in her so that the pain will go away. But all he can do is watch her as she brushes hair from his daughter's forehead.

"I'm…I'm sorry".

Carol doesn't move a muscle. She continues to whisper sweet nothings to her daughter. Billy is ignored. He steps forward and is about to put his hand on Carol's arm.

"Don't you fucking dare!" It's a warning, a vengeful, deep throated and primeval growl. "There's nothing you can say, you bastard. I mean, how, Billy, how? How can you be so fucking irresponsible? She's a child."

Carol is right. There is nothing that Billy can say, but he tries gamely.

"I'm so sorry. I didn't think…"

Carol's body is fixed and rigid. She dare not look round. It's only by concentrating totally on Bex's placid, sleeping face that she can prevent herself from tearing Billy's throat out. "That's your problem, Billy, you never bloody think. It's always someone else's fault. Poor Billy. You're a fucking liability."

"Please, Carol, not in front of Bex. What if she can hear us?"

"Then it's about bloody time. All through those years I expected it to be you. Every time you disappeared on a bender I half expected a visit from the police telling me you'd choked on your own vomit or were hooked up to this shit. I died a little bit every time you fucked up, but I thought you'd learned something, Billy, I really did. When you screwed us up I thought you'd learn. I should've known you'd never change. But this! Our little girl. Get out of here, Billy, just get out!"

"Carol?"

"Get out!"

Billy stands behind Carol and stares down at Bex. He feels torn. He doesn't want to leave her but equally he knows he can't stay. Whatever he says to Carol will only make things worse and Bex needs peace and love, not war. Billy has had time to think. If he stands toe to toe with Carol he will lose it. Bubbling beneath the sorrow there is vengeance and Carol doesn't deserve that. He has to find someone else to pay that price, the person responsible for all of this. Billy's rage is the rage of a dumb animal, a cornered, wounded beast with young cubs to protect. Carol sits quietly stroking her daughter's hand, telling her that everything will be just fine. As Billy edges around the bed he can see tears at the corners of her eyes.

Back out in the corridor Billy's heart sinks. He recognises the jacket. The name escapes him, but this must be Carol's new man. The recognition works both ways. Dave has seen photographs. Bex is proud of her father. Dave stops pacing when he sees Billy and walks up to him, offering his hand, gently and placatory.

"You must be Bex's dad. Shit, you look rough."

It's not quite the introduction Billy had imagined. Of course, he thinks, this man has just driven Carol down here. Any decent man would. A decent man. The thought turns Billy's stomach, not because he has any particular axe to grind about Carol's love life, but because the thought sticks bloody great pins into Billy's conscience. He looks down at Dave's offered hand. An apology for the situation. Billy almost takes it, almost accepts the olive branch, this badly needed gesture of friendship, but he can't quite make the connection. His head is burning. The lyric is on a permanent loop. He lets the cornered beast lash out one more time.

"Fuck off".

A snarl. The look of surprise on the other man's face turns to darkness. "On your watch, mate. Lay a hand and I'll sort you out."

Billy takes a proper look at Dave for the first time. He is ten years younger and as lean as an Olympic sprinter. The worst odds, the wrong place and time, a mistake, like so many others. Billy turns and stomps down the corridor in a foul temper. He needs a coffee and somewhere to think. A hot coffee this time. He sees a sign for the cafeteria and crashes through swing doors and down two flights of stairs to find a quiet corner where he can make some sense of the hurricane surging back and forth in his head.

In the cafeteria he pays for his coffee and selects a table by a window that looks out onto a small garden area. As he sits he sees Leona's reflection smiling at him from the wings at Snuggle's and quietly he starts to sing the song to himself again:

...The dreams we depended upon (2)

You're leaving a slow dying ember

I'll miss you, my love, when you're gone

I wish you joy, though teardrops burn

But if some day you should want to return

Please hurry back and we'll make a new start

Till then you're breaking my heart.

SITTING BY THE WINDOW

SUNDAY MORNINGS IN MONOTONOUSLY familiar hotel rooms are a perfect expression of the art of sterility. Stock photographs and prints on the wall. Every room is the same, a place where colours fade to a bland shade of blue. Alex Berisa opens his eyes and takes a moment to orientate himself. Through the double-glazed window he can hear the sound of cars braking at a roundabout. The traffic is clearly light this morning.

In the corridor outside his room he hears a door shut followed by the plastic rumble of a suitcase on wheels. Two or maybe three doors down he can hear a vacuum cleaner. A television is on with the volume raised fit for the hard of hearing. He lifts his head from the pillow and sees his reflection in the dressing table mirror opposite the bed. He is decidedly unkempt.

His head is muzzy and he feels heavy and slow. Too many miles and too many hours. Alex needs coffee. Before he thinks about the kettle he runs through the events of the previous evening. Signs and portents, or rather the lack of them. The streets of Barnstaple are like those of any other provincial town; badly lit and full of leery teenagers running at full throttle on tanks of alcohol and dope, the sign of a good night being the volume of vomit in the gutter.

Alex spent the early part of Saturday evening in The Monkey watching the boys and girls at play. Nothing much to report, just the usual backhanders in the gentlemen's lavatory, rounds of drinks and shouts and bravado. Girls on the prowl. Boys burning testosterone. Catfights and posturing. Conversation to die by. The only thing that Alex has learned from this particular venue is that the gear is cheap and badly cut, and that his clothes stink of cigarette smoke. The girl at the reception desk had been right in her assessment. The carpets were a disgrace.

Alex considers his position. This could be a wild goose chase. He has very little to go on. A sighting in a Spanish port and a copy of a ship's register, the Valentin, bound for Bideford, some days ago. A cold case. But Alex thinks it unlikely that his man has made any significant moves. Despite Arbnor Jasari's inherent dislike of provincial life he is too smart to make a beeline for bright city lights. He needs to lie low and, on balance, where better than Devon's mellow back lanes, especially if he starts cooking up exotic little snacks for the local clubbers and smack-heads. There is a vibration in the air.

Alex considers the innate strangeness of Barnstaple. It's not the fact that the place is full of kids and blue lights, fashion victims and binge-drinking that causes Alex to think this way. In many ways the old town is everything Alex expected, but he hadn't expected such a sense of fatigue. The place is old and tired, as if this part of the country is waiting for the good times to return. That same strangeness makes the dog-eared town seem familiar, as if he was at home on the Adriatic coast, watching lights over the border. Alex isn't sure that the local inhabitants would know what to do with good times if they ever came across them. Rednecks with attitude. Definitely just like home.

The Red Zone and Caligula's are dumps; one a converted cinema, the other an industrial unit in a sea of broken shutters and smashed windows. It's a question of scale, limited horizons, that 'make do and mend' mentality. He stuck it until one in the morning and then retired to his corner, punch drunk on warm juice drinks and boredom. By the time he returned to the hotel the girl behind the desk had given way to the night porter and any thoughts Alex might have had of relieving the boredom disappeared as soon as the young man appeared from his cubby hole. Nods and keys. Doors slamming. An hour of tossing and turning in a bed designed for people who find sleep through the wonders of Diazepam.

Alex swings his legs out of bed and pads over to the dressing table. He fills the kettle and pours coffee granules into a clean mug. He watches the kettle as it starts to sing. He relieves the ennui of commercial rest by switching on the television. The national news. The Premiership results. A cut back to the main presenters and then a signature tune. Graphics. A smiling girl in a red blouse. The news in your area at nine.

Alex hears the kettle click off as it spits water out onto the dressing table veneer but pays no attention to his primary need for stimulation. The lead story is about a tragic event at a nightclub in Bideford. The Basement. Two girls. A cocktail of drugs and alcohol. Rumours of something new to the area.

Overdose. Coma. Parents in bedside vigils. There is a report that one girl has died but this is not substantiated. The police won't release names until relatives have been informed. To Alex this is a signature. It is a reward for the days and hours spent without hope. This news, tragic for others, makes the price to be paid for the shirt in the white plastic dry cleaning bag by the door seem trivial.

He grabs the notepad and pencil left by the cleaner on his bedside table and makes hasty notes. The Basement. North Devon Hospital. Intensive care. That is the one thing about friend Jasari. He likes patterns, repeating patterns, fractal images. Alex is like a gifted collector, a divvie when it comes to spotting the genuine article, but he has no interest in modern art or landscapes. His abilities lie in far more practical directions. He has consummate skills in the field of collecting lives.

The newscaster breaks to a feel good story about a local farmer who has found a way to happiness and riches by selling some of his land to a well-heeled eco-warrior who wants to pioneer solar power generation somewhere in Holsworthy's wooded hinterland. Alex hits the button on the kettle again and waits for the gush of boiling water. He pours and takes the mug with him into the bathroom, where he draws a shallow bath. The water is hot but the bath is cramped and narrow. He sits up and stretches his legs out, closing his eyes as he sips thick, black caffeine.

Plans. Breakfast. It's one of Alex's rules; always make time for food, even on the hoof. He doesn't fancy the Wimpy at the services but remembers a golden MacDonald's sign near Sainsbury's. Egg and bacon McMuffins. Hash Browns. More coffee. And then the hospital. Then again, perhaps not. What's the hurry. The surviving girl isn't going anywhere according to the television news. She is in a coma. She can wait. At this stage of his little holiday Alex doesn't want to spoil the festive mood by getting involved with grieving parents.

Better, Alex thinks, to take a look at the club, maybe ask a few questions. He doubts that Jasari is dealing himself so there will be a link of one sort or another, a link that will chain him and Jasari together. He can smell it. Jasari is close. Alex needs a name, a location, somewhere to start from. A little gentle persuasion works wonders, especially when the Old Bill are crawling all over the corpse.

For the hospital he will need to assume a more subtle manner, something for the bedside. He bends his knees and slides down into the water, immersing his abdomen and chest so that his head dips down beneath the surface. It always feels good to be clean. He gropes for the bottle of complimentary shampoo that he put by the grab rail and lets the heat of the water soak into his soul. He wants to look his best when he walks out past the reception desk.

Maggie Heard visibly flinches when the local newsreader pops up on her television screen wearing a bright scarlet blouse. The girl is winter pale with mousy brown hair swept back tightly against her head. The colour is wrong. Continuity and make-up. Depressingly amateurish.

Maggie is sitting in the conservatory with Jock, who has buried himself in a copy of the Sunday Mail, which he has sent over on special order by the village shop so that he can feed his nostalgia for Glasgow. Jock has no wish to experience the reality of the place again, but from a safe distance he likes to keep in touch.

The newsreader smiles and begins her introduction at the top of the broadcast. "Tragic events at a local nightclub. Two girls have been admitted to North Devon Hospital following a night out at a club in Bideford. Police reports suggest the girls had taken a cocktail of drink and drugs. The police are yet to name the girls as they are at an early stage in their enquiries, but the families have been notified. Martin Gilfoyle reports."

The shot changes to an earlier video tape. The news reporter stands huddled in an overcoat and scarf outside Accident and Emergency. The dawn sky is clearly just breaking, meaning that the report is already some hours old. Behind him the strip lights of the entrance burn brightly and a member of the public can be seen to hesitate as he looks over at the television crew before disappearing inside the building.

"Earlier this morning two girls were rushed here to A&E having collapsed at The Basement club in Bideford." Inset: archive shots of Bideford High Street showing the entrance to the club. "Although there has been no official announcement, early indications from hospital staff suggest that the girls had taken a cocktail of Ecstasy and other drugs together with substantial amounts of alcohol. It is my understanding that one of the girls has subsequently died and that the second girl is in a serious condition in intensive care. Relatives have been contacted and are in attendance. The police have declined to make anyone available at this time to comment. Martin Gilfoyle, BBC Spotlight Southwest."

The shot cuts back to the studio and the girl in the red blouse pauses and looks sad for a moment before resuming her stock smile and moving to another story about the happy farmer and then another plan for the redevelopment of Plymouth city centre.

Maggie lets out a long sigh and puts her cup down on a glass-topped wicker table next to her armchair. "Bloody stupid kids. Won't they ever learn?"

She turns to Jock, ready for a general tutting about the youth of today, expecting him to be so engrossed in the back pages of the Mail that he won't have a clue what she is going on about. Instead she finds him perched on the edge of his chair, open mouthed, staring at the television screen. The paper is in a heap at his slippered feet.

"Are you alright?" she asks.

"What?" Jock shuts his mouth and tries to look bright and breezy. "Oh, yeah, yeah, Doll, I'm fine. You're right. Bloody stupid." He sits back but he can't take his eyes off the screen.

"You sure?" asks Maggie, "only you look like you've seen a ghost."

"Aye, sort of." Jock pauses. Time to think. Protection. "Just that some of the lads from the site out at Brownsham were there. A present from me for finishing on time. With their other halves. Sorry, Mags, just took me a bit by surprise. You never think about these things happening so close to home."

"Oh God, that's terrible." Maggie goes over to Jock and kneels on the floor by his chair. The laminate flooring is cold, even through her dressing gown. She puts a hand on his knee. "They said they weren't going to release any names. Do you think you should check up, make sure they're all okay?"

Jock is putting two and two together. Cocktails. Alcohol. Instructions ignored. Fuck, he thinks, it never rains… An idea. Jock needs to buy some time, to regroup. "Yeah, you're right. Would you do me a refill?" He hands Maggie his empty teacup and as she kneels up and reaches over to the coffee table to pour milk and tea, Jock gets up and goes to the phone in the living room.

"There you go, love, by your chair." Maggie settles back into her own chair and catches the weather bulletin. From the living room she can half hear snatches of an animated conversation.

"Morning, seen the telly? - Aye, bloody shite! - Everyone present and correct? - Any hassle from the Bizzies? - Good - Our mutual friends? - The farm - Eleven - The full complement, no excuses. - Okay."

Jock pretends to kill the call and dial again. He counts out the rings, settling on five. "That you, Ken? - Pick us up in thirty minutes, will you? - Aye, bit of a problem with the gutters."

This time he does kill the call. Jock returns to the conservatory, picks up his teacup and drains it in one, setting the back of his throat on fire. He can feel every millilitre of the hot liquid as it flows down his oesophagus. He coughs and swallows saliva..

"The boys are fine, and their girls. Didn't see anything, thank Christ. But…sorry love, bit of a problem out at Brownsham. Water leak. I'll have to go and have a look. Insurance and all that. Typical. Just when it's all sorted."

Maggie's look is like flying daggers. "Oh Jock, not today,

please. What about breakfast?" It's a pointless question. When he gets it in his head to go to work, there's rarely any stopping Jock Cascarino.

Jock bends and tries to kiss her on the forehead but misses as Maggie turns her head away. "Sorry, love. Business. You know what it's like. I'll be back by two, promise."

Maggie says nothing and continues to stare out of the conservatory windows at the green blur of garden. "Back by two, Jock. Don't be late."

"Ken will be here in a mo, so I'm off for a shower. Chin up, Doll."

Maggie manages to resist the urge to brain Jock with the crockery. Only just. Sunday. Bloody Sunday.

Ted Line is at home this Sunday morning. Ever since the incident in the club's kitchen, he has made a point of sleeping-off his little over-indulgences in his own bed. He feels safer that way. As he starts to surface, as he starts to come round after another night on the cheap stuff, he can feel rough edges on his tongue. He tastes dry peat and there is a damp patch on his pillow where he has dribbled during the night. Another Saturday finished off with a digital, corner shop romance and a strawberry yoghurt. Ted prefers yoghurt as a bedtime snack these days. His digestive tract is shot to hell and kebabs deliver a particular kind of misery. Gastro-oesophageal reflux. Judging by the colour of the stains on his shirt he spilled more of the yoghurt then he ingested.

The only cure Ted trusts in these days is the hair of the

slavering beast that he calls friend. He is still wearing yesterday's underwear underneath his yoghurt stained shirt. He has one sock on, the other being buried somewhere at the foot of his single bed. He sits up at the edge of the bed and retrieves a half bottle of supermarket scotch from the bedside table. There's one hefty slug left in the bottom of the bottle. Down the hatch. He coughs, in racking, phlegmy convulsions.

Ted grimaces and rubs his teeth with his forefinger. The room is in half light, protected from the outside world by shabby brown curtains that are almost drawn together. He stretches his neck, left and right, then rolls his head round in a clockwise circle.

Shit, he thinks, my head hurts. A quiet day today, that's what you need, old boy.

As he stands, the weight of last night's late finish at the club bears down on Ted's compacting spine. He walks the few metres from his bed, past a threadbare red brocade armchair, to the kitchenette. Bed-sit land. There is a narrow archway between the bed sitting room and the kitchenette, evidence that there used to be two rooms, the front one of which, the bigger room with the large sash window, looks out over parked cars and signs warning dog owners that they can be fined if their animals soil the pavement. All mod cons. Open plan living, a two ring electric hob and a microwave. A fridge. The enamel coating on the fridge has given up the ghost and brown chips of rust show through the face of the door. The light went ages ago, which, Ted thinks, is probably a good thing. God knows when he last cleaned the bugger. From the door he picks up a new litre and a half bottle of Coke. Cold. Sugar in the bloodstream.

He looks for a clean glass but can't find one, so he gulps straight from the bottle. The scotch has anesthetised some of the plaque and fur in his mouth but enough of it is still active and absolutely ready to fight back. As soon as he swills the Coke down he can feel a dry layer of fermenting chemicals coating his teeth. Ted Line perseveres. He needs half a litre to start opening up the constricted veins in his head.

The television remote is on the kitchen work surface. Sunday mornings, when seen, are a stream of unassimilated images. He flicks the television on from its stand-by state and, while downing more Coke, runs through the channels. A little luxury in an otherwise drab existence. Cable fun. Ted loves movies and pays for them. Other bills are limited by his lifestyle. Council Tax and single person discounts. He has no phone, no gas, just two rooms, a bed, second hand chairs and the essential audio-visual equipment. Money pays for light entertainment and darkly golden liquid forgetting.

On the wall above the bed Ted has a collection of photographs, some of them signed, mementos garnered from a life on the boards. Summer seasons and late night motorway cruises. Mike and Bernie, Bobby Ball, Cilla, Frankie Vaughan, The Chuckle Brothers and Lenny Bread. They're all that is left of a lifetime under the spotlight. Ted has progressively sold off the rest of his memorabilia on eBay, which forms an essential part his other little luxury. Broadband comes as part of the cable package, and it provides Ted with a window on the world and hard porn comfort when he is sober enough to be interested, which is less and less frequently these days.

It's twenty-past nine and Ted pauses to watch the local news. The bottle of Coke in his hand moves slowly down towards the stained melamine of the kitchenette work surface as he takes in the first item on the bulletin. Girls. Drugs. The Basement. Ted lights the first cigarette of the day and drags on it deeply. The tip flares and recedes at an alarming rate. Numbers and cogs. Ted Line is remembering conversations.

He takes the Coke, an ashtray and the packet of cigarettes through to his armchair and drags a small occasional table over so that he can write things down. On the back of an unopened envelope from a credit card company he scribbles down locations, times, dates and assumptions. No names have been mentioned by the presenter, but Ted is drawing conclusions; the club, Wednesday night, the tall kid who looked like a zombie, The Basement on Saturday night.

Everything seems to fit. Circumstantial calculations. But Billy had a point; how to gain an advantage that doesn't end with your kneecaps facing the wrong way?

"Maggie is the key", Ted mutters to himself. Maggie. But how do you tell a woman that her man is a callous, money-grubbing bastard? Right now Ted is in no fit state to plan anything so thoroughly. He runs a hand through his thin, grey hair and realises that he needs to wash it. It's still early and if he is quick he can probably get into the communal bathroom before the girls across the landing take up residence and all of the hot water goes. Ted takes one last swig from the Coke bottle and goes back to the kitchenette. Hanging on his front door there is a long, towelling bathrobe, a bath towel and a drawstring bag containing the basics required for his ablutions. There is usually a bottle of shampoo lying around in the bathroom that he can nick a couple of washes out of.

The door to the third floor bathroom at the back of the house is open and the light is off, a sure sign that the other residents are still sleeping off Saturday night excess. Ted closes the door to his bed-sit, puts the key in his bathrobe pocket and slips across the landing linoleum. Once in the bathroom he slams the door shut on purpose, locks it and pulls the cord that powers up the heated lamp unit and the extractor fan. The fan grinds through years of sticky dust and detritus, whining in complaint. Ted grins. It's bound to wake the poor little darlings across the hall.

The bath is, like Ted's fridge, a mosaic of scratches and chipped enamel. Brown water stains make teardrop shapes around the plug hole. Ted reaches up, turns on the electric shower and pulls the shower curtain down the length of the bath. It takes a couple of seconds before the shower spits and coughs, signalling the arrival of hot water, time enough for Ted to undress and roll his soiled clothing into a ball. Launderette day is Monday. He waits for the water to boil and then spends another minute adjusting the mixer.

The trick is to be quick. As soon as the other residents wake up and start making cups of tea or boiling their briefs, the water pressure goes to hell and you get scalded. The expensive advantage of living on the lower two floors is that the flats have en-suite showers and toilets, but Ted's circumstances and personal proclivities mean that he shares his facilities.

The shared bath is an old, cast-iron monolith on lion claw feet, the sort that middle-class homemakers pay through the nose for. As far as Ted is concerned the bloody thing is an accident waiting to happen. The sides are high and deep, which means a struggle getting in, given the general seizing-up of his joints. Once in the damn thing he has to concentrate. There is no bath mat. One slip and he will need a new hip.

But then the beauty comes, the effervescent restoration of hot water cascading over his head, onto his shoulders and down his torso. It reminds Ted of posh hotels and homes where he might once have remained had it not been for the dream of the starlight express. True to form there is a bottle of two-in-one anti-dandruff shampoo on the side of the bath. As he soaks and lathers under the hot stream he returns to thoughts of Maggie and Jock. He makes up his mind. It's got to be worth a punt. It's just a question of timing, a matter of recognising the opportunity. Ted will drop in at the club tonight and see if he can find an angle. There is always Billy, of course. The stupid bugger is in love with Maggie Heard, whatever that means, so maybe there is some room to manoeuvre in that direction.

"Okay", Ted says to himself, "a nice quiet day, a bit of thinking and a decent lunch. Kentucky, I think, old boy, push the boat out."

Lukewarm water, cheap tea bags and milk that draws spirals at the surface. There may even be lumps. Plastic mugs. Bright colours reminiscent of primary schools and puddles of orange squash. Charcoal Boomerang Formica. Plastic chairs and unguarded strip lights. Canteen culture in the Devon and Cornwall Constabulary. Sergeant Miller has finished his first stint on shift in the control room and is taking a break. Buttered toast and slightly stewed tea.

As he sips from the steaming mug he spots one of his uniformed officers enter the room and walk up to the counter, order a bacon roll and a mug of the brown stuff. Time for a chat. The officer pays for his breakfast and the sergeant beckons him over to his table.

"Nice start to the day, Jim. Although why anyone wanting to expose themselves outside Green Lanes would do it at seven-thirty on a Sunday morning is a mystery to me. What did he say his name was?"

The officer sits down, scraping his chair across scuffed grey linoleum. "Said he was the Vicar of Wakefield. Tosser. We thought he was on his holidays but he's a loony. With the M.O. now. Going to be sectioned if you ask me. Still, got me and Dave back here in time for this." He points to his bacon butty. "Bloody paperwork never ends."

The sergeant grins. "You'll be here for a while then. Where's Dave, by the way? Not like him to miss a tea break."

"Custody suite, with the M.O. and Duty Officer. Waiting for the guy's G.P."

Sergeant Millar nods. Procedures. Double checks and signatures. You can't just lock the loonies away anymore. Probably for the best, he thinks, most of the time, but there is a case to make for the exercise of peremptory powers in the case of a thirty-seven-year-old man waving his willie around outside a shopping centre.

"There was something else, actually. Remember our chat last week about the God Squad and those missing kids. I saw from the daily reports that you and Dave dropped in on them yesterday. Anything interesting?"

The officer is working his way through a mouthful of bacon and bread. He holds up a finger and raises an eyebrow. The question makes him swallow too quickly and he can feel the mouthful being forced down his gullet painfully, like a fist inside his chest. Sergeant Miller waits.

"Mmmmgh. Sorry, Sarge."

The officer takes a gulp of tea to try and wash away the blockage. "Yeah. We were passing their place on the way back from a call in Woodlands Close. Nothing much to report. The van seems pretty clean and they keep records, mileage, names, times, dates. The kids they pick up don't want to be found, though. Three Donald Ducks and Jeffery Archer. The head guy said they get lots of kids through but mostly it's a one way street. Food and a bed and bugger-off the next morning. A couple of them have stayed on, found God and all that, but it all seemed kosher."

"Anything odd about the place?"

The officer gives his sergeant a quizzical look. "What, apart from the bible-bashers and the unnatural quiet?"

"No! What about the drivers?"

The officer shrugs. "Same thing. Hand-picked members of their community. Everything logged, mileage, routes etcetera. They've even done police checks on everyone in case the kids are underage and start making accusations."

Sergeant Millar can taste milk on the turn. He sits back and crosses his legs. "Trouble is we don't really have anything to go on. Technically no one is missing. These kids drift in and out of the area all the time. Come summer the place is like a bloody drop-in centre. All we've got is a concerned social worker who, by his own admission, never really knows where the kids go, and it's not as though their parents give a toss."

"Want us to keep at it, Sarge?"

Sergeant Miller shakes his head. "No, lad. Eyes open and all that, but don't waste any more time on it. Anyway, there's plenty of other things to worry about. Did you hear about last night's shenanigans down in Bideford?"

The officer nods. Everyone has heard about the girls. A pervasive culture. "Yeah. Poor sods."

A look of sheer frustration crosses the sergeant's face. "Bloody stupid. Someone comes up to you and offers you something you've never seen before and you say absolutely fucking magic. And then, Jim, you wash it down with a crate full of booze."

The officer has heard it all before. The weary cynicism that comes through prolonged exposure to other people's stupidity and mean-faced barbarism. He tries to counter-attack, but it's half-hearted. "But, Sarge, one of them's dead."

"Tell me about it. Seventeen. Pretty from what I've heard. Bloody stupid. The boys who were on duty reckon she must have been three or four times over the limit. God knows what she thought she was doing."

"Does anyone have any idea about the gear?"

"Not yet, lad. CID are on the case. Whoopy bloody doo! I mean, who are they going to go after? It's a club. We all know the faces but there'll be nothing direct to link them all together. Kids dealing at the coalface. Intermediaries. We all know who we should be going after but making it stick is something else entirely."

"So who do you reckon it is?"

Sergeant Miller leans forward conspiratorially. He lowers his voice slightly. "Exeter boys possibly or maybe someone down from Bristol. Could be our local Scottish hoods. Not sure. It would be unlike Don Cascarino to mess with the cutting edge, though. He's old school, tried and tested. Anyway, from what I've heard he's selling-up. Spain. Shame in one sense, 'cos you know where you stand with JC. Soon as he's gone someone else will muscle in and who knows what shit we'll be dealing with then."

The officer traces the boomerang pattern on the tabletop with his finger for a moment before he replies. "Seems bad enough now. So what do you think the boys upstairs will do about it?"

"Nothing much. Nothing much they can do unless something falls out of the woodwork. They've got the stuff down at forensics so we'll get some idea what we're dealing with. Pray to God they keep the other girl alive until the boffins find out what she's taken. As for prints, probably smudged. All that sweat and sticky fingers. My guess is there'll be a few days, maybe a couple of weeks, when we crack down on the dealers, make some noises, hope the girl pulls through and then loads of shit in the press about the dangers of drugs."

The officer looks up. He drains his mug and places it carefully on the table, lining-up part of its curve with the pattern on the tabletop. "It's not right, though, is it, Sarge?"

Sergeant Miller is due back in the control room. He pushes his chair back and stands up, but before he goes he leans forward with both hands palm flat on the table. "No, Jim, it isn't. It's just the usual shit." He stands and is about to go, but stops and adds, "Although, if you want my opinion, what were the bloody parents doing letting seventeen year old girls out on their own somewhere like that? If you want to know who's really fucking stupid, ask yourself that one."

The constable rises too, but hangs back for a moment thinking about that last remark. After a few seconds grappling with another question he hurries forward and catches up with Sergeant Miller by the swing doors at the entrance to the canteen.

"Sarge?"

"Yes, lad?"

"You got any kids?"

"Boys, three of them. Why?"

"How old?"

"Nineteen, seventeen and twelve, why?"

The penny drops.

"Shit, that's different. They're boys."

Bedside vigils are, like Robin Hood and Ichabod Crane, largely the stuff of myths. The nurses working on the intensive care ward at the North Devon are polite but insistent, asking Carol and Dave to leave at twelve. They can return for two hours at six, otherwise the ward is closed to visitors so that the medical teams can carry out their duties. As they walk away from the unit Carol starts to feel the weight of absolute, emotional weariness in her bones.

"What do we do now?" she asks. "Six hours."

Dave steers towards the path of least resistance. "First thing let's get a cup of tea. Canteen's this way."

Dave guides Carol through the same scuffed corridors that Billy followed when she kicked him off the ward earlier that morning. The place is busier now, bustling with general ward visitors and staff. Trolleys move slowly congealing meals along in front of care staff, and porters wheel the infirm and the damaged towards toilets and x-rays. The smell of the place is institutional and cloying, especially now that the carefully controlled ambient temperature has been augmented by the bright spring sunshine that streams in through the corridor's large plate glass windows.

The canteen is in the basement of the hospital, not far from the mortuary. Unable to think about home with all of its reminders of Bex strewn about the rooms, Billy is watching the steam rise on a third mug of coffee. He is wired. Lack of sleep and a surfeit of caffeine threaten a short circuit. Like Carol he is desperate for the slide down into oblivion, but neither of them can contemplate rest at the moment.

On the till an older lady dressed in a dark blue smock and trews has started to watch Billy out of the corner of her eye. The object of her unsubtle surveillance is unshaven and rambling, singing to himself. If it wasn't for the fact that the psychiatric unit had recently closed down for major refurbishment she would have the man marked down as a resident. Not, of course, that there is a problem with that, not in this day and age, but she can't help her personal feelings about them. They make her uncomfortable. Nervous. There are trays of cutlery in plain view here, knives and forks, a veritable powder keg. Letting the medically insane into a canteen is, in her considered opinion, a tragedy in the making.

Dave holds the door open for Carol and they wander around for a moment or two trying to work out where the hot drinks are served from. The canteen has been organised along the usual time and motion lines; trays, soup and salads, hot cabinets, desserts, drinks. Dave picks up a tray. After a moment of brief inspection he puts it back and takes the one from underneath. He prefers not to dine from a tray with hard baked lumps of shepherd's pie stuck to its wipe clean surface.

Billy spots them from his window seat as they come in. The lyric stops and the music in his head fades out. Reality breaks through. He shrinks back against the wall and rests his forehead on the glass. Maybe they will not see him. Perhaps the nosy old beak taking the money will stop throwing him dirty looks. Billy wonders why everyone is blaming him. Complete strangers seem to avoid him and any of the tables in his immediate vicinity.

Reflected in the glass Billy watches Dave and Carol leave the serving area with a pot of tea on their tray and pay the old girl on the till. He loses sight of them as they collect cups, teaspoons and cartons of milk, which forces him to turn round to see where they are heading. As soon as he turns he sees that Carol is looking straight at him. Contact has been made. There is no way of avoiding the inevitable recriminations. Billy fully expects to be wearing his coffee within moments.

Dave is clearly reluctant to continue the conversation from the corridor but Carol, equally obviously, tells him to grow up. They walk over. Carol is the one who breaks the awkward silence. "Billy. Can we?"

She gestures towards the two seats opposite Billy and he nods. Dave slides in first. Billy moves back towards the aisle and sits opposite Carol. Billy closes his eyes and swallows. Where to start? He decides to deal with Dave first. "Look, about earlier. Sorry." He holds out a hand.

Dave looks at Carol and then returns the gesture. A handshake. "Yeah, me too. It's all a bit of a shock."

An outward semblance of humanity is restored and the old biddy on the till loses interest now that Billy has re-joined the ranks of the normal. Dishevelled, unhinged and severely in need of a drink he may be, but he is clearly able to hold a conversation.

Billy turns to Carol. "I really am sorry. She seemed so grown-up."

Carol breaks open the milk cartons and pours tea from a silver metal teapot into two cups. Sugar for Dave. She waits until she has taken a sip before replying. "I know. They all do."

Carol's voice is measured and even. She still wants to scream at the useless bugger sitting opposite her, but she has no intention of giving him or anyone else in the canteen the satisfaction of watching her lose it.

"Which is the reason why you should know better, Billy. Of all the people she could have been with you're the one who really knows what it's like out there. Not me. Not Dave. We're amateurs. You're the sodding professional."

Carol can feel the volume rising. With so much emotion screaming through her head she finds it difficult to hear one voice in relation to another, but she can feel the pressure wave. She pauses and takes two small sips of milky white tea. It's disgusting and she is in a state of shock. She decides that she needs sugar, so she breaks open a paper tube and adds its contents to her tea, something she has not done for nearly twenty years.

Billy has lived by himself for so long that he is out of practice. How do you argue with women you used to know so well? Lovers' tiffs and the odd bout of Dear Jane are one thing, but this needs reason, needs killer lines based in irrefutable fact. Billy struggles for words.

"I know…well…I think I understand a little of how you feel. It's the same for both of us. She's our daughter".

Billy turns momentarily towards Dave. "No offence mate."

Back to Carol, "I mean, if she'd asked you would you have stopped her going?"

It's Carol's turn to find words difficult to come by, so she chooses a simple strategy; anything that Billy says is irrelevant. Billy is the one fucking-up. But how can she deny the truth of what he is saying? Would she have said no? Probably not, although she would have arranged to pick them up from the club. She would have done something else. Done what, though? Carol recognises the fundamental weakness in her argument and changes the subject.

"Have they told you about the visiting hours?" she asks.

Billy shakes his head.

"Ten till twelve, six till eight, otherwise strictly no admittance, unless she's at death's door." Carol winces as she says this.

Billy can hear the first strains of the melody begin in his head again. "She's not, though, right?"

Carol's movement is involuntary. A reflex. Her hand reaches out across the table and comes to rest on top of Billy's. He is, after all, the father of her daughter. "No, she's not."

Dave watches, confused. He feels like a spare part, an interloper, a voyeur in a wedding chapel. It's his turn to stare out of the window at the hospital garden, where the warm spring weather has brought a few hardy lunch-time customers out to the tables on the patio. Their coats flap in a breeze which clearly gets funnelled through the hospital buildings and swirls around the garden.

Hands are withdrawn.

Leona is once again standing in the wings as mental Billy starts to sing. She smiles at him from behind a blackleg in Billy's internalised theatre of dreams, clipboard in hand, but her eyes are closed. There is a cold draft blowing from her side of the stage. Billy shivers. Carol is, he thinks, so wrapped up in Bex that she probably knows nothing about the other girl. Should he tell her? Should he open up the wounds a little more or should he bear them alone a little longer. No doubt the press will break the details about the tragic death of a teenage clubber before too long, and Carol will find out about more of the sordid details soon enough.

Billy is drawn back from the performance starting in his head by the sound of Carol's voice. "Billy, Billy...I was asking if you know anywhere that might have a room?"

His mind is a blank. "You could stay at..."

"No, Billy, thanks, but no. I couldn't do that."

"Oh, yes, stupid. Sorry. There's a travel place out by Tesco, you know where you come off the Tiverton road, or there's a lodge thing out at Roundswell. The lodge is brand new, just finished, I think, so it's probably the cleanest, if you don't mind looking out onto car dealerships or the Wimpy."

Carol grimaces. "Believe me Billy, I don't give a flying fuck about the view. Roundswell, where's that?"

Dave suddenly realises that he can do something practical. "No problem, babe, we can put it in the sat-nav."

Carol's hand movement is entirely voluntary this time as she pats Dave's leg and smiles. Billy is now the spare part. He drains his mug and makes a gesture of patting his pockets. He has no keys, so it will have to be a cab. He has no idea if he picked up his wallet, but what the hell. The cabbie is going to have the honour of transporting Billy Nero in the back of his motor.

Billy gets ready to leave and as he does so he turns to Carol. "Okay if I come back at six?"

Carol tries to smile, but her eyes are strained and the effect is thin and reedy. "Of course it is, you stupid man."

Billy walks out of the canteen with a vague wave in the direction of Carol's table and turns left. He has no idea which way he should go and heads down another light blue corridor more in hope than with any recognisable sense of direction. The melody in his head is muted but the disc is spinning. He walks past a man in scrubs who gives him an odd look but carries on towards the canteen. Odd looks. Why should that bother Billy? He is unshaven, dirty, slightly hungover and wearing yesterday's suit, a suit that he has slept in. Everyone is giving him odd looks.

The volume rises. Lyrics repeat. The loop builds. Billy is vaguely aware that he is heading in the wrong direction, but he seems to have no control of his feet. This is a compulsion, an inevitable consequence of his reading of hospital signs. One in particular. Mortuary.

He follows the arrow and comes to a pair of heavy swing doors set in the right hand corridor wall. There are two round porthole windows, which have been covered over with rose pattern curtains. Homely. He finds himself smiling inanely at this sweet and gentle touch. He stands by the door and lets Sensible Billy argue the case for retracing his steps. Mental Billy laughs out loud and turns up the volume.

A hand reaches out and lays itself flat against the wooden door. Pressure is exerted. The door holds firm for a second, during which Billy watches his internal conscience make one last plea for sanity. The panel of judges sitting out in the audience wave the boring little shit away and insist that the show goes on. The door shifts and then swings open. Billy enters an ante-room devoid of people. Two trolleys stand empty over by the far wall. Another set of swing doors are set into a white painted breeze block wall to the left. More porthole windows, uncovered this time. Billy walks over to the doors and peers in through one of the windows.

The volume cranks up to overload and Billy starts to sing as he slides down onto his knees. He is centre stage, in the spotlight, the apple of a thousand eyes, but he sees nothing beyond the footlights. The only thing that Billy can see is the body in the wings, Leona's body, laid out on a trolley in the main mortuary room, ready for inspection by the Coroner's Officer prior to Monday's autopsy.

In Billy's field of vision, in the image of the world that he carries with him as he sinks onto his knees by the mortuary door, Leona waves to him from the trolley and starts to tap her left foot in time to the beat of the music that is thumping through his throbbing temples.

SAY SOMETHING SWEET TO YOUR SWEETHEART

ALEX BERISA PARKS HIS hire car in Bideford's main car park at the far end of the quay, by a park filled with hassled parents watching kids on bikes and swings. The sun is breaking through the late morning haze and the ice cream vans are warming up for another afternoon of sticky fingers and vanilla-crusted top lips. A slight breeze hustles old crisp packets into the corners of vacant parking bays and there is enough of a chill in the air to make skin creep with goose bumps. Alex is wearing his suit jacket buttoned up, but not to guard against Easter's vaguely inclement weather.

The car park is a pay and display, and Alex has to juggle through the loose change in his trouser pockets to find the required fee. He scrapes together enough to make his parking legal for one hour, collects his ticket and leaves it on the Mondeo's dashboard. He walks past a statue with the name Kingsley on the plinth and he wonders who he was; a benefactor of the town, perhaps, or maybe a long dead, rotten borough politician who bought immortality in marble. It doesn't matter. The statue's eyes are made of stone and they can't see the sense of purpose in Alex's stride as he walks along the quayside.

The traffic is building up, a holiday lunchtime cruise into town for shops and pubs. The happy shoppers will be disappointed, though, as all bar the tackiest gift shops are closed. Bideford runs on an old punch card time clock, which has no means of recording time worked on the day of rest. If you want modern convenience you have to go out of town. The only shops that appear to be open are a tobacconist and an all-day convenience store.

Older couples amble along slowly, taking in the sight of a recently painted but still rust scarred cargo ship flying an Antiguan flag of ownership that's moored by the quay. A mobile crane stands idle, waiting for Monday and the unloading of ball clay. Family groups trundle pushchairs from which hang toddlers, flapping strands of fraying carrier bags and the escaping contents of baby changing rucksacks. Among the adults, the generations within each family wear an extra layer of clothing for each decade that they've been enduring English seaside town holiday weather.

At the bottom end of the High Street, where a queue is already forming outside one of the banks because all of the other cash machines in the town centre have run out of money, Alex spots the matt black security doors of The Basement. One of them is slightly ajar. He stands opposite the club for a moment and watches. Every so often someone tries to peer into the shadows, trying to add a little local colour to their morning stroll. There appears to be no such thing as bad publicity.

The place is quiet and sober in daylight. Alex crosses the road and walks up to the door as if he owns the place. The trick is to appear as though you belong. People only notice things that seem out of the ordinary. He opens the door and enters the building, closing the door firmly behind him. The door shuts with a definite weight and sound. Alex can hear voices in the interior of the building, voices that momentarily break off when they become aware of a change in the background wash of street noise. Alex waits, allowing his eyes to adjust to the strip lights shining from the ceiling in the main auditorium. A head appears from behind a wall, from where Alex guesses the main bar or the office must be. He waits.

The rest of the body attached to the head appears, followed immediately by another body, of medium height and build, heading for that middle aged paunch induced by a liking for pubs and real ales. The second person is short and squat, balding, with a neck built for breaking noses. The hired help are on duty. The first man stops a few feet from Alex.

"Who the fuck are you? Can't you see we're closed? Fucking press."

Alex says nothing. He watches as the bouncer walks towards him, chest puffed out, waddling in the way that only steroidal, over-muscled bruisers can.

"Like the boss said, time to go, pal".

Alex smiles. "Not the politest welcome I've ever had".

The older man, the aforementioned boss, folds his arms across his chest and scowls. The club is strangely silent, as if the scaffolding and the industrial ephemera that make up its skin are being sloughed-off by the reptile within. The shorter of the two men screws up his eyes and closes in on the intruder. His arms are rising from his side, ready to grab Alex and throw him out onto the street. Alex continues to smile but says nothing more. He lets the bouncer drop his full weight onto his front foot and as the man lifts his trailing leg to make the final step towards his prey, Alex moves.

It's all about the knowing, and Alex already knows how the man will shape up, knows where his weight will be, where his mass and energy are directed. Alex is no crouching tiger, but he is quick and definite. The fingers of the bouncer's right hand are reaching for the lapel of Alex's jacket and his left hand, balled into a fist, is drawing back to deliver a blow to the midriff. It is convenient that the man is a southpaw. It makes it easier for Alex to reach down to his belt, grab his handgun by the butt and slash the barrel across his assailant's nose.

The effect is instantaneous; barroom brawling at its most effective. The bouncer's head jerks to the left and blood showers out of his ripped face. Alex takes a step back, moves around behind his assailant and slams his bleeding face into the wall. The butt of the pistol cracks against the back of the man's head and the job is done. The body sags and crumples onto the floor. Alex looks over at the second man, who is standing quite still with his mouth open.

Alex points the gun at the nightclub owner. "Who I am isn't your concern. What I'm going to do to you is."

Alex takes his time. He knows that the man in front of him wants to run away as far and as fast as he can, but he also knows that the man is in shock, is physically incapable of moving, facing as he is the sharp end of a nine millimetre pistol. The man is in overload and it will take him a few seconds to regain control, more than enough for Alex to get close, close enough to make running or fighting-back an irrelevance. It's not all bad, though, thinks Alex as he walks towards his target. Judging by the stain spreading across the front of the man's trousers it is obvious that he has started to relax already.

After a little gentle coaxing Alex and his new friend move back to the bar. A fifteen inch colour portable television, mounted on a wall bracket above the optics, is playing on low volume. Alex reaches across the bar, picks up the remote and hits the mute button. As he slides the control back towards the night club owner, Alex asks him for his name.

"Stevie…Stevie Challinor". The man's voice is indefinite and thin.

Alex nods and continues. "Sit down, Stevie. You've probably guessed that I'm not the press. Not a cop either. All in all that makes me your worst nightmare. No rules, you see, no complaints procedures."

Stevie sits obediently on an old, bar stool. Although his view of the main door is obscured by a wall, he can see two feet sticking out from the entrance hallway. There is no movement. The guy in front of him has put his pistol back in his belt.

Alex stands by the bar, feet slightly apart, with his arms down by his side. He stands quite still, and using a soft and even tone of voice, makes sure that Stevie understands the basics of body language and purpose.

"I'm going to make this very plain and simple. I'm not going to torture you for information. I don't want your club. I don't want a cut or protection or drugs. What I want are answers to a few questions, answers that you'll give me straight away. Fuck me around, Stevie, and you won't have time wish your mother was here. Understand?"

Stevie nods. His mouth is as dry as the Gobi. He can feel the blood pumping though his arteries and throbbing at his temples. Whatever this man wants, he can have it. Right now, right here, he can take it all. Every time the guy says his name Stevie feels as though blades of ice are being dragged along his spine. First name terms. Stevie suddenly wants to sleep. He feels desperately tired and heavy, but he dare not look away from the stranger, even though the damp patch in his groin is growing cold and is a screaming embarrassment at his sense of manhood.

Alex leans against the bar, facing his new friend, and looks at him quizzically. His jacket hangs away from his body and the butt of the Glock is just visible in the shadows. "So, Stevie. Drugs. How's trade?"

Stevie is confused. Trade? How the hell should he know? He draws strands of thought together and tries to make them coalesce into something coherent. For the first time in years he tries not to swear. He feels like he is back in school, up in front of the headmaster, only this time punishment is spelled with a capital P.

"Not sure what you mean? We, er…I don't sell that shit, not directly. I couldn't say whether trade is good or bad, except the rent is paid." Stevie swallows. Now that he has started to talk his saliva glands have kicked into overdrive.

Alex checks his watch. He wants to be out of here in short order. There's no point in hanging around. In and out quickly. Make your point and leave. "Look, it's no skin off my nose, if you'll forgive the pun. Who, what, where. All the usual stuff. Nice and simple, nice and quick."

Life is measured in seconds and right now Stevie wants more of them, a lot more, and for the first time since he urinated, he feels as though he might have a chance. Words come tumbling out.

"Yeah, yeah, okay. Look, I don't deal. I have an arrangement with a few local lads, you know, they deal, I charge rent. Keeps it simple and no one gets hurt. The boys are just local kids, small fry, pushers."

Alex holds up a hand and shakes his head. He looks Stevie in the eye and brushes his jacket away from his hip, revealing the butt of the Glock in all of its cold glory. "You're disappointing me, Stevie, you really are. Of course you have kids in here dealing. That's not the point. I don't give a damn about the kids. You know what this is about. Names, Stevie, names, the real thing."

Stevie looks down at the ruined pair of jeans sticking to his legs, desperate in his desire for a moment in the shadows, for a moment out of the steady gaze of his interrogator. His trousers are cold and clammy against his skin and he can smell ammonia and the earthy dampness of soaked cloth.

"I couldn't tell you their names, well most of them. Come and go. The main bloke is Shaun, Shaun Lloyd. Tall lanky fuckwit, but he's good, regular and never gets into trouble. Doesn't use.

As far as I know he works out of Barnstaple. I've heard he works for the Scotsman. Word is that the Scotsman's selling up. Retiring."

This is what Alex wants and he smiles now. He doesn't need to prompt.

"Cascarino. Jock Cascarino. You can't miss Shaun. Skinhead. Always wears a long black overcoat. Looks like one of the Munsters."

Alex can feel the weight of the handgun against his groin. It's a tool and he is an artisan. He takes pride in his craft. "This Scotsman. And Shaun Lloyd. Location?"

"Dunno. Shaun does the clubs and pubs. Could be in any one of them. Cascarino hangs out at a cabaret club in Barnstaple. Not like this." Stevie looks at the décor. Home is where the heart is and he's not at all sure whether his heart is in this game anymore. "Old time stuff, you know, acts, singers and the like. Look, I really don't know what it's called. He sort of runs the place, with a couple of goons, Ken and Davie McCoist."

Stevie's eyes underpin his telling of the story. The man is telling the truth. Alex catches a flicker of light from the portable television behind the bar. The local lunch time news bulletin. The remote control is on the bar next to Stevie and Alex points towards it.

"Volume?"

Stevie hits the mute button and the presenter, the same woman from the morning broadcast, goes through the story one more time, the only difference being the release of names. She has changed her blouse, wearing pale cream this afternoon, although her hair is still tied back. Rebecca Whitlow and Leona Jeffery. North Devon Hospital. Alex makes a mental note of the names.

As the female presenter's voice cuts away to the next story Alex turns to Stevie. His hand goes to the butt of his gun. He watches as Stevie takes an involuntary breath.

"This is very simple, Stevie. No one moves from here for twenty minutes. You don't call anyone. You don't go outside. No one comes in. You lock up and wait. If you break the rules, I'll break you. You'll be out of business. Permanently. You understand me?"

Stevie nods. As Alex turns to walk out of the club, Stevie starts to follow him and then realises that this would be a mistake. He calls out one last question from the bar.

"What about Don?"

Alex walks up to the prostrate body on the floor by the entrance. He thinks about giving the guy a kick in the nuts but decides that it wouldn't be professional. Gratifying, but needlessly gratuitous. He will probably need surgery on the nose. Chances are that he will snore abrasively for the rest of his life.

Alex turns and looks round at the club owner. "Twenty minutes, Stevie. He'll need some ice when he wakes up."

Alex opens the door and steps out into the daylight, buttoning his jacket as he walks down to the quay and along past the tobacconist, past the convenience store and Mister Hu's Chinese takeaway. By the park entrance Charles Kingsley watches him in silence. Like the three wise monkeys, he sees, hears and says nothing. This is their little secret, a shared confidence, a matter of trust. Kingsley won't grass and that's just the way Alex likes it.

Jock Cascarino's silver Lexus is parked by the kerb outside a Victorian villa at the foot of Old Sticklepath Hill, an old terrace that has seen better days. The small front garden is still choked with last summer's weeds, a tattered bag of rock hard cement and the frame, minus wire basket, of a supermarket trolley. Paint on exterior woodwork is a luxury that the residents seem ill-inclined to afford. Traffic on the new bypass, which runs immediately behind the house, is already building up and Jock Cascarino, who is sitting in the front passenger seat, watches the cars and their drivers. He keeps a tally in his head of people absent-mindedly picking their noses. The brothers McCoist have knocked twice but no one has answered the door. Ken tries to peer in through a ground floor window while Davie returns to the car to get further instructions. At a tap on the glass Jock leaves off counting and lowers the passenger side window.

"No answer, Jock".

Jock looks weary. "Aye, but what do you expect? Place is full of smacked-up squatters. Just get the little fuck."

Davie whistles to Ken and points at the door. A size ten boot smacks into the woodwork, karate style, just below the latch and the door frame splinters but holds. Davie and his brother try again, together this time, and the frame splits as the door judders on its hinges and then smacks into the hallway wall. In the shadows at the back of the house someone slams the kitchen door shut and a chair can be heard scraping across a bare wooden floor.

Shaun Lloyd lives on the top floor. As the brothers walk up the stairs, they ignore shouts of alarm and looks of wide-eyed terror that appear on the faces of bleary-eyed kids peering out from behind psychedelically painted panel doors. The place is a mess. Carrier bags full of rubbish litter the stairwells. There is an ingrained reek of patchouli and stale dope in the air. As soon as the occupants realise that this isn't an official bust doors slam shut. No one wants to know. Honour among thieves.

There is a degree of status amid the anarchy. Shaun's efforts in the workplace are reflected in the fact that he has appropriated the whole of the top floor of the house for himself. At the top of the stairs he has installed a wrought iron garden gate, which is six foot tall and secured against a similarly heavy metal door frame with a padlock. As the McCoists walk up the third flight of steps they can see Shaun watching them through the lattice work.

"Morning, Shaun", Ken says in a matter of fact way.

"Fuck off". Shaun sounds flat and bored, but his eyes give away a distinct hint of unease.

"That's no way to greet your mates".

Shaun leans against a wall in a threadbare, olive green tee-shirt and paisley patterned boxer shorts. He has diamond-pattern ankle socks on.

"With mates like you, who needs fucking enemies. It'll cost a bundle to fix that bloody door. You could've knocked."

Ken looks at his brother and grins. "We did, Shaun, twice. None of your fucked up hippy cunts bothered to answer. Anyway, you've made more than enough to pay for the mess. Jock wants a word."

"I've got a phone. He can call me."

"Not that sort of word, boy. If I were you I'd get some kecks on."

"Or what? You got a key?"

Ken takes his mobile out of his jacket pocket. "No, pal, but I've got a lethal weapon. You see what I'm doing here. Amazing bit of kit. You press these numbers and it connects you to the Bizzies. Then, after they've busted everyone's balls, we'll come and find you and break both your fucking legs."

Ken has lost that ineffable feeling of Sunday morning grace.

"So why don't you be a good little boy and open up before Davie here gets really pissed-off."

There never was any doubt. Shaun knows the score. You have to stay in the game to be a winner, but on this occasion the underdog is exactly that and Shaun has the padlock key in his hand. He walks up to the door and unlocks the padlock. The boys accept his invitation and pay a house call.

Davie goes first, following Shaun into one of the three rooms on the top floor. There is a bedroom, an open plan living room with kitchenette, and a bathroom. Despite his own outward appearance, Shaun keeps the place neat and tidy. The three of them go into the living room.

Ken inspects the kitchen area. "Nice place."

"Don't have to live in total shit, you know. There's a point to what I do."

Davie runs a finger along the top of a Victorian cast iron fireplace. "There's more to you than meets the eye, Mister Lloyd. Housework?"

Shaun stands in the middle of the room, pulling on last night's jeans. "Whatever. Look, what the fuck does he want?"

"As I said, a word. About last night."

Shaun buckles up and reaches for his overcoat. "Last night? Sweet as fuck. Shifted the lot. Everyone seemed happy enough. Left at the usual time, no hassle."

Ken smiles and winks at Davie. "Aye, happy enough…until they started fucking keeling over. Jock's not a happy bunny on account of the punters fucking croaking, ye ken, laddie."

Shaun does not ken. He has certain habits and preferences in life. One is that he never uses the stuff he sells. Another is an aversion to television. He has no interest in the visual arts as delivered through the cathode ray tube. He hates PlayStations. Music and books are his bag, and this morning, deprived of instant television news, Shaun has no idea what Ken is talking about. He does, however, understand that dead punters might be a bit of a problem. He puts his coat on, picks up his wallet from the mantelpiece where Ken has been testing for dust, and follows the boys out of his top floor flat.

He locks the flat door and then the wrought iron door and, sandwiched between the brothers McCoist, descends to the ground floor. One of the residents braves this new Sunday morning world to ask if everything is okay, and Shaun nods, telling the boy to nip across to the retail park and get some wood and a new lock.

Once outside, Ken heads for the driver's seat while Davie and Shaun take the rear seats in the Lexus. As Ken starts the engine and heads out towards the main Bideford road in the direction of Sillick Farm, Jock turns to Shaun.

"We're taking a little trip, Shaun, to see a friend. We thought you might like a ride out to the countryside."

Shaun starts to ask a question but stops as soon as he sees Jock turn back to face the front. No one seems to be in the mood for small talk. Shaun sits back and lets his head rest on the glass of the rear window. The new bypass and the downstream bridge over the Taw flash by and all that Shaun has rattling around in his head is a single word that sums up his general state of mind; "Screwed!"

Jock has plans for a future, plans for a house built on solid foundations, capable of withstanding anything that Her Majesty's constabulary and court services might throw at him, at least until he is too old and feeble to care. As far as Jock is concerned, Ronnie Biggs had the right idea. Sit it out in the sun. Put two fingers up to the Crown Prosecutor over a long glass of sangria. When the day finally comes, when Jock's liver gives up the ghost, he wants to come home with a sheepish grin all over his face, rattling on about dignity, all the while thanking every bone in his body for the National Health Service. He'll love the Mediterranean weather but no grease ball surgeon is going to poke around near Jock's vital organs.

That was the plan, but behind every great man, once you have accounted for the inevitable woman, there is a fear of getting caught. Jock had it all sussed out, but, sitting in the front of the Lexus as Ken pulls into the courtyard at Sillick Farm, Jock is having to consider an alternative future, one with foundations made of sand. The doctor has been advised of their imminent arrival and is waiting in the doorway that leads up to the laboratory. He is still wearing his lab coat, and wipes his hands on the front of it as he watches them park the car. He was not amused when the call came in. There is little to choose between the scowls on the faces that Arbnor Jasari and Jock Cascarino present to the world. Both of them have developed an extreme dislike of the day.

Doors slam. Shaun is bundled out of the car and marched over to the entrance to the laboratory building. Arbnor Jasari looks the boy up and down once and stands aside. As Jock approaches the doctor turns to him and says, "Why the fuck you bring him here for?"

Jock looks at his pet chemist with disdain. "Inside. Now".

The dysfunctional Cascarino family are at home.

On entering the laboratory Shaun's eyes momentarily betray real fear. He recognises the place for what it is; the factory, the source of all this shit on a Sunday morning, and the seeing of it makes him feel very uncomfortable. He can imagine a scene in which Jock laughs as he tells him that he has no choice but to kill him now that he knows the route out to the fairground. Blindfolds in films suddenly make sense.

The McCoists put Shaun in one of the cells that the Doctor has used for his guinea pigs and make no bones about manhandling Helen, Jasari's recent recruit, into the same cell. Shaun and

Helen are told to shut up and wait. Davie then takes up station by the main door while Ken leans against the metal railings of the cell. Arbnor Jasari prowls around the room, pretending to inspect his scales and mixing table, while Jock sits in the doctor's chair by the computer desk. There are fourteen new Tupperware boxes full of sachets ready for distribution.

Jasari speaks first. "I asked downstairs, why did you bring him here?"

Jock ignores him and watches Helen. She fidgets nervously with her hair as she sits down on the camp bed in the cell. "First things first, Doctor A. I take it this bitch is the one Davie mentioned. If we're going to get shitty about guests, then we'll deal with her first. Did I say you could keep a pet?"

The doctor gives Jock a foul look but out of the corner of his eye he sees Helen shaking her head. He takes a deep breath and counts to ten. As he speaks he raises his hands, palms facing outward in a gesture of conciliation.

"No, you said nothing. But how do you think we made all this?" He points at the finished drugs. "And it's lonely here and she's a good worker. It costs nothing, just a few tabs, a little medicine. She keeps me company, stops me going crazy out here, and, as I said, we've made a lot of gear."

The McCoist brothers watch impassively as Jock smiles. "And afterwards?"

The doctor looks away and lowers his voice. "It's okay. I'll deal with that."

Jock sits in silence for a moment before sitting back in the chair and lightening the level of threat in his voice slightly.

"Let's get it straight, Doc. First, like you say, she's got a job to do. I can accept that, for now. Same with laughing boy over there. Works the clubs."

Jock turns and looks at Shaun. "Usually reliable. Let's hope she's the same, eh? Second, as you and I both know, when people like them become unreliable, people like you and me have to clean up the mess. Understand?"

The doctor understands all too well. It's not a threat, just the way of business. He understands that he too, like the couple in the cell, will be a mess that Jock will need to clear up one day. "Yes. Business. But like I asked, why are you here like this?"

Jock takes a second or two to frame his answer. He is still not sure how to play this. In the cell Shaun has turned an even whiter shade of pale than he usually manages. The girl is staring at the far wall, trying to make herself invisible.

"Have you heard the news today?" Jock asks.

The doctor looks confused. He walks slowly round to the front of the table where the tubs of Bliss are being stored and perches on the edge. "What news?"

"Bit of a problem last night. Seems two wee lassies got their brains fried at a nightclub. Now, the thing that bothers me is this. The television said it was a cocktail of drugs and booze. E and shit. Does that seem horribly familiar?"

"Why don't you ask him?" the doctor replies, throwing a dismissive wave in Shaun's direction. Deflection. He wants time to think because it does sound horribly familiar, and if Jock finds out about the contaminated batch the doctor doesn't hold out too much hope for Helen. He feels confident that he can deal with this sort of mess, but she is another matter altogether. He is growing used to having her around and it would be a shame to throw it all away now.

"Would you ask the boy wonder to step out here a moment?" Jock asks Ken.

Shaun is already on his feet as Ken repeats the request. He shuffles through the cell doorway, looking like a lost child wrapped in the folds of a filthy bag-man's coat.

"Can you remember last week, Shaun? The instructions."

Last week. Shaun racks his brain. Wednesday night. Something about booze.

"Yeah. No booze, Mister Cascarino. I told them, but I can't make them. I just sell the stuff. If they want to fuck up then that's up to them."

It sounds convincing enough, except Shaun has a pretty clear recollection of the weekend's dealing. He doesn't remember actually telling anyone to lay off the hooch, but thankfully Jock appears to be satisfied.

"True enough. Do you remember two girls. Seventeen. Pissed-up, by all accounts?"

Shaun makes a habit of forgetting faces in the clubs. He has a few regular clients, people he knows by name, but they rarely buy anywhere so obvious. He has no interest in the kids. All he wants to know is whether they have enough cash in their pockets.

"Fuck knows. Faces. I mean, you deal, wham bam, thank you. You don't get life stories, Mister Cascarino. It's possible. Most of them were blokes, though. I know it's all equal these days, but the guys usually do the buying."

Jock considers Shaun's explanation. What can you expect from the likes of Shaun Lloyd. Certainly not compassion. Whether or not he warned the girls, or their pimply boyfriends, is, anyway, irrelevant.

"Thank you, Shaun, you can sit down. You see, Doc, what worries me is we sell a hundred sachets and we get one dead cow and another stupid bitch in a coma. Two percent failure rate. Not huge in the great scheme of things but if we repeat that all summer there's going to be some heavy shit going down. The Bizzies will notice, know what I mean? So the question I'm asking is this. Is it our fucking mess?"

Arbnor Jasari stands and picks up one of the tubs full of sachets. He flicks his hand across the sachet tops, making a sound like an old playing card in a child's bicycle wheel. The Scotsman is working on circumstantial evidence.

"No, it's not our mess. This is good stuff. I've taken it. She's taken it every day since she's been here and there's been no hassle. In fact, we've both taken it and drank some wine and we're both still here. I'm a good chemist. Many things are possible. It's possible these girls took Bliss, but maybe not. I don't know. You don't know."

True lies. Jock sits forward in the chair and rests his head in his hands. He is frowning. "Is there any way they can find out?"

The doctor puts the tub back down on the table, goes over to the desk by Jock and picks up a bottle of water. He takes a drink before answering.

"Of course. They can test bloods. Maybe if one of the girls has a packet on her they can do a match, but they can't be sure. Everything in those sachets is normal stuff from the street. But, yes, I suppose they might work it out…if there's any link."

Jock sighs lightly and suddenly looks weary. "So, we do have a…"

The doctor cuts Jock off mid-stream. His voice is urgent. He must keep control of the situation before it gets out of hand.

"No. If you stop now, you have a problem. If the girls die and our stuff is out there for only one weekend they will make a link. You have to keep to the plan. If we flood the market and there are no more fuck ups, then they can't know. They can't make that link. Bliss is just some new stuff out there, the same as all the rest. Poor little girls. Stupid little girls. The newspapers run a story and then everyone forgets."

He returns to his perch on the edge of the central laboratory table and points at Shaun. "I still want to know about him? He knows we are here, knows too much. There are too many people getting involved and it's making me nervous."

Jock gets up and walks over to the cell doorway. "You hear that Shaun. You're making the good doctor nervous."

Time to get back to business. Jock asks Shaun a direct question. "What do you think? Keep selling. Bluff our way through?"

Shaun shakes his head. This is getting way out of line. "Don't know. What he says makes sense. Stop now and they might put two and two together. But then they might anyway if they do the tests. I don't know."

"Davie, Ken, any thoughts?"

Davie shakes his head.

Ken looks at his boss and says, "Fuck 'em. This shit happens all the time. We can't hold their hands. They buy and they use. If they don't follow the rules it's not down to us what happens."

Silence. Shaun is fighting an insistent urge to make a run for the door. Helen hasn't moved. She stares straight ahead as if she is trying to bore a hole in the wall above the staircase leading down from the laboratory. The brothers McCoist are doing what they are good at. Arbnor Jasari is thinking ahead, just like Jock, although their respective thought patterns are beginning to diverge. Jock goes over to the central table and picks out a sachet full of yellow powder, which he holds up to the light.

"Faint heart and all that. Pretty colour. There'll have to be a few changes. A few loose ends tidied-up after this, but we can still make it work. I've a few favours I can call in, find out what the boys in blue are thinking. In the meantime doc you carry on as normal. Shaun and the girl need to go on ice for a couple of days until we see how the land lies. Is that room downstairs still available?"

The doctor nods.

"Davie, will you get the key from the man and escort our guests to their new quarters."

Shaun is on his feet and heading for the cell door. Ken sticks out a thickly muscled arm and bars his way.

"Mister Casc..."

Jock smiles sweetly at the boy as he puts the sachet back in one of the plastic tubs. "It could be a lot worse, Shaun. All I want is you safely tucked-up overnight while I make sure the coast is clear. Everything checks out and you'll be back in your wee flat for milk and cornflakes. She's been down there before, knows the ropes. She'll keep you company, I'm sure."

Arbnor Jasari looks at Shaun and then at Helen. He doesn't like the boy and is a little taken aback by the feeling. The thought of them both locked in downstairs turns dislike into an instant hatred. Jealousy. He can feel trickles of sweat running down his torso from the damp patches growing at his armpits, under his lab coat. Jock retrieves the sachet he was looking at from the tub and throws it to Shaun.

"You won't notice the time if you try a little bit of what you sell to the happy campers. I'm sure your new roomie won't be saying no."

At the direction of the doctor, Davie takes a key from a small metal rack pinned to the wall by the computer desk and goes over to the cell. Together he and Ken pin their captives' arms behind their backs and push them down the stairs and into the ground floor room of the old barn, with Shaun protesting all the way. Helen remains silent throughout.

In the laboratory Jock walks up to the doctor and looks him squarely in the eye "I want you to double check every fucking bit of this shit. There's too much at stake, pal, for a fucking Dago screw up. We can all be winners or you can be dead. Simple. Comprende?"

It is all that Arbnor Jasari can do to stop himself from reaching out and throttling the ignorant little maggot in front of him, but he has to play for time. He needs money and he needs somewhere to lay low. For the time being it is, he thinks, better to be shafted by the devil you know. There'll be a time and a place for getting even.

"Yes", is all that he says. He looks away, towards his desk.

Jock leans in a little closer. He can feel the heat of the doctor's skin. Both men are sweating with tension.

"And don't go getting ideas about a little bit of nookie tonight, you dirty shit. I'm keeping the key with me until I get back."

Davie's head appears in the doorway.

"Snug as bugs in cowshit, boss".

Jock breaks away from his pet chemist and almost saunters to the stairs. "See you soon, Doc. Have a nice day."

Down in the car, as they head back up the lane towards the main Hartland road, Jock turns to Ken and says, "Tomorrow you two come out here and check-up. You can leave the girl for the time being, but Shaun is history. While you're at it you can get rid of the van in the other barn. No point leaving it lying around for the Bizzies to find. Torch it."

Tyres crunch on loose stones in the courtyard. Arbnor Jasari waits for five minutes to be sure that he is alone before going over to his desk and opening the central drawer. He picks up a broken blister pack that contained the padlock now being used to lock Helen and Shaun in the room downstairs. There is a spare brass key sitting snugly under the plastic wrapping.

"Stupid arsehole!" he says to himself as he pockets the key.

JUMP THROUGH THE RING

ALL THAT BILLY WHITLOW wants is a quiet life, that same untroubled groove of a life that is now being shredded right in front of his eyes. Sitting in the back of a cab in morose silence, Billy lets the music in his head fade to dull static. He is exhausted. When the mortuary technician found him on his knees in the mortuary's anteroom, he tried to help, making a sustained but weary effort to persuade Billy to sit down and have a cup of tea, assuming that he was related to the girl on the trolley, but there were no handles by which he could get a hold of the flaking singer. Grief unravels the knots that hold the fabric of everyday lives together, and Billy is a loose arrangement of tangled threads and regrets.

Billy should have behaved with more grace, should have recognised the compassion in the man's eyes, but he didn't. A hand on his shoulder shrugged off. Spitting venom into the face of kindness, shuffling away, unable to take his eyes off the porthole window to the main mortuary room, Billy had lashed out one more time and spurned this small moment of human kindness. Out of the static, circling and repeating comes a phrase that Billy has heard too many times. If he had a pound for every time someone had said it..."You're a shit, Billy Whitlow".

Billy needs a wash and a shave. Tyres thump on tarmac, leaving minute traces of themselves on the white lines that mark out road junctions. The Easter Sunday lunchtime crawl; bickering families on their way to The Big Sheep, fourteen hundred cubic centimetres of internally-combusting scenic country-lane driving, the flat cap and ladder-back glove brigade. Everyone assumes something. The cab driver tries to make conversation as they pull away from the hospital, but gives up before they hit Barnstaple town centre, only two miles down the road. Even Billy is aware of the odour; stage sweat, the remains of half cleaned Leichner, disinfectant, grime, sleep and sheer bloody terror.

Familiar places flash by, disjointed places, remote and out of context; the entrance to the picnic area just beyond Roundswell; a stretch of the coned-off dual carriageway. As the cab breasts the last hill before Bideford and slows down for the accident black spot at the Instow turn-off, Billy tries to get a grip. He starts to list the things he needs to do; shower, shave, shit. The order might change. Fresh clothes. A stiff scotch. He crosses the last item off the list. Bex needs him sober.

Billy gets the cab driver to make a detour to the supermarket where there is a twenty-four-hour cash machine. Once he is out of the cab in the fresh air, with the bustle of wire baskets under full strain all around him, he pays the driver and decides to walk back to the house. He buys a bottle of full fat Coke at the cigarette counter and heads back out onto the main road. A couple of happy shoppers mistake him for a tramp in someone's cast-offs, a missing person in a dead man's suit. Billy can feel their eyes crawling all over him. It is a perfect excuse for profanity, but he lets the moment wash away. The Coke sticks to his teeth and the sun is too bright, making him squint as he walks past the second hand car dealership at the bottom of the road where he lives. A Saab rag top catches his eye at a good price. It's a start, a little bit of the mundane seeping into his consciousness.

Hot water stings Billy's skin, restoring a sense of substance to the day and he feels as though he is being purged of sins, being exorcised. The demons lift away on red skinned wings and Billy is aware of external sounds and colours for the first time since seeing Leona's body. The simple act of scraping his fingernails through his shampoo covered hair restores a small aspect of his basic humanity. He lets the water fall for ten minutes in a cascade of absolution, and although he can still hear odd notes and bars of the melody deep in the primeval zones of his cortex, he feels as though he is regaining control.

He takes the time, while towelling himself dry, to look down at his body, allowing himself a moment of vanity, even in times of extremis. His belly is slipping south, expanding by slight degrees so that he can barely distinguish between the component parts of his torso; chest, stomach and abdomen. He is becoming unevenly cylindrical. He wraps the towel around the expanse formerly known as his waistline and squirts shaving foam onto the fingers of his right hand.

Steam from the hot water tap deposits an opaque film on the

surface of the mirror above the sink. Periodically Billy wipes a patch clean so that he can watch himself shave. As he draws the blades down his cheeks and follows the contours of his chin and neck he sees a familiar face emerge, but not one that he can immediately put a name to. The eyes are dull and the sideburns impossibly grey. Deep lines spread from the corners of his eyes, lines that reach down to dark bags that signify a definite lack of sleep. Billy wants to shut those eyes but they are stubborn. They won't rest.

He nicks his top lip shaving beneath his nose and dabs at it with toilet tissue, tearing off a small dot and sticking it onto the cut. The feather edge of the tissue tickles as he bends forward and brushes his teeth. Billy is forced to smile and toothpaste sprays off the head of his battery powered toothbrush onto the cold tap. He rinses and pulls the towel from his waist to wipe his face. The piece of tissue on the cut is pulled away with a sharp but brief nip.

With his hair gelled and armpits sanitised, Billy dresses; jeans and a white polo shirt. The putting on of clothes is an act of camouflage. He is going undercover, hiding behind a mask of typically bland middle aged scruffiness. The pressure is rising again and Billy can feel bubbles of nervous energy floating in his gut, as if, having descended into the depths, he is rising too quickly. Billy has the Bends. He hasn't got time to worry about the consequences of nitrogen embolisms. Socks and shoes, an overcoat grabbed from the hall, car keys retrieved from the living room, these are the components of ordinary life that he gathers unto him as he walks back into the nightmare.

Standing outside the house he takes a moment to breathe in deeply. Flashback. The Saab. He is looking at his battered old

Vauxhall, thinking that he really must do something about the heap on his driveway. Then he feels guilty. Bex is being kept alive by machines and he is thinking about a new second hand car. The relief provided by his shower evaporates as the horror takes hold once again. Billy feels like he is going to burst.

He backs the Vauxhall off the driveway and thinks about the radio. He needs something to occupy the higher functions of his mind while he drives back to the hospital. Thinking about music is like opening a trap door. Subconsciously the lunatic conductor in Billy's head taps his baton on a music stand, the record in his head flips over and Billy starts to hum to himself as he heads back out onto the main road to Barnstaple. Turning to face the outside world the mad conductor within gesticulates wildly and flashes Billy a wicked grin.

"Again, this couldn't happen again(3)

This is that once in a lifetime

This is the thrill divine"

Maggie has done most of the jumbo crossword in the Sunday newspaper. There are a number of clues filled in with made up words, but the key letters are correct. Septum has become Naptum. The difficult Sudoku lies untouched. The easy one is complete and Maggie has texted through her numbers in another attempt to win a case of champagne that she has absolutely no need of. Snuggle's provides her with as much alcohol as she could possibly want.

The beef joint for Sunday lunch is on the white ceramic kitchen draining board, still wrapped in the supermarket polystyrene tray. Vegetables have been prepared and sit in water waiting for the steamer. Potatoes have been sliced and par boiled, and the sherry bottle has been uncorked. She is quietly fuming, storing heat like a brick, ready for whatever hour Jock deigns to return. Maggie is keeping the home fires burning.

There is no point putting the roast in until she knows where he will be and when. To keep herself going she is listening to Tony Beard's Request show on Radio Devon. At the top of the hour the show breaks for a news bulletin. Maggie is standing at the pine kitchen table, flicking through the Sunday supplements, grazing the fashion pages in the magazine. She puts the schooner of sherry to her lips and lets the thick, sickly sweet amber wine from the Jerez region of southern Spain slide around her mouth. The news reader cuts from the lead report on Exeter City's vital game chasing promotion from the Conference to the story about the girls in the nightclub.

Maggie is dimly aware of the change of tone in the news reader's voice. She leans forward over the table, holding the glass aloft in her left hand, turning the magazine page with her right hand. She snorts. A stick thin model is wearing nothing but Lederhosen under a banner headline proclaiming that Austria is this year's chic summer fashion inspiration.

"I bet she hasn't shit in them", Maggie mutters to herself, a reference to ancient tradition that marks out the true devotee. The girl's makeup is stark and brutal; greys, browns and blacks. "Very Teutonic".

In the background the news reader confirms that two girls were taken to hospital and that one has died. There is something about a new designer drug. Maggie looks up from the picture in the magazine and checks the clock on the kitchen wall by the big, brushed-chrome American style fridge-freezer. It's just after one.

"Stupid kids", Maggie mutters as she drinks.

The bulletin cuts to a recording of a police statement. The detective leading the investigation repeats some of the previous details and then his voice breaks.

"Unfortunately… Leona Jeffery, aged seventeen, from Barnstaple, died early this morning. Her companion, Rebecca Whitlow, also seventeen and from Oxford, is in a serious condition in intensive care. The families have been informed and we are, at present, dealing with the incident with the utmost urgency."

Slow motion.

Special effects.

As Maggie turns her head toward the radio she can feel the resistance of the air. Her neck muscles strain against atmospheric pressure. Her left hand goes suddenly numb. The sherry schooner catches the edge of the table as it falls, snapping the stem from the bowl. Maggie is living outside of normal time. As she turns towards the radio Maggie's back foot slides across the kitchen floor towards the sink unit and the bowl of the sherry schooner shatters on terracotta tiles. The radio blurs. Sherry splashes her legs and hits the under sink cupboard doors. Maggie slips and jars her elbow on the edge of the sink.

Then the world snaps back into a regular timeframe.

"Bugger!"

Maggie slides down onto the floor, where a shard of glass cuts through her tights. A spiral of darkly purple blood mixes with the soft amber of the puddled sherry. She shrieks and clambers back to her feet, reaches for a tea towel and dabs at her leg. The glass shard is still embedded in the soft flesh of her calf and she swears viciously as it catches on the towel and jags through another millimetre of skin. She moves away from the broken glass like a hobbled goat, edging out of the kitchen towards the downstairs cloakroom where she keeps a first aid box, muttering distractedly to herself as she goes.

"Leona? Can't be. Shit, shit, shit. Ouch, that hurts."

Sitting on the toilet she manages to prise the sliver of glass from her calf using her beautifully manicured fingernails. She can smell the metallic harshness of blood on her fingers. She wriggles out of her tights and throws them onto the floor. Then she wets toilet tissue and cleans up the cut, which is no more than half a centimetre in length but it hurts like hell. She unclips the lid of the first aid box and tears open a square plaster, applying it firmly over the wound. When she takes her hand away the fabric of the plaster is already showing a small brown stain where the blood has soaked into the wadding. Maggie picks up the tights and the plaster wrapping and puts them in the bin under the wash basin.

With the dressing applied, Maggie scrubs her hands and returns to the kitchen, sweeps up the broken glass with a dustpan and brush, and then wipes the sticky alcoholic liquid up with reams of kitchen roll. She is in shock, working as quickly as she can to keep the starkly brutal images of Leona and Bex at bay. She mops the floor and hurls the broken glass and kitchen roll into the pedal bin by the back door. As soon as she has cleared up the mess, as soon as the unthinking physical activity is done with, her brain kicks back into life.

"Oh God. Poor loves. Leona and Bex. Billy, oh shit, poor fucking Billy!"

Maggie needs a drink, a real belter, so she goes into the living room and fills a tumbler with brandy. She has a list of people to call and at the head of the list is Jock. She flits from one facet of the story to another, running the thing back and forth through her mind's eye, editing the videotape, muttering to herself as she tries to piece the story back together; corpses, the girls, drugs, and worst of all, the link, there is one certain common factor in the story that stares right back at her.

"Not now, Jock, not now. We're so bloody close. Not fucking now!"

Maggie picks up the phone and hits the automatic memory dialler. Number one. Jock's mobile. As the phone rings she splices the images together in something approaching the right order, a documentary, biased but based in fact. There is no way Jock would rush off like that for a bloody water leak. No way. The deal is simple. One last hurrah. A big summer, sell up and piss off. If he screws up now what's the point. He can't screw it up. He just can't.

"Pick up, you bastard, pick up".

The phone rings out and clicks over to the mobile answering service.

The number you are calling is not available. Please leave a message after the tone. If you want to re-record your message press hash.

The tone. A moment of silence. Maggie feels suddenly impotent, but she focuses and manages to spit her message out.

"For God's sake call me back the moment you pick this up. The girls, Jock, the girls at the club. Leona and Bex. Our Leona. Bex Whitlow. Billy's Bex. Call me back!"

Hands free. Alex Berisa hits the early afternoon snarl in Barnstaple. Sunday is not a day of rest for the contractors working on the western bypass and the new bridge. Alex plugs the lead into his mobile and wedges the small round earpiece in his left ear. The cable tangles with his seatbelt and he has to try again. The traffic edges forward towards the roundabout and lights at Seven Bretheren. He flips open the clamshell and keys in a London number, glancing up in between digits to make sure that he is not going to bump the car in front, an eighties Sierra with a broken offside taillight and more dents than coachwork.

The phone hooks up and he can hear a ringtone. Alex stabs at the volume button on the side of the phone so that he can hear clearly above the noise of car engines. Five rings. An answer phone cuts in.

Hello. I'm sorry but I am unable to answer your call. Please leave a message after the tone.

The accent is unmistakable; Eastern European with a strangely formal telephone manner. Alex curses but waits for the tone nonetheless.

"Xhev, pick up the bloody phone, if you're there. If not..."

Frantic beeps and the sound of a handset being lifted out of a cradle.

"Alex?"

"Of course it's me. It's the work phone."

The voice in the earpiece is slightly distorted. "Okay, okay, how's the weather? How are the girls down there?"

Alex laughs. The man has a one track mind. "No time for girls, Xhev, not today. Look, I need some information. Have you got a pen?"

"No time for girls? You sad Mudack, Alex. Call yourself a man? Yes I got a pen. Fire away."

The line of traffic in front of Alex nudges forward a few car lengths. In the distance the two landward ends of the new bridge stand out against the horizon. In the middle of the estuary the concrete pillar that will support the central section stands bare. A blue van behind Alex crawls up to his bumper, urging Alex to fill the unnatural gap in the line. He waits for a few moments, watching the driver's disembodied arm tap impatiently on the side of the door.

"Xhev, three names. Jock Cascarino, that's C-A-S-C-A-R-I-N-O. Glasgow. Probably seventies. Same place for the others. Surname is McCoist, M-C-C-O-I-S-T. First names are Davie and Ken. Brothers, probably."

The signal dips for a second or two. "...that. Give me about an hour. I'll make a few calls."

"Thanks, Xhev. One more thing. There's a story in the news

this morning, two girls taking drugs in a club in Bideford, called The Basement. Can you check the names of the girls? I got something from local television but could do with confirmation. They're in North Devon hospital. It's probably on the net by now."

"No problem. You think he's still there?"

"Possible. Same old crap. Might just be kids, but it has that smell. You know the smell, Xhev?"

A pause. Alex lets out the clutch and the car rolls forward gently, edging up to the bumper of the Sierra. Three more cars and he'll reach the station roundabout.

"I know. I remember. For Rezarta. For our ray of golden sunshine, Alex. I'll call you back."

The line drops and Alex pulls the headset from his ear and throws it onto the passenger seat. Rezarta. Memories. Triggers. Alex can smell Rive Gauche. She danced like an angel, and smiled like one too. He can see her on a sunlit terrace outside the family home in Gjirokastër, diaphanous, drifting languidly through the early evening, laughing and cajoling. He wants to reach out and touch her.

Reality is the sound of a revving engine and the blare of a horn. The cars in front have moved. The driver of the blue van is so close that he can't pull out and swerve round Alex. The impatient arm is waving a single digit in the mirror. Alex whispers the name of his sister once, and, ignoring the imprecations pouring out of the blue van, he glides the car smoothly up to the roundabout and across the old bridge that leads into the heart of Barnstaple. According to the directions given to him by one of the cashiers at the petrol station at the services where is staying he has to hang a left along the old quay and then follow the signs to the hospital.

The traffic is flowing a little more fluidly now, but the town centre is a mess of small roundabouts and junctions. The blue van has taken a different route. As Alex follows the hospital signs the image of his sister changes. It becomes mechanical, one of drips, saline solutions and sterility. The smell of Arbnor Jasari overpowers Rezarta's favourite perfume and Alex has to open both of the front windows to stop himself from being sick.

The main car park at the North Devon Hospital sits between the accommodation blocks and the entrance to Accident and Emergency. A skeletal hedge is all that shields visitors from the reality of sickness within the buildings. Alex waits. He parks up by the entrance to the car park, well away from most of the other cars, which are crowded around the paths that lead to the main hospital buildings. His eyes are closed and his seat has been pushed back so that he can recline. The windows are shut. Alex looks like any Mondeo rep taking a break at a motorway service station.

A notebook lays open at a blank page on the passenger seat next to his mobile phone and the umbilicus of the hands-free cable. Alex has hung his suit jacket on the back of the passenger seat and the dark weight of the Glock has been spirited away to the glove box. Every so often, in between short bouts of half-sleep, when sounds lose their focus and distance is impossible to judge, he opens one eye and checks the white oval clock on the central dashboard console. Thirty minutes. Forty. Forty-five. Drifting off. Fifty-seven.

The phone rings. It takes a second or two before Alex gets his bearings. The angle of the seat back makes movement difficult and he fishes vainly for the phone, eventually grabs it and flips the clamshell open. The connection is made. Xhevat's voice is small and reedy. Alex fumbles with the earpiece.

"Alex…you there? Alex?"

"Sorry, vëlla, must have dozed off."

"It's alright for some, eh? I've been working my arse off and you've been grabbing some beauty sleep. Still, you need it more than me."

"Yeah, very funny, and you know it's not true. I take it you've got something?"

"I have. Basics first. Got a pen?"

Alex reaches across to his jacket and takes a matt silver ballpoint from the inside pocket. "Yeah, ready."

"Okay. Cascarino. Address. The Byre, Westleigh, Devon. No known address for the McCoists. Cascarino lives with some woman called Heard, Maggie Heard. Owns a pub or a club. Snuggles. Barnstaple. Am I going too fast?"

Alex writes down the name of the club. "No, that's fine, Xhev. Carry on."

"Cascarino is, officially at least, into property. Does up old farms. It seems he sold one of his holiday homes to one Joey Wallace, who got fifteen for importing the white stuff, which is where it gets interesting. Seems your Mister Cascarino has a few connections up here. Once upon a time he was into drugs, girls, protection, you name it. Rumour is that he's selling up. Most of the rackets have been transferred to other interested parties. Liquidated, although he's kept up a small franchise on the clubs. Uppers, downers, E, that sort of shit. Made a big purchase a few weeks ago. You think he might be connected?"

Alex makes notes, picking out the key words and circling them. He draws lines between the circles, mapping out the possibilities. "I don't know yet, but it's possible. The club where the shit happened is supplied by one of his runners."

"Well, you'll like the rest. The McCoists are his muscle. Basic meatheads. Seems all of them hail from the east end of Glasgow. Cascarino was born in fifty-two, usual shit, thieving, getting by, Borstal, gangs, eventually got mixed up with a local family by the name of Defries. Strictly small time. Late seventies it seems he got ambitious, took out a couple of competitors, only he got caught. Check out the scar running down his right side if you get chance. The McCoists were kids at the time, young punks doing a bit of heavy for him. Happily for all concerned he was given a choice; shut the fuck up, serve his time and piss-off or get a bullet. He did five years for manslaughter. When he got out he hooked-up with the boys again and ran. You didn't mess with The Licensee back then. You still don't."

"Thanks, Xhev. Sounds familiar, doesn't it. I've got some errands to run this afternoon, but I'll pay him a call later. Looks like the sort who'd be interested in the doctor. Worth checking out. Did you get the names of the girls?"

"Yeah. The dead one is Leona Jeffery. The one like Rezarta is Rebecca Whitlow. Interesting. I checked the Snuggle's website.

There's a Billy Whitlow on the cabaret, goes by the stage name of Billy Nero. Some sort of singer. My bet is he's related, father or brother possibly."

"Thanks Xhev. As you say, interesting."

"No problem, take care."

"Cheers."

The usual shit, except for Billy Whitlow. Alex grabs his jacket and opens the car door. He leaves the handgun in the glove box. As he walks across the car park towards the entrance to Accident and Emergency a dark blue Vauxhall Astra charges away from the ticket barrier and sweeps past him toward the knots of cars at the far end of the car park. Alex takes a quick step back. It's a good place to have an accident, but not today.

Paper bags full of grease proof paper and cardboard cartons, full of cold French fries and congealing slices of processed cheese, spill out of black and gold municipal bins. Seagulls and crows establish bragging rights over milkshake slops. Carol slams the door of the Range Rover and buckles up, tense and tight-lipped. Dave turns the ignition key and the engine kicks into life. Computer controls and warning lights flash.

Carol fidgets in her seat and turns her head, watching one of the gulls ripping at a slice of crispy bacon. "They're much bigger in real life, aren't they?"

Dave checks the slipway and nudges the car out of the car park. "Sorry?" Sunday afternoon on a retail park. MacDonald's. Temporary satisfaction, either way.

"Seagulls. Bloody great beaks. I don't like birds. Not close up", she explains.

"Can't say I've ever given it much thought. Suppose so."

Satellite navigation. Clear female enunciation. *At the next junction turn right.*

Family hatchbacks full of flat packs. The Sainsbury's store opposite the retail park is buzzing. The Range Rover burns through gasoline in the urban splendour of Roundswell; car dealerships, neon lights and estate houses themed on Spanish villas. At the main roundabout the lady behind the dashboard cuts into the silence. *At the roundabout take the fourth exit.* Dave obliges and is reassured. *You have arrived at your destination.*

The lodge sits behind a Wimpy and a bright red and white signed petrol station. Welcome to a new world of blue painted wood and flat glass walls. Heavy net curtains hang at every window. As Dave and Carol unload the car and carry their disrupted lives with them into reception they're greeted by the hum of vacuum cleaners. A trolley full of towels and sachets of tea, coffee, and sugar has been abandoned by the door through to the guest rooms. A bin on the lower platform of the trolley is full of used towels and bedding. Coffee stains on a pillowcase.

Reception is manned by a young girl, one of a team sharing shifts throughout the weekend. Her badge displays the name Davina, oriental eyes with hair tight at the roots. She has a frilly black scrunchie wrapped around the base of her ponytail. Blonde. Split ends. Short, dirty fingernails.

"Hello?" A slight west-country burr mixed with antipodean inflexions at the end of her sentences. She grates on Carol's sensibilities immediately.

Dave assumes the lead, fulfilling his hunter-gatherer role. Under the circumstances, seagulls and burger bar indigestion included, he is desperate to do something practical, something that might alleviate the sense of voyeurism that has engulfed him since the police called in the dark hours of this seemingly endless Sunday. He yawns.

"Sorry. We'd like a room if you've got one available?" It is a pretty safe opening. He can't help feeling that something more is required, but the girl behind the desk seems happy enough.

"Certainly sir. How long will you be staying?"

Dave puffs out his cheeks and looks across at Carol, who is studying the attractions stacked in a wooden leaflet holder; World of Barometers, Cobbler Honey Farm, Tractorland, Gnome From Gnome. Displacement activity. He is on his own. "Don't know…someone in the family is ill, so could be a few days."

Davina has a script. Item one for *ad hoc* guests is to establish exactly how long they will be staying. The computer requires a round number greater than zero. Her comfort zone is being compromised. "I do need to know exactly how long. It's all computerised nowadays?"

Dave notices the inflexion for the first time. He looks down at the counter, trying not to smirk. "Okay, five days."

"Is that four or five nights?"

"Sorry?"

Carol continues to look at tourist leaflets, although she hardly notices the words and phrases printed on them. Her attention is firmly focused on white paint on the wall by the door, just above the skirting board. Scuff marks. The place has only been open a few weeks and it's already starting to look down at heel. The nature of the trade, Carol thinks, itinerants with thick black rubber soles on their shoes, comfortable shoes.

"Five nights". Dave looks at the girl. Her eyebrows are dark black.

Davina taps on the keyboard for a moment or two. "Smoking or non-smoking?"

Despite the cigarettes and cigars in the car on the way down, neither he nor Carol usually smoke. If the strain gets too much for them they can always pop out to the car park if they feel the need. After dark the Wimpy car park will be full of luridly painted Fiestas and Corsas with polished alloys and drivers wearing Burberry baseball caps.

"Non-smoking", Dave replies.

He can imagine Davina clocking off at the end of another twelve hour weekend shift and climbing into something electrically purple with lowered suspension and bright blue diodes fixed to fake air scoops on the bonnet. The boy will be called Craig. Dave feels bad about the clichés, but as the saying goes, at least Dave's version of it, if the past is another country then the present is Southend on a wet bank holiday. Dave is comfortable, fortyish, and twenty years away from his Ford Cortina days and his Wolfrace addiction.

A few more plastic keys are pressed. "That's fine, Sir, ground floor, non-smoking. How will you be paying?" Dave fishes his wallet out of his jeans and selects a credit card. While the transaction is processed Davina wonders why they are staying here. If it is a family thing shouldn't they be stopping with relatives or with their kids or something. Weird.

Receipts. Instructions. "Through the door, turn left and follow the corridor. You're in number eight, at the end on the right."

Dave stuffs the paperwork into a compartment in his overnight bag and returns the credit card and wallet to his jeans. He nods once to Davina and says, "Thanks". Turning to Carol he asks, "Got what you want?"

She takes a handful of leaflets with her as they push their way through the fire doors and turn left. Numbers on doors. Spyglass. Identical prints on the wall. Everything seems hushed, as if the place is breathing out slowly, preparing for the Sunday night influx of workers. Dave opens the door to their room and Carol, stooping to pick up one of the bags, looks over her shoulder at the door opposite. Number nine. She hopes the occupant is quiet. The last thing she wants right now is a snorer or someone who insists on sitting up late into the night watching television. She shudders. Do they have soft porn channels in places like this?

Dave throws the bags on the double bed and checks out the bathroom. It has been cleaned and everything is in order. "Come on, love, you can have a shower and some sleep." He checks himself slightly. Carol is unlikely to find peace at the moment. "Well, a lie down. It'll do you good."

He pulls the curtains closed and wraps his arms around Carol. The shaking starts. She stifles the tears for a moment, but she can't hold them back for long. Somewhere along the corridor the sound of a vacuum cleaner resumes its low drone and Carol's defensive brusqueness breaks as Dave's shirt absorbs the moisture that spills from her eyes and onto her cheeks.

ON THE STREET WHERE YOU LIVE

THE GLARE OF FLASHBULBS is the last thing Billy expects as he heads down the walkway from the car park towards the main hospital entrance, and he takes a few seconds to realise that his name is being called. The quiet of the early morning, when a local news reporter and the television crews from Exeter were fumbling in the dark, has now been replaced by a small but determined pack of news hounds. The local press have been joined by agents and freelancers from the nationals. Two kids wired up after a nightclub overdose is worth the shoe leather and the petrol receipts.

Déjà vu. Billy gets a momentary flashback; night clubs, the steps of a courthouse in the mid-eighties, being charged and tried for possession. Then he realises that the girl's names must have been released. The reporters from the local rags, who have put two and two together, have given the boys from the red tops the scent of 'D List' celebrity. Billy Nero, The Don of Doo Wap, made famous once more by the vicarious activities of his teenage daughter. Billy can see the headlines. Like father, like daughter.

A shout. "Billy? Billy? Over here, Billy?"

Cameras. A small explosion. Security guards hover just inside the doorway. Innocent visitors get caught up in the moment, rubbernecking, straining to catch a glimpse of the star of the show. One older lady, in a blue rinse and purple stockings, has to grab hold of the parking ticket machine to stop herself from falling onto her already heavily bandaged knee as the small tangle of hot gossip merchants lurches forward. A voice recorder is thrust out towards Billy's face as he tries to turn away, as he tries to hurry past.

Local news; "Billy, how are you feeling?"

Red Top; "How does it feel to have a daughter who's a junkie, Billy?"

Local news; "Anything to say, Billy, come on, mate?"

Red Top; "Is she dying, Billy? Is she a vegetable?"

Billy only has a few steps to go until he is safely inside the hospital reception area. He is chilled to the bone, but not by the baying of the press-pack intrusion. Billy is drawn towards the cameras. He feels the pull of the flash bulbs, like it was seventy-nine, and he wants to stop, wants to make a statement, the statesman, the doting father with a sparkle in his eye, and he is disgusted with himself. Not one of them cares about Bex. Not one of them wants to know what he's been doing all these years, but still he craves the attention.

Collar up, he picks up the pace and pushes past a small family group, muttering curses under his breath, and disappears into the hospital foyer, where the interminably waiting stewed tea and bun brigade stand and stare.

Bex has the easiest ride. It's the waiting game that cuts away your life in small slivers. Carol and Dave kill time with bitter coffee and an old film in a room full of other people's slaked-off skin.

Billy shrugs off the press pack but not the inner loathing around half three, and the innocent are occupied with the wasting of time. Canteens and cheap hotels. Corridors and unfamiliar smells.

Alex Berisa has an alternative way of pacing out the empty expanse of Sunday afternoon. He watches the minor fracas at the hospital entrance from the edge of the car park, and once he is sure that the poor unfortunate soul who sparked off the flash bulbs has gone for good, he follows the signs to the main enquiries desk in Outpatients. Quickly checking the ward names on the board behind the porter's head, he asks for Bassett, explaining that his sister has just had her second little boy. He is directed to the first floor of the Ladywell building on the far side of the hospital, and taking the advice of the porter, Alex heads off in the direction of the link corridor on the ground floor, two floors down from the current level. When Alex looks at him oddly the porter explains that the hospital is built on the side of a hill.

It is, for most wards, a popular time for visiting. There's nothing much on television until after six. The majority of people in the main reception area are middle aged or older, which, Alex thinks, is how things should be. The young have no business getting sick. He thinks again of Rezarta, about the sheer bloody injustice of it all. As he walks through the crowd, heading for the lifts and the central stairwell, he reflects on the case of his intended target; Doctor Arbnor Jasari. This is the sort of place the man should inhabit, but somewhere the wires crossed. Alex has no illusions about the situation. The want of money and the crushing boredom of provincial life make for a poor bedside manner, but there is something else about Jasari, something brutal. The man has never shown an ounce of compassion. How he came to choose medicine as his vocation in life is a mystery to Alex, a puzzle that he's spent too many hours trying to unravel.

He tries to focus on the job in hand. Here and now is not the time for reflection. Ever since Rezarta failed to respond to treatment, Alex and Xhev have pursued a single goal. Since the doctor abandoned the old family business, Alex and his brother have been doggedly persistent in their pursuit. The smell of the man is in Alex's nostrils as he pushes through the swing doors that lead to the main hospital staircase and he heads up to the third floor to start his search for the Intensive Care Unit. Blue signs indicate Capener Ward and Surgical. Choices. Then Alex spots a smaller sign pointing to his right: ICU.

In a vain attempt to soften the clinical nature of the environment the main reception desk is surrounded by fake potted plants, and behind the desk sits one of the ICU nurses, checking notes in a large buff folder. Alex has a thing about young women in blue scrubs. Uniforms. He prefers women dressed when they're not in his bed and this one is a honey, clean and fresh, stripped of make-up and falsehood. It's time for the smile.

"Hi, I wonder if you can help me?" Broad and open. Under the strip lights, which do nothing for pale skin, Alex looks dark and tanned. The girl spends too much time locked away in the low dusk of the dying in the rooms beyond the security doors.

She looks up and returns the smile. "I'll try".

Alex looks round, making a show of confusion, acting dumb, but not too dumb, almost puppyish. "Only I was looking for the, Erm, Intensive care and I seem to be lost."

A slight shake of her head. The grin fades. She has dark brown eyes under a swept back fringe. Brunette. "Intensive care?"

"Yeah". The smile. Full power.

"You've found it. This is ICU, but we don't allow visits until six." She looks Alex in the eye. She has a strong gaze, clear and deep.

Professional, be professional, Alex thinks to himself. Time to play a hunch. "That's fine. Actually I'm looking for my cousin, Mister Whitlow, Rebecca's Dad. Only he's not at home and we're all dreadfully upset about last night." The smile is less intense, headlights on low beam. "I had hoped he'd be here."

The nurse's shoulders drop slightly. Names. The relaxation is momentary. Mister Whitlow doesn't ring true. The Billy Whitlow she met earlier that morning didn't seem to expect formality.

"Are you from the press?" she asks defensively.

Alex is thrown for a moment. He thinks back to the scene

outside the main entrance that he witnessed a few minutes previously and feels a little offended that she could think that. The smile drops away. "No, no, I'm not. Believe me, this is a family thing." Alex can tell by the hardness around the edges of her eyes that she doesn't believe him.

She confirms Alex's impression, reducing the conversation to a formally official negative. "I'm sorry but I'm going to have to ask you to leave. We're very busy. I haven't got time for this." She turns back to the file that she was reading when Alex first approached the desk.

Now or never, thinks Alex, time to get a few things straight. "Look, it's me who should apologise."

The nurse sighs and flashes Alex a hard look that says; I knew it all along. "Would you please leave." She reaches for the telephone receiver. "I'm going to call security".

Alex leans forward. He can smell the alcohol gel on her hands. "Please don't. I'm not from the press. I'm not Mister Whitlow's cousin, either, but I do have some information for him, something that might help, you know, with the police." He looks over at the security doors. "It's wrong, what she's going through. I really do need to speak to him. For her sake. Please?"

The nurse lifts the receiver, but stops before dialling. The look on the man's face touches her. His eyes are on fire. She hesitates and then drops the receiver back into its cradle. "I can't help you. I can't give out personal details of patients or their families. I'm sure you know that."

She pauses, considering, but the way back to official silence is already barred. "All I can say is that he went home to change.

Said he was coming back this afternoon. His first name is Billy, by the way, mid-fifties, pretty trim. If you've really got something useful you might find him in the canteen or you could come back at six. That's all. Now, please leave."

Alex nods and smiles. Six o'clock is out of the question. There will be too many people about, and family too. This time the smile is faint and pained. Alex has carried Rezarta with him for months, determined to see that Arbnor Jasari pays the full price for his cavalier drug-making. Alex has grown cold and hard on a diet of vengeance, but being so close to another victim, to one so young, brings the ache back.

Alex has something to think about on his way down to the canteen. A hunch. Is Billy Whitlow a way to reach Cascarino and Jasari?

Billy has just over two hours to wait until visiting time. Despite his rising antipathy for the lure of the press pack he couldn't think of anything else to do but buy a paper in the hospital shop and now he is sitting in the canteen nursing another cup of coffee. He feels wired, on caffeine overload, but it is better than the void, better than the numb impotence that curls around the edges of his world. He is facing the main serving area at the entrance to the room and tries to lose himself in the football reports, but he's never really followed any one team. The words in the match reports merge together and he can't remember the scores.

The weather is turning. Billy keeps glancing out of the window. He feels like a goldfish in a bowl, peering out at a world that he can't understand, a world for which his own experience strangely provides no point of reference. It should do so given the nature of his personal history. The morning's sunshine has been smothered by a blanket of grey clouds and a breeze is whipping-up stray chocolate bar wrappers in the courtyard. Billy is vaguely aware of someone approaching a table a few metres down from his and asking a question but he doesn't hear what is said. The questioner moves away and looks round the room. Billy is next. He shrinks down into his coat collar.

A soft, sun-tinged voice. "Excuse me, but you wouldn't be Billy Whitlow, would you?"

Silence. Brooding. Billy can see jeans and boots. The bottom of an expensive looking suit jacket brushes against the table. The stranger doesn't move away from the table, which means that Billy is going to have to answer. He looks up into a dark face. Eyes lock.

"No".

It's too late. Billy should have kept on reading the football reports. There is something about the stranger's face, about the way those eyes bore into him, that unnerves Billy. He looks away and pretends to read about Charlton Athletic.

Feet under the table. The jeans and boots disappear as the young man slides in opposite Billy. There is no escape now, save the obvious defence of sheer, barbaric vitriol, a rapier thrust, the ball down to the by-line and a whipped in cross.

"What the hell are you doing?"

A tilt of the head and a smile in return. "Pleased to meet you too, Billy".

"Fuck off. Bloody press. I've got nothing to say. I told your lot out by the main entrance, so just piss off back to whatever shit hole you came from."

Billy stares at the newspaper resolutely. He can see hands, long slender hands, well-groomed and clean. The hands fold into each other.

"I'm not the press, Billy. You don't mind if I call you Billy, do you?"

"Yes I bloody do." Billy can't help but raise his head. The young man has presence and Billy can't help himself. He has to look into those eyes again. Billy can't shake the insane feeling that somewhere behind those eyes there is an answer.

Alex leans forward and whispers. "Sorry. Mister Whitlow it is. I'm not the press, Mister Whitlow. I'm not a nutter and I'm not the police...but I can help you."

Billy leans forward too. Their faces are inches apart. There is recognition, something primeval in the way the two men look at each other and smell one another. The young man has that same cornered animal smell that Billy tried to wash away in the shower, something maleficent, somewhere between terror and desperate fury, only this stranger seems to be able to control of his emotions, to subjugate the primal.

Billy is jealous and awestruck, feeling raw and feral, and now he is caught in the man's headlamp gaze.

"How can you help?" he asks, low and whispered.

"I saw what happened just now, out there. Let's just say I know what you're going through. I have information that might help. Can we talk?"

"Information?" Billy has been so wrapped up in the tragedy of Bex and Leona that he has no idea what the man is talking about. How can information help Bex? "I don't understand. What do you mean, information?"

Alex sits back and checks out the canteen. This is not the place. Alex needs somewhere quiet, away from prying eyes and ears, where he can manage the situation. He recognises in Billy the same confusion and anger that he felt all those weeks and months ago back home on the Adriatic coast. Does Billy have the strength? Can he channel the demons? Alex knows from personal experience that there's no easy path through this, that there's only one way to find out.

"Not here, Mister Whitlow. The car park. I have some papers in the car."

Billy leads the way as they walk through the main hospital concourse, anxious to get on with the business of understanding. Alex hangs back a little, keeping some distance between them. He believes firmly that if you walk slowly then people seem not to notice you. There have been one or two glances directed at Billy as he hurries out through the plate glass doors that lead to the drop off area, glances that follow a marked man. Some of the foyer wanderers recognise Billy from the earlier scenes with the press, while others notice how frightened and nervous he looks.

Once outside Billy stops and turns, but Alex ignores him and walks straight out towards the car park. Before Billy can turn again to follow him he is accosted by the reporter from the local rag. The rest of the pack has disappeared, canteen bound, not expecting any action until the intensive care unit chucks out at around eight o'clock.

"Mister Whitlow? Billy? Anything to say? Come on, give me something."

The economic necessity of world paper shortages and rising print costs mean that the man's face is half hidden by the digital camera that he is using to take shots of a poor, comatose girl's grieving Dad, and Billy, spurning the chance to thrust out a hand and drive the camera back into the man's nose, hurries away from the main hospital entrance, shoulders hunched, almost tripping down the kerb.

Billy is out of breath as he reaches the top of the short rise to the car park, and stumbles, catching his shoulder on the edge of one of the car park ticket machines. He curses loudly, looks round and sees Alex standing next to a parked Ford Fiesta, watching him.

Reaching the stranger, Billy takes a moment to catch his breath before speaking. "You're not from round here, are you?" The question takes Alex by surprise, and Billy jabs him in the chest. "So, who the bloody hell are you?"

Alex takes Billy's arm and leads him across the car park.

"No, Mister Whitlow, I'm not from round here. Not from this country as a matter of fact. As for who I am, it's better you don't know. Not yet."

Billy tries to pull his arm away and Alex releases his grip.

"What the fuck is going on? How come you speak such good bloody English?"

Questions.

As they walk to the far end of the car park Billy fires question after question at Alex but gets no real answers. Members of the general public stop and stare at the two of them as they argue. Alex swears that it will be worth it, but won't say any more in public.

At the far end of the car park Alex flips the Mondeo's remote, climbs in and clears the passenger seat of notebook, pen and mobile phone earpiece. Billy falls into the seat and slams the passenger door.

"So?"

Alex consults the notebook, taking a few seconds to familiarise himself with recently recorded names and circumstantial evidence. It's strange, he thinks, that the world turns but there's never anything new. You clear up one piece of shit knowing that all you have achieved is a moment of sweet air while you wait for the next piece to be dropped in your path.

"Okay, Mister Whitlow…"

"Jesus, cut the Mister shit. You've dragged me all the way out here. You'd better call me Billy."

Alex nods. "Good, Billy. You can call me whatever you like. It's enough you know I'm here and I'm looking for whoever did this to you, to your daughter. First, I have to explain…"

Billy wants a name. Any name. He picks one out of the ether. "Vic. I'll call you Vic."

The song playing in Billy's private sound studio is by Vic Damone. *On The Street Where You Live*. Billy needs a hero.

Alex looks at him and shrugs. "Sure. Look, I'm going to tell you a story."

Billy can't sit still. Caffeine and nerves. The world has stopped making sense. To Billy there is no rhyme or reason, no pattern to day and night. He needs something to hold on to and whoever Vic is, he seems to be the handle.

The words don't come easily. Alex wants to keep the personal nature of the story at arm's length and not just for selfish reasons, but he needs to treat Billy gently. Too much, too soon, and the man will flip. Alex has to judge just how much information will open up the right lines of communication. They need to share a little pain, he decides.

Alex begins. "Late last year my youngest sister, a little older than your daughter, took something in a club and it hurt her very badly. In my own country I found out who made the drugs and tracked him down, but he got away. For the past few weeks I have been following him, following his trail, and I think he's here. I think your daughter has been hurt in the same way as my little sister."

Billy stares at Alex blankly. Thoughts spin around inside his head; is Bex going to get better? Will she be a vegetable? Will she ever wake up? Of course he knew there was a drugs scene in the clubs, there had always been a drugs scene in the clubs, but he never believed that Bex would get involved. That sort of shit happened to other people's kids. How do you deal with this sort of stuff?

So far all that Billy has wanted to do is make time slip backwards, to protect his little girl, but the words sink in and he realises what the man sitting next to him is saying. There's some bastard out there with a name, with a face, alive and kicking, some shit who made the gear that has put his darling girl into a coma.

Alex pauses, letting the confusion in Billy's eyes subside a little, before continuing in a measured and gentle voice. "This man is, or was, a doctor. Hard to believe, I know. He got involved with bad people and made drugs. Makes drugs, I should say. I've tracked him to England and, I believe, here. I have a few leads but I need to check some things. The dealer in the club last night was called Shaun Lloyd. Is that a name you've heard, Billy?"

Billy's mind is blank. He is suffocating under the weight of revelation. He shakes his head slowly. Shaun Lloyd? "No, doesn't ring any bells".

Alex waits to see if the fog will clear. He repeats the name and Billy repeats his answer. Alex moves on. "I have one other name. This one you might know."

Alex pauses and looks at Billy, who is staring straight ahead through the car windscreen.

Alex speaks softly and slowly. " Jock Cascarino".

It takes a few seconds for the name to register and then the impossibility of it overwhelms Billy. Not Jock. It couldn't be Jock. As he repeats the name over and over in his head he realises that it could be and he starts to swoon. His head fills with thick black smoke and everything solid starts to turn to sand, swirling around him in a stinging, biting storm. His skin fades to a pallid white and he feels physically sick, feels the heat rise and sweat break out on his forehead. Something thick and heavy rises in his gullet. Billy turns and stares at the dark-skinned man and tries to scream but there's no sound. He wrenches open the passenger door and leans out. His throat burns and he gags uncontrollably, depositing bile and half-digested coffee over the sill and the tarmac. In his head the music stops.

Alex waits quietly, patiently. In that one moment when Billy looked into his eyes he got what he wanted. It most certainly could be Jock Cascarino. He leans over and puts a hand on Billy's shoulder as the man continues to retch and vomit, but Billy shrugs him off. Alex sits in silence, watching Billy until the spasms abate. Billy clambers out of the car, falling onto his knees. Saliva and bile drip from his chin. He wipes away the mess and then turns and looks back at Alex.

"Fuck off. Just fuck off!"

Alex leans across the passenger seat and grabs hold of the door. "I've got some calls to make, Billy, but I'll be seeing you again. I promise."

The door closes and Alex drives away gently, as if all is right with the world and the heavens are just peachy.

Billy wipes his chin on his coat sleeve and hauls himself to his feet. The afternoon has turned distinctly chilly under the cloud cover and he starts to shiver. His head is full of names and faces; Jock, Maggie, Bex, Carol, the cadaverous boy in the club, Ted Line and his nasty little comments, the McCoists grinning like Cheshire cats, and Leona. Little Leona laid out cold on a slab. Just when he needs the music to drown them all out everything has gone deathly quiet. He staggers back to his own car and, revving the engine like mad, lurches out of the parking bay. At the traffic lights at the entrance to the hospital he turns right and heads away from Barnstaple towards Exmoor.

Muffled but distinct feminine tones. "What bloody time do you call this?"

Jock is halfway out of his jacket. He raises his eyes to the roof of the porch and takes a deep breath before extricating his left arm and hanging the jacket with the other coats on a rack fixed to the wall. He slips his moccasins off before opening a heavy, Georgian-style front door, which is off the latch. The lowering weather makes the hallway of The Byre dark, a darkness made more pronounced by a deep red carpet over which hangs a mood of quietly seething malice. A radiator runs down one side of the hall as far as the door to the kitchen with a slatted cover over it on which sit a collection of miniature cottages and village shops. Jock walks in his socks halfway down the hall and peers around the door into the kitchen.

It dawns on him as he pokes his head round the door frame that the smell of roasting meat is entirely absent from the house. The extractor hood is silent. The steamer sits quietly on top of the gas range. He can hear the clock ticking on the wall as he steels himself for the inevitable rekindling of Maggie's midweek fire. Maggie is perched on a chair by the kitchen table staring straight at him in absolute silence. A bottle of brandy and a half full tumbler are on one of the yellow Royal Doulton placemats. He walks into the room and waits.

Maggie twitches her tail like a hungry cat in a field full of voles. "Well?"

Jock walks around the table and gets another tumbler out of one of the glass-panelled kitchen cupboards. Oak, rustic, with loads of brass.

"Sorry, babe, just lost track. You know how it is."

He walks over to the table and reaches for the bottle of brandy but Maggie clamps her hand around the neck and pulls it toward her chest. It's petty and she knows she will give in, but the look on his face makes it worth it.

"Oh come on, Mags, it's been a hell of a morning. Do you think I like getting called out to deal with this shit on a Sunday?"

Maggie keeps the bottle close. "I know, Jock. Too many years, too much shit. I know what's going on."

She tops her glass up, leaves her seat and goes over to the sink. She leaves the bottle on the table and Jock pours himself a stiff shot. Maggie leans against the worktop and folds her arms.

"As you can see, you'll have to wait for your dinner. Two o'clock... did you get the leak fixed?"

It takes a second or two for Jock to tune in. The leak? "Aye, aye, well, the boys turned the water off. The contractors can do the fixing tomorrow. All sorted. Look, I'm really sorry, babe, but some stuff just has to be done. You know why I'm doing all this. For us, Mags, for us."

He pulls out a chair and sits at the table. There's no need, he thinks, for Maggie to get bogged down in the details, not now it's all sorted.

Maggie is on her third large brandy and she can feel the edges of her thoughts curling up like dry leaves. She has to concentrate to stay cool and focussed. "I know why you're doing what you're doing, Jock." She pauses. "It's the way you're doing it that worries me. Why can't you come home when you say you'll be home?"

Jock drinks and lets the liquid warm its way into his bloodstream. "I said I was sorry. It's just you can't always hurry this stuff. You should have called."

Bait. Maggie sees it hanging in the water. She wriggles away. Still calm, "I did call but your mobile was off." She knows that Jock turned it off because he didn't want to be disturbed with the trivialities of domesticity. "And that's not your first stiff one this afternoon, is it?"

Jesus, thinks Jock, it's like playing fucking chess. The best option is to keep the opening gambit simple. "No, you're right, but I had the boys up to their elbows in shit. The least I could do was pop in somewhere and buy them a drink. Anyway, you've been on the sauce yourself."

She can't argue with that. The boys. Sometimes it seems to Maggie that he cares more for his Glaswegian protégés than he does for her, but she lets it go, preferring to move another pawn into position.

"So, everything's hunky dory out at Brownsham then?"

"Aye. Have it sorted tomorrow, then finish the kitchens. We can get the agents round and start selling the units. Cash in the bank, Mags, one step nearer to sangria and sunshine."

In complete silence Maggie turns and takes the joint of beef from the sink drainer and walks behind Jock. She puts the meat back into the fridge and turns to the cooker. She drains the water from the vegetable pans, kicks down on the pedal bin and empties green beans and carrots into the black plastic mouth of the bin.

"I'm not in the mood. You can get us a Chinky tonight. If you want something now you know where the bread bin lives." She looks at the pan of parboiled potatoes and decides that she can't be bothered clearing them away.

Jock watches in quiet amazement. "You can't waste good food like that."

Maggie walks back to the sink and takes up her former position. Waves of resentment, fuelled by the heat of the alcohol already in her blood, break through. The volume rises. "Your choice. You want roast beef you bloody cook it."

Jock has lived with Maggie for long enough to realise that the conversation so far has just been a preamble, that there's more to come. Trouble brewing. He decides to back off.

"Okay, Chinese it is. They open at five. I can wait. I really am sorry about this morning."

The tipping point.

"Not as sorry as Leona. Not as sorry as Billy's kid, you know, Bex, little Bex."

Jock is confused now. Getting it in the neck for spoiling Sunday lunch is one thing. He can handle that. What the hell it has to do with two silly little girls is another thing entirely.

"Come again?"

It's lame and he has an instinctive feeling that he should be sitting up and taking more notice, but his moral insensibility is ingrained.

Maggie's voice dips again, but this time the words are barbed with vicious steel tips. "The two stupid little girls last night. The club. Your builder mates you were so concerned about this morning. Turns out the girls are our Leona and Bex. Leona is on a slab, Jock, a fucking slab in a fucking mortuary. God knows what poor Billy is going through." The words flow like a tidal bore. "She only came down for a break and some revision. Exams Jock, you know, the things you never bothered with, too busy friggin people over, learning at the university of life. Little Bex, only she's not so little now, got wasted last night. Leona. Sweet, lovely, air-headed Leona has been fucked over for good. That's what I'm on about."

Jock lowers his glass slowly, staring at Maggie, open mouthed. He has no defence. Too late he realises that his pieces are wide open. This is too close to home. He should have something to say, something constructive, an easy way to deflect, but all he can manage is, "Fuck!"

Maggie leans forward so that Jock can hear her clearly. Her head is suddenly very clear and her tongue has lost the rough edge induced by the brandy.

"The point is, Wee Man, that your leak might turn into a bloody great flood. This isn't Noah's Ark, Jock, this is one hundred percent drowning. Do you understand me?"

Jock feels like a naughty schoolboy caught nicking milk cartons for his poor mother. His knees go weak and he can feel the blood in his veins pumping harder and harder. It makes him feel faint. He finishes the glass and waits for the relief to set in but it doesn't come. Random thoughts spill out of his mouth and across the kitchen table; too close to home, that bastard Shaun, that fucking incompetent Spic doctor, what am I going to do? What am I going to do? His mouth is still wide open. His eyes have glazed over.

Maggie's head is now very clear and ordered. Since she heard the radio bulletin she has had time to think. She knows who Jock is, she understands his hinterland and his history, and has lived with him through the inevitable darkness induced by his business interests. Maggie made a choice when her husband went away, when he was given the ultimate choice, and nothing is going to get in the way of the good times. She has worked too hard.

"What you're going to do, Jock, is sort it. I've worked my arse off all these years and I'm not going to let you screw it all up now. I don't care how you sort it, I don't care what you have to do, but I'm not throwing all this away because you've got careless. You close down your little project, Jock, do you understand me? No more sodding gangster shit. Get rid of it. We'll have more than enough from the properties and the club."

A keen sense of self-preservation is a necessary part of survival in the underbelly of the world. Jock starts to catalogue his options, thinking aloud.

"Can they trace anything?"

Maggie can feel the alcohol kicking back in and she feels suddenly very weary. She sits heavily in her chair.

"You tell me, Jock, you tell me. The radio said there was a new drug. The Old Bill are bound to work that one out given enough time."

Jock's fingers are tapping out an irregular rhythm on the pine tabletop. He starts to pick at a scratch on the edge. Thinking by numbers. Reading aloud.

"Aye, they'll work the club, get names, the dealers. If they do that properly then everything unravels. Can't pay to keep that clean. Liquidation's the only way. Whole kit and caboodle. Still, everything's in one place, on ice till the morning. The only real link to us, to me, is that lanky git, Lloyd, but he's already taken care of. I need some time to think, Mags. I need tonight. Got to cover it all off. Do you think that's possible?"

Maggie swirls the last of her brandy round in her tumbler. "That you can sort it out or that the police will crack it overnight? I don't know, Jock, but I don't imagine the boys in blue will be knocking on our door just yet, not if everything's already on ice, like you say it is."

The look of panic on Jock's face is infectious. Maggie can feel her own heart fluttering. Could they really lose it all now?

Jock takes a deep breathe.

"Aye, lucky and safe. That's always been the way. Everyone who knows about this is under lock and key, well out of harm's way. I'll need to make some calls and speak with the boys, but we can get it sorted first thing tomorrow. Right now I need another drink and some time to think. Do they deliver out here? I can't remember."

Maggie thinks for a moment and then gets up and fishes a menu out of a pile of paperwork at the end of one of the worktops.

"Yes. Taxi. Any idea what you want?"

WAR AND PEACE

BEYOND THE IMMEDIATE SPRAWL of the hospital buildings Barnstaple fades quickly in Billy's rear view mirror, not that he is at all aware of the mirror, signal, manoeuvre process. Images of Bex merge with shots of junkies in their Trainspotting brutality; threadbare interiors, screams and shouts, blue lights, shadows, blank faces, anonymous dealers, and spliced into the sequence he sees Jock Cascarino's smug face as he tells Billy to buck-up his ideas and get a plan. A plan. Billy can barely see the road through his tears. Planning requires forethought and Billy is running on blind instinct.

Houses give way to fields, to the high banked hedgerows of the rural Devon landscape, to broken down fences and dilapidated field gates. Trees, where they stand in thin knots, are bent and misshapen, pointing out the path of least resistance to Atlantic squalls. Global warming turns Easter daffodils paper brown. Clumps of primrose are already bursting through the early grass heads as cows lay down in fields under a changing sky. Late lambs follow their mothers, blissfully unaware that this brave new world of ovine possibilities and green, green grass is short on time. Billy wipes a sleeve across his face and gets a noseful of his own odour, of dried bile and mohair. Lambs to the slaughter. The images of Bex in her hospital bed, wired and comatose, loop back inside his head and the tape plays again, but there's still no soundtrack.

Diversification. A neatly hand painted sign outside a farm entrance proudly boasts that you can hire ball gowns and hats as well as buy the obligatory free range eggs. Billy reads it as he flashes by and he starts to laugh out loud. Ludicrous bloody people. The madness of taffeta and slurry cuts into his thoughts; maids a-milking dressed in chiffon and silk, wearing elbow length gloves and tiaras. Billy has to jink right as he approaches a hard right hand bend, narrowly avoiding the chevron signage in the hedgerow, and, oblivious to the state of the road behind him, he slams on the brakes, white lining, and slides to a halt. Autopilot kicks in. He manages to edge the car onto the hard packed ruts of a field entrance and, bending forward, he rests his head on the soft plastic of the steering wheel. The car lurches and stalls as Billy's foot slips off the clutch, its bonnet buried in a thickly matted wall of hawthorn and beech.

Billy sits hunched over the steering wheel for five minutes, letting the tears fall. He gulps back the sobs, but his entire being is in shock. He wants Bex to wake up so badly and tries to imagine her opening her eyes, tries to will her awake. Every time he sees her invented face open its eyes he also sees his dishevelled self-sitting by her bed holding her hand, but no matter how many times he wills her back into the waking world, the daydream is spoiled, is broken apart. Every time that Bex wakes, Jock walks into the room and whispers in Billy's ear; 'Got to have a plan, Billy, got to have a plan'. Strangely the dream Jock has no trace of his usual Glaswegian guttural harshness.

The road is quiet and Billy is vaguely aware of bird song, of blackbirds and robins marking territory and singing out loud to keep their tiny little hearts from bursting. A couple of cars whoosh by, the occupants clearly unwilling to take to notice of the shape of a man's torso abandoned in the cockpit of an old blue Vauxhall Astra that is wedged into greenery. Eyes front. Ignore it and it never happened. Except that the third car to approach Billy's hedgerow head butt slows as it passes, flashing brake lights in the late afternoon gloom. A question. The answer, however reluctant, is given with hazard warning lights and the whine of a transmission in reverse. The car draws level with Billy's Vauxhall and the driver and his passenger peer in through Billy's window.

Contact. A tap on the glass. Billy sees dashboard lights swimming in front of him. His car is still in gear, with partial ignition engaged. He powers down his window and looks out, red eyed and snivelling. He sees a man and a woman looking back at him, the man leaning forward in his seat to get a clear view past his partner. A wife, Billy guesses, and he tries to smile, returning a small sliver of basic human kindness that, for once, Billy recognises through his tears.

"You alright mate?" A Welsh accent. Holiday makers probably.

Billy is transfixed. How the hell do I answer that, he thinks? Faces stare at him from the shadows. He has to find an answer. "Yeah, thanks, yeah I'm fine. Just needed a... in gear, foot slipped. I'm fine, really".

"Only you don't look so great. Sure we can't help?"

Billy reaches down into the driver's door pocket and fishes out a burger bar napkin; a souvenir of one road trip or another. He blows his nose. He sounds nasal.

"Really, thanks, both of you. Anyway, you don't want to hang around. Some dick-head'll shunt you up the rear. Please..." A star of stage and screen smile this time. "...thanks, but I'm okay."

The woman moves away from Billy, pressing herself back into her seat. She won't say anything until she and her husband are back on the road with the windows powered up and with the safety of half a mile of tarmac between her and the crude mouthed yokel. That's the trouble with holidays. The natives need your money but resent your presence. Her husband nods to Billy.

"No problem. As long as you're okay".

The window, under his wife's control, slides shut almost as soon as he finishes his last sentence. He checks his rear view and side mirrors, indicates and pulls away smoothly.

As the sound of the Good Samaritan's engine fades into the daffodil banks Billy lets birdsong wash over him. The shrill repetitions break the rhythm of the dream, and he sits back and looks at himself in his own rear view mirror.

"This is no good Billy, my old son, no good. As that scheming Scots bastard says, I need a plan. First of all, though, I need a drink."

It takes two attempts to reverse the car out of the hedge. Billy finally gets himself together and, driving with a little more of the required due care and attention, he turns the car around in the next farm entrance and heads back into Barnstaple.

At the traffic lights by the entrance to the hospital Billy intends to hang a left so that he can be with Bex, but as much as he thinks about indicating and joining the filter lane his hands refuse to obey and he heads straight on into town. He could turn round and double back at any one of the inner ring of roundabouts, but he doesn't. He drives along the quay and swings up past the Seven Bretheren retail park, up the hill opposite the new bypass and on towards Roundswell.

At the Fremington junction he makes a firm decision to take the first exit and hit the main trunk back to Bideford. He has time for a wash and brush up before seeing Bex and he wants to look his best when she wakes, which she surely will. Instead, his hands keep the steering wheel pointing straight ahead and he drops down into Bickington and then Fremington, where he pulls into an off road parking area in front of a Spar shop. He hasn't eaten all day and his stomach is screaming at him. He decides that he needs something to line his gut before having that drink.

The sandwiches look as though they have been on the shelf since Friday morning, but beggars can't be choosers. Billy's body is telling him that he needs something with starch and carbohydrates, so he selects the least offensive option; tuna and cucumber, together with a packet of salt and vinegar crisps. At the checkout he gives the spirits a quick once over and asks for a bottle of Fundador. The girl behind the counter gives him one of those 'poor sod' looks as she hands him his change, but Billy ignores her. Perfunctory manners. A mumbled thanks and he's out of the door and back in his car, driving hard for home where he will have a quick shot with his sandwich, wash and then hit the road again. He doesn't care about having the odour of brandy fumes on his breath when Bex wakes up.

The reason that Billy rarely takes the Fremington road is because of the speed restrictions, forty miles per hour all the way. It's not even as though the view makes up for it, he thinks. It's all bungalows and boats with flowers in them on street corners. He trundles through Instow in a pulse of traffic, holiday weekenders heading back to caravan parks, and tries to decide whether to cut up to the main road or drive down through East-the-Water and over the old bridge. Before he comes to a decision he finds himself turning off at the sign for the Exeter Inn. A quarter of a mile up a narrow, twisting lane there is another sign, half buried in sprouting greenery, that bids him welcome to Westleigh.

The lane splits at the start of the village and Billy takes the left fork, manoeuvring slowly through the narrow streets. Cottage walls bulge into the constricted lanes, and he eases the car round each corner, expecting to meet a four-by-four at every blind spot. He passes the pub and snatches a glance through one of the windows. He would love to stop and have a long cold pint of cider, letting the close confines of old wood and brass wrap him up like a corpse in a coffin, somewhere to rest and sleep, but he has to get home. He drops a gear on the hill rising out of the village and points the car in the general direction of Bideford, but the innocence of his journey is fading. Billy knows this road.

Just outside the village, on a lightly wooded hillside, there are a series of large houses, each with the obligatory shingle driveway full of Sunday's bright and gleaming German engineering. The houses are a mixture of thirties interpretations of the arts and crafts movement and more modern boxes designed to show the character and originality of their owners. One has fake Doric pillars either side of the heavy, wooden front door. The last of these houses breaks with automotive tradition. A silver Lexus is parked in front of a double garage.

As Billy slows and lets his idling engine drag the Vauxhall up to the entrance to The Byre, he sees, through the thickening foliage of ancient rhododendrons, snatches of the good life; brick and timber, dark wooden frames around the windows, which are Georgian in style with multi-paned panels of glass. There is a pair of five bar gates across the main drive, both of which are open, and as Billy passes he sees a taxi turning in front of the house. Lights are on in the kitchen.

Billy knows the basic geography of the place. Being one of the select few at Snuggle's, the lock in few who are mates with the owners, has its advantages; summer barbecues, Christmas parties and informally alcoholic dinner parties. Billy endures these minor social events because it brings him closer to Maggie, and he also has to admit that he loves the house, although he finds the contents a little twee. In the late hours, when he, Jock and Maggie have sat nursing tumblers of liquid gold, Billy has often wondered why people collect anaemic porcelain figurines and display them in wall cabinets. It hardly fits with Jock's external persona.

Reality bites. The trance is done with. Thinking about the white and grey porcelain figures waltzing under a G-Plan spotlight brings Billy back to the conversation he had in the hospital car park. He snaps his head away from the view, changes gear, accelerates slowly and pulls into a small car park in the woods, the sort of place frequented by dog walkers in daylight and hurried lovers by night. With twilight rapidly approaching the space is empty. He parks up and sits for a few minutes, letting the ticking of the cooling engine mark out his time.

Without music in his head Billy can't stand the silence. He starts to talk to himself as he breaks open the plastic triangle containing his sandwich.

"How could it be Jock? Maggie? Does she know? Of course, she doesn't, how could she?"

The edges of the bread are hard and starting to curl. Definitely Friday's stock. Billy wolfs down both of the sandwiches in sixty seconds flat.

"I know, I know, Jock's a cunt, but he's not that sort of cunt. He wouldn't do it, not to Bex, not to Leona...would he?"

The screw top snaps away from the metal ring around the neck of the brandy bottle. Billy absent-mindedly checks the centre console and the glove box, looking for a glass, before remembering where he is. He up ends the bottle and takes a long, hot swig.

"Shit. I mean, who was that guy this afternoon, anyway?"

The conversation replays in Billy's head as he takes another gulp and then another.

"Jesus. I called him Vic".

Billy is freeing his mind, letting the thoughts flow through him in rapid, staccato succession. He thinks out loud, communing with no one, with nothing that matters, revealing to the woods, the badgers and the bats a simple logic.

"It's too bloody fantastic, too much of a coincidence, except… except the look in the man's eyes, Jesus, did you see those eyes. Shit, if it was my sister I'd want the bastard responsible."

It dawns on Billy that he hasn't got a sister. He is an only child. He has a daughter, and that burns his soul far more deeply than the cheap Spanish hooch burns in his throat.

Snuggle's has lost none of its glamour in the week since Billy's last performance. If anything the smoke aged patina of the ceiling seems a little darker and a little thicker, but maybe that's just a trick of the light on a quiet night. Sunday night is a wind down, a chance for the odd local and Ted Line to down a few more bevvies before the week starts rolling. There isn't a single person in front of the bar under the age of fifty. Not one of them has an early morning alarm set. Ken McCoist is on duty behind the bar, Sunday nights being part of the deal; free accommodation and food in return for simple menace and a shared shift on the pumps with Davie. Ted is perched on Maggie's stool at the end of the bar by the main door, wreathed in smoke which curls around the tassel fringes of a red-shaded table lamp.

One of the locals walks in, early doors, red faced with the exertion of the walk from the family hearth, and stands at the bar by Ted.

"Pint please, Ken"

He turns to Ted and unzips his fleece to reveal straining shirt buttons barely containing the enthusiastic expanse of his belly.

"Shit, d'you 'ear about them girls? Leona, they say". Mickey's accent is broad and obvious, even when he's trying to be measured and sombre.

Ted has been thinking about nothing else all day, or more precisely, how to turn the situation to his advantage. Like everyone else he was upset when he found out just how close to home it all was, but he hasn't let it get under his skin. They say that if you talk to enough acquaintances and friends you'll find a link to pretty much everyone else in the world. The proximity of death has, Ted believes, made things that much simpler, especially where Billy is concerned.

He acknowledges his impromptu drinking partner. "Yeah. Tragic, Mickey, tragic. Poor lass. And Bex, you know, Billy's girl, she's the other one."

Ted can hear the sound of air being sucked in through clenched teeth. Ken places a pint of bitter on a towel on the bar.

"Cheers, Ken. What about you, Ted?" The inside track is lubricated with a large one. "Billy's kid? Jesus."

A twitch of the head in the direction of Maggie's office.

"So, how's Mag's taken it? You know, with Leona gone and Billy being a mate and that?"

Ted's top-up appears and Ken hands Mickey his change. Ted downs the last of his old drink and immediately takes up the new glass.

"Cheers, Mickey, you're a gent. Difficult to say, really, except she called in this afternoon. You know what women are like. Too upset to come in. Ken's had to open up and everything."

Ken tips Ted the wink and busies himself with glasses. The old duffers are going to rattle on about it whether he likes it or not so there's no point in saying anything. Ken doesn't want to get involved in the speculative, alcoholic rumblings of the walking dead. There's every likelihood that there will be enough of that in the morning. Jock has called in too. Crack of dawn stuff. Sale of the century. End of the line. Everything must go.

Mickey pulls up a bar stool. "So, what 'appened?"

Ted looks into Mickey's eyes and sees the glossy shine of expectation. Insider dealing. The redness in Mickey's cheeks is fading, leaving the veins on his nose as a rough guide to the state of his liver and coronary function.

"Well, pretty much what they said on the telly. I don't know what goes on in these clubs, it's not like when you and me were at it. Well, don't know about you, but I was up in the smoke then and you could get a bit of dope and stuff, but I was doing the clubs up north by eighteen. Missed out on the summer of love."

Mickey is nodding. They're both of an age that has shared the vicissitudes of the Three Day Week, the Winter of Discontent and New Labour's protracted birth pangs amid Thatcher's dose of social realism, but the horizons on view throughout their shared histories have been very different. Mickey worked the farms, milking and labouring, while Ted steamed forward on the light entertainment express to Eastbourne, Morecambe and Scarborough. It doesn't seem to bother them when they reminisce, that Mickey manned the secondary strikers' barricades while Ted was a true blue supporter of capital punishment. In these fading years they can share a drink and these days Ted does most of the milking.

"Anyway, as I was saying, seems they were stacked-up to the eyeballs. God knows what's in the stuff they take these days. I mean, LSD could be a bit shit, but we weren't fucking idiots, no disrespect, but it's all synthetic crap these days. I'm sorry, of course, especially for Leona. She did a good job, in a basic sort of way, and was always very… erm…pleasant, but kids, eh? They never think about anyone else. I mean, what about her mum and dad, and Billy?"

Mickey leans in closer and tries to whisper, but the rest of the drinkers, should they wish to, can hear every word that he says. "I know. My own lad, well 'e don't do that sort of stuff, but 'e does smoke a bit a pot. Tells me I should, like, for me arthritis, but I tells 'im a pint and a fag'll do me fine, so long as I'm able. I don't reckon 'e's…"

Ted has his back to the door, but can feel the draft as it opens. Mickey stops talking in mid-sentence and looks over Ted's shoulder. The other drinkers in the bar, mostly solitary males, are all drawn to the stranger entering their domain. Only Ken seems to welcome the intrusion.

"Evening. What can I get you, pal?"

Alex wants to laugh. The bar looks like a waiting room for the terminally depressed, somewhere that the Grim Reaper might park his latest charges while he goes off to collect the rest of the damned. Tired is a word that Alex would use about his home country. Snuggle's isn't tired; it's amateurish. God knows, he thinks, as he smiles and walks up to the bar, but is it any wonder Jock's selling up. He returns Ken's greeting.

"Hi, just an orange juice, please".

Raised eyebrows amongst the hardened drinkers. Ken grins at one of the guys at the bar. "Coming up. On your own?"

The stranger is a good looking man, early thirties and Ken wonders whether he has a bird in tow.

"Yeah, just me. Down on business. I heard there was music here?"

Ken takes a closer look at the man. He's not just good looking. You do enough weights, spend enough time in gyms, and you get to recognise the signs. His neck. The wrists. The stomach. The man works out.

"Not on a Sunday, pal. Wednesday through Saturday there's something on every night. Sunday we're just a pub." Ken points at a couple of the men at the bar. "Hardly what you'd call night life". Ken drops ice cubes into a half pint glass and pours two bottles of fruit juice into it, holding both bottles by the neck with one hand. "Two quid, please".

The silence worries Alex. He needs people to talk. A quick glance around the bar reveals a world of lonely pints and silent boredom. A middle aged couple are pumping coins into a fruit machine. It's the only sign of life.

"Nice place. Yours?"

A snort from the end of the bar. Ken scowls.

"No, I just work here. Owner's night off"

Ted raises his glass to the stranger. "Yeah, nice place. Threadbare fucking carpets, the stage is wank and the boss pays peanuts. It's a really nice place."

Ken looks over at Ted and shakes his head. To the stranger he says, "Pay no attention to him. He's pissed."

Alex looks quizzical. "Already? It's only seven."

"Aye, but he's been on the sauce. Park benches probably. Sherry and cider mix."

Ted, glass in hand, stands up, pats Mickey on the shoulder and walks over to where Alex is standing. He has to look up to speak to the man.

"Not true. Not today." He tries to give Ken a withering look, but it falls on stony ground. "Things to think about today". He taps the side of his nose.

Ken is having fun. Ted-baiting. It livens up a Sunday night once in a while. "The only thing you think about is which way up you have to sit when you need a shit." To Alex he says, "Stupid old bastard. I don't know why the boss puts up with him."

"Because, my friend, I am the best bloody comedian in Barnstaple". Ted thrusts out a hand and Alex grips it firmly. Ted winces but soldiers on. "Ted Line. You may have heard of me. The Bread Line. Saturday night variety shows and all that."

He downs the last of his scotch and places the glass firmly on the bar, ensuring that Alex has no option but to notice.

Alex duly obliges. "Another?"

"Don't mind if I do, thank you. Mickey, you alright back there?"

Mickey takes his cue, walks up and joins the group. A regular party. Alex buys drinks all round, including a half for Ken, and then decides that orange juice is out of place. He orders a vodka. Neat. An hour passes during which Alex gets Ted's life story, with interjections about local farming history and the kids from Mickey. Ken gradually loses patience as Ted begins to lose the thread of stories but continues to take his drink on the strength of the stranger's money.

"…which is how, how, I ended up here."

Ted has finally got to the twenty-first century. Mickey has filled his boots and toddled off home. By now Ted and Alex are perched on bar stools, with Ted looking distinctly worse for wear. Alex has matched him, shot for shot, and still looks as sober as the day is long.

"It's a nice place, Ted, I mean, it's not the Pallodeon…?"

"Palladium".

"Palladium, sorry, but it's alright. Sort of family, which is good at your age."

"Might be a nice place, might very well be, if it weren't for the Scots git. If I had my way I'd bury him, I would. Big Ken over there, he don't like it when I say things like that, but fuck him, fuck him with a pitchfork, that's what I say. Sideways. It'd be alright without the Wegie scum. Him and his deals. Sitting at the bar being rude when I'm on stage. Forty-five years, man and boy…"

Ken is no longer amused. Without the distraction of too many other punters, Ted Line is now most definitely the focus of his attention and Ken is getting really pissed-off. Ted is verging on the indiscreet. Ken doesn't care if Ted drinks to oblivion as long as he keeps away from certain subjects. It's like Wednesday night and the business with Shaun. The old bugger is becoming a liability, one that he and his brother are probably going to have to deal with.

"You're getting boring now, pal. I'm sure your new friend has heard it all before." Ken mouths the word sorry to Alex.

"My new friend." Ted considers the phrase for a moment. "My new friend. Can't be calling him that. What's your name?"

Always a tricky one, but Billy Whitlow has given Alex his name for the day, "Vic".

"Vic. Good name. Vic. Well, Vic, a blind's as good as a wink to a dead horse. It's like them girls, the dead ones. See, there's always a link."

"A what?" Alex looks to Ken for some help.

Ken has heard enough. This is getting too close to the bone.

"That's it, Ted. You've had enough. Time to go home."

It's not a polite end to the evening. Ken has a way of speaking, a way of making his intentions clear to people that leaves nothing to the imagination. This will all go back to Jock.

Ted finally gets the message. He manages to put his forefinger to his lip at the second attempt, and then as he slides off his stool he says, "Nice to meet you, Victor. Victor, Victoria. Good film, that. Maybe see you here Wednesday. Battle of the…whotsits. Yours truly doing the proper job. Ta ta."

Ted continues to slide all the way to the door, where, having fathomed out the intricate operation of the swing handles, he pulls his jacket collar up and weaves his way out into the night.

Ken wanders up to the end of the bar where Alex is sitting. "Sorry about that, pal. He's fucking lost it. Used to be quite good back in the seventies, but he's a complete waster now. Off his trolley. The boss keeps him on 'cos she's sorry for him. Same again?"

Alex shakes his head. "Not unless you're doing coffee?"

"No, kitchen's closed and the machine's buggered, sorry."

Alex hangs around for another five minutes, just long enough to seem relieved that Ted has finally disappeared. As he chats to Ken about training regimes and about how he will need a full session to work off the vodka, he puts the pieces together; Snuggle's, Jock and Maggie, one half of the brothers McCoist and a pissed-up comedian who seems to know something. Alex recognised the look on Ken's face when Ted was harping on about dead horses, the sort of look that you give a man who doesn't yet know he's going to get a solid beating.

"You off then?" Alex clears away the last shot glass.

"Yeah. Thanks, and don't worry, he hasn't put me off. I'm sure he's very professional on stage."

"No. No, he isn't, but he'll retire soon. I think the boss has just about had enough. I know I have."

Alex takes his final bow, "Yeah, know what you mean. Cheers."

He walks out into the car park and fumbles in his jacket for his keys, feeling slightly muzzy, but he can still function. It's all about training. Anything other than vodka and he'd be on the floor. It's a family trait. He drives out of the car park and heads slowly into town looking for an old comic who is having trouble walking. An act of charity. Maybe the old rogue would like a lift home?

Helen is sitting on the edge of one of the camp beds, letting the tensions of the last couple of hours dissipate. She looks down at her bare feet. She has black ringed toes where the dirt from the lower barn floor has become ingrained. The doctor has eased the pain a little and she is feeling calm again now that she is back in the light.

Doctor Jasari is torn between two conflicting emotions and it is all that he can do to ask a civil question. "Is he alright down there?"

He left Helen down in the darkness for an hour after the Cascarino boys departed and memories of the other boy have unnerved her, even though Shaun was far more talkative and comprehensible in his urgent whispering of escape plans. Shaun seemed to assume that she would be on his side, but all she wanted was some light, and the simple ease of chemical contentment.

The doctor has thought things through since the visit. Shaun Lloyd is the least of his problems. The boy can rot for all he cares, which is a symptom of the conflict that he feels inside. Leaving the boy to rot is inconsequential. It's the fact that he cares about this girl that doesn't make sense. This is basic jealousy, he tells himself, and he can't help colouring at the thought of Shaun and Helen alone together. The boy will rot.

Helen is easing down now that she has her synthetic happiness in train. "Yeah, yeah. He looks like he needs a good night's sleep."

The conversation feels stilted and awkward. She and the doctor sit slightly apart, feeling their way across the distance that Jock and his splintered visit has introduced between them. Most of the production equipment has been stacked on a couple of tables at the far end of the upper barn room. The two central tables have been cleared of the drug sachets, which are in their tubs on the floor in front of the cells. On the tables the doctor has laid out a holdall, clothes, two piles of dollar bills, a cobbled together collection of syringes and bottles, and his Beretta with its single clip of ammunition holding two bullets.

Break point. Helen watches the doctor as he packs his clothes, wrapping the American currency in his boxer shorts. He puts all but two of the syringes into a plastic carrier bag before filling the remaining two from one of the small, dark brown bottles on the table. He sheathes the needles in their plastic covers. The process of packing-up has an air of finality about it that is mirrored in his eyes.

Helen wonders who the syringes are for. Two. Janet and John come tumbling down the hill.

The doctor reads her mind. "No, Helen. You're coming with me." He smiles and puts the syringes back onto the table. "Insurance. Now, let's get you sorted, yes? What clothes have you got?"

It's a simple answer. Helen has the clothes that Davie brought over; a couple of tee-shirts, a pair of jeans and her trainers, two pairs of knickers and the bra she was wearing when she arrived. The sum total of her life. She packs them on top of the doctor's clothes in the holdall.

The doctor continues to pack away the tools of his trade as he speaks. "Over there in the desk drawer you'll find your purse and some money. Take one of the kitchen knives and put it in this jacket." He hands her a man's suit jacket from a coat rack by the door. "You'll need a jacket when we go away."

Helen does as she is told, as she has done for the last week, palming a few sachets of Bliss with the doctor's consent and stuffing them into the jacket along with a dull edged paring knife. She knows that she will need some relief, something to cover-off the stress.

With everything packed and the Beretta tucked safely in his jeans, the doctor goes to the kitchen and fetches the last bottle of red wine and two glasses, which he wipes on the bottom of his shirt. They sit on the edge of the table, next to the holdall. The tension between them is not as acute as it was when Helen first emerged from the lower barn, the packing has helped, but there is still a sliver of ice to melt.

"Are you going to tell me what you're thinking, Arbnor?" asks Helen, as the doctor pours wine into the glasses.

Helen edges along the table so that her left shoulder and hip touches the man that she is coming to rely on. He has, in his own way, treated her better than most of the shits out on the street, not exactly as an equal, but he does seem to recognise her humanity. It's a crazy, screwed up world, she thinks. I'm lost in a fucking nightmare and I've never felt this safe, not for…not since…

The doctor drains his glass of wine in one gulp and refills. He likes the feeling of Helen's body next to his. Thinking through the likely outcomes after Jock's last visit, he almost decided to cut free and leave everything behind, including Helen, but the thought was never serious. She has become part of his life, a part that he wants to keep warm and alive. For the sex?

Certainly, but she is more than that. He needs someone to hold his hand from time to time because she wants to and not because he has paid for it. He knows, in his heart, that he is paying this time as well, but not in hard currency. The dependency is different and if he is totally honest with himself, he likes the element of control.

He looks her in the eye and says, "It's all screwed up, Helen. I don't mean the girls. Shit happens. Of all people, you know that. It's Jock who is fucked up. He's just small-time. He panics, can't think straight, and he's going to get us all in trouble. I told you about Tirana, about the prison. Never again. Never. You and me, we take off."

Helen looks into his eyes. "Now? This minute?"

He shakes his head. "No car. We need to get out, to a city, to a proper place, London or Birmingham, but if we steal a car out here everyone will know about it. I've been thinking it through. When they come back tomorrow, we'll be ready."

He pats the two loaded syringes.

"The gun is okay but it makes too much noise. We'll empty these into them. Nice and quiet. Very quiet. Forever. Do you understand?"

She knows. She remembers the baying of the slaughtered in the barn.

"What's in them?" she asks, picking up one of the two syringes.

"You really want to know?"

Helen nods.

"Okay. It's a mixture. MDMA, methamphetamine and cocaine.

Very pure, very highly concentrated. Empty one of these into a main artery and you'll give someone permanent brain damage or a heart attack. They'll be out of it in seconds, dead pretty quickly afterwards. Inject into muscle and it takes longer but the effect is probably the same."

Helen shivers and the doctor takes her hand in his and squeezes it gently. "Yes, you see, they'll be very nervous, jumpy, making mistakes. We'll get out, take our chance, and, I think, because of that lovely yellow stuff over there, they won't have told anyone where they are going, so we'll be free for a few hours, maybe a day or two. Jock's car will be clean for a while, so we should have enough time to get away. The basics are simple. If we don't do this, then we'll be joining the bodies in the pit."

Helen stiffens.

"The question, Helen, is this. Will you come with me? Will you, if I ask you, help me kill them?"

This is it, this is the point of no return. She thinks of films full of grim heroines, in particular Ripley and the alien mother, sees herself as the little girl screaming in the lift. Life on the street. Decisions. Self-preservation. It should be a simple answer. Choose life. She imagines the tip of the needle breaking skin, sliding into muscle, the bulge where the liquid pools as she presses on the plunger, and the spasms, a face, a rictus grin. She can feel a tear on her cheek as she starts to nod slowly. She whispers her answer softly. The words, spoken too loudly, would change their fate.

"Yes".

The doctor shifts, crooking one leg up onto the table so that he can face her. He leans forward and takes both of her hands in his.

"Look at me."

She stays stock still for a moment.

"Look at me, Helen."

She moves slowly towards him until her eyes lock onto his. His face is long and thin, his hair receding and lank, unlike anyone that she has ever been close to before, but his eyes pierce her. He looks so intense and there is something in his eyes, something in the soothing way that his voice modulates, that draws her in.

"Good girl. You're my good girl."

He cups her chin with his left hand and draws her face to his. She closes her eyes as he bends his head forward and kisses her on the lips. Their smells mingle and he tastes the salt water on her cheek.

"In my own way, you know, I love you…" he says, and he too sheds a tear.

MUSIC FROM BEYOND THE MOON

ALEX BERISA IS CRUISING, kerb crawling in the sodium glow of evening as the provincial streets wind down towards late night walks, the pad of paws and the rustle of plastic bags. Pubs hang on the cusp of closure, barren underneath their illuminated signs, weary of a week that has run on too long, stale and stained. Alex Berisa scans the thin filaments of life on the streets, looking for the tell-tale flicker of old skin.

Ted is on autopilot, swinging through the blue street-side shimmer of late night television, Midsomer Murders and Melvyn Bragg. He is slow and slightly unsteady on his feet. His hands are thrust into his jacket pockets, and he sneaks quick glances through sitting room windows, sneering at the décor of tidy lives. He is a metronome. His right fist rises up to his lips at every third lamp post, and he tugs on his hip flask, a little something to warm the bones now that the Spring chill is settling. The sky is clear and car windows are beginning to glisten with condensation.

The route into town is as worn as Ted's shoe leather, his feet fitting the grooves and shallows in the pavement sweetly and snugly. He prefers to stay in the light in these troubled nights of binge drinking chaos and unprovoked menace, although in his head he can still see the hard fist of his youth dealing out a solid and immediate form of justice to the kids in the hood. The hugging of hoodies and cash point fines are signs of a soft underbelly, of the yellow streak running through the modern world. Wars. Polished steel. Kids today don't know they're born. A Nissen hut and battledress, that's what Ted would prescribe, although he forgets, as he hunches up his shoulders and completes the last hundred metres of his walk home under broken streetlamps, that he was just too young for National Service.

It's a close run thing. The Mondeo is very nearly past the turning before Alex spots the tell-tale weave of the old comic as he disappears into the shadows. He parks up in front of a solid nineteen-thirties semi-detached house, its bow front belly and mock Tudor adornments standing proudly against the night sky, a cipher for deep suburban, middle-aged contentment. The curtains in the bay window are closed but the tell-tale haze of passive entertainment sparks through the cracks. He closes the driver's door gently and hits the remote. Lights flash and the interior light dims. As he walks round to the pavement he makes a quick check for the handgun tucked into the back of his jeans and does up the middle button of his suit jacket. The houses change as he follows Ted at a safe distance. Victorian villas and a row of doorstep cottages take over from the solid urbanity of the slightly more modern, semi-detached conformity where he parked. The villas were once substantial residences, a world or parlours and roast meat, of the girl in service and the rustle of long skirts, but now they host the two-ring lives of students and people like Ted, people screaming silently, inwardly, as splinters drive under their fingernails as they claw their way up or slide their way down life's serpentine ladders.

Alex pauses in the shadows of a box hedge on the opposite side of the road as Ted fumbles for his keys under the last of the working streetlights, takes another hit on his flask and pushes open the gate in the small front garden of one of the villas. Unwanted solitude peels from the eaves. The chequerboard tile-work path is cracked and overgrown with tufts of new grass, the pale, washed-out petals of long dead hydrangea flowers and the straggling, early season buds of pink Campion. He slides his key into the lock and pushes open the heavy front door. It's Sunday but he checks an old kitchen table in the hall for post. The light is low rent, forty watt and unshaded.

Ted is silhouetted by the light from the bare bulb and Alex watches a charcoal sketch of the old man through the frosted safety glass as the door swings closed. The shape shuffles down the hall and gradually disappears from view, like a ghost floating upwards through the ceiling. Alex watches for lights in the upstairs windows. He imagines a hand groping around a door frame for the light switch. After a minute or so a light goes on. The third floor, at the front, on the left hand side of the building. He takes a moment to check the street and then crosses the road, walks up to the front door and with a minimum of fuss goes about the business of breaking and entering. A faint click is all that the ancient family ghosts hear.

Alex checks the layout downstairs; two flats, one either side of the hall. Treading carefully on the left and right edges of the stair treads, he goes up two floors. Wooden joints complain and the carpet slips where the runners are broken, but the sound of canned laughter covers his footfalls. He checks the landing. Flat five, left hand side, flat six, right hand side and a shared bathroom at the back of the building. White tiles and stained grout. Flat six is silent. The door to flat five has, rather conveniently, caught on the latch. Alex pauses and then hears the sound of a man relieving himself unsteadily in the bathroom. Perfect cover. He slips quietly into the flat.

Ted zips and washes his hands, drying them on rapidly disintegrating toilet paper rather than using the roll of pull down towelling on the wall. He chucks the remnants of the toilet tissue into the toilet bowl but doesn't flush, a present for the girls in flat six. He pulls the light switch and pads across the landing in his sock feet. As he pushes open his front door the timer on the landing light clicks and the bare light bulb hanging from the faded glory of the servants' storey ceiling rose snuffs out. Ted has lived here for five years and he knows the layout of his tiny, threadbare flat like the back of his hand. He hits the main light switch, smothering the bed-sit in darkness and as his eyes adjust slowly, he fumbles for a lamp on top of the fridge, preferring soft shadows at this time of night.

The chill on the Spring air seems to have followed him into the room. As he reaches out for the flex and the switch, Ted is suddenly aware of something awry, something other, in the room. He is suddenly aware of an echo, as if the world around him is breathing in shallow draughts of air slightly out of time with his own inhalation. Ted hesitates and breathes in deeply.

He can feel his pulse racing and to reassure himself, to break the spell of suspense, he mutters, "Stupid bastard, messing yourself up. Victorian houses are full of ghosts, full of shit, don't be a complete twat all your life."

He laughs at himself in that hollow way that people do when they want to bolster themselves when the hairs on the back of their necks stand on end. In the moment that his thumb depresses the switch and light blossoms in the kitchen Ted's faith in boundaries is shaken to the core.

A voice. A sudden rush of blood. His heart thumps into busy life in his chest. A half turn. An open mouth and abrupt silence within.

Alex steps out of the bed-sitting room shadows and into the black frame of the connecting arch way. He speaks in a whisper, one finger up against his lips.

"They shouldn't make you live like this, my friend."

Ted staggers backwards, ramming the base of his spine against the corner of the fridge, rocking the lamp, making Alex shimmer. He wants to shout, but the shock and the manic swelling in his chest make him mute. The intense, suffocating moment of panic is long enough for Alex to reach Ted's side, put a hand over his mouth, and for their eyes to lock.

Alex's grip on Ted's arm is firm and he instinctively recognises that familiar look of fear and confusion on the old man's face. To the untrained man, to the casually aggressive, violence is a blunt instrument wielded on a whim and a skin full, but to Alex it is a tool employed with the loving care of a master craftsman. He looks into the old man's eyes and without having to say a word he knows that Ted understands. This isn't the brute menace meted out by the muscle-bound barman at the club; this is the real thing.

Alex takes his hand away from Ted's mouth. "There's nowhere to go, my friend. All I want to do is talk. Shall we?" Alex leads the old man towards the other part of the room, towards Ted's bed and the armchair.

Ted can feel the hard walls of his arteries flexing in his chest, their brittle inner surfaces flaking and cracking under the pressure, under the wild torrent of liquid being forced through them by the flood of adrenalin in his system. He nods and Alex releases Ted's arm slowly. Ted can't tear his gaze away from the young man who has been buying him drinks all night down at the club. He tries to think, tries to imagine how he could have given any cause for this to happen, but his head is full of worms. Ted sits in his armchair, pallid and feverish. His chest feels like it has a metal band clamped around it. His mouth is dry and he can barely breathe.

Alex moves up behind him and bends down so that he can whisper in Ted's ear. He can smell cheap scotch on the man's breath and the last lingering scent of medicated shampoo. "A real shame".

He shifts so that he is squatting down by Ted's side.

"It's all quite simple, Mister Line. I believe you can help me find someone. In return I'll try to help you."

Carefully, gracefully, like a predator breaking cover, Alex stands and looks down at the old man in the armchair.

"I'm forgetting my manners, Mister Line. Would you like a drink?"

Ted can barely move, can barely speak. His head aches and he feels as though he is sliding down into the cold earth. He can smell damp soil, but he manages to summon-up the last flickering embers of his youthful vigour to whisper, "Kitchen. Above…above the sink."

Alex returns to the kitchen and opens the cupboard above the sink. He selects a bottle of malt, one of two or three that Ted keeps for high days and holidays, Old Pulteney, a delightfully peaty distillation. He selects a cut glass tumbler. Light refracts. He pours a stiff measure. Before returning to the bed-sitting room he takes the Glock from his jeans waistband, reaches into his jacket pocket for the silencer, and slowly screws it onto the barrel of the gun. Alex loves the simple, solid sound of tightly engineered metal and lets the comforting resonance of it wash through him. It is a sound that must, he thinks, fill the world with a thousand shades of death for the old man in the armchair.

Ted can't look. He sits rigid in his chair, staring at the open curtains. Perhaps someone will see them, he hopes, but he knows in his heart that they won't. Alex puts the pistol back into his waistband, picks up the drink and the bottle and walks back into the bed sitting room. He hands Ted the glass and puts the bottle on a side table next to the chair. Alex sits on the bed, but before he settles he takes out the handgun and puts it on the duvet. Ted's eyes follow the movement of the gun instinctively.

"I think you know how serious I am, Mister Line, but I want to make sure. Shall we get down to business?"

Ted's eyes are wide and he can feel another rush of adrenalin hitting his body like a sledgehammer. He feels faint and cold.

Sweat is breaking out on his forehead and tears are forming. His throat constricts and he throws the Scotch down hard, hard enough to burn his gullet and bring tears to the corners of his eyes. He wants to feel the burn and the heat as an antidote to hurricane forces pummelling his chest, but when the alcohol bites he feels stone cold sober. Bravado. Ted is a fighter and the odds are always stacked against him. So many odds. He discovers a little morsel of fight-back lodged somewhere deep and dark.

"Who the…the fuck are you?" he asks, hoarse, pleading.

"Not relevant Mister Line. All you need to know is that I'm here."

A second slug of malt helps Ted regain control of his voice. Indignation. This is his home, such as it is. How dare the bastard do this.

"I've met your…your sort. All the bloody time. Fucking agents and wide boys friggin me over. Why the fuck should I help you, big man, why? Got a gun? My dick's bigger than that!"

Alex smiles. "Well done. That's more like it, more like the real you. As I said earlier, it's a shame, all this." He looks around the room. "A real shame. So much to offer and they do this to you."

"Like you care." Ted snorts and pours a third shot.

"Oh, I care, Mister Line, more than you know. I'd have to care quite a lot to come to a place as squalid as this. Jock Cascarino, Mister Line, tell me about Jock Cascarino."

That bloody name. Ted can't think straight. It's always Jock bloody Cascarino, screwing up lives, pissing people off, hurting people. It's not bloody fair. The focus of Ted's anger shifts and he sags in the chair. The moment of bravado, his moment in the limelight fades, just as it did all those years ago. The spots dim and the sound of canned laughter dribbles into the dust. Flames and ashes. There's no point. Ted is an old man and the boy has a gun. Anyway, he thinks, if he's after that Scots shit, what does it matter.

"You said you'd help me. What did you mean?"

Where there's hope there's life, Alex thinks to himself. It really is a shame. He smiles again.

"A fair exchange. You tell me what I want to know and I'll help you. A little something from a grateful friend, something to make a difference, perhaps?"

"What?" Ted looks genuinely shocked. A moment of silence and it dawns on him; a joke, sick realisation, but then Ted thinks about it; cash from the Scots bastard, cash from this arsehole, it's the same thing.

"What do you want to know?" he asks.

Alex thinks for a moment. There seems little point in prolonging the agony and the old man will get himself royally pissed before too long. "Where can I find Jock Cascarino?"

Ted points at a reporter's notebook and a tatty old address book on the side table. The scotch and the fear coalesce and make Ted gabble out a stream of disjointed thoughts and words.

"It's all there. Notes. That bastard is always fucking me up and now he's baling out, leaving us all in the lurch. What am I going to do? Billy's alright, saint bloody Billy, but what about me? Then there's these girls. Put it all together and you can't escape the conclusion Jock's a cunt…but I thought Maggie was my friend."

Ted shrugs once.

"Goes to show. It's all there. Home address is in the book. Details as best I remember them on the notepad; Shaun Lloyd, some new drug, doing freebies or something, everything. "

Alex picks up the notebook and the address book and puts them down on the duvet next to the handgun. There is enough sense in the old man's slurred and peevish outburst for Alex to fit the pieces together, enough sense for him to make those all-important connections. He smiles at Ted and says, "Thank you. If I were you I'd sit there for a few minutes and have another drink."

Ted pours a regular measure this time and, instead of gulping it down, he stares into the glass, savouring the colour and peaty aroma. He sniffs, wipes a tear from his cheek and takes a sip, rolling the warm glow of the fireside around on his tongue as Alex gathers up the books and his handgun and heads back to the kitchen. Before Alex leaves the bed-sit he turns and watches Ted for a moment.

"I'm sorry, Mister Line, but the truth is I never carry much cash and even if I did pay you, you'd only piss it all away. It's time for a change, Mister Line, time for a change."

Smoke. The smell of oil and cordite. A clean head shot. Ted line takes his final bow, slumping forward in his chair, bent double, dying for the last time in the silent applause of the ghost audience. From the Gods, Mike, Bernie and the rest of the alumni mark Ted's passing with glossy eyes. Alex waits for a few moments, letting the barrel of the Glock and the silencer cool a little before unscrewing them and sliding them away, safe and tidy, ready for another day. He waits to see if there are footsteps in the hall, but the Sunday night world of television and sleeping heads is undisturbed. He is safe in the knowledge that no one will miss Ted Line until the job is done. Alex wonders for a moment if perhaps he should have been kinder to the old fool, but it is just a momentary thought. Ted Line disgusts Alex. This is definitely the best thing for the remaindered comic, and it stops his drink fuelled tongue from wagging.

Condensation dribbles down the windscreen. Cheap Spanish brandy spills from the corner of Billy Whitlow's mouth. He is half-way down the bottle, drinking for the sake of it and the temporary warmth that the liquor gives to his body. He can feel the ache, the chill that will, if he sits in his car through the night in an alcoholic stupor, turn his joints into rusty spokes. He has cried a river, has sung the song to himself over and over again, and with every chorus, with every verse, he has felt himself slide down, inch by inch, into a bottomless well of self-pity.

Every so often he turns the ignition key so that the dashboard lights illuminate the unnerving darkness. Bex. He cries for Bex and Leona. Images of the poor girl's blue skin keep flashing through his head. Another slug. His hands are growing numb and the bottle slips from his grasp as he tries to set it back down on the centre console. He catches the gear lever with his sleeve and the bottle upends in the passenger footwell. The last straw. Cocooned in the deadening field of metal and safety glass he howls.

"B-E-X!"

In the rising fog of alcohol fumes, fumes that will fill the car for weeks to come, Billy makes a decision. The car door slams and Billy stumbles out into the night, blind and raging. The air slaps him in the face and he holds still for a moment to let his head clear. Spots before his eyes. Dizzy, he slips onto all fours. Stony ground. Grit under his fingernails. He crawls to the side of the car and hauls himself upright, running a mud stained palm across his eyes to wipe away the tears, leaving brown tracks, a primeval war paint, across his cheeks. He breathes in deeply and, orientating himself by the position of the car, he starts to walk towards the road. His sense of direction is clouded by the hour and the alcoholic dilution in his bloodstream. His foot slips in the mud by the side of the track leading into the parking area and he falls into a blackthorn bush, which whips at his hair and impales him on its thin black barbs.

Tearing himself free, he emerges into the clear space of the country lane and turns a full circle before he is able to pinpoint the direction that he should be heading in, towards the target location, the focus of his anger; Jock Cascarino. As soon as he gathers his wits he starts to jog towards the gate and the parked Lexus. The back of his polo shirt is hanging down over his jeans, and his left knee shows through a jagged tear in the denim. Mucus drips from his nose where he has been crying, and it joins the mud on the back of his hand.

He reaches the gate and stops, standing in the middle of the entrance to the gravel driveway and stares at the house. The carriage lights on either side of the porch are on and the glow of table lamps in the sitting room filters out through the glass in the main door to the house. Billy is suddenly calm. Everything has suddenly become clear in his head. He takes another deep breath.

"Cascarino! Jock fucking Cascarino! Get your fat, gobshite arse out here now!"

As Billy shouts he starts to walk up the drive. His hands are balled into tight, quivering fists. He kicks at the gravel with every step.

"Cascarino! Can you hear me. I'm coming for you, you bastard. I'm coming!"

A light comes on in the hall.

"You murdering cunt, I'm coming for you!"

The kitchen light goes on and Maggie is framed in the window looking out onto the drive. The inner porch door opens. Billy bends and picks up a handful of gravel.

Jock opens the front door. He is in his slippers. Billy launches grapeshot at the Lexus and grins as the stones ping off the metalwork on the rear driver's side wing.

Jock has picked up an old putter from the umbrella stand in the porch. The outer porch door opens and Billy starts to run. Maggie starts to scream.

A Ford Mondeo crawls past the open drive entrance, the driver peering through the passenger window at the names of houses painted on logs and cast iron plates. Headlights sweep away beyond the hedging at the front of the house. Billy has cut the distance between himself and Jock in half. Jock has the porch door open and is raising the club, ready to swing it into his assailant's midriff. Maggie has disappeared from the kitchen window. As Billy closes in he is vaguely aware of a woman's voice.

"Jock! No..."

Speed takes on a substance all of its own in the final few metres of Billy's charge. He is aware of everything and nothing. He can see individual bricks in the wall of the porch in front of which the putter's head is hovering. He can feel the air between himself and Jock vibrating. His footsteps sound like thunder in his ears and he can almost sense the weight of the club pressing against his ribs, but he can't stop now. The club moves back and Jock's face is set. Muscles stand out in his jaw.

Billy turns his left side towards his target and he readies his left arm so that he can try to absorb the worst of the impact. He needs to get closer. The club starts to swing forward and Billy winces in anticipation but the blow never arrives. The club seems to hang in the air just behind Jock's right shoulder and Billy has sufficient momentum to twist as he steps inside its lethal arc, pull his right arm back and launch his fist into Jock's shocked face.

Bone on bone. Skin tears and Billy can feel Jock's cheek flatten and rip inside as it is compressed against his jaw. Billy's knuckles are pressed in towards the palm of his hand and he can feel cartilage buckling. The blood begins to flow and Jock staggers back into Maggie, who is still hanging onto the shaft of the putter with both hands. Jock's falling body slams her back into the door frame. All three of them collapse onto the cold stone chippings of the driveway and lay there, stunned and still, as early season moths flap and flutter against the glass of the carriage lamps.

Wrapped in the cloak of bloodlust, none of them are aware of headlights coming to a standstill in the lane. None of them notice the headlights reverse and swing into the parking area where Billy has left his car.

Maggie is the first to come to her senses, and although she is winded, she is able to shake off the intoxication of violence. Jock is on all fours coughing and spitting blood out onto the gravel. Billy has rolled away and is sitting with his head in his hands, sobbing as the blood from his torn knuckles trickles down his arm.

Maggie rises from the dirt, wincing, her back feeling as though it should have hoof prints all over it, but she ignores the pain and grabs Jock by the shirt collar. "For Christ's sake, Jock, give me a hand."

Jock is still groggy from the punch. "Wha...Shi..."

His tongue is swelling up and his cheek is raw, the bruise already rising. He shakes his head a couple of times and crawls over to the porch doorway, where he uses the windowsill as a crutch, hauling himself upright. "Tha bas'ard jus tried to kill me an' you wan' me to hel..."

"Inside, Jock, help me get him inside. The last thing we need is the bloody neighbourhood watch!"

Jock knows that Maggie is right, that she's the only one here with her head screwed on. He feels the inside of his cheek with his tongue and whimpers as an electric charge spikes through the side of his face, but still he does as Maggie asks. Taking one arm each they manage to heave Billy to his feet and half drag, half carry him into the house. They get him to the kitchen where they sit him down on the floor. Maggie soaks a tea towel under the cold tap and starts to wipe away the congealing mess of mud and blood from his hands and face.

"Jesus, man, look at him."

Jock sits at the table. He can't quite get at consonants. "Loo' at him, wha' abou' me?"

"Flesh wound, Jock, you've had worse. You're a soldier, remember, you keep telling me. Billy here is a ponce, a fucking artiste. Look at him. What if it was your daughter?"

"I don' have a daugh'r."

"For fuck's sake, Jock, you know what I mean. We've got to sort this."

Maggie hates the smell of iron in the blood and nearly gags. She can smell a pint's worth of brandy fumes on Billy's breath. Maggie turns to Jock, who is sitting at the kitchen table nursing his own wounds, together with an entirely inappropriate sense of injustice, and she screams at him, "Will you open the friggin window?"

Jock does as he is told, pulling a wad of kitchen roll from the holder on the wall by the microwave, which he too wets under the tap so that he can clean himself up. His shirt is ruined and as he resumes his seat at the kitchen table he gives Billy a weather-eye, a knowing look that says; I'll get you, pal, your card is marked.

Billy's tears have dried, leaving tracks of clear skin on his cheeks. Specks of mud and blood line his fringe, but his hand is bathed and his face wiped. He either won't or can't say anything. He just sits on the kitchen floor, his back against the cupboard doors underneath the sink, and stares at Jock. The kettle is filled. Maggie takes the plastic bag containing the empty cartons of Chinese take-away from the table and sits opposite Jock.

"So, what do we do now? How did he know?"

Jock shrugs. He is going to look like a goon for a week. The boys will have a field day. He thinks about Maggie's question for a moment before answering. "Does he, though? I mean, who, how? Doesn' ma' sense."

Billy is still staring straight at Jock, unspeaking, glass eyed, locked in a state of alcoholic futility, submerged by the catatonia of ineffectuality.

Jock returns the stare for a moment. He turns to look at Maggie and puts a finger to his lips, nodding in Billy's direction. "Walls have ears an' all tha'. He doesn't know 'cos there's nothing to know. Asso...ciation. I have a reputa'ion and his girl's in shit. Lash out. Firs' por' of call. The guy's sick, Mags, not a vigilan'e."

The grass in the front garden is soft and fresh. Jock and Maggie don't own a dog and there are no geese to warn of approaching danger. The birds see no just cause to fly from the treetops. Alex Berisa moves across the lawn quietly and stands in the shadows just to the left of the kitchen window. He is screened from the road. Because of the angle anyone looking out of the kitchen window would have extreme difficulty spotting him, but he is close enough to listen to the conversation in the Cascarino inner sanctum.

Maggie starts to sag, coming down from the rush. "Okay, but what are we going to do? We can't leave him like that all night."

"Aye, you're right there. We've go' to talk to him, but…"

Jock turns to face Billy. He lets out a long sigh as he looks into Billy's vacant eyes. "Hey, pal, tha's a mean right hook you've got. An' yeah, I know I sor' of deserve it for all the nee'le, bu', well, it's all been a bit of a shock. To all of us. Loo' we're really sorry about Bex, she's a lovely wee lass, but you can't go lashing out like tha'."

He looks at Maggie and raises an eyebrow. Brain lock. Maggie tries to break through.

"Billy love, Billy, I'm so sorry. But she'll be fine. She's young and strong. She'll be back and shining like the little star she always was in no time."

Silence. Billy sits and stares. He can hear voices but none of the words make any sense. He feels dead inside, gutless, as though the world has stopped and thrown him off the carousel. Things are starting to spin around him again but he is on the outside watching the gallopers waltz round and round, straining to catch sight of his little girl as she bobs in and out of his field of view. He feels drunk and hopeless.

Maggie gets up from the table, kneels on the floor and takes Billy's good hand in hers.

"Billy, when did you last sleep, love? You look knackered. You've been drinking as well. Why don't we get you to bed. A good night's sleep and you'll feel better."

Jock looks at Maggie questioningly, but she ignores him.

"Come on love, we'll get you to the sofa. You can sleep it off."

Billy feels the warmth of Maggie's hand bleeding into his own skin, and the strings that tether him to the here and now are pulled taut. He blinks, and as he does so a tear forms. He sniffs and breaks his gaze away from Jock.

"Bed", he slurs, and lets himself be led into the sitting room, where Maggie clears cushions from sofa. A duvet from one of the spare bedrooms is thrown onto the sofa and Billy's coat and shoes are removed. Jock and Maggie tuck him in, switch off the lights and return to the kitchen, leaving the doors open in case Billy stirs.

Jock's train of thought is heading for the buffers. He needs help and he turns to Maggie, to ice cool Maggie, and asks, "Shit, Mags. It's okay now, but wha' abou' the mornin'?"

Maggie shrugs her shoulders and fills two mugs with boiling water, dropping a tea bag in each mug in turn.

"You'll have to sit with him tonight, Jock, to be on the safe side. I'll take over in the morning, sweet talk him, keep him on side while you do what you have to do at the farm. We've got to be clean tomorrow Jock, that's the main thing. After that we can deal with Billy."

A dash of milk. They sit quietly, contemplating the night ahead, a night that will see Maggie twisting the duvet around her legs in her bed and Jock dozing uncomfortably in an armchair. Determination is one of Maggie's more pronounced character traits and is one of the things that Jock loves about her. They are too close to let it slide now.

Alex waits until the kitchen light goes out. He checks his watch. Twenty to twelve. He makes his way back to his car and sets the alarm on his phone to four forty-five. He wants to be up and awake in plenty of time to get the stiffness out of his bones before he has to deal with Jock Cascarino and, he hopes, his friend, Arbnor Jasari. Before he lowers his seat back, settles down and shuts his eyes to the chill of the night, he checks the Glock and makes sure that he has two spare clips ready for the morning. He takes another handgun from the bag in the boot and puts that in the glove compartment. A good workman always makes sure his tools are clean and keen.

Shadow and light. At the back of the traveller's hotel at Roundswell, across a thin strip of grass and beyond a six foot high chain link fence, beyond a car park full of new model Peugeots waiting for eager buyers, the dark hulls of low rise industrial units lie at anchor. The window to the room that Carol and Dave are staying in is shut, causing Carol to lie on top of the duvet. The air is still and thick. A line of sweat breaks out on her forehead. The sound of cars and late night hauliers making time and distance ready for Monday morning crawls through the wooden frame of the double-glazed window. Every so often a room door opens and shuts.

Dave is laying on his side facing Carol. He too has kicked off the duvet and cannot sleep. He puts his hand on Carol's shoulder. "Can't sleep?"

Carol shakes her head. "She looks so lost in there, Dave. My little girl."

Fingers tense. Dave rises up onto his elbow and strokes Carol's fringe out of her eyes. He feels the heat in her forehead. "I know. We've got to hang in there for her, though."

Carol rolls over to face Dave. "I know". She traces the contours of his arm with a fingernail. "I know, love. Thanks, by the way. I've been so wrapped up in it all. You're a good man."

Dave lets the words wash over him like cold surf on a hot June afternoon. He wants Carol right now, but stays silent, stroking her cheek with the back of his hand.

"Makes you think, doesn't it", she says softly, moving her hand to her lover's chest and letting her fingertips wander through thick curls of his greying chest hair. "This place. Full of people getting pissed, having affairs, living lives and any one of them could stop, could be snuffed out, just like that. Another mother, a wife, a husband, kids, the list goes on, any one of them could be where we are now, at any time. It's all so fragile. You don't realise, do you."

There are times when you listen. Dave keeps his reply short. "No. No, you don't".

Carol dams the flood of words threatening to overflow her defensive walls. To go on now would break the thin barrier of control that she has erected around the flowing water of her life.

"Hold me?" she whispers.

Dave reaches out and draws her to him, enfolding her despite the heat that rises from their closely-coupled bodies. He can smell Carol's hair and a faint trace of body odour. He breathes in deeply and wraps himself around her. The quiet comfort of softly embracing bodies should go on forever, but Dave has a question that he can't help but ask. He waits, feeling the fidget start in his toes. It crawls through his limbs, dragging with it the impenetrable barrier to love. He has to ask.

"Billy? Where was he tonight?"

Carol leans back slightly so that she can look up at his face. "Where he usually goes at times like this. He's never been strong."

Dave can't see any logic behind Carol's answer. How would he react in similar circumstances? Can you really know anything before it happens to you? He tries to be Billy, to see the world through the man's eyes but he can't.

"Bex is his daughter. I don't understand how he could be anywhere else?"

"He's not anywhere else. He's not anywhere. He's full of good intentions, love, always was, it's just that things get in the way. He's probably sitting at home in his coat and shoes, having a last drink, with his beloved Vic Damone crooning away in the background. He'll be crying by now. Tomorrow. We'll see him tomorrow. First thing he'll say is sorry for fucking-up again. He's never going to change."

A swing door further down the hall opens and anonymous shoes brush across carpet. Carol is getting hot. She stretches her head up towards Dave's face and kisses him softly on the lips.

"Night, love."

She rolls away and closes her eyes, trying to think herself into unconsciousness, as if concentrating on a word will close her mind down. It usually works, but not tonight. In her head Bex is grinning at her and turning over prompt cards, one after the other, all of them showing the word 'Sleep' written in shaky black marker pen. A Dylan song starts to play in the background. Carol knows this is basic thought association and tries to let the image fade, but there is no chance of anything working so simply, so effortlessly, not tonight. In the background Dave mutters good night and he is asleep before his head hits the pillow.

Carol will look like the wreck of the Hesperus in the morning. She resigns herself to the long hours of dead waking, and as she tries to settle, as she tries to find a position of relative comfort, she asks herself a simple question; "Why, Billy, why can't you do something useful for a bloody change?"

EBB TIDE

THE CORDED TASSEL OF an embroidered cushion is imprinted on Billy's cheek and his earlobe hurts where it has been bent back by the awkward angle that his head has been lying at. The curtains are open and bright sunlight is crashing into the sitting room through the conservatory. Pillars of dust rise on thermals. As Billy tries to sit up his temples start to throb, joining a chorus of complaint from his joints and his stomach. He needs water and the toilet.

Billy reaches behind his head, searching for the familiar comforts of home, for the water bottle that he keeps by his bed, but his hand swings through cool, clear air. The room, largely unnoticed in Billy's slow crawl back towards consciousness, suddenly spills out of the night shadows into daylight. The pillows seem impossibly small and square. The duvet is the wrong colour, the wrong pattern, and the space, the sheer openness of the room makes him giddy. Billy is not at home.

It takes a moment or two for him to assemble his thoughts and turn the random instructions flashing through his head into a coherent pattern of command. He props himself up and swings his feet out from under the duvet so that he is sitting. His head swims. Memories; the car, a passenger, sitting in the eye of the storm with a bottle, Jock's face crumpling, Maggie taking his shoes off. The image of Jock's flattened skin under his fist kicks the pain receptors in his hand back into life and Billy's hand starts to ache. He looks down at his grazed knuckles and tries to flex the joints. Stabbing pains ricochet through his wrist and up his arm. The flesh wounds are clean and are starting to scab over at the edges.

A movement to his left. A twitch and a low snore. Billy has to twist round in his seat to find the source. He sees outstretched legs, red diamond pattern socks and a swollen eye. Jock is asleep in a reclining armchair. Place and time coalesce and Billy remembers. Bex and drugs and wild stories in a car park, but last night's urge to hurt, to exact vengeance in blood, has been replaced by a desperate urge to pee. Billy can't face the awful prospect of waking the Cascarino household. Yesterday's conversation replays in his head and he can smell bile again. He's too tired, too worn out to deal with it. All that Billy wants is to escape, to get home and shut the door. He needs time to think after Sunday's lunacy. Billy fumbles along the edge of the sofa and finds his shoes, slipping them on without doing up the laces. As he stands he catches sight of the torn knee in his jeans. The smell of dry mud rises as he stretches the creases in his clothing.

Billy grabs his coat off one of the kitchen chairs and walks on tiptoes to the front door. Bolts and deadlocks. He slides the top and bottom bolts back, expecting them to be stiff, but they slide easily. The deadlock catch snicks. He pauses before opening the main house door, listening for the sound of footsteps, for the sound of Jock or Maggie in hot pursuit, but the house is silent, save for the ticking of a mantelpiece clock in the sitting room. Time to go. Billy eases out of the front door, giving the porch door frame a wry glance as he leaves.

Once outside he takes a deep lungful of air, and lets the cold, clean brightness of the morning fill him with hope. He checks his watch. The hedges around the house are alive with early morning chatter and squabble. Sometimes, he thinks, it's just good to be alive, and despite the waves of nausea that wash through his shattered body, the thought hangs in the air in front of him. He has to get home, has to wash and get himself straight for visiting time at the hospital. The beauty of the morning fills Billy with a warm sense of anticipation, convincing him that Bex will wake up today.

That rare silence, the natural silence of a crisp Spring dawn full of noise keeps Billy company as he walks back to his car. His head is clearing and he is, for the first time, starting to think about the story he was told yesterday in the hospital car park. He has a vague recollection of a conversation in the kitchen, a conversation about survival and knowledge. Billy can't quite believe that anyone could be that stupid, not even Jock. The morning is too sharp and too glorious to allow anybody to be that dumb.

Turning the corner, Billy walks into the car park and sees his car. He pats his pockets but finds no keys. Stupidity, he decides, can't be changed by the colour of bright blue skies. He can't remember if he has left the keys at the house or left them in the ignition of his beaten up old Vauxhall.

"Either way", he says to himself, "You're a stupid bastard, Billy boy."

He hurries round to the driver's door, which is open, and seeing his car abandoned in such an out of the way spot, Billy fully expects to find ripped out wires and a gaping hole in the facia where the CD player used to be. There are no keys in the ignition, but the player is snug in its black plastic housing. A moment of confusion. Blackbirds mark their territories and added to their song is the jangling sound of bright, shiny metal.

Tucked up against the roadside hedge, backed into a protected spot that has full command of the car park and anyone approaching, there is a silver Ford Mondeo. The driver's window is down and an arm hangs out of the window. A set of keys hang from the driver's fingers. Billy turns to face the sound and as he does so the Mondeo's door opens. Billy has to squint to make out the driver's face. The sun is behind the Mondeo, still low, scattering itself through budding branches.

"Hello, Billy."

Billy struggles to fit shapes together but slowly the pieces lock into place. The man from the hospital car park. Vic. There's something ordained about the moment, as if the light and the freshness in the air makes their meeting holy.

"It's you, isn't it, from yesterday."

"Yes, Billy, it's me. Get in the car, please."

It's a politely phrased command. Billy has neither the strength nor the inclination to disobey. His stomach is complaining, a mixture of sour guts and emptiness, and he is sweating. He hopes that there's a bottle of water in the car.

"How was your evening?" the driver of the car asks.

As he squeezes between the car and the hedge, Billy starts to map out the landscape of the man's face. Apart from a thick layer of black stubble, the boy looks fit and well, which makes Billy feel even more dishevelled and wasted than he did when he woke up on Jock's sofa.

"I've had better."

"Yeah, I know the feeling. I didn't catch everything last night, but it looked as though you gave Mister Cascarino a bit of a thump. Did it make you feel any better about things?"

Billy stops and looks at the man. How much did he see? Where was he? Is this what police surveillance feels like?

"Not really", Billy answers, feeling the skin stretching across his bruised and grazed knuckles as he tries to make a fist.

"It never does. To get anything back from bastards like that you have to hit them a lot harder than that."

Alex ducks back into the car and puts Billy's keys on the top of the dashboard. As Billy climbs in Alex opens Ted Line's notebook.

"I made some calls. Your friend is…well, let's just say he has a few questions to answer. These are connections, Billy, circumstantial, but in my line of work most things are. It's not the proof that matters, it's the connections and there are a lot of them. A weight of evidence."

Billy sits back and shuts his eyes. He's too tired to think any more. The stranger sitting next to him in the silver Ford is confirming his worst nightmare, but all he can think about is a hot shower. He could have throttled Jock as he lay sleeping in his chair this morning, but he didn't. It wouldn't help Bex. Billy doesn't have the strength to spare.

"So, Billy, this morning I need your help. A chance to settle things, for Rezarta and your daughter. What do you know about farms, Billy, about Jock's farming interests?"

Billy's mouth is dry. "Have you got any water?"

Alex reaches over to the back seat and fishes a half empty bottle of mineral water from a plastic bag. The water is night chilled and feels like heaven to Billy. He finishes the bottle in three long draughts, wiping his mouth with the back of his already soiled jacket sleeve.

"Not much", he says, adding, "but he did say something about tidying up this morning, but not where or when."

Alex reaches back over to the plastic bag and pulls out a plastic sandwich carton. The wrapper is open and one egg and bacon sandwich remains, slightly hard at the edges. Alex passes it to Billy.

"You look like you need this more than I do. Anyway, we've got a little time to kill. If Mister Cascarino is paying house calls this morning, I think we should drop in too."

Billy shrugs his shoulders and tucks into the stale bread. As he eats he looks at Ted's scrawled notes and the map of connections in Alex's notebook. Fair enough, he thinks, as Alex gets out of the car to watch the entrance to the house through a gap in the hedge.

"So long as we get back in time to see Bex", he says with a mouth full of egg, bacon and dry bread.

Maggie wipes a grain of hourglass sand from the corner of her eye. Sunshine streams in through the bedroom window and she has woken to the clock radio on her bedside cabinet clicking into life with the BBC news, the Today Programme, and a Monday morning story about death, another British soldier killed in the Middle East. Six fifteen. Five minutes pass, five minutes spent in slow waking, in reacquainting herself with the world, and she decides that she needs a cup of tea. Death, she thinks in her drowsy, half dreaming state, must sound like John Humphries, and then remembering Bex and Leona, Maggie suddenly finds herself brightly, anxiously awake.

As she pads down the stairs in her dressing gown and slippers, the house feels strangely empty. Maggie fills the kettle with water and the teapot with three tea bags. The first brew of the morning needs legs, needs that extra dose to stiffen it, ready for the buffeting winds of the day. She walks into the living room expecting to see Billy lying comatose on the sofa, expecting Jock to be looking like hell, sad and tired, looking like a man nearing sixty who hasn't slept, but instead she sees the inevitable celluloid image, the night watchman sleeping on the job and the turned back duvet from under which the renegade has made his frantic escape.

It's a head in the hands moment. She wants to scream, but like Jock she is getting too long in the tooth for tantrums. Of course he went to sleep, she thinks, and finding a moment of calm amongst the dust motes, she decides that she can't blame him for that. She wants to, though.

Spilt milk on the kitchen worktop. The sound of a teaspoon on the rim of a mug hauls Jock into the world of daylight. It takes a few seconds for him to get his bearings, a few seconds more for him to unwind his aching limbs from the chair and for his neck to loosen, and then comes the second inevitability of this fresh, young morning.

"Fuck!" Jock spins on his heels. The conservatory; the hall; the stairs. "Maggie!"

She appears in the kitchen doorway, carrying two mugs of tea and Jock visibly sags as the adrenalin coursing through his veins loses the fight with the sheer bloody fatigue that he feels in his bones.

"Come on", she says and they both make their way past the rumpled duvet at the foot of the sofa and sit down in the conservatory. The sun is still low in the sky and Jock has to squint to look at Maggie. He gets up and lowers the blind in the window behind her.

"Screw him, Jock. You can deal with Billy later. Right now we've got other things to think about."

"Screw him…are you serious? He's a liability. I can't have him wandering the streets shooting his mouth off."

Maggie takes quick sips of hot tea, feeling the brew on her lips, almost scalding her, but she needs the hit. Her body is accustomed to waking slowly, with Jock being the first to rise. Making the first brew is a blue job.

"He won't", she says quietly. "Billy won't do that, Jock, not yet."

"I don't understand", Jock says, washing his mouth out with tea to get rid of the fur on his tongue. The liquid burns the cut on the inside of his cheek where Billy hit him the night before and he whimpers slightly.

"Priorities, love, it's all a question of priorities. Billy won't do anything until Bex wakes up or...well, let's just hope she wakes up. After that he'll be a problem, but not until then. Right now he'll be hurting because he missed her yesterday, because he screwed up. All he wants to do right now is get himself straight and be at the hospital for her."

Jock grimaces as the hot tea burns the back of his throat, but he continues to drink it in large gulps, using the pain to clear his head. "You think so? Aye, you might be right. So, what now? Do I get out to the farm?"

Maggie nods, staring past Jock's left shoulder at the line of trees that separate the garden from the lane that runs along the front and side of the house. A slight breeze shifts the bright greens of Spring and she feels calm. Her anger has subsided, replaced by a quiet sense of purpose.

"Yes, out to the farm. Priorities. Bex is in intensive care, right. Remember when Mum was in there after her heart attack? Remember the visiting hours? Billy won't be able to see her until late morning, which means he'll be occupied until then. That gives you time to get out to the farm and do whatever it is you need to do to sort this bloody mess out. I'll go down to the hospital at lunch time, around twelve, lend Billy a shoulder to cry on. You know how he feels about me, Jock. Between us we can manage the situation."

Jock finishes his tea. "Shit. You've got it all worked out."

Maggie flashes him one of those wither and die looks, but she doesn't flare. She remains calm and considered. "Got a better idea?"

Jock shakes his head, picks up his and Maggie's mug and goes to the kitchen for refills. In the minutes that pass while Jocks boils the kettle and tops up the pot, while the tea brews and the fridge door slams, Maggie sorts out the day. Clean and tidy. It's what women are good at. Men make the mess and women clear it up. Jock puts her refreshed mug on the table next to her and sits opposite her again.

"We've got to stay focused, love, just you and me. We're this close." Maggie holds her world, her future happiness, in an inch of space between her thumb and fore finger. "We've been through worse."

Jock nods, remembering her husband and muffled sounds that came from the boot of his old Mercedes. He remembers the wasteland that some people are forced to endure after a sudden, unexpected divorce. Poor bloke.

Maggie continues. "We'll need a couple of days to get everything sorted. Cash, Jock, we need to get as much cash together as we can, run the businesses from Spain or wherever for a while, let the lawyers handle the sales. Take a long holiday. I'll sort the bank this morning, move money out of the country, into the Spanish account. You sort the farm and get clean. Then Billy and Bex. I don't know, maybe a pay-off or something?"

After last night's debacle Jock very much wants it to be something, but that can wait. Maggie is right. Deal with the matter in hand. Put Billy on ice somehow and take a long break.

"Aye, you're right, babe. I'll get on to the boys, arrange a pickup."

He slides over and joins Maggie on the two seat wicker sofa.

Picking her hand up in his and stroking it he says, "I'll not let you down, love. Everything I do is for you, you know that, don't you?"

Maggie leans across and kisses the bruise on Jock's cheek. "I know", she whispers. "But you don't need to do quite so much of it. If you screw up, if you ruin everything because you got greedy, I'll never forgive you. It's my time now, Jock. I want my reward."

The traffic on the roads is light at seven, made up of early shift starts and the twenty-four hour grind of the haulage industry. The Easter holidays mean that there's no school run and the tourists are still asleep or locked in the paralysis of leisurely breakfasts and television kids. There is enough traffic on the roads, however, for Alex to follow Jock's Lexus with a couple of vehicles in between the two cars, and it becomes clear that Jock is making for the club. Billy tells Alex to wait by a bus stop on the main road because Jock and the boys will have to hit the main Lynton road back into town before they head out into the countryside.

Sure enough, ten minutes after disappearing into the narrow streets that run along the bottom of the hill on which the hospital sits, the Lexus reappears, three up, with Davie McCoist at the wheel. As Alex eases out into the traffic behind an articulated lorry, Billy sneaks a glance in the passenger side mirror at the road disappearing behind them. Bex pulls him towards her, but Billy has made a new resolution. He promises her that he'll be back as soon as he can, blows her a kiss, and settles back into the passenger seat. He won't let the bastard in the car in front of him off the hook that easily.

As Davie manoeuvres through the road works in the centre of the town, Billy keeps Alex in the right lanes. They head out to Roundswell and join the main trunk through Bideford and on towards the border with Cornwall.

With the pace and distance settled, Alex relaxes his grip on the wheel and starts to think about his next move. "So, Billy, tell me again, what do we know?"

Since their dawn meeting in Lover's Lane, Billy has twice told Alex about the encounter at Jock's house. It doesn't seem to get any clearer with the repetition and he sighs, stares out of the side window at the hedgerows and the fields, and goes over it again.

"Not much to say. You blew my world apart yesterday afternoon. I got drunk, lost it, went over there to knock seven shades of shit out of the bastard and that's about it. All I could see was Leona on that trolley. Couldn't even get a grip on my daughter's face. Just Leona. As soon as I saw the bastard I knew I had to hurt him. After that it's weird. Fuzzy. I remember odd bits, odd snatches of conversation, something about sorting it out this morning, but that's all."

Alex leans over and fishes the notebooks out of the glove compartment. "What about these?"

Billy flicks through the pages once again and says, "Like you said, Jock's a shit. Drugs, racketeering, girls. Respectable now, or so he says, and then this, my little girl."

Billy looks at scribbled notes. "I saw this one yesterday." Then Billy holds up Ted Line's notes. "But not these. Where did you get these?"

Alex slows down as they reach Horns Cross and the village's flashing neon speed warnings. Up ahead the Lexus starts to pick up speed as it nears the top of the hill and the open country lanes. He looks at Billy, gauging the strength of the man sitting next to him. "Ted Line. I met him last night. He had some interesting things to say about your friend."

Billy doesn't bat an eyelid. Apart from the hangover, apart from the nearly overwhelming urge to lay back and sleep induced by the hum of the engine and the compulsive sense of motion, he feels numb.

"Ted is a wanker first class. I mean, he's right about the kid on Wednesday, but he's bound to be making five, you know, getting his sums wrong. Ted has always got his sums wrong, that's why he's such a loser."

Alex considers this for a moment. "I tend to agree, but not, I think, this time. As I told you yesterday, the club, Ted, everything points to your Mister Cascarino and my old friend, Doctor Jasari."

They reach the top of the hill and Alex changes down and floors the accelerator. The lane twists and dips past Hoops restaurant, turning sharply left, and as the Mondeo swings through the curves and Alex catches a flash of brake lights up ahead, Billy starts to feel nauseous. The last thing he wants to do is be sick. Billy doubts that the man sitting next to him would worry about the mess, but he would definitely be pissed-off if they lose the Lexus because Billy has soft guts. He swallows a couple of times and opens the window by a couple of inches to let the slipstreaming air hit his face.

With his mention of Jasari, Alex tightens his grip on the steering wheel again, hammering through bends to keep the Lexus in view. He can feel the good doctor's body heat, can feel his presence drawing closer. Alex breathes in deeply, practising self-control. Now is not the time to let emotion overrule his head. Cold and efficient. It's the only way to deal with the situation.

The silence in the car is a reflection of their thoughts. Billy is with Bex as she lays on her hospital bed with heart monitors and breathing tubes plugged into her body. Alex is with Rezarta in the family villa in Albania, watching her as she is spoon fed soup and porridge. Much to his own surprise, Alex is the first to break the silence.

"I think you understand me. Billy. Where you see your daughter, I see my sister. The difference between us is you have hope. Rezarta has no hope. Jasari is a true killer. He is without compassion. He kills my sister every day, bit by bit. With every second that her skin ages and she becomes old, she dies, just like you and me, but he killed her soul. If I seem odd, like a cold fish, it's only because I have become like him. I have to be like him so that I can find him and make him pay. For you, he is faceless. For you it is Cascarino. For me it is my old friend."

Billy wants to be shocked but he simply can't feel it. He doesn't feel anything right now. Even Jock seems a million miles away. Billy is sitting in a warm cocoon, protected by velour and side impact bars, by a plastic facia and the reassurance of the internal combustion engine, and he feels nothing except the suspension flexing and jerking across potholes and worn patches of tarmac.

"You're going to kill him, aren't you?"

Alex frowns for a moment and then smiles. "Yes, Billy, I am going to kill him".

"What about Jock, what about the boys?"

"That's up to you, I think. Do you want me to kill them too? Is that something you can handle?"

For the first time it occurs to Billy that the man sitting next to him would have no qualms about putting a bullet in his head. Vic would happily snuff out someone like Ted without a second thought but still he doesn't feel anything. It would almost be a relief to die, except for one thing. Bex. He can't allow that to happen until Bex is well again. Billy shuts his eyes and tries to imagine perfect silence, but as he does so he realises that he is wrong, that this man, Vic as he has called him, will not kill him. They share a cause, a bond, a purpose. When all is done and dusted this strange man will simply leave Billy to deal with the fall out. Billy knows this and he doesn't care anymore.

The Lexus shoots through Buck's Cross, sliding a little on the left hander opposite the Bideford Bay Caravan Park. Alex slows as a Fiesta approaches a junction and the driver starts to pull out. The Fiesta rocks as the driver slams on the brakes when he realises that Alex is not going to keep to the speed limit. Billy sees road rage on the face of the driver, a sign from another world, and he feels as though he is a character in a second rate gangster film.

"I couldn't kill Jock", says Billy, "I just want to make him understand. You know, anyone else but not my little girl."

The Lexus slows for the hard right by the Milky Way amusement park and Alex backs off a little. "Yeah, I know what you mean. It was always okay when Jasari was in the family. You do understand what I mean, don't you?"

Billy looks blank.

"The family. You know, the same shit as your man in that car. Jasari was the family doctor. He cooked up junk for us to sell all along the Adriatic coast. That was fine. Then he blew away one of his own, my sister, Billy, and it stopped being okay. When that happened Jasari fled and me and my brother swore we'd do one thing before we die. We swore we'd make the bastard pay. So here we are."

Clovelly Cross. Straight across the roundabout and at the Hartland turning the Lexus peels off to the right. Alex is caught by oncoming traffic and has to wait for twenty seconds before he can turn. The Lexus disappears round a hard left hand turn, but the road slopes down towards a converted chapel and Alex manages to keep the target car in view all the way to a small stand of cottages on the left. The road bears right and then left again and he loses the Lexus for a moment.

"Shit, not now!"

The Mondeo slides violently as he kicks down and tries to cut the distance between the two cars. Immediately past the cottages there are two derelict pillars on the right hand side and as Alex powers the Mondeo forward Billy just spots the snub rear end of the Lexus disappear down an unmade lane beyond the pillars and swing into what looks like a farm courtyard.

"There!" he yells, thrusting an arm across Alex's chest.

Alex continues down the Hartland road until he comes to a junction signposted for Hartland Point, turns the car round and drives back past the farm entrance. He finds a field gate with a large turning area and parks the Mondeo there.

"No point in advertising. Anyway, I prefer to arrive on foot. Less obtrusive."

Alex motions towards the door and Billy takes the hint. He gets out and waits while Alex checks his Glock and the spare clips. Then Alex takes the spare handgun from the glove compartment and checks that too. A full magazine. Nine shots. As he and Billy walk down the lane towards the farm Alex checks to make sure that there are no cars approaching and hands Billy the spare gun. Billy nearly has a heart attack when he realises what Alex is suggesting.

"What the hell?"

Alex talks quietly as they walk on towards the farm entrance. "Just in case. The safety is on. If you have to use it you flick the catch on the side down."

Billy stops in mid-step, in the middle of the lane, and stares at the gun in his hand. Alex continues walking towards the farm. Billy shuts his eyes, hoping that silence will finally come, that the gun will disappear or morph into something more useful, a bottle of brandy, perhaps, but nothing happens, nothing except for the sound of his on board stereo system breaking through the hangover haze in his head.

Alex turns briefly and watches Billy as he stares at the handgun. "You can tell yourself whatever you like, Billy, but you know the truth, you know what you really want to do, don't you. It's the only way to be sure, the only way to get your little girl back safely."

The first melodic strains of a new song start to play in Billy's head and he can see the words forming again like super tanker bows emerging from the mist on a dead calm sea. He puts the gun into his jacket pocket but dare not let go of it. As he hurries to catch up with Alex he starts to sing quietly to himself.

You're breaking my heart 'cause you're leaving (4)

You've fallen for somebody new

It isn't too easy believing

You'd leave after all we've been through

It's breaking my heart to remember...

A hand appears from under a duvet and reaches for a glass of water. There are no curtains at the window of the downstairs room in the old farmhouse and the duvet is pulled up to the headboard. Light sneaks in under the heavy duvet, in through a gap made by her arm, and Helen's eyes open. There will be no sleep now. The day is underway and she needs a hit, a little something to get her going. The doctor's supplies, the impromptu picnic hamper that he brought over from the barn the previous evening is empty, save for a couple of sachets of Resolve. It will have to do. She has strict instructions not to touch any of the stuff in the bags that they packed last night, which are stowed by the front door. She takes a deep breath and smells sex, smells her deathly lover's body odour and the aroma of the blood in his veins. Helen takes strength from it, drinking deep at the well, and feels safe.

She takes the plunge and pulls a corner of the duvet down, forcing her eyes to open so that the sunlight makes her pupils grow wide. The light hurts and makes her squint, but she ignores the discomfort and hauls herself up so that she can rest her back against the headboard. The Resolve is on a chair next to the bed. Helen tears a strip off both sachets, dumps the contents into a half full glass of water on the floor by the bed, and, shutting her eyes, she listens to the fizz of dissolving chemical compounds. The sensation of being half full is a luxury bestowed upon her by the thin man lying next to her.

Helen pulls the duvet back a little further and reveals the back of his head. Arbnor Jasari is on his side, almost foetal in his unconscious state. His breath is shallow and soft. She strokes his head, running her finger along the edge of the bald patch on his crown, and she wonders how it could come to this, how it could happen that she would start to feel wanted, to feel needed by someone so alien to her. She has a vague memory of stories about kidnap victims turning to the dark side, but she dismisses them as irrelevant.

The lime green effervescence settles in the glass and she swallows the potion in one long gulp, wiping her mouth with the back of her hand before putting the glass back on the chair next to the bed. She rolls over and folds herself into the man's back, spooning, and with her left hand she reaches over his hips and glides her hand across his abdomen towards his morning erection.

Arbnor Jasari, the good doctor, is aware of her movement and he prescribes for himself his favourite pick-me-up. He deserves it, he thinks. After all, he has given her life and a little luxury, a real bed and fresh linen. He pretends to sleep as Helen plants gentle kisses on his back and slowly moves her hand up and down his penis. He thanks God quietly for this woman and lets the warmth in his groin spread throughout his entire body, but the thrill of her touch is too much to bear with anything approaching stoicism and, despite a valiant effort, he is compelled to roll onto his back, to roll into her and pull her down towards him.

She adjusts, props herself up on one elbow, never losing her touch, and the first things that Arbnor Jasari sees of this new day are Helen's eyes. Her pupils are deep and black and wide. He groans and raises his head from the pillow. Their lips meet and the world takes on a soft focus glow for a moment, before thunderclaps roar and the heavens open on the dry spring meadows. A moment, an idyll, a place of worship, and in that moment he truly loves her, briefly and without question, and continues to do so until he recognises the sounds of the promised land for what they are; tyres on ribbed concrete, car doors slamming and leather soles on gravel.

The slow arousal of his waking breaks like a cobra strike, and his hand shoots up and covers Helen's mouth. He is up on his knees in a second, leaning over her, staring into those bore hole pupils, pupils that have been shocked wider still by his sudden movement and alarm. He puts a finger to his lips and then points to the window. He takes his hand from the girl's mouth slowly and points to the clothes that litter the floor. Then, rolling away from her softly he moves quietly away from the bed, unhooks his jeans from the back of the door and pulls them on. Helen throws him his shirt and, holding her skirt in front of her chest, she scuttles into a corner, away from the glass eye in the wall. She dresses hurriedly.

It's impossible to tell from the makeshift downstairs bedroom in the old farmhouse how many people there are outside and precisely where they are located, but Jasari makes an assumption; three people and one car. They have a couple of minutes at most to get ready. Jock and the boys will check the laboratory and the locked downstairs barn. They'll find stacked equipment, most of the drugs, but no cash and no clothes. They'll find Shaun Lloyd, but they won't find their immediate prey. Then they'll come looking for the lovers and he doubts whether they'll be reading the banns.

"Come here", he whispers to Helen, who crouches low as she manoeuvres around the foot of the bed. "Okay, you remember last night, our little chat?"

She nods.

"Nice and easy, yes? Cascarino will be pumped. He'll be pretty rough, but we'll just say we wanted a decent night's sleep."

Helen pulls on a pair of trainers as he speaks. She watches him as he runs through his instructions. He told her last night about the guards, about the problems he had with goons in his home country, and about how, God willing, they will be able to do the same again today if they have to.

"We'll leave the bags here. Money and supplies, yes? We'll leave them here. You have the syringe in your jacket pocket, remember, and I have one here." He pats his own jacket pocket as he puts it on. If they go too far, if they look, if they smell wrong, watch for my signal. Then, just do it. We'll only get one chance. The right moment. And remember... I have this."

He tucks his Beretta into the back of his jeans.

Helen is wired, feeling freaked by the sudden change in mood, by the sudden lowering of shadow over the land.

"But you showed me. You've only got two bullets".

She can feel the weight of the syringe against her thigh as she stands up. The moment, the idyll has become an endless suffocation. She wants to run, run now, run anywhere. The thought of killing a man, even one as odious to her as Jock Cascarino, has been a game until now, a fantasy in which she has been the badly-wronged princess in disguise. She can feel her hands shaking. She needs to pee. This is the harsh reality, the black downside of the fairy tale.

Jasari is focused. He takes her free hand and kisses it. "For us. For me. For you. An end to this shit, you and me, together. I need you."

Helen wants to cry. He needs her. She steadies herself, breathing deeply, holding each breathe for five seconds. Slowly her pulse subsides and the feeling of panic that has been tightening across her chest releases its grip a little. She is still wired, but the circuits have hardened and she won't short out on him. She won't. She promises herself that she will see this through. For him. Helen lurches forward, ungainly and awkward, but determined, and throwing her arms around his neck she kisses him hard and deep.

Arbnor Jasari lets her do this one last thing. He needs her, at least for as long as it takes to deal with the three stooges in the courtyard and hit the up country roads. He needs her now, and as her tongue searches for reassurance, as her lips force the blood from his own, he hopes that he can find it in himself to need her for a lot longer than that. Right now, however, he has other things on his mind, and he breaks their embrace.

"Shhh! I know, I know. But now, my love, we have work to do."

He straightens and leads Helen towards the front door of the farmhouse. It's always best to get bad news over and done with, he thinks, as they walk out into the lane and turn left towards the courtyard where the Lexus is parked, doors ajar, and the sound of shouting echoes from inside the upper storey of the old barn.

GOD'S COUNTRY

JOCK CASCARINO STANDS IN the middle of the laboratory on the first floor of the barn and balls his fists, driving his fingernails into the soft flesh of his palms. The place is neat and tidy, too neat and tidy. The simple outlines, the bare essentials, the cleanliness of the place irks him. Doctor Jasari is second guessing him, is thinking on his feet, thinking in a foreign language, out manoeuvring him, out flanking him. Jock stares at the lie of the land and curses.

"Keep it simple", he says to himself as he surveys the tables around the walls. The equipment is stacked and ready to ship out. The bulk of the product produced so far is packed and ready for the likes of Shaun Lloyd, but right now, in the heat of the moment, Jock doubts that the little shit in the locked ground floor room will ever see the benefit of it. Jock tells himself it's not about the battle, it's about winning the war, and wars are won by taking small victories. Shaun Lloyd is a prisoner of war on the bullet train. Shaun Lloyd is the least of Jock's worries. Where in the name of hell is the doctor?

The cells in the upstairs laboratory are clean and empty, the camp beds made up and clearly unused. The brothers McCoist are watching Jock, waiting for orders, making their own assessments of the situation. Ken is staring straight ahead, channelling his energies for the business to come. Davie is getting agitated, is starting to feel the flush of tension that always comes when he can sense that his brother and his employer need some heads cracking open.

Jock hates the presumption of the doctor, the foreign bastard, making him look small in front of the hired help. Losing face. It's bad enough that Billy has marked him, and Billy will pay for that. When the dust settles and Maggie has worked her magic, Jock will see to it that Billy walks with a permanent limp, but right now he has to get a grip. He spits on the bare wooden floorboards.

"Davie, you get over to the far barn. I want that fucking bus out of here. Hartland point, anywhere you can tip it over the edge. Get it under water. Understand?"

Davie nods slowly before asking, "You sure?"

Jock is keeping it simple. The raw wound on the inside of his cheek is throbbing. "You can't torch it, not here. Last thing we need is the Bizzies poking around. With a wee bit of luck it'll be down there long enough to get wiped clean, long enough for us to be away, sunny side up."

Davie is working it out. Methodical. Mechanical. Grinding sawdust between the gears. He begins to see daylight. A Transit painted in the lurid colours of the God Squad. It's hardly what he would call inconspicuous. Monday morning, even out here in Hicksville, is full of eyes. He moves slowly towards the door and then pauses with his hands thrust into his jacket pockets. There is a chill in the air. The numbers don't come quickly, but he can carry a ten given time, and something doesn't add up.

"Yeah, I get it, but shouldn't we wait, you know, till dark and that?"

Jock walks over to the cell that Jasari kept the girl in and sits on the camp bed. It sags visibly under his weight. He runs his hand over the carefully folded blanket. Filthy bastard. She's just a junkie but she's one of his own, a native of this sceptred isle. Jock dismisses the image in his head and sighs. Keep it simple, he thinks, Jesus, keep it simple for the boys...

"You're right, Davie. We should. But don't you think maybe time's not on our side?"

Jock picks at a bobble of wool on the blanket's surface. Rolling the ball of fluff between his fingers, he stands up again and walks across the laboratory, walks up to Davie and, looking down at the man's black polished shoes, says quietly, "But then thinking was never your bag, was it? Remember the old days, remember the troubles. I was right then and I'm right now. There's no such thing as a perfect crime, Davie, no way. There's getting away with it, there's having balls, that's all, and right now I need you to pack the full pound, know what I mean?"

Davie takes half a pace back towards the door. When the boss goes quiet you don't screw around. Davie remembers the troubles, remembers the muscle on the streets, the deals and the cut throats, the reasons they came south. Jock got ambitious, went too far, but when the knives were out he was the one who got them away, Jock was the one who worked it out with the

Licensee.

"No problem", he says. The moment passes, a moment of joint recollection, a moment of brief understanding. Davie is caught on the cusp of action, but waits.

Jock looks up. "Now!"

Davie knows what to expect but still jumps. He fumbles in his pockets for the keys to the Transit, realises that they are not there and starts to feel sweat breaking out on his forehead. The veneer of affection, the camaraderie of violence, of shared experience, is ripped away from the carcass of their relationship. Davie is twice the size of the man in front of him, he could rip him apart if he wanted to, he feels sure of it, but the reality borne out by years of experience is that he is impotent.

Jock's face is reddening. Ken laughs and throws the keys to the Transit towards the door and open staircase. A second passes. Indecision. The keys hit the wall and Davie stumbles as he bends to pick them up. He is back in the school playground, the stupid lump in the corner, never picked for games of footie, the boy in the blue Proddie shirt left until the last knockings, included in the world of Fay Knights only because his younger, smarter little brother would have murdered anyone who took the jokes too far. Davie's eyes are smarting as he hits the steps and lumbers down towards the courtyard.

Jock is on a roll now, on familiar territory. He knows that most of it is bluster, done for effect, but he carries it well, a seasoned campaigner with scrambled egg on his shoulders. There's no secret to it, no magic potion, nothing God-given. It's about balls. It's all sleight of hand. He turns to face the other brother, the smirking, would-be Spanish-Fly bartender.

"You always were a bastard to your brother, Ken. Mind, he was tying his shoelaces when the man upstairs was giving out the brains. You ready?"

Ken packs his sibling face away, sets his expression for business and nods. "Aye. Shall we deal with Mister Lloyd?"

Jock turns towards the door, shaking his head. "No, he's on ice. No need. First thing's first. Let's find the Albanian Fuck. We'll see where his head's at. Down a hole I dare say, or soon will be. Then we'll clear this place. With a bit of luck we can be out of here by opening time."

Ken follows his boss down the stairs, stopping for a moment by the door to the ground floor area of the old barn to listen for signs of life. All quiet. He thumps the door once, a little act of kindness, a reminder of the tender caresses to come. Ken can smell the salt on the warm air drifting into his beachside bar. Today is just a minor disturbance, a short, sharp Atlantic squall. It's like the old days, all wrapped up with the 'local lad made good' dreams of his teenage years. The setting has changed. East Fife rain turns to Spanish sun. It's all just another game of cowboys and Indians, and Ken has the biggest gun. He walks out into the courtyard and joins Jock Cascarino just as the good doctor and his little girl walk round the corner from the farmhouse. Ken starts to hum a childhood favourite, something about Mary and her little lamb. The feeling is almost purely childish and Ken loves play time.

The lane narrows as Alex and Billy approach the stand of

cottages just before the Sillick farm gate. Country folk. Early risers. Billy and Alex have to hug the kerb, walking along the hedge line, as much to keep out of the way of oncoming cars as to keep out of sight. A huge, blue New Holland monster growls under wheeling planes of gull wings in a field on the higher, inland side of the road. Kitchen lights still glow despite the clear blue of the sky. A South-westerly skips across the open fields and whips through breaks in the blackthorn. In the banks upon which the wind-stunted bushes bend, daffodils huddle together, ragged and bleeding at the edges of their two-tone trumpets. The first outbreaks of Campion are scattering their pink flower heads like the talents of cheap tarts on a bank holiday weekend, and their first, early seed pods are breaking open, the vanguard to their annual invasion of the field edge. Magpies chatter in the branches of short stubby trees, swivelling greedy eyes on fresh roadkill, waiting for the two men to pass, waiting impatiently for the hop, skip and intermittent flutter of fresh meat served on cold tarmacadam.

Alex moves quickly ahead of Billy, ignoring the fields of glass through which he might be recognised, through which he might become a reconstruction on prime time television. Billy tries his best not to be noticed, collar up, dishevelled, instantly identifiable. The song remains the same. The words become a blur in his head, as if they are being sung through a layer of damp gauze, but the melody stays with him. He follows in his master's wake, hands thrust deep into his coat pockets. He feels like 'The Monster', like the freak, brought to life in the middle of a storm, except the weather is fine and the birds are singing and the lump in his throat is made of flesh and blood.

He realises as he listens to the dull rubber soled thud of his feet on the road, as he moves in time with the beat of the bass line, that the monsters have never been that far away. If his skin had seams it would be unravelling. The gun in his hand is alternately heavy and light, a thing of solidity and vapour. Billy wonders, as he struggles to catch up with the man who has given him this gift of death, whether he will ever be able to stop the music in his head.

There are no other considerations for Alex. He hears no music. The birds sing in vain. Flowers bud in darkness. Each step is a winding-in of the reel as the fish is played out and drained of its strength. Jasari is close. He can smell the man. The air seems to be thinning as he approaches the gates. Months of casting out, months of blind navigation, are made worthwhile by the sight of cloud banks over land. The lions on top of the pillars are laying down with the lamb, and Sillick Farm breathes softly in the quiet drift of the morning, but Alex is intent on one thing only, on the hauling-in of the long line of revenge. He can see the shimmer of scales reflecting sunlight a fathom beneath his feet. The dazzling play of light on the water that has drowned his memories reminds him how Rezarta used to smile.

He reaches the far edge of the garden of the last cottage. 'Vacancies'. A skinny, lime green Fiat, pure rust on wheels, bears down on the gunfighters like an ancient western stagecoach, flinging up clouds of dust as the driver puts the wheels into the gutter on the bend by the farm. Alex reacts, slamming his back into the arrow headed branches of the hedge, and the driver, open mouthed, heart racing, swerves out across the white lines in the middle of the lane. A squeal of tyres. Brake lights. Blood on a collar. A thorn in Alex's neck.

The flick of net curtains in the guest house. A pause. Heart rates spike and settle. Alex looks back at Billy and puts a finger to his lips.

Billy plods on regardless, just grateful that he can catch up with Alex. He feels like a five year old being taken on a long bike ride by an older brother. This is a foreign land, a street on which other boys, bigger, harder boys, rule, and for all of his natural bluster, Billy is suddenly aware that he is lost, lost in a world that doesn't fit the soundtrack in his head. He watches as Alex motions down the line of the hedge towards the pillars. The farm track runs down for twenty or thirty yards between two fields and then opens out into a wider, gravelled area in front of a derelict farmhouse. Beyond that there are huge stone barns.

Billy and Alex crouch low as they move carefully past the pillars. The only cover is a lichen covered two bar stock fence running the short length of the lane to the farmhouse. The lower rung of the fence is just beginning to disappear beneath the first growth spurt of the season, with knee length clumps of nettle and dock running along the borders.

The house is substantial, essentially Devonian in its Victorian solidity and state of grand decline. The window frames are held together by condensation. But for the fact that the front door is wide open and there is a black holdall on the threshold of the hallway, the place looks as though it has been standing idle for fifty years.

The bag in the doorway makes a difference. Alex stops as soon as he sees the bag and seems to melt into the background. Billy almost trips over him, and is only stopped from crying out in surprise by the swift movement of Alex's hand across his mouth. He is pressed down and back into the damp, dewy fringe running along the farm lane. Alex is already looking away, calculating distances, making assessments and assumptions. There are no signs of movement in the farmhouse and the Lexus is out of sight.

The bag in the farmhouse doorway momentarily stops the music in Billy's head. A distant voice breaks in, a news flash in the middle of a Saturday night variety show. People. Real live people. Billy has drifted along with some vague sense of justice in his head; this is for Bex, an abstract Cascarino motivation. Scenes from a film; Josey Wales; Wyatt and Doc walking into the OK Corral. The bag breaks the celluloid in the projector gate. Billy can smell the iron bitters of fresh blood. Wheels spin. This is the moment that a pheasant becomes carrion, the moment when you lose sight of the outside world and feel the dull thud of bone on a chassis. Billy turns away from Alex and tries to breathe in clean air, a reflex action at odds with the harsh reality of this brave new world.

Alex moves away and blends into the background, merging with shadows and foliage. Billy knows that he is there, knows that he should be able to see him, but it is as if Alex is able to shape shift. The movement in Billy's gut is unstoppable. He swallows twice, desperately fighting the burn of reflux, but he has no choice. It comes. He is on his knees, retching. The world dislocates. Wide open prairies and one horse towns require broad, open spaces and borderless, sun kissed imaginations, but this is England. Rural, retiring, dense little England, and Billy has a real live gun in his pocket.

The curtains across the road flicker. The sound of car tyres, the hedgerow waltz of the dude ranchers and the sound of bile, all of these things are congested, in shadow, and in the absence of breakfasting travellers, the owner of the cottage nearest the farm steps out onto her drive to see if the world on her doorstep really is as depraved as the *Daily Mail* describes it.

Mental images of the immediate future, premonitions based on the reality of cold blood, are stopped in their tracks, are brought up short in the sudden confluence of bodies in a courtyard. Arbnor Jasari has a picture in his mind of what is about to occur, an image in which he is, inevitably, victorious. There are no doubts or grey areas in the simulation. He has balanced both sides of the equation, and the result is, like statistics, weighted in favour of the statistician.

The sudden appearance of Ken McCoist and Jock Cascarino in the doorway to the laboratory is like finding that a decimal point has been misplaced. He falters and slides to a stop on the loose gravel. To his right the engine of the Lexus ticks and cools. Helen sees the two men a split second later and is unable to stifle a short, sharp scream of surprise. She too stumbles to a halt behind the doctor, and peers around his shoulder, eyes wide and mouth open, waiting for the next move. Morning is broken on the adrenaline rush.

Ken is caught momentarily off-guard, but years of practice, years of experience, kick in and he moves forward again with languid efficiency. There is a lump in his throat and his heart rate has jumped up a notch, but he hides it well. Practice makes perfect. Never let your opponent see the fear. This is the final round, the bell sounds and mentally he rises from his stool. He fixes the shape of the doctor in his eye, squares up and waits for Jock to touch the gloves and say the word.

Jock, too, is primed. He has a purpose, a reason to be here, and the people he most wants to see have run right into the net. He can begin the cold blooded process of gutting and filleting. Jock slows up as he draws level with Ken and smiles briefly, more to himself than to his newly arrived colleagues or to the fine Spring morning. It's time to land the catch, pack away the bait box and get the gasping little fish into the freezer. Permanently.

"Morning, doc", he says, maintaining the Cheshire grin just long enough to reveal a chiselled, canine intention. "Going somewhere?"

By his side Ken has already slid his right hand into his jacket pocket. He pulls out a pistol and levels it, waist high, aiming in the general direction of the stalled doctor and his lover.

"Aye, I guess so", continues Jock, walking slowly towards them. "and you know what? It's a lovely morning for it. Mind if we walk with you?"

Ken keeps a measured pace with his boss, watching the doctor all the while, waiting for a movement or a look, anything that might suggest a rush of blood to the head. You can never be sure how people will react. Some of them recognise the futility of it all and never say a word. Others in his experience shit themselves and beg some unseen, disinterested God for help or mercy or some such irrelevance. Occasionally, just occasionally, they believe in fate, believe that they are untouchable.

The reality, as far as Ken has been able to determine, is that you stay calm and do what has to be done. He has fought before and he has run before, and he has no doubt that he will fight and run again before he dies. He, Jock and his brother are sort of running now, just like they did back home when the Licensee was the one with the upper hand, but Ken has an instinctive feel for what is right. This is not a time for losing.

The doctor can feel Helen's heart beating against his upper arm as she presses herself into him. His breath is shallow. He reaches out behind his back, locates Helen's hand and gives it a faint squeeze. He turns slightly towards her and whispers, "Remember."

Helen stares straight ahead, fixated by the muzzle of the pistol in Ken's hand, but the doctor sees her dip her head slightly. Good girl, he thinks. They might just do this. He has to concentrate. No sudden movements. It's all a question of timing. One mistake, either way, and the last thing that he and Helen taste will be cold, hard grit.

The doctor clears his throat and takes half a step forward, palms facing outward. "You've seen upstairs, yes? I thought maybe we'd be moving. You can't be too careful after what happened to those girls. We slept in the farmhouse last night. A proper bed, that's all. We're here now. We're waiting for you."

Jock motions to Ken to get the girl. Helen is as good as gold, even when the man grabs her by the arm and hauls her away from the doctor's protective shadow. She tries not to trip as he pulls her in between himself and Jock. Her free hand, her right hand, is in her coat pocket. Fingers and thumbs. Plastic. She locates the twin lugs at the top of the cylinder and grips the syringe in her fist, keeping her thumb free and loose. She looks at the doctor, and is unable, despite telling herself to stay frosty, to keep the tears from her eyes. She wills him to give her a sign, but he just stands there waiting for Jock to say something. The grip on her left arm tightens. Ken McCoist has hands like baseball mitts and she can feel her skin bruising under his fingertips. All the while Ken keeps the gun pointed at the doctor, at the main target, at the clear and obvious danger.

Jock looks at the girl and shakes his head. "Pretty enough, doc, but hardly a good bet for a long and happy future. Too much baggage, if you get my drift. Dirty little shag, though, I bet."

The doctor looks down at the floor for a moment before answering. When he does he moves slowly forward, his hands still palm out in front of him, and he looks directly into Jock's eyes.

"Sure. But you know what it means? Nothing."

In the courtyard, the doctor is suddenly aware of the echo. His voice is strong and clear, bouncing off the old, pitted brickwork.

"She's nothing to me. Keep her, kill her, I don't care. All I care about is money and freedom. I've worked hard for you. Briefly, yes, but hard. It's a shame it hasn't worked out, but I think it's time to go. You keep her, give her to your boys, whatever. All I want is to go. It's taken too much effort to get here, too much suffering, too much pain, to waste it all now."

Helen is burning up inside. She hears the words and they are words that she has heard so many times before. No one ever gives a damn about her. They're all the same, each one as cold and heartless as the last. One fuck and they think they own her. The tears in her eyes are like chlorine now, smarting and stinging. The fear, the unknown chill that has been seeping into her bones, is suddenly overwhelmed by a surge of sheer, bloody-minded indignation and fury. Not anymore, she tells herself, not anymore.

The doctor watches the colour rise in her cheeks. He catches a shower of sparks from her eyes and he lets them fall onto his upturned palms. He stops walking forwards a metre away from the short, squat Scottish gangster and slowly moves his hands behind his back, as if he is about to stand at ease. His left forearm brushes against the butt of the revolver tucked into the back of his jeans. The second syringe is primed and dosed in his jacket pocket. A stand-off, and the boys from the North are making basic mistakes. He always said that they were amateurs and he is convinced that he is right. It's the same the world over. They are just like the blood-soaked Berisa family. Arrogant and stupid.

Jock is on edge and the connection between him and Ken is almost telepathic. They share hard experience and body language, a shared sense of survival bred by years of brutal intimacy. Ken raises the gun and aims it at the doctor's upper torso. A heart shot, with the arm extended, making the distance all but point blank. Jock steps to one side and offers the doctor a position next to his girlfriend. "I thought we'd take a stroll round to the back garden. There's some interesting stuff your wee lass might like to see."

The pit with the bodies. The doctor has no wish to introduce Helen to his inglorious but necessary recent past. It would, he feels, put something of a dampener on their future lovemaking, should they be lucky enough to have a future. This is no time for sightseeing. A walk around the barn is a death sentence. He tilts his head slightly and looks into Helen's watering eyes. She gives him steel. She is, he decides, worth more than he thought. He tries to reassure her, to speak to her with his eyes, to make contact through the anger, to restore her confidence and remind her that he is simply playing the game.

Jock is still beckoning him forward and the doctor has to turn slightly away from him, towards Helen and Ken, to make sure, despite the cover of his jacket, that the gun tucked into his jeans stays out of Jock's sight. It's now or never. There are simple moments of trust required in every life and this is one of them. Pure and simple. He moves between Jock and Helen, keeping his back slightly turned. Helen is now between him and Ken and the big man will have to readjust his position to keep a clean line of fire. The doctor bumps into the girl and as he feels her pull away from him in disgust, he hisses one word, "Now!"

In celluloid terms, the next moment should be like a flash of lightning, but the real world works through simple, individual sparks of light, and through basic synaptic connections. The world hangs in rolling suspense. One, elephant. Two, elephant. Then the thunder hits, the thought made real, crashing overhead, shaking the foundations of the old stone barns to their deep, black rotted roots. Everything depends on speed of thought.

The doctor steps forward as soon as he speaks, making Ken reach round the back of the girl with his gun. As Ken tries to keep the doctor in his line of fire Helen steps back with all her weight and employs the heel.of her boot on his shin. The gun goes off once, wildly, bucking into the air with the recoil. Ken yelps and feels the sting of cold metal in his neck.

Helen has made the right connections. A thumb depresses a plunger. Ken staggers back. He swings the gun round, past the girl and aims at the thin, side-on figure of the mortal apothecary, but as he tries to aim he can feel his eyeballs start to swell. He swims in darkness as his pupils flick up into his skull. He strains again to see the world as it should be, but staggers backwards, hitting the brick wall of the barn with his head as he falls. The gun spills from his hand and he hears a straw donkey braying in one last brilliant shaft of sunlight.

Jock has a simple view of life. He is armed and dangerous, but the act of firing guns is one that he leaves to the boys. There are no traces that way. There's no point in being a criminal mastermind if the Bizzies can run forensics and trace a bullet to a magazine or the particular scratches on the inside of a gun barrel with his fingerprints plastered all over it. His piece is purely for show. He turns and starts to run for the car, yelling for Ken, yelling for Davie, as he pumps his legs, desperate to build a head of steam so that he can get away.

Age and conceit make him a poor sprinter.

The doctor is on him in a second and Jock's legs are taken out from under him. Jock hits the dirt, face down, screaming as his left wrist snaps under his weight. The retort of shattering bone echoing off solid Victorian walls is like a second gunshot. He tries to turn round and look at his assailant, but the man is on his back, pinning him to the floor. He feels his hair being ripped from his skull as the doctor yanks his head back and shows him the tip of the second loaded syringe. He feels hot breath on his face.

The doctor spits the words out, venom on hot skin, "A special gift, just for you. A little cocktail of my own, and I'm going to give you just enough, just enough to know that you should've retired a long time ago, old man. You're going to need plastic pants for the rest of your miserable life."

Jock is aware of pain, aware of the needle being stuck into his buttocks, but he is in that quiet moment of shock when a broken body fails to connect with the receptors in the brain that describe a wound. Then the weight from his back is gone. He hears footsteps running across the gravel courtyard. He tries to look up, tries to will Ken and Davie to appear, shining and white, but all that he sees are two pairs of legs hitting the ground, and then the doors of his Lexus slam shut. He hears the engine fire.

He tries to make a mental note not to leave the keys in the ignition next time, but the words won't form properly in his head. Stones fly as the car is put into gear and wheels spin. If only he could move, he might be able to watch events unfold, might be able to see what is happening, might be able to assess the damage.

As the car turns round at the far end of the courtyard Jock tries to shout at the driver to stop, but his mouth won't work. He can't feel anything. He can see a narrow strip of dirt and gravel, he can see across the courtyard to the opposite barn where Davie is supposed to be getting the van sorted out, and he can, if he swivels his eyes upwards, see sky above the barn roof. For the first time in all the years that he has owned Sillick Farm, he notices the ornate ridge tiles that run along the apex of the barn roof and he tries to smile, but none of his facial muscles seem to work anymore.

Jock is facing the wrong way as the Lexus speeds up to the corner by the barn and the old farmhouse and turns right, heading up the lane towards the main Clovelly road. The noise of the revving engine starts to fade as the crumbling stonework and render of the old farmhouse blocks the passage of sound waves.

Jock suddenly remembers a dog that the family had when he was nine years old. The dog died out in the backyard one afternoon, died of old age and poisoned kidneys, and Jock was the one who found her. Bonnie. She was a good dog, always ready to chase a ball or a stick. The thing that Jock remembers most about Bonnie was the smell. When the old mutt died her bowels loosened and she smelled like a dysentery ward. Jock can't quite get a handle on why, after forty odd years, he can smell Bonnie now.

Billy emerges from the grass verge, stained green at the knees. He is starting to hate the smell of his coat sleeve. He feels faint, as though he is standing at the leading edge of a storm front, vainly attempting to hold back the wind. Inevitably, the world clouds over and Billy hears distant thunder break over the swelling surf at the foot of the Clovelly cliffs. The roar in his ears gets louder, turning into a high pitched whine. Now it reminds him of televised motor sport, the sound of rubber in distress, of boy racers on the streets.

He wipes his chin with the back of his sleeve, shudders, and looks up from the patch of grass that he has been staring at for the last few seconds, desperately trying to control the movement of his stomach muscles.

Alex is a couple of metres further down the lane towards the farmhouse, crouched down by the fence. He has his gun raised in front of him, holding it in both hands to steady his aim. Billy remembers something about life flashing before your eyes just before you die, but is confused by the images flickering though his head. His black and white personal history seems to be stuck on the last frame. He is almost sure that the soundtrack that has been running through his head since he first saw Leona on the mortuary slab is running backwards, delivering subliminal messages, but he can't understand a word. This would be a good time for miracles, he thinks, and sees a sudden flash of silver on his low horizon.

He can feel tremors in the grass under his hands. It takes a second or two for the real world image to register. Silver and chrome. A radiator grille. Colour coordinated wing mirrors. Tinted glass. The rumble of thunder tyres. He blinks and watches the beast slide to its right, picking up speed with sudden jerks, slewing towards the line of the fence. This would be a very good time for a miracle.

Then Billy has another strange thought. In real life guns don't sound like they do in films. He tries to get grips with this rare insight, but instinct rips its way through the Saturday morning cinema screen in Billy's head, spilling plaster and dust from the smashed proscenium arch onto his trousers. A car. Drug dealers. The getaway. Driving straight at the fence.

The echo from the single shot that Alex Berisa manages to get away as the car speeds towards Billy finally hits home, snapping him back into the here and now. Billy jumps back towards the fence, catching the base of his spine on the lower rung of the post and rail fence behind him. He yelps and falls sideways. He is facing head on oblivion and all that Billy can think to do to save his life is raise his arm in front of his face. The car suddenly slews left and snakes up the drive. In that brief moment between blue sky thinking and absolute, black ignorance Billy sees a face staring out of the shattered driver's door window.

Clunk click nearly every trip. Good advice, but not appropriate today. Leaving Jock and Ken McCoist for the crows, the doctor slams the car round the corner leading into the courtyard and fights with the gears, desperate to feel the wheels bite. He is on the wrong side of the car and can't quite get to grips with the British way of driving. He misses a gear and grinds metal.

As he straightens the car and looks up and out of the windscreen he sees a body in the lane, a live body where there should only be grass and weeds. He has no time to wonder at the vagaries of fate. Why a body should be there is an irrelevance. Sillick Farm has been a place of ghosts for too long for there to be a welcome on the doormat. The doctor makes a quick decision, floors the accelerator and points the car at the fence line. He is not taking any chances.

The tyres grip and the car jolts forward. Helen is still looking out of the back window at Jock's prone, unmoving legs in the courtyard. They appear to be disembodied by brickwork. She is in shock, but it's not the shock of killing a human being. Helen is admiring the strike. She enjoyed doing the bastard.

The car swerves and she is slammed against the glass of the passenger window and then back into her seat. She lets out a squeal, and then screams as she realises that they are heading straight for the fence. She grabs at the steering wheel, yelling at the Doctor, and he fends her off, pushing her forward into the dashboard.

The world around him explodes. Colours change. Black leather is stained with the deepest red wine. Glass shatters into a thousand jagged little cubes in his lap. Helen's arm snags in the steering wheel spokes and as she falls back into her seat the wheel is yanked to the left, hauling the car away from the anonymous body by the fence.

Caught between two stools. The doctor stares at a complete stranger through the open window on his side of the car. Then he turns to look at the girl, ready to lash out but there is no one to hit. He makes an immediate mental adjustment. There is nothing to hit. The damage is done and she, Helen, his one true love, is dead meat. The girl who felt so warm and alive last night has left him. She is slumped against the passenger door, spilling bits of her face onto the upholstery. His foot slips off the clutch and the car kangaroos. Helen's head lolls forward. Muscle control. The rear window shatters and the doctor twists round in his seat. His foot tangles with the brake and the accelerator. The car slows.

Alex is on his feet and running past Billy as soon as he sees the car lurch to the left. He raises his gun again and as the car snakes up the lane he fires a second shot through the rear window, destroying the perfect symmetry of Japanese automotive design. Alex has made an assumption. His friend, the good doctor, Arbnor Jasari, is in the passenger seat. Job done.

The car slows. Brake lights. Red mist. Water drips from the exhaust pipe. A head turns and Alex sees a silhouette, thin and long haired, turn to look out of the rear window. Mutual recognition. Cold realisation. The body in the passenger seat, twice dead, is not his target.

Alex is catching up with the car. The body count is immaterial. This is payback time. Revenge is a dish to be enjoyed at any temperature, just so long as it is served. Alex slows down too. His heart is racing. He breathes in deeply and tries to focus. One more shot and the thing is done. For Rezarta. He brings the gun up into his eye line, stops and spreads his feet. Balance. A deep breath. Squeeze gently.

Just in time the doctor realises that the engine is going to stall, dips the clutch and floors the accelerator. As the tyres grip and the engine drops its guts, Helen's body slides down into the passenger seat footwell. Her knees wedge under the glove box. There is a pool of blood on the stage and she is a limp marionette, her strings cut. A third shot whacks into the radio on the central console and sparks fly. Smoke fills the cabin, but the rush of air streaming through the smashed windows clears it immediately. The doctor hits the junction and accelerates through the left turn, swerving across the road as he heads out towards the main North Devon trunk road.

"Vdeksh!" is the last thing Billy hears as Alex sprints up the lane and disappears from view, heading back towards the Mondeo that they parked a little way up the main road. Those few brief seconds of lunacy, of boisterous, burning Bedlam, subside and the world returns to its normal silent, brooding state. Billy's ears ring with the repeat of gunshots. There is an unnatural lull in the morning bird song. Around him, below his audible register, there is only the sound of grass growing. Billy looks up and sees housemartins swooping across the rooftops. The guy in the car was a mess, covered in shit, but he wasn't Jock. Billy uses the fence to haul himself upright, wincing as he feels the bruise at the base of his spine bite and swell.

A frantic phone call; triple nine, garbled words, gunshots, men, cars without windows. Staccato bursts; calm down, blood and guts, one of them is still there. Where? What? Where? When?

"Sillick Farm, Higher Clovelly, by the garage, the Hartland road."

"Lock your doors and windows. Is there a room at the back of the house? Good. Stay there. Don't speak to anyone! Don't answer the door unless it's one of our officers. Keep away from the windows!"

On their way. Please God, just get them out here. Guns. Easter. Idyllic. Richard Littlejohn. Kitchen solitary with a boiling kettle. Brandy. Medicinal. The sun is over the yardarm in Singapore. Confusion, a world tumbling out of control. The landlady's worst fears have finally, gratuitously, thrillingly, been realised. She knew she was right.

A revving engine in the barn at the back of the courtyard buries the sound of death in a diesel cough of thick oil and cold metal. The lump under the bonnet of the Transit takes four twists of the ignition key to fire. Flooding the injectors. Eventually

Davie kicks the beast into life and holds the accelerator in the mid-range for a few seconds. The barn fills with the reek of diesel fumes and he lets the engine idle. He holds his hand over his nose and mouth as he makes his way to the back of the barn to open up the double doors that lead down on to concrete hard standing at the entrance to the top field. A car backfires in the distance. Davie ignores the bark and concentrates on doing his job. A second backfire. Only this time the sound of the exploding exhaust seems to shift, seems to echo off the walls. Davie stops by the doors and waits, listening. The Transit needs a minute or two to warm up. A third backfire and tyres squealing.

Davie decides to take a look, to check on Jock and his brother. Something doesn't quite feel right. The sums still don't add up.

GOING OUT OF MY HEAD

IT'S A WEIRD KIND of silence in the eye of the storm. Billy is torn. Alex is the only person he trusts, the only person who seems to know what is going on and Billy needs that reassurance. There is something else, though, something heavy and deep, that prevents his feet from moving back up the lane, something dark and compelling drawing him down towards the farm courtyard.

As far as he could tell, the occupants of the Lexus were strangers to him, which means that Jock has to be on the premises somewhere. He has an uncomfortable feeling in the pit of his stomach, as though lidless eyes are staring at him as he straightens up and turns to face the barns.

The old farmhouse looks cold and uninviting, brooding over the loss of past generations of pig breeders. The place is a mess of broken fence rails and overgrown hedgerows. Gates hang loose, buried in bramble runners and the first spurt of cow parsley. He shivers slightly. The emptiness of it all drills down into Billy's marrow. He puts the feeling down to the river of bile that he has deposited in the gutter.

A vacuum. Abhorrent. Nature has a way of dealing with emptiness and Billy has no real choice in the matter. He is drawn downwards, taking slow steps, descending the slight incline of the lane, past the farmhouse door and on towards the courtyard. The travellers' abandoned trousseau on the threshold adds to the absurd sense of loss that is hollowing-out a space inside Billy's head.

The song has to come. Billy believes in the song and the melody. He has faith. When all else fails he always has the sure procession of notes to lead him into the light like a line of biscuit crumbs in a smugglers cave. Billy has always relied, even in the darkest times, on his own personal gospel as performed by Saint Victor Damone, except that Mother Nature is playing games this morning. She has filled the hollow space in his head with the static interference of little voices.

At the far end of the farmhouse a low wall sticks out from the front of an old coach house. Billy has to swing out into the lane, away from the comfort of the fence at the front of the farmhouse garden. Exposure. He walks hesitantly forward, the irregular rhythm of his footsteps a direct consequence of the mute in his head. He notices the earth packed into the right angle between the low brick wall and the concrete strip of the lane. The dry weather is already turning it to dust. Footsteps echo in his head where the music should be, kicking up clouds of fine powder to obscure his view of the wider world. Tunnel vision.

As Billy approaches the corner of the coach house and the

courtyard starts to come into full view he sees feet. He pauses for a second. The voices tell him to turn round, tell him that if he wants it badly enough he will wake up in bed and hear Bex making coffee in the kitchen, but Billy is running on Josey Wales time. He has to go on. For some absurd reason it's what a man has to do.

He walks a little further and sees legs. A prostrate body in a dark overcoat. The angles become more obtuse. Lines of sight and changing perspectives. There is a second body slumped by the wall of a barn. Billy feels as though he should be doing something other than walking slowly up to the body in the middle of the courtyard but he can't quite get a handle on what it is. He tries to hum the song that he has been singing to Bex these last couple of days but he can't remember how it goes.

The small voice deep inside his head tells him that he should be running, that he should be putting distance between his own aching body and the wreckage in the courtyard, that he should be calling the cops, anything but walking towards Jock Cascarino. Billy knows instinctively that Ken is dead, just like he knows without a shred of doubt that Jock is still alive.

His inner conscience is getting agitated, yelling at Billy that he should take his hand off the butt of the pistol in his pocket, but Billy shuts the last open window to his soul. Double-glazed, it cuts the voice off completely. If Billy is going to walk in melodic silence he doesn't want the moment ruined by a rational prick in a cheap suit shouting at him from an upstairs window.

Billy feels strangely lightheaded, as if the world is fine and all is right in Heaven. The storm front is lifting. Ken has broken his last head. The odd arrangement of his limbs is an apt epitaph for a man who has dedicated his life to breaking other people's' arms and legs. The man must be double-jointed at the knees. Glass eyes. No sweat. Billy can deal with Jock. He has the grazes on his knuckles to prove it.

He wonders why his blood isn't boiling, but then he remembers; this is for Bex, Bex is the reason and this sick bastard is the cause. Josey Wales had a cold heart when it came to dealing with scum. Without the words to explain it to himself, or to Bex, who seems to have joined him in the courtyard, Billy starts to understand why he is here. He imagines that Bex is six years old, and that she is holding his free hand. In the real moment, in the breaking of the spells that bind us to the wheel, when the world spins slowly and feet move inexorably towards the end of days, you see everything clearly. The silence breaks. Infant Bex smiles at him and birds sing. It's almost a cartoon moment and Billy finds a new song. Infant Bex tells him to do it.

Davie McCoist sees everything clearly, too. The car is gone, his brother is a pale shadow of his former self and something that looks like the Boss is lying face down in the dirt. Standing over Jock Cascarino is a middle aged crooner pointing a gun at his head. Davie is unarmed. He stands in the shadows at the back of the barn where the Transit is ticking over and waits for the shot. He heard two, maybe three backfires. Ken and Jock. Billy Whitlow has clearly shot his brother and his employer.

"Fuck me", he whispers, and holds his breath.

Jock must need a final bullet. The seconds pass and Billy just stands there. Davie can hear the Transit idling. Sparrows chatter on the barn roof. He has to think about this. He should be running across the courtyard, grappling with the crazy bastard and saving what is left of this sorry life, but that's the point, he realises; this sorry life. He is sick of it. He wants to go home.

Davie wills Billy to finish the job. "Jesus, man, just do the cunt".

Billy stands and points the gun at Jock's head. Surreal television. Suspended animation. It feels as though someone has pressed the pause button on the remote. Davie breathes out and feels a sense of relief wash through him. It's the only form of emotion that he seems to feel these days. Seeing his brother on the floor, unmoving, impossibly silent under the circumstances, is like having the keys to the cell door thrust into his hands. The madness of it suddenly strikes Davie as funny and he fights to hold back the laughter. Billy bloody Whitlow, he thinks, fuck me!

Second thoughts. Gun fire. Rural England. Men in suits. The Old Bill are bound to be making house calls. Davie's next impulse is to slide back, to slip away unseen and walk across the fields. He wants to fill his lungs with solid country air. He doesn't care if he has to walk all the way back to Ibrox, just so long as he gets there, but he can't fight the macabre fascination of the scene in the courtyard, he can't just walk away. He has to see, he has to be there when the final act goes down. Laughter and tears. He has to be there because Billy has a daughter and because he, Davie McCoist, has a lost childhood. He blinks back a tear. He always liked Bex.

Davie has no choice, just like the bounty hunter in the film. Billy shoots or he lets him go. Davie needs the choice to be made for him. Davie needs Billy to set him free one way or another. There's something about the old man with the gun that impresses Davie. He walks out of the shadows and starts to cross the courtyard to where Jock is lying in the dirt. He holds his hands up in front of his chest. He doesn't want any shooting, at least until he can look Billy clearly in the eye. As he approaches the death scene he realises that Billy is singing to Jock, singing softly, a lullaby, a simple little song of farewells.

He sees Billy look up. The gun never moves from Jock's head. Billy sings quietly and it's only as Davie gets close that he can make out the words. For someone of Billy's talents the lyric is all over the place. The man's voice is cracked and the notes waver and spiral. The words make no sense, not in this context, but then Davie considers the situation. Killing is a funny business. The song goes round and round:

Cincinnati dancing pig (5)

He's the barnyard mister big

Cincinnati dancing pig

with his riggedy, jiggedy, jiggedy, jiggedy jig-a-jig-jig!

Children yell and clap and sing

When he does his buck and wing,

Cincinnati dancing pig

with his riggedy, jiggedy, jiggedy, jiggedy jig-a-jig-jig!

Dancing bears and kangaroos

have a lot on the ball,

but until you dig that remarkable pig

You ain't seen nothin' at all!

From Duluth to Birmingham

He's the pork chop Dapper Dan,

He's the keenest ham what am,

Cincinnati dancing pig

with his riggedy jiggedy jig-jig-jig!

Impaled on the horns of a dilemma, two men stand over the conscious but unmoving body of the recently retired Jock Cascarino. If Billy Whitlow and Davie McCoist decided to reach out they could touch each other's fingertips, but the small space between the two men is as wide as the Grand Canyon is deep. The song dies and the chatter of sparrows in the hedgerows spirals outwards. Somewhere in the bright blue sky a buzzard calls, searching for carrion, unaware of the rich pickings that lay prostrate on the courtyard floor at Sillick Farm. Fresh, warm meat.

Davie checks Billy out at close range. The only word that he can come up with to describe Jock's assailant is, 'frayed'. Billy looks like a ripped-up carpet, soiled, trodden into oblivion, the threads of a life hanging together more out of habit rather than any tightly bound weave.

Billy's voice is dusty. "Hello, Davie".

Davie looks at the gun, which is still pointing at Jock's head. Billy's hand is shaking slightly, but his grip looks firm. Davie keeps his voice low and soft, without threat.

"Billy?"

Billy casts a quick glance towards the other man. He can see shoes and the bottoms of jeans. There is a line of mud around the sole of Davie's left shoe. Birdsong. The sound of a chainsaw across the fields. Bright emerald bodies drift towards the barn wall. Flies on the make.

Davie is aware of time, aware of the slow dripping down of fragile existence, aware of the need to make himself scarce, but he is fascinated by this montage, by this still life. He has to know how this ends. He has to know that Ken and Jock are history and that the slate is clean, or, if not clean, that at least the chalk marks are illegible.

Davie feels as though he is going to choke. Mercy is a quality that he has largely forgotten about, tagging along through life in his brother's wake, abjuring any responsibility for things that have happened with the excuse that he has only been following orders. Simple Davie. Knuckles on the floor Davie. Not anymore, though. One way or another Billy is going to set him free.

"So, Billy, what happens now?"

Billy seems oblivious. His head nods every so often.

"You in there, Billy? You still singing to yourself?"

Another bar. The melody repeats over and over again, worming through the verse towards the heart of the chorus. A pause at the end of the line.

"Whatever you do, Davie, whatever you do, don't say her name".

Slow Davie. He has to think for a second before the penny drops. In the working out he almost asks out loud, "What, Bex?"

But Davie is methodical. Davie, the kid in the adult body, takes a little while to work things out, but he usually gets there in the end. His heart is thumping in his chest. He can feel waves of nausea and relief washing through his body, but he manages to keep everything under control, manages to stay silent. Davie looks away from Billy, glancing quickly across at his brother and then down at Jock. Eyes swivel at ground level. The man on the floor is dribbling, a pig snuffling in the dirt. Davie is caught off guard by the realisation that his former master is impotent, and he takes a step back.

Billy doesn't move.

"Shit way to finish don't you think?" says Billy. "He's in there, somewhere. The bastard who killed my little girl is in there. The only reason I haven't pulled the trigger is I want him to know it's me. I want him to know it's me, Davie, do you understand?"

Davie understands. Full circle. End and beginning. It's time to walk away from the past.

"Aye", Davie replies, gathering his thoughts and his composure. Remember the Bizzies, he thinks, time to go home.

"Did you do Ken?" he asks.

Billy looks up for the first time since Davie walked out into the courtyard. He shakes his head. He feels the warmth of the climbing sun on his face. George Harrison; *Here Comes The Sun. A Perfect Day.*

"Fuck off, Davie, fuck off home".

Eyes meet, cold and grey under the cloudless pillars of ozone. Davie can't hold Billy's gaze. He starts to say something but the words catch in his throat. You don't get many chances in life and somehow he knows that this is one of those important moments.

Davie clears his throat and whispers, "Take care, Billy".

Then he turns slowly and walks back towards the barn where the Transit is coughing its guts up in a cloud of diesel exhaust. He doesn't look back. He is free. Turning the corner and walking down the length of the barn towards the open double doors he makes a sign of the cross on his chest and whispers the word sorry to the boys and girls blocking the soak away at the back of the laboratory. Davie walks on past the open doors and across the concrete hard standing by the top field. He walks out into the damp tufts of thick meadow grass and away towards the coast. The land slides down to the sea and Davie can think of no better place to begin the process of getting lost.

Billy watches Davie disappear behind the barn at the far side of the courtyard. The pig at his feet snuffles, blowing tiny saliva bubbles mixed with grit. Billy looks down and smiles.

"Time to sing, Jockie boy, time to sing. Maybe we can sing

together. Have you got a plan, big man, remember?"

At that moment Billy understands that his own singing days are over, that he will never croon again. The only singing to be done here is the singing of the baritone in the full metal jacket.

"You always were a shit. Just so you know, Jockie boy, this is for Bex, my little girl, and for Maggie, who should have been my big girl. One way or another, you've screwed both of them. Take note, big man, this is me screwing you."

Frantic bubble blowing. Jock tries to beg with his eyes. He tries to move his tongue, but he can't feel anything. His breathing is becoming laboured and he can feel his body slowly but inexorably shutting down.

For the shortest moment.

Colours don't register at speed. The passenger window of the Lexus is fading to pink. The human eye is designed to notice distinct movement, not background colour and no one seems to see the aftershock. Doctor Jasari has forced Helen's body as far down into the foot well as it will go. Wind streams through the cabin, whistling on the jagged slivers of glass that cling to the window frames front and back. The tank is half full and the satellite navigation console is chiding him firmly but softly with a slurred, slow voice, bleeding to death electronically.

As far as the immediate future is concerned the doctor has neither the time nor the inclination to consider the finer points of interior automotive décor. His thoughts are focussed on geography, on the panorama of survival. Instow. East-the-Water. He has a vague impression of shapes, of coastal bulges and inlets, but the place names on the road signs might as well be written in ancient Greek. The Bideford bridge disappears as he climbs the ascent to the top of the first stretch of dual carriageway on the main trunk road east. Rolling Devonian metal to his left. Rusting Rovers and clapped out Citroens. Speed. He has one aim. Follow the green. Find the blue. Blue means motorway, means north, means city streets and anonymity. The question for Doctor Jasari is this; where does he ditch the Lexus and find an alternative means of escape?

Alex Berisa shifts uncomfortably in his seat, reaches between his thighs, and fishes the Glock out from between his legs. Speed limits. A safe braking distance. He has already been passed by two unmarked police cars running in suicide mode. Up ahead he can hear sirens. He keeps the Mondeo on the straight and level, losing miles and minutes in the quiet pursuit of his prey. Arbnor Jasari is getting away. As Alex hits a tail of traffic following a JCB on the rise out of Woodtown, he realises that he has a couple of hours of grim frustration ahead of him before the trail goes cold.

Arbnor Jasari. The doctor. The good doctor. Doctor Albania. The shit, the murdering bastard, the man who broke Rezarta, the man who turned his little sister into a vegetable, makes another exit from Alex Berisa's life. The sequence of events is becoming tediously repetitive. Alex can't quite believe that he got this close and missed. Atlantic Village. The Big Sheep. Road signs and tourist attractions. Shooting ducks at a funfair. Alex wants his cuddly toy, but the carnie boys always have an edge, always seem to bend the barrel when you take the last shot. The bastards always have a line and an underlying threat.

Roustabouts. Life on the road. The questions in Alex's head are these; which damned road? Where now?

Sirens are the backing track to Billy's silent vigil. He hears sirens in the lane, hears tyres on gravel and is aware of heavy footsteps in deep, menacing stereo. He sees shapes by walls, crouching shapes, shapes covered by car doors and brickwork. Billy is vaguely aware of caps and flak jackets, of chequerboard stripes and barked orders.

Jock's body lies bleeding on the courtyard floor. Ken McCoist sits, uncomfortably relaxed, by a barn wall. Ken McCoist and Jock Cascarino, late of Barnstaple parish, formerly and briefly infamous for being run out of Glasgow city's nether regions by the Licensee, gaze out dumbly at a world fundamentally changed, and like dinosaurs grazing in the shadow of the comet, like the Romanov family in a cold country house parlour, they have no understanding of the revolution. Extinction comes abruptly. Nuclear Winter.

Billy is aware of death, aware of the metallic smell on the breeze, and with little Bex by his side, with the ghost girl in his arms, he sits next to a piece of rusting, fang-toothed farm machinery with a gun barrel pressed against his temple. One simple squeeze, a reaction, a muscle spasm, and he can be with Bex. The infant Bex, insubstantial and flowing, kneels by his side and he looks into her eyes. Freckles. Her soft hair drifts idly in a halo of spring sunlight. Her skin shines like marble in a Vatican courtyard. The faintest whisper of Leona waves to the two of them from the back of one of the police cars in the lane.

Billy spins the disk in his head one more time. He feels women in his arms. Bex starts to fade and he remembers cocaine wraps and Jack Daniels. Threads of life spill out of his fingers, spill into the dissolving ghost of Bex, and all that Billy wants to do is stop the world. He doesn't want Bex soiled by his own frailties, by the genetic code that unravels every time he feels the faint twinges of happiness.

Maggie is singing in the background, a fabulous, wealthy tart, the love that dare not speak its name, a love made real by eternal distance. Unrequited. Impossible. Billy knows in his heart, deep down in the well, that he could never love Maggie, but the superficiality of his longing for Jock's mate is what makes it real, is what made it seem so suitable. The smell of cordite is in the air and Billy has finally woken up to another home truth. She knew. This is about Bex, and Billy feels ashamed that his last words to the prick on the ground included bloody Maggie.

His right arm is aching. The pistol slips a millimetre, dragging against his skin. He hears a voice, calm and controlled.

"Put the gun down".

This is the moment for the final gesture, the final telling of truths. This is when Billy does something real. Thoughts appear, real thoughts; you've fucked up for the last time, Billy. A farewell. One last smile, one last look into her blue eyes, and there she is again, his little Bex, the only true love of his life, the girl holding his hand in the brilliant blue morning light, except that she is telling him not to come over, telling him not to twist against fate. Sudden clarity. Brilliant blue vision. A head free of static.

"Put the gun down and lie on the floor with your hands behind your head, or we will fire."

Bex floods away, downhill, bound by gravity. Billy is alone in the courtyard with Jock and Ken. His finger twitches on the trigger and he has a choice to make. Do it. Do it now, or accept the blindingly obvious facts of life; you never really had it in you, Billy, you were never really a player.

The voice sounds like Carol. The rigger boots in her hall. All of the things that he should have had, the simple things, the boredom and the warmth, all of these things sit at his right hand. To his left he has the drugs, the girls, the glittering spots and gels, all of them wrapped in shades of scarlet, shades that smell of grease paint and stale cigarette smoke.

There is, Billy realises, no choice to be made. He has always gone with the flow, with the least path of resistance, and today is no different from every single one of his yesterday's. Josey Wales splits. The gun spins through the air. Billy falls forward. His head hits the ground a few inches away from Jock. Billy can almost taste the last decaying spots of Jock's saliva. For the first time Billy notices the smell, a rank mixture of expensive cologne and faecal matter. He has time to smile. Got the bastard.

Boots on gravel. Knees in his back. Cuffs. He is manhandled into a kneeling position, his arms pinned and locked behind his back. Marksmen. Blues. A moment shared with the cadaverous Jock. Billy can feel the imprint of gravel on his cheek, can taste worm earth on his teeth. He can't hear a thing. The music is dead, the words a vague shade of grey, the melody a childhood memory. He feels hands under his armpits and he is hauled to his feet. Now that the job is done, now that the ghosts have faded and Billy is alone amid a sea of uniforms and flashing lights, all that he can think as he is pushed down and forced into a squad car is that his shoes are ruined. He feels hollow, as though he has forgotten something important, and as the rear doors of the police car close, as he feels the weight of the law on the seat next to him in the back of the car, he wants to cry but he is as dry as a bone.

AN AFFAIR TO REMEMBER

BLUE AND WHITE TAPE. Black and yellow stripes. White suits and latex gloves. There is a patrol car parked across the entrance to Sillick Farm, and a traffic cop leans against the door with his arms folded across his chest. He is watching the house opposite, the bed and breakfast, watching and waiting for the uniforms to finish a cup of tea and make their notes.

A statement. Descriptions. Vague impressions of height and weight. Hair colours. Skin hues. Makes of car are always a problem. The number of shots. Clothes. Blood on the broken tarmac by the front wheel of the patrol car.

"Shit", he mutters to himself as he jerks away from the car. "SOCO!"

A world of samples and dust. The lane is rapidly filled with crouching bodies, bodies intent on tracing every last splash of blood on the unmade farm road, on grass and fence posts. Glass shards are bagged. A bullet casing is picked up gingerly between the folded edge of a uniformed cuff. More tape.

Chalked outlines around blood stains.

In the courtyard the bodies are being zipped away. Identification. James Charles Stuart Cascarino. Kenneth Graham McCoist. Two-thirds of a firm. A board meeting gone wrong, but still quorate. Supposition. A bullet to the head is an easy spot, but for the body sprawled up against the barn wall there is no apparent cause of death. Instructions are given. The mortuary. Scenes of crime. Post-mortems. Ambulance crews slide black plastic onto stretchers and push them into waiting but redundant resuscitation bays. Certification. Dead at the scene.

One of the plain clothes boys wants a search of the fields. The uniforms will get to spend sunny Monday in the country, searching in lines. Fine tooth combs. Another group emerge from the laboratory on the upper floor of the barn with arms full of plastic evidence bags. Samples. Test tubes. A computer carcass. Dishes and scissors and spoons. Blankets. A music player. Toiletries and a pair of flip flops. Tubs and tubs of neatly prepared sachets of something yellow. The flash of a camera bulb sneaks out through the gap in one of the upstairs window shutters.

In a squad car parked over by the far barn wall two detectives are talking to a sallow-skinned youth, who is taking long drags on a bottle of still mineral water. Shaun Lloyd is taking the greatest pleasure in giving the boys in blue a full description of events, about how he was dragged out here against his will and was being framed. The look of utter disbelief on the officers' faces is blatant. The questions twist and turn. The bottle is drained and Shaun is cautioned. He is left to stew in the perverse juices of random fate while the detectives consult their superior. A quiet little room and a tape recorder beckon. Shaun is just grateful to be out in the open air.

There are insufficient officers at the scene to perform a detailed search, so the Inspector in charge splits the uniforms up and sends them off in different directions to check on the basic lie of the land. No heroics. They are told to watch out for someone called Davie, one David Alan McCoist, the missing member of the triumvirate, noted for acts of outstanding bravery in the face of impossible odds. Davie is a simple bruiser, none too bright, but neither is he malicious. That was the *modus operandi* of his older and recently deceased brother. There are no tears being shed.

South along the back of the far barn, walking slowly, looking into angles of shadow and watching for sudden shifts in light, one of the uniformed constables makes his way toward the field at the bottom of the farm complex. There is a smell of diesel in the air, but he can't hear the sound of combustion. As he approaches the end of the barn he becomes aware of a subtle shift in the outline of the building. A door is open and pushed flat against the wall. The officer checks behind him but sees no one. He edges forward slowly and peers into the gloom. His eyes take a second or two to adjust from morning sunlight to dusty, exhaust laced shadow. Colours begin to merge, a ragged paint job, primary bright and flecked with rust at the wheel arches. He edges into the barn, carefully checking the corners as he approaches the van. On the side of the Transit there is a bright flash. He recognises the symbol and the legend from a house call made a few days previously.

"Shit".

The Eureka moment. Discovery described as simply as that.

The officer pulls his radio up towards his chin. No bloody signal. The North Devon coast is a digital nightmare. Time to get back to the courtyard, time to get support.

The huddle. Reports. The old lady at the bed and breakfast has proved to be no better nor worse than the average witness. She is, apparently, generous with the tea bags and the biscuit tin. She saw two men on the road, and then in the drive, one of them shooting into a silver saloon, and then running after the car. That was when she too ran for the safety of her kitchen, when she rang the triple nine and then remembered to lock her doors.

The sound of cars and sirens, the sound of someone knocking on her front porch was one hell of a fright, but not half as bad as the sight of the man running up the old farm lane with that gun in his hand. She thought that he might have been in his early thirties, maybe a bit older, with dark hair, nicely done, expensive. He definitely had dark skin, a suntan, like she remembered all the boys had from that summer in seventy-six. A stifled, embarrassed giggle. Really dark. She wasn't sure about his height. Maybe six foot. Clothes were a problem. Jeans. A jacket. Brown or black. Maybe blue. It was difficult, she said, with so many images and thoughts in your head.

The car was a mystery. Silver and messy, but that was all she was able to tell them. Apart from the windows being smashed. She had no idea where the car or the man had gone. Back to Barnstaple probably, she had said, in a tone of voice that suggested that it was no surprise.

All points. Descriptions are broadcast. Police computer checks suggest a Lexus. The hunt begins.

At about the same time that the first officer is reading the words on the side of the Transit, a second officer is kneeling on the cracked earth at the back of the laboratory barn, running his finger through a trace of white powder. Quicklime. The place stinks to high heaven and he has a bad feeling about the day. The ground is rutted with the imprint of old tractor wheels. Up against the barn's back wall there is an upturned wheelbarrow. The officer can see a smaller rut leading up to a plastic manhole cover. It's nearly two weeks since the last rains, so the track has to be at least as old as that. On the ground next to the manhole cover there is length of metal. An invitation.

The smell reaches out and makes a grab at his nose and throat as he moves closer to the plastic cover. The officer is swooning under a heavy cloud, in a melange of earth and metal, of maggot meal and black decay. His mind is already reeling, but the compulsion to see, the compulsion to witness, is overwhelming. He starts to shout for help, and as he does so he reaches out for the metal bar and inserts one end into the lip where the plastic cover fits snugly into its hole.

The thing has been opened before and the seal is already broken. The lid lifts with relative ease and flips over. Flies. Green bellied emerald flies swarm up and out of the blackness, causing the police officer to throw himself backwards. He gags as he falls, spilling his guts onto the front of his flak jacket and then onto the floor, and he turns away and starts to crawl as soon as he feels solid earth beneath his spine. His head is full of the swarm, full of the buzz and drone of putrefaction, and in the middle of the swarm he can see an empty eye socket staring out at him from this heart of darkness in the middle of a Devon farmyard.

Boots. Hands on his shoulders. In the background he can hear the sound of grown men retching. He can feel men he calls friends, men who he would normally rely on, men accustomed to the sights and sounds of mean lives, momentarily falling apart. He is filled up to the hilt by the empty eye socket. Tears fall. The involuntary twitch of sleeplessness starts.

From the direction of the barn, moving closer, impatient and caustic, comes the voice of the detective in charge at the scene. "What the bloody hell is going on?"

A ring tone. Plastic vibrations. Personal effects rattle in an evidence bag. A mobile rings four times and cuts to voicemail. There is nobody home, nobody taking calls this morning, nobody except the Scene of Crime officer who is tagging the collected exhibits. Gloved hands fish around in one of the evidence bags and pull out a silver and black Samsung. Call history. Missed calls. The late James Charles Stuart Cascarino provides a telephone number and a voicemail trail.

… speak after the tone. To re-record your message press star at any time.

"Jesus, Jock. Now's not the time to go AWOL. Call me as soon as you're done out there."

Maggie slams the phone onto the kitchen table and paces the kitchen tiles. She wants to know what is going on. Left to her own devices, left to her wild side, where the imagination runs in a slow riot like bindweed, she has already worked her way through a dozen fanciful scenarios; the femme fatale, terrible injuries, a car in a ditch, another deal, another retirement, the McCoists suddenly getting ideas above their station.

One call, one sound, that familiar voice, that mixing of emotions, is all that it would take to settle her. Then she could be sarcastic or she could chide Jock for his unthinking bloody alpha male priorities and hormonal negligence, and then, as soon as he tries to pour oil on her troubled waters, as soon as he infuriates her with his calm, business voice, she will know that everything is fine and dandy.

Coffee. Tea. Maggie decides on tea. Electrodes at her temples. Maggie feels like Elizabeth Taylor, like a cat on a hot tin roof. Southern heat and boredom. Tension in spades. She is caged in the middle of an electric storm, and for all of her venom Maggie feels toothless and naked. She hates the waiting game and this is the biggest game of her life. She breathes in deeply and tries to focus. The kettle starts to hum. Poker face. She needs to practice her poker face.

In the background radio voices fly brightly through the morning; a discussion about breastfeeding, the subject of this morning's podcast, downloadable, and absolutely, totally annoying. The kettle starts to crank up towards the hubble-bubble of boiling. Maggie reaches across the work surface by the kitchen window to turn off the radio, but she decides that she needs music. Music soothes the savage beast. She hits the station button a couple of times and gets the latest boy band dross. Summer loves and broken hearts. She listens for a moment or two before deciding that silence is golden. It's all too twee and infantile.

The click of the automatic switch on the kettle. Maggie throws a tea bag into a mug and lifts the kettle up and forward.

"Bloody hell!"

The boiling water has not yet settled back into a calmer state of simple hotness and the water jumps from the spout and misses the cup, spilling white hot blisters of water across the countertop and down the cupboard doors. Maggie's cup hand is splashed and the burn bites. She slams the kettle down onto the work surface and pushes the cold tap to maximum so that she can stop the skin on the back of her hand from staining red with the scald.

A morning gone from bad to worse, and all that she wants is word from the outside world, a word that says, "Book the flights, love, we're on our way".

Maggie grabs the house phone from the table and wills it to ring. It's not fair. The faceless systems that underpin the digital communications revolution aren't playing a straight bat. It's not too much to bloody well ask, is it? she thinks.

Maggie sinks into one of the chairs by the table. Where did all of her dreams go? What happened to the brightness of expectation, the shine on her skin when she first walked out into the big wide world? All gone. Some of the desiccation is caused by the inevitable dimming of youth's first blush, that inexorable slide into tiredness and ill temper that comes with the slow physical disintegration caused by free radicals, some of it, but not all of it. That's the tragedy of the human condition; eighteen in your head and incontinent in an NHS bed.

This is the chance to put things right, the last chance to escape the chains put around her limbs by a world that spins down through other people's lives. Her bastard husband. The bruises and the excuses. Jock fixed that and she will be eternally grateful to him for it. She will love him after a fashion for that, but she won't forgive. In a way she is almost glad that Leona and Bex are being sacrificed. Part of it is spite, but she is also relieved that they will be spared the same old shit.

She punches numbers into the phone and waits. The lines and airwaves hook up. The phone rings. Once. Twice. Hearing the third ring Maggie fully expects the carefully chosen words of the voicemail lady to lay down the usual barriers to direct communication, but Maggie's rattling train of thought is rudely derailed by a male voice.

"Hello?"

Maggie is silent. Shock. Where is the Glaswegian overtone? She can't think.

"Hello?"

The irresistible impulse to fill the spaces in between the words pulls her forward. "Who's there?"

Silence at the other end.

"Is that...Maggie?"

Overtime. Cogs and wheels. Two plus two. Caller

Identification.

Maggie hits the red button and slams the phone back down onto the kitchen table. She has to hack away at the undergrowth to reveal the lost city of her imagination. Wilderness is rampaging through her skull. She hears but doesn't really notice the sound of tyres on the gravel driveway outside. Confusion. Jock has lost his phone, the stupid bugger. Stolen. Taken away. Panic. Everything is being taken away.

She gets up and looks out of the kitchen window, expecting to see Jock and the boys climbing out of the Lexus. Instead, she sees white, blue and Day-Glo yellow. She sees blue and red and checkerboard green.

Traced. The wilderness is suddenly spreading out and dragging her down, right here in the kitchen. She is pinned to the harsh walls of the domestic mausoleum by creeping vines, smothered in the leaf mould decay covering the floor of the untamed land at her feet. The bad thoughts have come true. The femme fatale? The car on its roof in a ploughed field?

She instinctively knows that impersonal tragedy is a myth. The McCoists? For a fleeting second she believes it, but then the simple truth comes bursting through. Jock has really screwed it up this time.

Maggie bends forward across the worktop. Her head sinks down onto the polished granite surface and she starts to cry as the doorbell chimes.

"Oh God. Not now, not…"

*

There is a little secret that Bex hasn't told anyone. The secret tells of a short lived moment of peace, a brief interlude, a space between the blip and slide of the monitor soundtrack that pervades every spare inch of the intensive care unit. Bex is aware. Her eyes remain closed, but she can distinguish shades of light from under her eyelids. Nothing much makes any sense and her head feels as if it is wrapped in cotton wool, but she is rising, she is cognisant.

In her thoughts she throws open the patio doors at her father's house and takes a slow step around his garden, shuffling past flowerpots full of cigarette butts, one more casualty on the mend, a dressing-gowned remnant of the whistling generation. The electronic pulse to her left rattles like howitzer fire, a distant memory causing a Pavlovian response. She screws her eyes tightly shut and tries not to remember. The cotton wool in her head is surprisingly strong, but she slowly starts to surface. She breaks through into clean air.

Crêpe footsteps. A weight on her left arm. The skin on the back of her left hand tingles slightly. Catheterised. Saline infusions. Clipboards. A strip of brighter light above the waterbed. Bex can hear sounds washing over the ramparts of her consciousness, humming notes, staccato glissades, particle waves, and she is both reassured by their proximity and confused by the language. A sideways tongue. Accents of angels. Angles of expression. Something in the tone, some vague sense of timing and cadence overcomes her sense of displacement and turns the amplifier up a notch. Familiarity.

With the shapes and sounds come pictures, spooling reels in her head, the ticker tape grains of memory. Oxford. Dreaming spires come to mind and seem strangely appropriate. Edge curled snapshots, photographs that have been bent back and forth so much that the polished gloss of the paper has cracked right across a face. The melody of her years plays in time with the memory of her father's dulcet tones. Vic Damone on black vinyl. The cracked background hiss of ancient treble. As far as the immediate world goes, Bex can remember a car door slamming and the sound of the doorbell. Ding dong, pussy in the well.

Rapid eye movement. The flicker. A muscle spasm. A finger moves and Carol looks up. Dave's reactions are a second behind Carol's sudden movements, a video voice out of synchronisation. Carol grips Bex's hand that little bit tighter. A long breath drawn in and held. The trumpet involuntary.

"Bex?" Broken and cracked. Strangled.

Rising from her seat, Carol is brushing hair from her daughter's forehead. One of the nurses attending the intensively ill spills across the opposite side of the cot, reading vital signs in the colour of the girl's cheeks and the dilation of her abruptly open eyes.

Tears. Carol is repeating her daughter's name over and over again, burying her head in Dave's shoulder as medical staff run checks and ask questions, moving Bex into the first stage of waking. A wall of simple questions, names and dates and observational logic. Dave is crying too, overwhelmed by his proximity to other people's lives. Throats constrict. Smiles tighten and teeth are bared. Emotion overload. Relief. Sheer bloody relief. God-forsaking, heaven-praising, ball-breaking relief. A world of inner promises and deals, the life changes writ large for a moment, meant truly, forever, anything now that prayers have been answered.

The moment passes in a bewildering array of tests and mechanics as drips are changed and monitors checked, as wires and plugs and tubes are realigned and removed from flesh. The process and method of recovery is definite and measured. Explanations. Words. Bex is largely oblivious to anything other than the sense that the world is solid again. She emerges from a black hole, from the amniotic warmth of coma, and smiles the smile of birth. Carol's face is split apart by a wild, untameable grin as the unit doctor tries to explain.

"…not out of the woods, although the signs are encouraging. To use the vernacular, she's been on a pretty bad trip, but with time and care there's no reason why she shouldn't make a full recovery. There will be tests, of course, just to make sure, to make sure that there's no lasting side effects, as it were, but I'm sure Rebecca will be up and about in no time…"

White noise. Dave tries to pay attention, tries to take it all in so that he can give Carol the low down when she eventually climbs down from the cloud, but he really only grasps the basics. Checks. The possibility of brain damage. Probably not, but they have to be sure. It might take a while to be certain and he has a vague sense of another conversation taking place. University. Wanting to be a vet. Probably have to take a gap year. Lab reports. Lethal combinations of drugs. Acid freaks and flashbacks.

The doctor withdraws and leaves the family to their reunion. The tests can wait; five minutes; an hour; they have all the time in the world. Except that Bex is looking worried. She tries to speak but the cells that form her mouth and vocal chords seem to have rearranged themselves to form a child's sand pit. She coughs and tries again, then manages to make a gesture towards the locker beside her cot . Water. Warm water, but it tastes. It's as simple as that; it tastes.

Bex whispers once but Carol shakes her head and leans forward.

Bex tries again, "Where's Dad?"

That's when the tears turn to monsoon rains. Carol hugs Bex tightly and sobs. Dave stands behind Carol and tries to put an arm around her shoulder, to put his hand on her back, but he finds it impossible to complete the manoeuvre. His hand dangles in the space between their lives, a few inches away from his lover's skin. The moment is gone and he smiles the spare part smile of embarrassed exclusion.

Carol fusses and worries, "You'll see, love, everything will be fine now."

There is gratitude on both of their faces, but Bex insists, "I know. I'm sorry, Mum, so sorry." Tears and hugs. Then the inevitable, "Where's Dad?"

A lump rises in Carol's throat. There are a thousand things she wants to say about Billy but this is simply not the time.

"You know your Dad, love. He's never where he's supposed to be. He'll be along in a minute. He's been here with you. Probably just popped out. It's not his fault, love."

And the thought comes with an inevitable predictability; it never is, darling, it never is…

Billy sits alone in paper slippers and overalls. They have taken his clothes for forensic tests. He sits on hardwood. The white tile acoustic. Shoes without laces. The melody is gone and his head is full of random lyrics divorced from their arrangements. Anyway, who needs an audience when you have the only real people in the world within your eye line. The six year old ghost of his beloved Bex is standing to his left. Vic Damone, dashingly-smooth in a dark-grey, double-breasted suit, is standing to his right. This is the day that old crooner's dread, the day that the music dies. While Billy sits quiet and still amid the heavy metal sounds of the custody suite, his companions reach out and take his hands in theirs and the three of them begin to mime and mug like savant idiots, and with the sound turned down, with the picture fading to a single white dot, they start to belt out Billy's favourite song without shifting a single molecule of air:

Again, this couldn't happen again (6)

This is that once in a lifetime

This is the thrill divine

What's more, this never happened before

Though I have prayed for a lifetime

That such as you would suddenly be mine

Mine to hold as I'm holding you now and yet never so near

Mine to have when the now and the here disappear

What matters, dear, for

When this doesn't happen again

We'll have this moment forever...

ABOUT THE AUTHOR

Clive Gilson was born in 1962 into a household steeped in sport and rhythm. His father was a senior amateur and lower-league professional footballer, while his mother, equally formidable, was an award-winning ballroom dancer. Their spirited household didn't just hum with ambition, it danced to it.

After earning a degree in History from Leeds University, Clive took an unexpected turn into the then-nascent world of information technology in the late 1980s. Yet, the call of story and stage never left him. Alongside a thriving tech career, he freelanced as a journalist and book reviewer, earning one small by-line in the national press, and also spent over a decade performing in village halls and professional theatres across the south of England.

A true inheritor of his family's sporting zeal, Clive later pivoted into live sports broadcasting. In the 1990s, he became a trusted rugby 'stato' for the BBC, ITV, EuroSport, and TVNZ, bringing insight and analysis to major tournaments including the Heineken Cup, Six Nations, World Sevens, and Rugby

World Cups.

As a writer, Clive has made his mark across genres. His debut novel, *Songs of Bliss*, was published in 2017, followed by *A Solitude of Stars* in 2019, and the companion piece to *Solitude*, *A Symphony Of Sorrows*, in 2026. He has released four acclaimed short story collections, *The Mechanic's Curse*, *The Insomniac Booth*, *Melodies in Black Ink*, and most recently in 2026, *Proud Jenny Jay*.

He is also an award-winning poet and the author of a biography detailing the life of a former professional footballer, namely his father. Since 2018, Clive has served as Managing Editor of the Firesides Tales Project, a global storytelling initiative that has published over 30 collections of folktales, fairy tales, myths, and legends from around the world.

Today, Clive continues to write fiction rich in folklore, memory, and quiet transformation, combining his deep love of narrative with a lifelong fascination with the human spirit.

For more about his work, visit clivegilson.com, where stories are always waiting to be found.

ORIGINAL FICTION BY CLIVE GILSON

- *Songs of Bliss*
- *Out of the Walled Garden*
- *The Mechanic's Curse (short stories)*
- *The Insomniac Booth (short stories)*
- *A Solitude of Stars (Cry Havoc, part 1)*
- *A Symphony Of Sorrows (Cry Havoc, part 2)*
- *Melodies In Black Ink (short stories)*
- *Proud Jenny Jay (short stories)*
- *Acts Of Faith*

AS EDITOR – *FIRESIDE TALES* – *Europe*

- *Tales From the Land of Dragons* – Welsh Folk & Fairy Tales
- *Tales From the Land of The Brave* – Scottish Folk & Fairy Tales
- *Tales From the Land of Saints And Scholars* – Irish Folk & Fairy Tales
- *Tales From the Land of Hope And Glory* – English Folk & Fairy Tales
- *Tales From Western Europe* – Folk & Fairy Tales from France, Belgium, The Netherlands and other Western European traditions.
- *Tales From Northern Europe* – Folk & Fairy Tales from Germany, Scandinavia & Baltic traditions.
- *Tales From Southern Europe* – Folk & Fairy Tales from Spain, Portugal, Italy, Greece and other Southern European traditions.
- *Tales From Eastern Europe* – Folk & Fairy Tales from Poland, Hungary, Romania and many other Eastern European traditions.

AS EDITOR – *FIRESIDE TALES* – *North America*

- *Okaraxta* - Tales from The Great Plains
- *Tibik-Kizis* – Tales from The Great Lakes & Canada
- *Jóhonaa'éí* –Tales from America's Southwest
- *Qugaaĝix̂* - First Nation Tales from Alaska & The Arctic
- *Karahkwa* - First Nation Tales from America's Eastern States

- *Pot-Likker* - Folklore, Fairy Tales, and Settler Stories from America

AS EDITOR – *FIRESIDE TALES – Africa*

- *Arokin Tales* – Folklore & Fairy Tales from West Africa
- *Hadithi Tales* – Folklore & Fairy Tales from East Africa
- *Inkathaso Tales* – Folklore & Fairy Tales from Southern Africa
- *Tarubadur Tales* – Folklore & Fairy Tales from North Africa
- *Elephant And Frog* – Folklore from Central Africa

AS EDITOR – *FIRESIDE TALES – Middle East*

- *Tales From The Meddahs* – Turkish Folk & Fairy Tales
- *Tales From The Hakawati* – Arabic Folk & Fairy Tales
- *Tales Told By Balebos & Gusan* – Jewish & Armenian Folk & Fairy Tales

AS EDITOR – *FIRESIDE TALES – Asia & The Far East*

- *Tales Told By The Kathaakaar* – Folk & Fairy Tales from India
- *Tales Of The Gùshì Yuan* – Chinese Folk & Fairy Tales

AS EDITOR – *FIRESIDE TALES – Animal Tales*

- *Dog Tails* – Folk & Fairy Tales featuring our canine chums
- *Cat Tails* – Folk & Fairy Tales featuring our feline friends
- *Horse Tails* – Folk & Fairy Tales featuring our equine friends
- *Pig Tails* – Folk & Fairy Tales featuring our porcine friends

AS EDITOR – *FIRESIDE TALES – South & Central America*

- *Tales From The Caribbean* – Folk & Fairy Tales from Caribbean islands
- *Tales From Central America* – Central American Folk & Fairy Tales
- *Tales Told From South America* – South American Folk & Fairy Tales

Reviews

I have edited Clive Gilson's books for over a decade now – he's prolific and can turn his hand to many genres. poetry, short fiction, contemporary novels, folklore, and science fiction – and the common theme is that none of them ever fails to take my breath away. There's something in each story that is either memorably poignant, hauntingly unnerving, or sidesplittingly funny - *Lorna Howarth, The Write Factor*

Ragged A Ruffian reviewed on Amazon in the United Kingdom on 27 January 2021 - A truly heartwarming, interesting, story with a wonderful narrative. Unquestionably a splendid read

A Solitude of Stars: With deft turns of phrase and an imagination that would make Philip K. Dick jealous, Gilson foresees a dystopian future, the seeds of which are definitely being sown right now. The story is a chilling glimpse of what may come to pass, warmed by a thread of love that raises the narrative beyond despair. I found the stories disturbing and breath-taking in equal measure. The Apparat and Dirigiste tribes are ranging across our solar system seeking peace by waging war, raising the question; is humanity actually capable of peace? A riveting read. - *Rob Swan, The Write Factor*

Songs of Bliss gripped me from the start - I had to read right to the end. Loved the humour. Impressed by the surprising empathy that I felt for rather - on the face of it - unlikeable characters. Look forward to seeing it in print. - *Maighdean-Mhara, commenting on Authonomy*

I just wanted to thank you once more for your help acquiring this beautiful collection. It's found a new home at the top of my library. I've already stumbled onto some wonderful stories in a couple of the collections, and I can't wait to get more. Have a wonderful holiday and a great new year... - *Richer Daniel Laporte, California, December 2021*

Melodies In Black Ink: A collection of darkly captivating short tales, each inspired by the melodies that move us, the lyrics that linger, and the stories hidden between the notes.

Gilson (editor of the international Fireside Stories series) offers a dark, poignant collection of genre-crossing stories, all inspired by songs, that explore the fragile intersections of love, loss, resilience, and the shadows we carry. Ranging from children with superpowers to accounts of blossoming love, abusive relationships, unexpected pregnancies, and the isolating rhythm of a machine-driven society, Gilson's stories capture raw textures of the human experience in a key suggested by their musical inspirations, which include lushly brooding tracks from Kate Bush, This Mortal Coil, Angel Olsen, The Cure, and Youssou N'Dour (the sublime "7 Seconds," a duet with Neneh Cherry.) Gilson has a gift for moment-to-moment storytelling that grips and then lingers, like Gorilla Glue stuck to one's fingertips, resisting even the harshest solvents of reason.

Life goes wrong in unpredictable yet resonant ways throughout these 26 compact tales, and Gilson's vivid portrayals of scenery and emotion make it easy to lose oneself in these narratives, drowning in a wave of feeling that refuses to let go. From the Scottish Highlands to space travel to the blood-soaked earth of Danish-Viking battlefields, told from the perspective of Ulfhednar and his sacred wolf, Ulric, these stories span wide imaginative terrain. Despite some big ideas and SF elements, characterization is compelling. "The Jakey and the Nae Chancer" introduces Elliot and Fiona, who have perfected the art of detachment, the latter of whom "was almost certain that her heart was too delicate to risk breaking again." One of the most heart-wrenching stories, "Be Well," is inspired by a devastating loss. It's a piece that does more than tug at the heart, it reaches in and seizes hold with unrelenting intensity.

Adding a unique dimension, each story concludes with a toast to the song and artist that inspired it, an invitation to experience these briskly potent stories on another sensory level, with a soundtrack tying words to melody, emotion to rhythm. Melodies in Black Ink is not light reading, but it is deeply moving, with haunting emotional rewards.

Songs Of Bliss

Searing, surprising stories of urgent feeling, inspired by beloved songs.

The US Review of Books
Professional Reviews for the People

Melodies in Black Ink: This work is not just another set of tales linked together by a myriad of characters who sometimes appear in more than one narrative. In fact, this is much more than just another short story collection. It is also a reflective, musical journey. Accompanying each story is an explanation of the song that inspired the writing. Most impressive is the wide expanse of musical genres, artists, and songs included in this book. From Wardruna to Metric to Blue Oyster Cult to Dot Allison, the book's audience will experience a musical journey unlike any other. The incorporation of the notes discussing each inspirational song provides an informative background. It also provides historical context, along with the author's personal anecdotes, about each song.

What makes this book even more realistic is its honest, vulnerable, and sometimes gritty portrayal of the characters and their existences. One story in which all of these themes and characteristics culminate is "Going Underground." It is a story in which even the main character's name, Daniel Grimes, reflects the character's harsh, gritty environment and existence, as well as the difficult decisions Daniel must make. Daniel embodies rebellion against the status quo after having lived a life in which he originally "played by the rules. All it got him were ration credits and a little coin, enough to rent a bedsit and eat slop." "Going Underground" is a daring story with a dystopian tone. Deepening that dystopian tone is the fact that the author cleverly disguises the story's time period, and the tale can be read as either occurring in the past, the present, or the very near future.

Music lovers will appreciate this book because of the role music plays in each and every story. The stories, too, are a testament to not only the power of music but also of the necessity of interdisciplinary studies and the humanities. The stories are a novel type of ekphrastic writing in that, rather than responding to visual art, the stories are responses to music. The fluid, poetic writing in each story mirrors the magic and lyricism inherent in the songs the author utilizes. These stories are powerful, emotional, and moving. Most of all, they are beautifully and unquestionably human.

RECOMMENDED by the US Review

Book review by Nicole Yurcaba

Lyrics:

Songs Of Bliss

1 You're Breaking My Heart, Vic Damone, - words and music by Pat Genaro and Sunny Skylar

2 You're Breaking My Heart, Vic Damone, - words and music by Pat Genaro and Sunny Skylar

3 Again, Doris Day, later Vic Damone, Written by Dorcas Cochran and Lionel Newman

4 You're Breaking My Heart, Vic Damone, - words and music by Pat Genaro and Sunny Skylar

5 Cincinnati Dancing Pig, Vic Damone, Written by Guy Wood and Al Lewis

6 Again, Doris Day, later Vic Damone, Written by Dorcas Cochran and Lionel Newman

www.ingramcontent.com/pod-product-compliance
Lightning Source LLC
Chambersburg PA
CBHW030658190726
48286CB00001B/83